Cover art and creation by:
Mark Bussanich, Illustrator,
mbussani@att.net

Author's photo by:
Dawn Malone Photography,
dawnmalone@mac.com

Published by:

Lawless House Publications
2699 Blue Spruce Drive
Hemet, California 92545
Kim's Story: Murder in the Everglades
Copyright 2012

ISBN – 13-978-0615691091
ISBN – 10-0615691099

ACKNOWLEDGEMENTS:

I owe much to my friends, The Interrobangs of Hemet, California, a group of talented writers lead by the skillful and dedicated leadership of our moderator, Ann J. Dunham.

I want to thank my wonderful family, extended family and friends who have all encouraged me to follow my dream at this later time in my life. They helped me prove that "it is never too late to discover a new you".

Above all, I must thank my eldest daughter, Donna, and her gifted husband, whom it is my good fortune to call my son-in-law, Mark Bussanich. Without these two stubbornly tenacious and dedicated people, I fear my novel may have died a lonely death in some forgotten drawer.

I also wish to thank you, my dear readers for buying my first book. I hope you enjoy reading it as much as I enjoyed writing it.

KIM'S STORY
Murder in the Everglades

By Loie Lawless

BOOK DEDICATION

Kim's Story: Murder in the Everglades

It is my privilege to dedicate this novel to my late husband, Don Lawless, whom I think I have loved forever. He encouraged me to attend a writing group where I could receive help to achieve my goals. He read each and every segment of Kim's Story with pride as I completed it. He always handed it back with a smile and a "Well done, Honey" comment and never a criticism. He didn't live long enough to see the finished product, but I know his spirit is still with me, cheering me on.

PROLOGUE
In the beginning

Was it a nightmare that awakened her with a start? She opened her eyes to darkness. Only slivers of moonlight filtered through the lacy curtains of her second-story bedroom window forming pattern pictures on the wall next to her bed. An owl hooted from the magnolia tree just outside, interrupting the amorous chirping of the Everglade geckos.

Alien sounds had infiltrated her unconsciousness: muffled thumps and thuds had brought her crashing to reality. With a fear that washed over her like a tidal wave coming ashore, ten-year-old Kim Alexander scooted deep under her covers. Perspiration seeped from her scalp, dampening her auburn locks. She wanted the comfort of her parents; to know they were here for her, to protect her from the wicked dreams, to shield her from herself. But fear kept her frozen beneath the sheets where the silence became suffocating.

Now, something new demanded her attention. This time it wasn't a dream. The stillness was broken by footsteps, barely audible, as they moved down the hallway toward her bedroom. She pulled the sheet from her head and peeked in the direction of the door. The soft glow of the hallway nightlight flowed beneath it as she watched a shadow pass, return and hesitate on the other side. The pause was long enough for Kim to leap from her four-poster bed into the safety of the built-in storage area beneath her bay window. The lid with its heavy padding and gingham cover settled over her like a camouflaged haven when the bedroom door exploded inward.

Dead quiet reigned momentarily as Kim pictured the intruder trying to establish her whereabouts. She lay motionless, afraid to move an eyelash, or draw in more than short breaths lest he detect the expansion and contraction of her lungs. She knew if he didn't hear her, he probably would never find her.

Forcing herself to crack one eye open, she pressed it against a tiny slit between the boards of her hiding place, below the gingham frill. She saw movement in the filtered moonlit interior of the bedroom.

Then the rampage began. Drawers opened and slammed shut. Treasures on top of her dresser crashed to the floor. Inside the closet, hangers, shoes and boxes from the shelves banged and clattered across the room. Glass shattered. There was rage in the way her desk chair hurtled through space, and the table lamp smashed against a wall.

A massive thud above her shook her refuge when the intruder leaped on the window seat. Had he sensed her hiding place? She could only pray he hadn't. She jammed a fist into her mouth to squelch the sobs she felt rising in her throat. She heard him tugging and ripping at the screen. Did he think she had escaped through the window and onto the magnolia tree?

Where were her parents and why weren't they coming for her? She wanted to scream to let them know something was terribly wrong, but quickly dismissed this foolish thought knowing it would reveal her hiding place. She squeezed her eyes shut, praying this was all a part of the cruel dream that had broken her sleep.

Kim sucked in tiny breaths, fearing another explosion of violence. It came all too soon. Now she heard the curtain rods being yanked out of the wall, material being slashed. He sprang to the floor again, this time savagely attacking the bed. Wood splintered as the madness gained momentum.

When the furor finally subsided, silence became master.

Still fighting her terror, Kim lay in her fetal position, trying to quell the violence that continued to shake her body. Where did this madman go? Could he be lurking behind a closed door waiting for her to reveal her hiding place? Too afraid to abandon her shelter until she knew for certain he had left, she could only wait for her parents to come to her rescue. They would discover the invasion and devastation and call the police to find this monster.

At last sleep overtook her as exhaustion claimed its victory.

Sunlight crept through a crack in the boards of her hiding place. Outside mockingbirds welcomed another beautiful day in the heart of the Florida Everglades. As Kim slowly became aware of her environment, fear again flooded her every sense.

Once more chills spread through her body like an evil plague. She was still alone. Her parents had not come to her rescue. She peered through the cracks of the storage chest but saw nothing but remnants of what had once been her cherished bedroom possessions. Everything she could see had been destroyed. Other than the songs of nature slipping through her window, the place was as quiet as death itself.

She closed her eyes, tried to think what to do next. Should she make a dash to her parents' bedroom and take a chance that this monster was not hiding behind a closed door waiting for her?

Questions nagged at her subconscious. Where were her parents anyway? Had they not heard the frightening disturbance in the middle of the night? Even in a house so huge and rambling as this one, they couldn't have slept so soundly.

Mother and Daddy's bedroom lay at the opposite end of the long, second floor hallway. Walls, closets, and two guest bedrooms occupied the space between. Could that have possibly been enough to muffle the devastating disturbance?

She imagined Daddy already gone to work and Mother sitting at the kitchen table drinking coffee and reading the Miami Herald. She had no idea of the time since her clock lay smashed on the bedroom floor.

Quietly she crawled out of the window seat, cautious to skirt the broken glass and splintered wood. Peeking around the open hall door, she made certain no one lingered there. Dead silence and emptiness greeted her. Could someone be hiding in one of the doorways? One foot followed by the other, she tiptoed down the corridor, past the two guest bedrooms, past the large linen closet, and hesitated by her parents' bedroom door, still closed.

They must be asleep because her mother always left the door open after they were up and she had made the bed. Kim tapped lightly, but there was no response. She twisted the knob, and the door swung open. A ghastly sight met her face on.

The same devastation that had befallen her own room awaited her here with one exception; blood covered much of the bed and floor. As the acrid metallic stench of it assailed her nostrils, she reeled backwards, groping for support from the door frame. Clasping her free hand over her mouth, vomit erupted through her fingers.

Her mother lay still on her side of the bed, eyes open and unblinking, Daddy on the floor in the middle of the room lying in a red pool.

She screamed. Screamed again and again. The sound of her own hysteria propelled her down the corridor to the curving stairway that led to the main floor. She felt herself trembling, stumbling down the steps and grabbing at the railing to stop her fall. This time she reached the bottom where instinct guided her to the hall phone. She dialed 911.

Even before it all happened, Kim felt she should have been forewarned. Her sleep that terrifying night had been fitful as she tossed and turned trying to find a comfortable position in the four-poster bed her grandfather had built for her. When sleep finally came, it distressed her with a repetitious dream that someone pursued her, stealing her away to a frightening and unfamiliar place.

The unsolved murder of her parents was a memory that periodically burst from the misty depths of her mind and rattled her sense of being as Kim Alexander grew from a curly headed ten-year old to a responsible young adult. The nightmare lingered in her memory like a scab over proud flesh. When it surfaced, it was clear and undiluted, a picture burned into her soul with indelible ink, one that would direct her life toward a sworn commitment: to bring the responsible party or parties to justice.

Kim's only living relative became her new guardian. Her mother's unmarried sister, Patricia Sanderson, lived and worked in the northwestern part of the country. Seattle, Washington, was as far away from her place of birth as one could physically get and still be in the continental United States. This city her aunt had made home and established her career after graduating from Miami University. Patricia's substantial salary afforded her the privilege of hiring a full time housekeeper to ease the burden of her new position as a substitute parent.

Kim struggled with the loss of family, friends and climate as she and her aunt slowly adjusted to their new lives together. While Kim threw herself into her schooling, Patricia had acquired more than a niece to raise: she'd been left with the responsibility of Kim's inheritance from her grandfather, Margaret and Patricia's father.

In his will, George Sanderson had left his entire fortune, which included a successful air boat business and the family estate, nicknamed SandHill, after part of his last name and Sofia's maiden name, Hill, to his only grandchild, Kim. With the stipulation that her parents, Margaret and Charles Alexander, would operate the SawGrass Boat Tours and live in the home until Kim came of age, George felt assured his assets would be safe.

By appointing a longtime employee of the Sanderson business as new manager, Patricia felt reassured that the place would still flourish. She hired a reliable garden service to maintain the grounds around the estate, and the Glade City police were commissioned to keep check on the state of the property to avoid vandalism.

This situation stood for fifteen long years, waiting for the rightful owner to grow to adulthood and take charge of her inheritance with its accompanying responsibilities.

Chapter 1

The once handsome three-story Sanderson estate stagnated for nearly fifteen years near the back roads of the Everglades on the outskirts of Glade City, Florida. Boarded up and sealed off from the public by an eight-foot chain link fence, the only thing that kept the home and grounds from being swallowed by the sub-tropical overgrowth was the staff of gardeners hired by Patricia Sanderson. What once had been a proud homestead now clearly begged for someone to love and care for it again.

Surrounded by ten acres of south Florida real estate which embraced an area adjacent to the mangrove wilderness, the estate home designed by George Sanderson had been constructed after he and Sofia were first married. Planning on having at least a half dozen children, the couple settled for the two they had been blessed with, since Sofia's health had precluded having more. Here the couple raised their two daughters while George established an air boat tour business in Glade City.

The estate, tagged as SandHill, became the best known and most talked about landmark of the Everglades, featuring an enormous entryway with a winding staircase and a crystal chandelier from Italy which hung from the center of the third floor ceiling. The spacious first floor's kitchen and butler's pantry covered the rear of the main floor, while a generous living/sitting room focused on a baby grand piano. George had designed a sizable library with an attached, private office. A powder room, plus a full sized bathroom, strategically placed, completed that floor.

The second floor consisted of an immense master bedroom, its private sitting room and bath area, and a room size closet with sliding glass windows. Storage rooms were located at both ends of the hallway, along with a roomy guest quarters with private bathroom, which later became young Kim's bedroom. Two more guest rooms lay between.

The top floor housed the bedrooms assigned to the two daughters, plus a number of rooms which could have been turned into more bedrooms when necessary, but were left as storage areas for the time being.

The exterior of the estate had been left entirely to the discretion of Sofia who designed it to emulate a beautiful tropical garden to be viewed with pleasure from the full wraparound porch of the home.

Glade City, not more than a spot on the map in those days, still attracted plenty of visitors. George and Sofia, like the tourists who answered the call of the Everglades, loved the proximity to nature. Sofia never tired of the variety of birds abounding there. Herons, egrets, anhinga, and an occasional American bald eagle often graced the gardens surrounding the home. They were not far from the Cypress swamps that, from time to time, rewarded them with glimpses of alligators, bobcats, black bears, raccoons and Florida panthers. Not a welcome sight was the possibility of encountering a deadly coral snake, a predator to be reckoned with and feared.

Kim Alexander parked her airport rental car in front of the fence surrounding the Sanderson estate and slipped her five-foot-six inch frame from under the wheel. When she stepped out onto the gravel pathway, her heart thumped as she viewed the property through the metal links. Fifteen years had changed a lot of things. Boards covered the windows like blindfolds. She could still see Grandfather's old cane back chair on the porch, a treasure with which he could never part. A small child's rocking chair stood beside it.

As though it were yesterday, Kim could still visualize her grandfather sitting on that chair carving a pumpkin for her the Halloween before she started school in Miami. "Come sit beside me, sweetheart, and I'll show you how this is done. Put the seeds in that pan on the floor," he instructed. "When we finish we'll find one of Grandma's candles and put it inside the hollow. After that I'll take you fishing."

"Can I have my very own pole, Grandfather?"

"You can have anything you want, my little one."

Would the halls still echo with his exuberant personality?

All the memories of her life here in the Everglades and those very special ones of her grandfather would remain forever in the recesses of her mind and always be a part of whom she had become.

Perspiration trickled down Kim's neck as the heat of the Florida Everglades cruised through her veins, reminding her that she was back in the semi-tropics and no longer in cool Seattle. Removing some tissues from her handbag inside the vehicle, she wiped away the dampness and twisted her auburn curls into a small ponytail, fastening it with a clip high on her head.

The time had come to prove she could overcome the fear that plagued her whenever she remembered the night her life changed in a matter of moments. Unanswered questions stoked a determination to unravel mysteries long a part of her psyche.

With sweaty hands she played with the keys she'd brought with her. One would open the gate, the other, the front door of the house. Excitement momentarily masked the memories she had never been able to erase.

"May I help you, young lady?"

Kim spun around. The voice from behind startled her, shaking her from an intense concentration. Her eyes focused on a brown-uniformed policeman. Two sharp pleats ran down the front of his short-sleeved shirt and through one pocket that displayed a shining badge. He held his hat under his left arm, staring at Kim with unsmiling, piercing blue eyes.

"I'm Kim Alexander, Officer. I inherited this place from my grandfather, George Sanderson," she replied. Feeling intimidated, she reached back into the rental vehicle for her purse and papers she'd brought with her from her aunt's lawyer. "I just arrived from Seattle and wanted to see how everything looked."

"I need to see your ID, ma'am." He extended his hand. "Your driver's license, please."

Kim opened her purse, withdrew the wallet with the license and handed it to the officer.

"Thank you, ma'am." He carefully examined it, and then handed it back to Kim. "So, you're Margaret and Charles Alexander's daughter."

"You knew them?"

"Of them," he corrected. "I was a rookie back then when they lived here." He studied her face. His pale eyes, intense and unwavering, revealed a hint of arrogance. "I'm Officer Grey, ma'am. This place is on my beat, and we check it regularly, a request from Miss Patricia Sanderson of Seattle."

"My aunt," Kim replied as she replaced the driver's license into her wallet. "She's been in charge of this property until now."

"Just doing my job, ma'am. Can never be too careful these days, you know. A lot of folks around would be happy to take advantage of a … situation.

"I see your home address is also Seattle. You live with your aunt?"

"Past tense. I did live with her. However, I'm back here now on a permanent basis."

"Well, welcome to our fair city." His eyes softened somewhat as he added, "If I can be of service to you in any way, just call the station, and they'll forward a message."

Replacing his hat on his head, he turned and retraced his steps to the squad car. When he reached the door, he looked back at Kim. "Come to the station at your earliest convenience, Miss Alexander. We'll confirm the details so no one will be bothering you again on this same issue."

"I intend to, Officer Grey. I have a letter with me from our lawyer making everything official. And, no doubt my aunt has or will be calling to advise the proper authorities of my arrival."

After the squad car left, Kim took her cell phone from her pocket, brought up the address book, found the number and pressed the send button.

An answering machine picked up. "This is Gloria. Please leave a message."

Chapter 2

At least a full hour remained before Gloria would be home from the real estate office where she worked. Kim knew her best friend in the world wanted to accompany her on her first inspection of the estate and its property, and she welcomed the thought of having a buddy along to help fight off the demons that played in her mind. Visiting the police station in the meantime with the legal papers on the property should satisfy the authorities.

She cruised down Lincoln Avenue, the main street in town, past the Glade City Motel, a number of fast food restaurants that had sprung up since she'd left, a Wal-Mart, another recent addition, and on past a number of small shops she couldn't remember existing before. The town had definitely changed in the years of her absence.

Kim recalled the police station had been on the north side of town, somewhere along the main drag. She couldn't miss it, she thought. But somehow she had.

"Guess this calls for a cup of coffee and some local information," she murmured aloud as she pulled into a small strip mall with a variety of stores, a restaurant and an ice cream shop.

After she slid into a booth of the Glade City Family Restaurant, a waitress came for her order.

"Just a cup of coffee, please, no cream. I need the caffeine."

"No problem, sweetie. Anything else I can get you?" The waitress's short, dark brown hair framed tanned skin deeply lined from an over abundance of Florida sun.

"There is one thing, if you don't mind? I'm looking for the police station. I used to know where it was when I lived here as a child."

"Well, welcome back ta Glade City, darlin'. My name is Marsha, and I understand why you can't find it. They tore down the old station house a few years back. The TropiCal Hotel's on that spot now." She tucked a pencil back over her ear. "The city had a brand new buildin' put up 'bout two years ago on a much larger chunk of property. Guess the big wigs was bustin' their socks tryin' ta figger out where ta put all their 'hard earned' tax money. They decided they needed a bigger place 'cause they wanted to combine City Hall, the police station, the courtrooms, and new jail quarters. Now it sits on a whole city block. So, go back two blocks, turn left and you'll see it on the corner of Palm Drive and Everglade Road. Can't miss it." She gave a toothy grin. "It's the million-dollar pride of our fair city."

"Well, thanks so much for your directions, Marsha, and I'm also happy to meet you."

Kim finished her coffee while thinking about the friendliness of her waitress. What a difference there is in people from a small town and those who have been used to living in a large city like Seattle, she thought. You wouldn't find that down home earthiness in most city people. Not like this, anyway. A smile worked its way across her lips as she headed out to locate the new police headquarters.

When she found the new station house, she understood why the waitress had called it the million-dollar pride of Glade City. It looked more like it should belong in the city of Seattle than here in the Florida Everglades. The three-story edifice consisted of a glassy blue exterior that mirrored and reflected the sun, which probably helped keep the building cooler.

To gain entry to the building, Kim had to go through security similar to that in the airports. Quite up-to-date and modern, she reflected.

Police headquarters occupied the front portion of the main level. The rear half housed the jail. City offices inhabited the second floor while courtrooms filled the top floor.

A female officer at a desk directed her to the proper authority. The officer in charge of "Security Patrol" was a big man, six-foot something and weighed in the 300-pound range. A plaque said he was Sgt. Ben Nelson. His prominent desk occupied one complete end of the large entry area.

"Help you, ma'am?"

"Yes, sir. I'm Kim Alexander from Seattle, … formerly of Glade City." She reached into her handbag and withdrew an envelope. "My grandfather, George Sanderson, willed me his estate." Kim handed him the legal papers from her lawyer in Seattle. "I need to notify the proper authorities so they know I'll be working on the place as soon as I can hire a cleanup crew. My aunt, Patricia Sanderson, has been the party in charge until I could assume control."

The officer took the document. "See some ID, ma'am?"

Kim's handed over her driver's license while he thumbed through the four sheets of legalese.

"I've been on the force for twenty years, ma'am," he said, looking up at her through thick lenses. "I remember your mother and father lived here and ran the Glade City Air Boat Tours … until …" He let his words slide away quietly, picked up a can of pop he had setting on his desk and took a big swallow. "So, your grandfather was the original owner of the estate? I just assumed it always belonged to your parents. Not that it's any of my business, ma'am. Guess it don't make much difference at this point, anyways."

"The deeds for both the estate and the business are in my name." Kim fidgeted with her shoulder strap as Officer Nelson finished scanning the papers. "I have them with me if you need to see them."

"No problem, Ms. Alexander. This letter from the lawyer is sufficient. I'll see the force is aware of the changes. Will you still be wantin' the place patrolled … like your aunt was havin' done?"

"Yes, please, for now, Sergeant, until I'm able to hire some help to clean the place. I'm not certain what sort of time schedule will be involved here, but I'll be sure to notify the station when I find out."

Officer Nelson copied the papers and handed them back to Kim. "Thank you, ma'am. 'Preciate your coming in."

Chapter 3

By the time Kim finished at the police station and returned to her rental vehicle, it was well after five o'clock. Before she turned the ignition, she took out a hand drawn map Gloria had sent her. Finding her place would be easy with Gloria's detailed instructions. As she studied it again to refresh her memory, a tap on her window startled her.

"Finding everything you need, ma'am?" Officer Grey bent over and peered inside her vehicle.

She rolled down the window. "That's the second time today you startled me, Officer."

"Sorry. Just thought if I could be of some assistance …" He grinned and Kim felt her cheeks heat up. His smile illuminated a handsome face. With his eyes focused on her hand-drawn map, he said, "Why don't you tell me who you're trying to find, and I can lead you there?" His expression seemed much softer now. "After all, that's my job … to assist the residents and any newcomers to our town."

"I think I'll be okay, Officer Grey. My friend has drawn me a very thorough map, so it should be no problem."

He reached through the open window to take the map from her hand, but Kim held it tightly. "If you're quite certain, ma'am. It's just what being a police officer is all about. May I just have a look?"

Reluctantly Kim allowed him to take the piece of paper. He studied it for a moment. "It would appear that your friend is quite good at drawing directions. It looks accurate."

"I'm sure I'll be fine, but I thank you very much anyway."

Kim started the car and watched in the rear view mirror as the policeman stood there focused on her departure. She thought afterward she should have accepted his offer, but his scrutiny left her feeling self-conscious.

When she pulled up in Gloria's driveway, the front door flew open and her friend came bursting out before Kim could turn off the engine.

"I thought work would never end today. I couldn't think of anything but you. It's so good to have you back." She opened the car door and grabbed Kim, giving her a lung-crushing hug. "I'm never going to let you leave Glade City again, Ms. Kim Alexander." Several tears of joy slid down her cheeks as she brushed a golden curl from her brow.

"I hope I never have to go away again, Gloria. This day has been a long time coming. And here you are in a brand new home of your own."

"Well, I've been in it almost a year now, and I love it here."

Gloria was just as pretty as Kim remembered her when they played together as little girls. The blonde ringlets, now stylishly shorter, framed a pert, attractive face with a turned up nose and blue eyes. Snapshots she had sent over the years did not do justice to the young woman who had wrested her from the car and squeezed the breath out of her.

"I've never known an afternoon that dragged so," Gloria said breathlessly. "Let me help you with your things, and we can get started with our catching up. I've made a big chicken salad, and iced tea is ready."

"I've seen the estate, Gloria," Kim said, as she opened the trunk, "from the outside only. It looks pretty lonely and unkempt ... timeworn, to be exact." The two of them started to pull out suitcases and boxes. "I packed all the rest of my worldly belongings for Aunt Patricia to send when she knows I've settled."

"Don't worry about the estate house, honey. You'll have that taken care of before you know it." She hit a button on the garage remote in her hand. "Let's go in this way. Easier access to the bedrooms. I've made room in the garage for you to park after we get you unpacked."

Gloria's home reflected the modern construction of Florida living: pale green stucco-covered cement block, topped with a gray concrete tile roof and built to resist the possibility of extreme wind velocity. Young, colorful blooming plants followed the perimeter of the building: hibiscus blossomed near the porch area while a tiny Bougainvillea with rust-colored blooms climbed a trellis next to the garage door. Several groupings of pigmy date palms lent a tropical finish to the front lawn.

Inside, the place was a compliment to her friend, with feminine touches everywhere. The guest bedroom was a pale pink with white eyelet curtains and bedspread. The girls opened Kim's suitcases, hung up skirts, slacks and blouses in a small walk-in closet and put lingerie and personals into dresser drawers.

"Come on, honey, I'm starving." Gloria grabbed Kim's arm and marched her into the kitchen nook where she had set the table for supper.

While they ate and later cleaned up, the two women talked as though they hadn't had any communication since their childhood separation, though letters and phone calls had kept them in constant touch. But being physically together again brought up endless questions and answers. Before they knew it, it was two o' clock in the morning.

"Gloria, I'm so sorry. I've kept you up way past your bedtime. Work tomorrow as usual? You'll be dead tired."

"Not to worry, honey. I'm taking tomorrow off. I wouldn't be able to concentrate on work, anyway." Gloria reached over and squeezed Kim's arm. "It's hard to believe we're finally going to live in the same town again after all these years. Best of all, you'll be staying here with me until you finish work at SandHill. So, what's the plan of attack for tomorrow?"

"I have the keys," Kim said. "We can go there in the morning and have a good look around. I'll make notes and you can help me find the right people to do the cleanup work. But first … ." She hesitated for a moment, concentrating.

"What?" Gloria prompted.

"It's just this old thing of mine. The unsolved, the unexplained, uncalled for… "

"Don't say another word," Gloria interrupted. "I know what you mean. I'm here to help you all I can, friend. We'll go over the place with a magnet, if necessary. We'll leave no stone unturned, as the saying goes. So, let's just do it."

Chapter 4

The next morning arrived sooner than the girls would have liked. Cool showers, strong coffee for Gloria and brisk tea for Kim helped their thinking processes. Each had a bowl of cold cereal and a half grapefruit for extra starting power. Gloria grabbed a notepad and pen and the two headed out in her white Sedan Deville.

The sun was brilliant by the time they arrived at the estate. All the better, Kim thought. It should help to dispel the seriousness of the occasion and brighten up an interior thrust into isolation, and shrouded in darkness for years.

When they reached the property, Kim stepped out of the car, unlocked the iron gate and pushed it aside to allow Gloria access. She pulled through and parked in front of the porch steps while Kim closed and barred the entrance behind her.

Once a masterpiece in gleaming white with a typical southern-style wrap-around porch, the house sat partially draped in wisteria planted by Kim's grandmother. The vines now clung to one complete side of the place, immersing everything in a maze of lavender and green. Although hibiscus, bougainvillea, plumbago and other exotic tropical plants and shrubs no longer graced the garden, the place still held Kim's heart captive.

As she mounted the seven stairs to the porch, Kim turned to her friend. "I didn't tell you yesterday, Gloria, but when I first arrived here and was standing outside the gate surveying the property, a police officer stopped by to check on me. His name is Officer Grey. Do you know him, by any chance?"

"I do. His first name is Chase ... very good-looking. The kind I would call handsome in a very cool way." Gloria rolled her eyes. "I met him last year at the Policeman's Ball, a charity for underprivileged children. He asked me to dance."

"He struck me as being all business, but then he <u>was</u> on duty," Kim said

"Chase can be very charming when he wants to be. I believe he's around thirty-five, never been married, kind of has an eye for the ladies, I've been told. He came across to me as a bit ... controlling. Outside of that, I don't know a whole lot about him. Neither Brad, my boss, nor I have been into much dating. Been too busy making a living and keeping the real estate office in reasonable shape, so we don't get around to seeing how the other half lives." She stopped, turned to Kim and said, "When we have time, I'd like to take you into the office to meet Brad. He's a great partner and a good friend."

"I'd like that," Kim said as she unlocked the heavy oak door, at one time her grandfather's pride, but now showing signs of age and assault from the sun. When it creaked open, an overpowering musty odor assaulted their nostrils, and dankness wrapped them like a wet cloak. The two stood side-by-side peering into the immense entry hall. A curving stairway led to the second and third floors. The whole interior would have been in complete darkness except for the huge skylight that dominated the third floor ceiling. It allowed sunlight, dimmed only by layers of accumulated dust, to illuminate the grand entryway and ooze into the adjoining rooms. Next to it, a cobwebbed crystal chandelier hung on a heavy chain.

Cautiously, the two entered the hallway. "Wow. This is kinda creepy, girl." Gloria scanned her surroundings.

Tables, chairs, the grandfather clock, bookcases, every piece of furniture in their sight had been covered in white sheets, including the baby grand piano.

"Thank goodness for that skylight," Kim added. She left the front door open for fresh air and additional light.

The hall didn't seem as ostentatious as it had when Kim was younger, but the sweeping staircase still looked as imposing as ever. Mildew had established itself everywhere, and more cobwebs claimed their share of the area, as well. With her initial survey, Kim surmised it would take a sizable crew to get rid of these problems.

"The place needs a lot of refreshing, I'd say." She wrinkled her nose.

They walked into the large living room where the covers concealed most of the massive, baroque furniture that Grandfather and Grandmother had purchased and cherished, and Kim's parents had chosen to keep.

"We need to open the drapes and get more light in here." Kim moved toward the windows and began to slide the long curtains aside while Gloria followed suit.

"Brad will know just the outfit to come in here and clean this place," Gloria said as she touched a cover on one of the chairs. A billow of dust spewed into the dead calm air, and Gloria jumped back from the cloud of grime. "Wow! This place needs it big time." She covered a sneeze with one hand.

"Sorry about that, Gloria, but before I can have anyone touch anything in here, I'm going to have to go through the personal belongings that were left when Aunt Patricia came for me. She hired a firm to close up the place after the authorities finished all their investigations. So, nothing has been touched since." Mentally, Kim assessed jobs that needed to be done.

"Everything was left just as it had been," she continued, "with the exception of the two bedrooms which couldn't be touched until the police finished collecting evidence. She also hired someone to pack my clothing and personal items. That was it. Grandfather's records and personal papers have been locked in the library storage closet since my parents took over the place after he died. Those are the things I especially want to look into. My mother never wanted to bother with any of that stuff, and Daddy was always too busy at the boat tours."

"So, basically, everything has been sitting here waiting for someone to take over." Gloria put her arm around Kim and gave her a squeeze. "I can get a few days off to help you, honey, if you'd like."

"Thanks, Gloria. I'd appreciate that. Just seeing this place again brings back such mixed emotions; my wonderful childhood with my grandfather, … right up to the … loss of my parents." She took hold of Gloria's hand and lead her into the formal dining room. "I'm so glad you could come with me today."

The two women moved on through the butler's pantry and into the kitchen.

"After living with Aunt Patricia in her condo, this kitchen looks like it could hold her entire place," Kim said, taking in the extent of the room.

Dust laden pots and pans still hung from their hooks above the island range. The refrigerator door had been left open after being shut off and cleaned out. A built-in desk occupied one corner of the room beneath a large window that opened onto an expanse of what had once been a beautiful garden. Kim sat down in the desk chair and glanced at the row of recipe books on a shelf above her. Pads of paper and a flowered glass that held pens and pencils sat on one corner of the desktop.

She pulled open the large drawer in the center as Gloria checked out some of the cupboards and examined the pantry. Small piles of unorganized paper filled the inside along with paper clips and a stapler. There were a few notes that her mother had written as reminders for certain events. Some recipes in her mother's handwriting had been clipped together and stashed to one side. Kim thumbed through them. She recognized some of the dishes her mother had prepared when the housekeeper had not been around to cook. There was a recipe for barbeque sauce in an unfamiliar hand with an added note, "You'll love this. It's my own special formula for the best sauce this side of Miami." Kim wondered which one of her mother's friends had given this to her since the other recipes were all tagged with the donor's name. This one had no signature.

There were three drawers on either side of the knee hole. Those on the right contained housekeeping information; work schedules for the Ramons, repairs to be made and new equipment to purchase. The left side held an assortment of old mail, photos, unused and canceled checks, and a jumble of unrelated items. Kim could only assume that the authorities had dug through these searching for clues and answers.

Examining all these items, one piece at a time, wasn't going to be easy.

They spent the balance of the morning checking the rest of the house from the ground floor to the second and third story. The second floor held five very large bedrooms. Mother and Daddy's, the master bedroom, was the largest. Each had its own private bath quarters. Kim's and one next to it, were equal in size. The remaining two had been used as guest rooms. The third level consisted of another five large rooms, three of which had never been finished and had been used as storage areas. Margaret and Patricia's childhood bedrooms had been on opposite ends of the third floor hallway.

"Let's break for lunch," Gloria suggested. "We can stop at the office and I'll introduce you to Brad. He can give you some ideas for a cleaning crew."

"Great idea. I hadn't realized how famished I am."

When the two women arrived at Glade City Real Estate, Kim followed Gloria past several stalls of real estate dealers to a back office where her friend knocked briefly on a door and then popped her head into the room.

"Brad, I want you to meet Kim Alexander, my best friend ever, and … "

"You don't have to say another word." Brad stood and put out his hand for Kim. "I think I probably know this young lady almost as well as you do, Gloria." He chuckled and gave a warm smile. Looking directly at Kim, he said, "Ever since she found out you were coming back to Glade City she could talk of nothing else." He held her hand tightly as he studied her face.

"She's been pretty useless waiting for you to get here. Maybe I can get some work out of her now." An infectious grin crept across his lips.

His lean, six-foot-three figure stood well above Kim's. Silky chestnut hair framed a square, ruggedly handsome face with hazel eyes that exuded fire. With an affable smile and warm handshake he put Kim instantly at ease. He looked vaguely familiar, and she wondered if he might have a connection to her past.

Gloria ignored Brad's remark and went on. "Kim, this is my good friend, my business partner, and the company broker, Brad Kimbal."

"Kimbal," Kim repeated, staring intently at the young man still grasping her hand. "Not, by any chance, Leslie's brother?"

"None other." He smiled again, showing a row of even white teeth.

"I thought I recognized you as someone I may have known before. Leslie and I were friends at school and slept over at each other's homes on occasion."

Brad grinned. "Well, back then it was my job to get out of the house before Leslie brought over any of her pesky little girlfriends for pajama parties. No offense intended, please. You know how high school boys are. Not a bit interested in little grade schoolers."

Kim suppressed a smile remembering how most of Leslie's friends had crushes on her handsome, big brother.

"Does Leslie still live here?"

"No, she went to college in Miami and married a guy she met at school. She gets back now and then to visit with our parents. They're still here in the same house they've been in forever."

Brad's phone rang and he answered. "I'll check it out right away and get back to you as soon as I find out."

Gloria tugged on Kim's arm. "Let's get out of here. We'll talk to Brad later."

"Nice to have met you again, Kim, after all these years. Let's get back together soon."

"Don't worry, Brad. We'll be back and forth for the next few days," Gloria said. "We're not finished with you yet, but right now, we're starving." She grabbed Kim's arm and hauled her out of Brad's office, closing the door behind them.

"I knew he looked familiar, but fifteen years has a way of changing people; for him, even better than I remember. Not that he wasn't good-looking before, but now he's no longer a boy."

"Come on. Enough about Brad for now. I'm taking you to the local watering hole where you get fast service at a reasonable price, and, if you're lucky enough to get Marsha, some of the local gossip for free."

Kim laughed as Gloria dragged her along to the car. "I think I've met that one. She's a very down-to-earth person."

"We call it 'homespun'." Gloria put the key in the ignition and they were off before Kim finished buckling her seat belt.

After they had eaten, Gloria made a suggestion. "Let's get back to SandHill, Kim. We can start checking out the personal stuff you mentioned. I'll pick up some boxes at the grocery store, and we'll sort the things you want to keep as opposed to those that go to the dumpster."

"That's a very good idea." Kim sat back and relaxed as Gloria made her way through a town Kim barely recognized anymore.

"I realize I have to get the place ready to bring in a cleaning crew, but the most important thing to me now is making certain I check everything. There must be overlooked clues. I know the police were supposed to have combed the place, but they never, ever came up with any suspects or leads. I believe they put the case to rest just to get it out of their hair."

Gloria pulled up in front of a Winn Dixie and parked.

"For my own peace of mind, I have to try and find something, anything that might give me some sort of closure. Outside of Aunt Patricia, I'm probably the only person who has anything at stake in wanting to bring a monster to justice." Kim looked over at Gloria who had switched off the engine and was studying her friend closely. "This thing has haunted me for so many years it seems to be a part of me. I believe with all my heart the police just weren't interested enough, lacked technology … or both."

"I'm with you, honey. You've waited long enough. You deserve some answers. I'll help all I can. I just wish I had more time off, but at least we can get a good start."

"I love you, Gloria. You're a true friend." She reached over and squeezed Gloria's hand tightly.

From one of the store's box boys, the two women picked up five large fruit containers, threw them into the trunk and back seat of the car and headed out of town toward the old estate.

"I only hope you won't be too disappointed if nothing turns up," Gloria said as they passed the few remaining homes on the outskirts of town. "According to the local paper, the police did a pretty thorough search after your aunt took you back to Seattle. I remember my mother discussing it with Dad. In fact it was the talk of Glade City; around town, in our local paper, and even a blurb in the Miami Herald."

"Stop!" Kim said as she seized Gloria's arm. "Let's go to the newspaper's morgue and check out the information they have on record. That should give me some sort of good starting point."

"Great idea, pal," Gloria said. Swinging the car around, she retraced her way back to town and to the Glade City Globe.

Chapter 5

Gloria and Kim sat in front of a microfiche where the past newspapers had been recorded. They sped through hundreds of pages until they reached the date of the murders. Pictures of the estate, Kim's parents and Kim spread below bold headlines: MURDERS ROCK GLADE CITY.

> "Well known local family, Margaret and Charles Alexander, owners of the city's popular Glade City Boat Tours, were found murdered in their beds yesterday morning. Miraculously, their only child, daughter Kim, was spared. City police are still searching the home for evidence and have not yet released any information as to their findings. The County sheriff's office will be aiding in the investigation of this grisly crime."

Another article from the following day read:

> "Local senior officer, Max Young, and his partner, Chase Grey, have been assigned to the Alexander

murder case for further investigation. The home has been posted off-limits until a thorough search can be completed.

The couple's ten-year-old daughter, Kimberly, has been placed in police custody awaiting the arrival of her aunt, Mrs. Alexander's younger sister, who currently lives in Seattle."

"What about this Max Young?" Kim continued checking out details. "He was the chief investigating officer. Do you know anything about him, Gloria? Is he still around?"

Gloria shrugged her shoulders. "I just know that he retired years ago."

"And Chase? Maybe we can start with him. We know his whereabouts." Her heart beat a little bit faster as she anticipated the possibilities.

"I think that sounds like a great idea," Gloria said while she busied herself printing out copies of important pages from the old records. "Best said, we can try. Chase might be willing. He loves talking about himself. He might still have some contact with Max, as an old partner. If not, maybe he at least knows where he is now. Personally, I have no clue." She placed the Photostats in a manila envelope for safekeeping.

"Let's get whatever else we need copied and then go home." Kim stood up and stretched. "We've had a pretty busy day, and I don't know about you, but I need a break … and some fresh air. This place is pretty stuffy."

"And musty smelling, too," Gloria added. She gathered up her purse and keys. "I'm ready. We can have an early night, get a good sleep, and be off to SandHill as soon as possible in the morning." She giggled. "Let's try to round up Chase and see what information we can squeeze out of him."

Chapter 6

The following morning Kim and Gloria were up by seven, prepared toast and freshly squeezed orange juice. While Kim enjoyed a dish of strawberries and cream, Gloria dialed the police station to inquire about Chase. The officer who answered said he was on duty, but would see that her message reached him.

They gathered up what they anticipated needing for the day, made some sandwiches, put the cooler packed with ice and several cans of root beer into the back seat of Gloria's Sedan Deville, alongside the extra fruit box that had not made it into the trunk yesterday. Gloria locked the house, and the two set off for the estate.

When Gloria pulled up to the iron gates, she stopped and let Kim out to open up, then drove in and parked in the same place they used yesterday.

"Let's have a quick walk around to the back of the property, Gloria. That's another area that needs much attention," Kim said.

They made their way to the rear of the home where the gardeners had managed to keep the Florida overgrowth under control. A jungle had developed beyond the fenced area.

Both girls wore flat shoes and shorts in preparation for a good day's work. As they made their way through the course Floritam grass, it seemed to reach out and bite bare skin through the open sides of their sandals.

"I used to hate this grass when I was a kid," Kim said, remembering the tough, almost weed-like ground cover that had the ability to withstand Florida's harsh sun.

"Keep your eyes open, Gloria. There could be snakes on the loose," Kim cautioned. "My grandfather found a coral snake in the back yard during one of my summer visits. He trapped it in an old piece of PVC pipe." She shuddered at the memory. "Since one end was already capped, he chased it into the opening which he stuffed with steel wool and wire to prevent it from from getting back out."

"I'd say that must have been a pretty scary experience," Gloria said.

"It served as a lesson and a reminder," Kim added.

"What did he do with the snake?"

"He kept a little wild animal sanctuary at the boat tours, a kind of fun place for tourists to see. The coral snake added to the mystique."

"Glad I didn't have to feed anything like that," Gloria said.

As they circled the estate, Kim took a notebook and pen from her pocket and began making notes. Some of the old bushes and trees needed to be torn out and replaced. She intended to hire a horticulturist to draw up some plans for new plantings and flowers. The exterior of the building cried for paint, but that would have to wait until the grounds were redone.

The two girls were deep into discussing possible businesses to hire for the variety of rejuvenation projects needed when they heard tires on the gravel driveway out front. Kim had left the gate open and someone was already trespassing. Gloria heard it as well, and put her index finger to her lips.

Kim nodded knowing she should remain calm, but the estate was several miles out of town, and there were no neighbors nearby. After locating her cell phone in her shorts pocket, she wrapped her hands tightly around it and proceeded to move slowly toward a corner of the house, Gloria at her side. An old Queen Sago with sprawling fronds afforded them a safety shield while Kim peeked around the side of the building. A police car parked adjacent to

Gloria's Caddy. A uniformed policeman stepped out and put on his cap.

"Good Morning, Officer Grey," Kim said with a sigh of relief as she came out from behind the sago.

"And to you, Ms. Alexander. I stopped by to see if everything is okay. From the road I noticed the open gate." He removed his cap and placed it under his arm. "I didn't see the vehicle until I reached the fence and realized it wasn't yours."

"Everything is fine," Kim said. "We're just checking on the condition of the grounds and taking notes." Gloria stepped up closer to Kim. "Did they give you my message at the station?"

"Morning, Ms. Latham," he said, nodding his head and smiling as he switched focus to Gloria. She acknowledged his greeting with a wave of her hand.

Turning back to Kim, he said, "I haven't been back to headquarters since I went on duty, and no one has radioed. But if it wasn't urgent, they would just let me know when I got back to the station.

"What was the message, Ms. Alexander? Can I be of service in some way?"

"As a matter of fact, I had a question to ask you … not pertaining to my property here, but in regards to an old partner of yours, Max Young. I wondered …" She hesitated, then continued. "Would you possibly have any idea where he could be located?"

Chase was quiet for a moment while he studied the young women. "I haven't heard from Max since he left Glade City." He removed his sunglasses, took a handkerchief from a back pocket and wiped a speck of dust from one lens. "Originally, he told me that he had requested a transfer back to Miami, and it had been accepted. Said he wanted to be there when he retired."

He put his glasses up to the sun, inspected them, and then put them back on.

"I just thought you might know how I could get in touch with him. I … I know that he and my parents were old friends, and I'd like to talk to him about them." She watched Chase closely. He had an air about him that made her feel a bit intimidated and distracted.

"Well, I don't really know more than that, but … " His voice softened. "I'll be happy to make some inquiries, though."

Kim began to relax. "I'd appreciate it."

He started toward the squad car, and then turned back to face Kim. "Perhaps you wouldn't mind my asking you something?"

"Please do."

"My shift is over at four. I'll have some time to see what I can do to locate Max's whereabouts, if possible. We could discuss it over dinner tonight … my treat. What do you say?"

"I … I don't really know if I could do that, Officer Grey."

"Chase. Please."

"Well, … Chase, I'm staying with Gloria, and I don't know what she has planned for the evening."

"Kim," Gloria interrupted, "it doesn't matter to me. Do whatever you need to do. I'll be fine."

Kim looked from Chase to Gloria and back. "I appreciate your invitation, Chase. You've been very kind to offer your help, but I don't want to put you out in any way."

"It's not putting me out … trust me."

Kim looked at Gloria again. "I really don't want to leave Gloria so soon. After all, I've only been here a few days."

"I certainly understand, Ms Alexander. Perhaps another time."

"Why don't you come over later to my place this evening?" Gloria said. "For some coffee or iced tea, perhaps."

"Thank you." He smiled, and the sternness seemed to melt away. "I'd like that. Is eight o'clock okay? I'll see what I can dig up on Max for you, Ms Alexander."

"Just call me Kim, Chase." She glanced at Gloria who nodded. "Eight should be fine."

As the squad car left, the girls walked back to the Caddy, got out the packed lunches and the empty boxes.

"I think I'd like to start in the library storage closet first. That's where Grandfather used to put all his accumulated papers, important or not. There could be information in those boxes, things that might answer some of my questions."

"I'm with you, honey," Gloria said as she carried the cooler up the front porch steps.

Kim followed with three of the empty boxes and the house key in hand. They left the front door open and hauled the rest of the things into the library. A healthy stash of built-in bookcases lined two walls. A large desk, some easy chairs and floor lamps occupied the opposite corner of the room while a pool table stood in the middle of the room, all still covered in their ghost-like sheets. Grandfather's passion for pool had led him to try and teach Kim to handle a cue stick as soon as she was tall enough to see over the edge of the table.

From home, Gloria had brought two large oil lanterns, the kind local folks kept in case of power outages. She set them in opposite corners of the oversized storage closet to distribute the light as much as possible. When she lit them, they peeled away most of the shadows.

The girls brought in their boxes, set up two folding chairs, and sat down to begin the immeasurable task of sorting through each and every paper. Clues could be lurking almost anywhere in this unorganized conglomeration of papers.

The desk drawers held a few old letters, envelopes with bills that had been taken care of long ago by Aunt Patricia. Most of these Kim tossed into the wastebasket since they were no longer needed and had no relationship to the present time or the death of her parents. Papers that neither of the girls were sure about were carefully packed into some of the boxes they had brought with them. These would be taken to Gloria's and examined later at their leisure. Both girls worked diligently until it was time to break for lunch.

By five o'clock, Gloria stopped and looked at Kim. "If you've had enough for one day, honey, we can get this stuff loaded in the car and head for home. I'll start supper while you sort what you need on the dining room table."

"I'm more than ready to call it a day, Gloria, but I'll help with dinner and then we can both get to the boxes before Chase arrives."

Chapter 7

That evening, after dinner and cleanup lay behind them, Kim and Gloria spread the dining room table with the newspaper copies they'd made the day before and the papers they'd brought back from the library closet today. At eight sharp, the doorbell rang, and Gloria got up to answer. Chase stood at the front door casually dressed in a pair of tan safari-style shorts with a cotton shirt displaying a variety of alligator designs. He wore navy blue dock shoes and a billed cap imprinted with "Miami Dolphins".

"I found some information for Miss Alexander ... Kim." He removed the cap and put it in his back pocket.

"Come on in, Chase. Kim's working in back."

Gloria led him through the house to the table where Kim sat. She had covered up the photocopies, but left her pad of notes open beside her.

"Hi, Chase." Kim looked up and smiled.

Gloria pointed to a chair across from Kim. "Have a seat. Could I get you a cold drink?"

"Would you have any ice tea?" Gloria nodded, and he settled himself in the chair she had offered him. "I did find out a bit more about Max Young," he began.

"Several years after his transfer to Miami, he took an early retirement. According to our former chief of police, Max was burned out and needed a change of pace." He reached into his shirt pocket and pulled out a piece of paper. "Chief Laslow said Max gave him this address and phone number at the apartment where he would be living. Said if he ever got to Miami to look him up. The chief never had the opportunity to make the contact and doesn't even know if Max is still there." He opened the folded sheet and handed it to Kim. "If he's still there ... you might be able to track him down. There's a phone number, but after all these years it may not be in service anymore."

Gloria returned with a tray holding three glasses of iced tea, some sliced lemon, a bowl of sugar, napkins and teaspoons. She placed the tray in the middle of the table away from Kim's papers.

"Thank you so much, Chase. I appreciate your effort." Kim smiled as she accepted the paper. "I'll try to follow up tomorrow."

"Happy to oblige. Just a word of warning, though. If you're going to be doing anything around the old homestead, it might be wise to notify us. The place has been known to attract would-be vandals and freeloaders."

"I've not heard anything about that." Kim put down her glass of tea. "My aunt and I were never informed." She studied the young officer.

"Probably because the police have kept a close watch on the place. There never seemed to be any reason to worry your aunt when the department could effectively handle any situations. But, please don't worry. Nothing unusual has happened lately. I just don't want to see you get into any trouble." He took the glass of tea Gloria handed him and squeezed in some lemon.

"I'll be sure to call the station when I'm ready to go there again. But tell me, Chase, has anyone really managed to get past the fence and gate?"

"When vandals want in, a gate and fence won't stop them. Most are pretty creative. No one seems to have broken into the house yet, but we posted signs stating that surveillance cameras are set up and monitored at the police station. This happened to be false, actually, but it helped to frighten off would-be criminals. The place is always checked by patrol cars." He drank his tea in several swallows. "I might add that your aunt has been very generous in paying for our services. The estate has always been top priority with us."

He got up, raised his empty glass to Gloria, and thanked her. "I'll be on my way then. No need to take up anymore of your time. It's been a pleasure."

Kim pushed her chair back and stood. "I'll see you out, Chase, and again, thank you for the information." They walked down the hall to the front door.

Kim stepped out onto the porch as Chase was leaving.

"Beautiful car you have," she said, surveying the small red Mercedes convertible parked at the curb. "Growing up, I always had a yen for one of those."

"My feelings exactly." He hesitated at the bottom of the stairs. "If there's anything else I can do for you, please call me." His eyes were warm and friendly, reflecting the glow of the porch lights. Before he turned to leave, he said, "I'd like to ask you something ... "

"And that would be?"

"I would still like to take you out to dinner some evening when you have the time." He paused, waiting for her answer.

"I ... I have some things I feel are very important for me to get out of the way, Chase. Let me see how my time is going, and I'll get back to you soon."

"Good enough. I'll look forward to it." He turned, opened the car door, got in, and was gone in moments.

Kim closed and locked the door behind her. She went back to her seat in the dining room where Gloria was sorting some of the paperwork they had collected.

"I still can't believe you're actually here, honey. It's been such a long time getting to this point in our lives." Gloria got up from her chair, stretched and yawned. Reaching for Kim, she gave her a big hug.

Kim hugged back. "Get to bed. I want you to be bright and chipper in the morning."

"I hear you, honey. I do feel a bit weary. You would do well to get some extra rest yourself."

"I won't be too long, Gloria. I'm just so anxious to get into more of this stuff," she said, pointing to the piles of paper.

After Gloria retired, Kim picked up an expanding file folder marked Sun Bank of Florida. When she opened it, she could see that it was filled with months, no, perhaps even years of canceled checks that Grandfather must have stashed all together. At least they appeared to be arranged in chronological order.

She sorted through a few that dated back to the 1970s. Randomly, she picked out the year of 1978, thumbing through several months. There were checks to her mother and father when they must have been living in Miami. Notations in the memo area stated: Patricia's room and board. She remembered Aunt Patricia attending college in Miami. Grandfather paid for schooling and for her to stay with Margaret and Charles instead of having her board elsewhere. Long ago, her aunt had told her that it was Grandfather's way of helping his family financially. Some checks were made personally to Patricia, probably for college needs and spending money.

She was looking through the checks from 1979 when she discovered one made out to a Dr. Warren Wagner. No memo. Then another. No memo. She continued looking over the canceled checks, but most seemed to be for ordinary living expenses, groceries, household items and clothing.

More checks turned up to this Doctor Warren Wagner. The first ones were a nominal fee, probably for office visits. The next one dated in May of 1980 was made out to him for $40,000.00. Then one to the Palm Medical Clinic and Private Hospital, shortly after Wagner's check, for $55,000.00. Someone in the family must have been seriously ill, or it could have been for an accident. She couldn't remember anything having been mentioned before; neither Aunt Patricia nor her grandparents had talked about a sickness in the family ... or an accident. It couldn't have had anything to do with what had happened to her parents. The dates were far too early.

She considered it best not to leave anything to speculation if she could possibly dig up some answers. She would try to track down this Dr. Wagner, if he were still practicing. Depending on his age, he could be retired. In that case, she hoped a phone listing might be available. If not, perhaps ... she didn't really want to ask Aunt Patricia, unless there was no other way.

She kicked off her shoes and put the file aside. Tomorrow was another day.

Chapter 8

In the morning Kim found Gloria in the kitchen cutting grapefruit. "Last night after you went to bed, I found these canceled checks in one of Grandfather's file folders. They're all made out to a Dr. Warren Wagner." Kim waved a large brown envelope in front of Gloria. "No one has ever mentioned that name before, and I don't remember talk about anyone being sick in the family."

"Don't you suppose people go to doctors on occasion for a physical or simple little things like blood pressure checks or a cut finger?" Gloria laughed at the seriousness in Kim's voice. "Most folks don't bother to mention their regular everyday, ordinary medical problems."

"Gloria, I hardly think that these represented everyday problems." She fanned out a handful of canceled checks. "Most of them to the doctor were minimal, as for an office visit. But look at this one, for $40,000.00. They're all dated in the same year. Then a large check for thousands of dollars to the Palm Medical Clinic and Private Hospital. Take note of the dollar amount here. Someone in the family must have either had a bad accident or been seriously ill."

Gloria moved away from the sink and stood next to Kim. Putting her hand on Kim's shoulder, she looked at the display of checks in her hand. "You separated all these from the files?"

"They sent up a red flag; something unusual going on, not just an everyday, or monthly occurrence. It made me more than a little curious."

Gloria took the checks from Kim, thumbing through them one by one. "Hmm ... Was there anything else that would give you a clue as to who, in the family, it was for, or why?"

"Nothing I could find."

The two young women stood in silence, looking first at the checks and then at each other.

"What now?" Gloria asked. She passed the checks back to Kim.

"I want to track down this Dr. Warren Wagner. He might be willing to give me some information about the family."

"I wouldn't get my hopes up, Kim. A lot of years have melted into the sunset since all that happened. He might not be living anymore, or he could be in a nursing home." With a droll smile, she added, "Perhaps even on another planet."

"Right!" Kim said. "I am serious, though, Glo. I've given this a lot of thought, and basically, I have to go with whatever leads I might get." Kim got out plates and silverware to set the table. "Someone has to have known this doctor. If this gets me nowhere, I'll check with the hospital."

"That might be more apt to get results. Businesses don't always fade away. If they fold, usually someone knows why or where."

"I'll do what it takes," Kim determined.

The two sat down with the fruit and some cold cereal. "What can I do to help?" Gloria said, taking a big spoonful out of her grapefruit.

"My lap top won't pick up the internet here. How about your office computer?"

"Reception there is great." Gloria replied. "Come in with me this morning and we'll have a good look."

"I'll also try the number Chase gave me for Max."

Chapter 9

Gloria sat quietly staring at her monitor. "I've looked through everything and can't find a Doctor Warren Wagner or even just a Warren Wagner. Have you found anything?" Gloria turned around to where Kim sat at a small table in one corner of the office. She had several large telephone books beside her.

"No, I haven't located anyone by that name. But, when I looked under 'Physicians,' there is a Doctor Jillian Wagner listed. I wonder if they could be related?"

"Well, I know one way to find out," Gloria said. She snatched up the book Kim had open in front of her and dialed the number. She put on the speakerphone.

"Dr. Wagner's office," a female voice answered.

"Is the doctor in, please?"

"She's with a patient. May I ask if you have an appointment or wish to make one?"

"Actually, I was wondering if you might know the whereabouts of a Doctor Warren Wagner?"

"He was Doctor Jillian's father. He passed away several years ago. Is there anything we can help you with?"

"If possible, I'd like to speak to the doctor on a personal matter. Do you think she could call me back sometime today when she has a few minutes?"

"I can take a message for you. Your name and number, please."

Gloria gave the receptionist Kim's name and cell phone number and winked at her friend. "I'd really appreciate it very much. I'll wait to hear from her."

Gloria hung up and sat back in her chair. "This is fun," she exclaimed. "I like this detective work stuff. I think I missed my calling." She chuckled as Kim smiled and shook her head. "Maybe we're getting someplace."

"I hope so. Thanks, Gloria. You can be my Dr. Watson ... or maybe, you be Sherlock and I'll be Watson." They both laughed heartily until Brad stuck his head in the room.

"What's going on in here?" He smiled. "Business, I hope."

"Not quite," Gloria said. "I just want to let you know I'm giving you notice. I've been offered a new job."

Brad's mouth dropped. "You've got to be kidding me. You're not serious, are you, Gloria?"

"Yeah, I'm kidding. But, mind you, Kim and I are going to put up our shingle one of these days. It's going to be Alexander and Latham, Private Eyes."

Kim's cell phone rang. Dr. Wagner was on the line.

"Ms. Alexander, I have a few minutes before my next patient. What can I do for you?"

"I'm looking for answers to some unfinished business that dates back to your father's practice. It's important to me and very personal. Is there some way I could meet with you and discuss this in person?"

"You're living in Miami?"

"No. I recently moved to Glade City from Seattle."

"Glade City, huh? By any chance are you related to the Alexanders who used to live in Miami ... a number of years ago?"

"They were my parents. Did you know them?"

"I knew of them through my father. I was in premed at the time and used to help him in the office when I had time off. He thought it would be good training for me to get accustomed to long hours. I really think he might have been trying to discourage me." She gave a little laugh. "In fact, I think I was in his office one day when your mother came in for an appointment. A very attractive woman with lovely auburn hair."

This time Kim giggled. "That must have been my aunt. My mother's hair was dark brown, but auburn hair runs in the family. My grandfather had rather sandy red hair."

"Sorry, my mistake." She paused briefly. "My last patient on Saturday is at 11:00 AM. I should be finished about noon. If that time would work for you, I'll have my receptionist give you directions to the office."

"That time would be perfect, thanks."

"So, if there's nothing else for now, I'll see you on Saturday, Ms. Alexander. Here's Janeen."

"Wait," Brad motioned. "I don't think you should go alone. Let me drive you. I'm not unfamiliar with Miami, and I have some business there that I've been putting off."

Kim nodded and spoke into the phone. "Janeen, this is a friend of mine who is more knowledgeable on getting around in the city." Kim handed the cell to Brad.

After Brad took the directions, he turned to Kim. "Hope you didn't mind my interrupting, but I can't see you driving to Miami by yourself on a weekend. It can be dangerous if you happen to get into the wrong part of town."

"Brad, I'm grateful for the company. I know Gloria has a full schedule this week-end and I've taken up enough of her time."

Gloria looked at Kim. "Boy, I'd trade a dozen of those Johnson clients of mine to be with you any day, Kim. But, I guess I'll have to deal with them sooner than later." She winked at Brad, "Or the big boss would probably fire me."

"It's settled then," Brad said. "Saturday it is."

After Brad left, Kim turned to Gloria. "Now that we have that established, I'll try that phone number Chase gave me for Max."

She took out the paper and dialed. After two rings, a recorded voice answered. "The number you have dialed is no longer in service. Please check your phone book or call information."

"Darn!" Kim said.

"You still have his old address," Gloria said. "Why don't you and Brad go to Miami early on Saturday? You'd have time to look up that address and maybe find some info on Max. You never know. Someone there might know or remember him."

"That could work," Kim mused, pleased with the idea.

Just then, Gloria's office door opened and Brad popped his head in. "How would you like to see my folks again, Kim?"

"I'd like that, Brad." She smiled.

"Mom just called, and I mentioned that you were back in town. She said she and Dad would love to see you again after all these years. They're coming over Thursday evening. Would that be okay with you?"

"Perfect."

"And you, too, Gloria. Let's make it a really good evening."

"I'll try to squeeze it into my busy schedule." Gloria said, a smile crossing her lips.

Chapter 10

Tuesday morning Kim planned a trip to the estate to go through things in the Master bedroom. She found Gloria in the kitchen, dressed and ready for work.

"I have to be in the office this morning, but I should finish sometime early afternoon." She set her empty cup in the sink, and picked up her purse and keys. "I can meet you at SandHill then. Need me to bring you anything, or will you be tired and ready to quit?"

"I want to work as long as possible. I think I'll just take a peanut butter and jelly sandwich along. Call me on my cell when you're on your way. I'll unlock the front door for you."

"I'm off then."

Kim walked down the hall with her. Gloria took one last look in the entryway mirror. She's every bit as pretty as I ever imagined she would be, Kim thought. Her naturally curly hair hung down to her shoulders in golden ringlets. She never seemed to have to do anything more than comb them out to set off her oval face and compliment her attire. This morning it was a red silk jacket and skirt that showed off her trim, curvacious figure.

When Gloria opened the door to the garage to leave, she turned and gave Kim a huge hug and said, "I have a very important client today, honey. It's the pits to try and understand his English, but he's rolling in dough and wants to spend some of it. I'll do my duty and try to find him a home he can't pass up. I'd love to shake him loose from some of those greenbacks."

"Well, lots of luck. Sounds like you may need it. I'll see you this afternoon then."

After Gloria left, Kim dressed and grabbed a banana to eat while she prepared her sandwich. She gathered some supplies, including a flashlight, a notebook and pen. She placed three large flattened boxes in the trunk, and set off for SandHill.

Her heart pounded when she pulled up to the large double gate. Seeing the home with Gloria by her side had not seemed so intimidating as it did now. She inserted the key, unlocked and pushed the heavy gate to one side, drove through, and parked in the circular driveway.

Armed with her small bag of supplies and purse, she stepped from the rental vehicle and mounted the seven steps to the wrap-around porch. Picture memories filled her mind as she fumbled slightly getting the old key into the lock; images she'd managed to keep in abeyance for fifteen years.

Passing through the entryway, Kim walked into the living room, one large enough to accommodate a studio apartment, she thought. Spanish tile and a large accent rug covered the floor where the upholstered furniture had been arranged. Her mother had complained about the large rooms and over-sized furniture being too much for her to keep up. That's when Dad hired Luz and Felix Ramon: Felix would care for the grounds, and Luz cleaned, cooked and watched young Kim when her mother worked or was gone.

Putting anxiety aside, Kim determined she would blot out those terrifying images from her past and start clearing out her parents' bedroom. She retrieved the three empty boxes from the trunk of the car, locked it and the front door of the estate behind her.

When she started up the circular staircase to the second floor, her thoughts took her back to the morning after the murders. She slowed, then stopped completely. Although the skylight washed golden rays of sunshine into the area, the memories just wouldn't fade away. She needed to pump up her courage. If she busied herself downstairs for an hour or two, perhaps she could shed the feeling of fear that had encased her.

She went into the library to Grandfather's storage closet and desk. There was plenty to go through here. She could fill up another box to take back to Gloria's with her.

She worked about two and a half hours, packing and tossing what she considered as unnecessary paper when she decided to again make the attempt to go upstairs. Her mind had begun to relax and shut out the demons.

Halfway to the second floor, her cell phone rang, startling her, but the familiar voice put her back on track.

"Kim, how are you making out?" Gloria sounded concerned. "Are you okay? You handling it being alone?"

"Okay, I guess."

"You don't sound okay. What are you doing now?"

"I'm just on my way up to the bedrooms. Everything seemed to be all right 'til I reached the stairway." She bit her lip. "That's when it hit me. I'll be okay. I think I have a handle on it now."

"Why don't you leave that part 'til I get there, honey? I'm waiting for Mr. Vu to come back from the men's room. We just had coffee at Cora's Café, and he wants to go back to the first place I showed him."

"Really, Gloria? Sounds positive. I'm glad for you." She took a deep breath and went on. "Just come as soon as you can. I'll be upstairs."

"I'll be there within the hour."

Gloria hung up and Kim continued her upward journey. The stairs now seemed a bit less formidable knowing that she would soon have company.

When she opened the door to her parents' bedroom, it no longer looked like it had that horrific day so long ago. Aunt Patricia had hired a cleaning crew to come in and get rid of the blood and destruction once the police released the home back to the family. The bed had only a box spring since the mattress had been ruined.

First she opened the drapes and windows to allow sunlight and fresh air to enter and chase away some of that musty odor. Her mother had kept a mahogany dresser and matching bureau that Grandmother imported from Italy, although she recalled her complaining about the dark color and felt the furniture should have been lighter and of more exotic tropical wood. Two overstuffed chairs still sat in front of the large floor-to-ceiling windows.

The roomy closet had a forty-eight by thirty-six inch window with panes that slid open horizontally to allow air circulation inside the room. During the day no additional light was needed for good illumination.

She opened up the flattened boxes and began removing some of the clothing from the racks. Dust billowed into the air making her sneeze. She would have to shake them out later or have them laundered before she could donate them to a worthy cause. The last container she used to pack shoes. Later, she could bring more equipment to handle the odds and ends she'd encountered. She pushed the filled containers into one corner of the closet to be dealt with later and brought the flashlight with her to the bathroom.

Focusing on the medicine cabinet, she pulled out two prescription bottles made out for her mother. One bottle contained Valium, the other, Tylenol with codeine. Was the Valium for depression? If so, why had her mother been depressed? And, Tylenol with codeine happened to be strong medicine for a pain reliever. Why? She would check out the telephone number for the pharmacist and the prescribing doctor in the local phone book.

Nothing else looked out of the ordinary: toothpaste, a lady's shaver, some band aides, rubbing alcohol, the normal things one placed in medicine cabinets. As she wondered about the reason for the drugs, she heard movement downstairs. Thank goodness Gloria had finally arrived, she thought. She could discuss the puzzling questions about the prescriptions.

"I'm upstairs in Mother and Daddy's bedroom," she called out. No response. Now she heard footsteps on the stairway. "In the bathroom," she said loudly.

Wait! She froze. She'd locked the front door. Beads of perspiration instantly broke out on her forehead as she realized it couldn't be Gloria. But who and how? Instinctively her hand fumbled on the counter for the flashlight. Not much of a weapon, but it was all she had.

"Getting right into it, are you?" a man's voice said behind her.

Kim swung around, startled. Chase leaned up against the doorway into the bathroom with a smile on his face.

"You frightened me half to death, … again." She gasped, then straightened up, slightly mortified at her own weakness. Studying the handsome officer in his neatly pressed uniform, she tried to steady her breathing. "I locked the front door," she said. "How did you get in?"

"Remember? I have keys." He stepped inside the room, jiggling keys in front of him. "I'm sorry, Kim, if I startled you. I'm on my regular rounds and noticed the gate open, drove up and found your car parked in front. Since you hadn't informed the station, I felt I should make sure you weren't in harm's way. I apologize."

"I guess I should be the one to apologize." She flushed, still feeling shaken. "I'm sorry I forgot to call the station. Too many things on my mind, I guess. And, I know it's for my own protection." The corners of her mouth turned up slightly as she began to breathe easier.

"Come in the bedroom and sit down. I've upset you, and I'm not leaving until I know you're okay."

He walked her over to the box spring, motioned for her to sit down, then stood in front of her. "I want you to know that what I did today is partly in the line of duty, but also because I have concerns for your safety."

"I understand. I need to learn not to be so jittery."

"Well, under the circumstances … "

"You up there, Kim?" Gloria's voice echoed up the stairway.

"Mother and Daddy's bedroom. Come on up."

Chase, his hat still in his hand, said, "I'd better be going, get back to my patrol. I'll see you later." He turned to leave as Gloria walked in the room.

"Chase?" Kim said.

He looked back.

"Thanks for your concern. I'll try to remember to call the station from now on."

"No problem. I'll lock up on my way out. Afternoon, Gloria."

"Good afternoon to you, too."

After Chase left the room, Gloria said, "What was that all about?"

"He was on his rounds when he noticed the gate open. He came in to see if I was all right." Kim sighed and looked at her friend. "I foolishly had forgotten to inform the station that I would be here today. I'm sure he means well."

"And, that was it?"

Kim got up from the box spring. "That was it. He's so striking with those penetrating blue eyes of his. He really has a way of flustering me." She straightened her shorts and headed back to the bathroom where she'd left off her search. "I'm surprised he's managed to stay single all these years."

"Maybe he's had that same affect on other women, and it frightens them off."

Both girls started to laugh. Then Gloria stopped, looked around. "Enough about our friend Chase. Let's get to work. Where do I start?"

"I've been working here. Maybe you could start on the linen closet and pull out some of the sheets and towels. I don't want to throw them away, so I'll need to launder them. I'll clean out the rest of the medicine closet. I found two old prescription bottles I want to ask the pharmacist about."

"Gotcha." Gloria pulled a hamper close to the linen storage.

"Do you remember the Ramons?" Kim dumped the rest of the items from the medicine chest into a wastebasket.

"I sure do. Luz made the greatest chicken enchiladas I've ever tasted." She dropped the towels and washcloths into the hamper and started on the sheets. "As a matter of fact, I just saw their son, Justin, the other day at the post office. Said he came back to see his fiancée. They're getting married in a week or two."

"What a coincidence. Will the wedding be in Glade City?"

"I'm sure it will. She's a legal secretary for Hayden and Michaels, and most of her family members live around here."

"Well, I've been thinking about Luz and Felix lately, wondering if I could locate them. If the wedding is to take place here in town, perhaps they would spare me a little time. They worked long enough for my parents to know them quite well." Kim got down on her hands and knees and began emptying the cabinet below the sink. "They might have seen things no one else did, … know if they had any enemies or anyone who held a grudge."

"I'm sure they'd be happy to see you and tell you anything they could remember. Those two were a special treasure to your mom and dad." Gloria pulled out the last set of sheets and reached to the back of the cupboard to make sure she had it all. "Hello, what have we here?" She pulled out a small shoebox tied with red cord. "This was on the back of the shelf behind the linens."

"Let's have a look." Kim took the box, untied the cord, and pulled off the lid. A stack of letters filled the inside. "I need to sit down, I think." She went into the bedroom and sat on the box springs. Gloria followed, sitting beside her.

The top letter was addressed to M. Sanderson at a box number at the Miami post office, dated May 19, 1979.

"The year before I was born," Kim said. "You, too, Glo."

As Kim pulled the letter from its envelope, she said, "My mother's maiden name, of course, Margaret Sanderson. But, according to the date, she had already been married almost four years."

"Maybe it was from an old acquaintance who only knew her by her maiden name."

Kim looked down and read aloud:

> "*Hi Honey,*
> *I sure miss seeing you at the coffee shop. I know you've been busy with work and home, but I don't dare come to the library anymore. That woman at the checkout desk is pretty nosy. I believe she's getting suspicious. She always gives me that 'What are you doing here?' look.*
> *I guess for now, mail will have to be our safest form of communication since the coffee shop is even more risky.*
> *How is it going with Patricia? Is she still attending college, and does she like Miami any better than home? I'm sure it's been difficult for the three of you living under the same roof. Is she planning on returning to Glade City at the end of the semester or will she stay here in town and look for a job?*
> *Please drop me a note in our post box and let me know when and where we can meet. I miss you more than you know.*
> *Love,*
> *Me*"

Kim looked up to see Gloria observing her reaction. "What on earth could this mean?" she said, questions in her eyes. "This letter is definitely not from my dad. So, who then?"

Gloria reached over and placed her hand on Kim's. "I hate to say this, honey, but what else could it be but an affair? Do you mind if we look at a few more of the letters? Maybe we'll get a clue."

"Gloria, you're my best friend. Of course I don't mind. Just having you here for support in light of this … is comforting." She turned the letter over in her hand, tried to keep it from shaking. "I am crushed, to say the least."

She pulled out another letter and opened it. It was dated May 12, 1979.

> *"Hi Honey,*
>
> *I'm sure glad I had the chance to slip you the note and key to the post office box last week. Since your hours have been cut, I'm never sure when you'll be at the library, and I don't want to give that old biddy at the desk the opportunity to get you in trouble.*
>
> *Does Charles know yet about your work schedule being shortened? It gives us more time together as long as he doesn't suspect anything. Is he still working those ten-hour days?*
>
> *They've changed my hours again. I'll be working graveyard shift for the next month so we'll have to make other time arrangements. Please just use the P. O. Box to keep in touch. I've paid for it in advance.*
>
> *I've been thinking about renting a small apartment on my own if my partner can afford to go it alone. It would give us somewhere safe to meet. Let me know what you think.*
>
> *Love, Me"*

Kim folded the letter, replacing it in the envelope and wiped her eyes with the back of her hand. "I just can't believe what I'm reading, Gloria. I never expected to uncover anything like this."

"It's okay, honey. Stuff happens in the best of families. Yours is probably no exception. Things could have changed when your mother got pregnant. Maybe it made her realize the value of her marriage. This … unknown person … could have up and disappeared from the picture years ago. After all, if the letters were placed in the box as they were received, they must have stopped with the one written in May of 1979."

"If that were so, why would she have kept them all those years? That was when they lived in Miami, and now, the letters turn up here, hidden away." She touched a tissue to her eyes. Gloria put one arm around Kim's shoulder and squeezed her.

She pulled out the rest of the letters, looked at them and said, "I can't read anymore just now. I feel like I've had the wind punched out of me." She put the two notes back in the box, retied the ribbon, and placed it with the items she'd put aside to take home.

"Would you like to take these things and leave now? I'll fix dinner while you sort things out to look at later." Gloria stood up and straightened her skirt. "I think you've had enough for one day."

Chapter 11

Gloria's suggestion to go home early had been the right thing to do. Kim's day had struck the gamut of emotions. She followed Gloria home, her mind spinning on her latest discovery. Her own mother in an affair? Kim could deal with many surprises, but this was more like total shock.

What had happened with this love affair to seemingly bring it to a close? Had the unknown lover left town, or died, perhaps? Maybe Daddy had discovered what had been going on, confronted her, and forced an end to it? Or had it ended? Based on the fact the letters did not continue, would not necessarily mean the affair was over. Her mother could have disposed of further correspondence, maybe forgotten about the box. Her father might have discovered the letters and … So many questions bounced around in her head. Would she ever uncover the whole truth?

Another thought jolted her; could Aunt Patricia have known?

According to Kim's father, Aunt Patricia went to Seattle immediately following college graduation. He said she'd had a great job offer, too good to pass up. After she moved to Washington State, her aunt only returned twice to Glade City before her trip to pick up her orphaned niece; the first time had been for Grandmother Sofia's funeral, the second time, when Grandfather died. Could Aunt Patricia have been sent away to squelch the truth?

In the years Kim lived with her aunt, she'd never mentioned a word about an affair between her sister, Margaret, and the 'Me' of the letters. Maybe she knew nothing. Maybe she chose never to cast a shadow on Margaret's reputation.

Somehow, Kim planned to tell her aunt about her discovery. If she had any knowledge about the affair, Kim was certain she'd know by Patricia's reaction.

But something else pricked her subconscious but wouldn't quite come into focus.

Her mind continued to dart from one unanswered question to another. Would she ever achieve satisfaction on that score?

They were within a block of Gloria's home when a new thought smacked her; if Mother's affair began more than a year before her birth, it could be possible that her dad was not her biological father. It might be the "Me" of the letters.

Kim shook her head and pulled into the garage next to Gloria's Caddy.

"Are you okay, Kim? You look washed out." Gloria reached into the small extra freezer in her garage and removed a bag of frozen shrimp.

Kim hesitated. "I'm … handling it, I guess, but I just had the most unnerving thought. What if Dad was not my real father, after all?"

"I'm surprised that hadn't occurred to you before this, from the date of the letters." Gloria walked over to Kim and took her arm. "Come on in and relax for an hour or so while I fix us some supper. You'll feel better then."

"That was the last thing on my mind, I guess. I'd been thinking about what Aunt Patricia would know about all this, never about my father."

Kim reached into the back of her car and took out the box of letters. "Leave the other things. I'll get them later"

"How about your birth certificate, Kim?" Gloria opened the door into the house. "Wouldn't that name your real father?"

Kim stopped, staring intently at Gloria. "I think you may be right on that score, Gloria.

The problem is, I've never laid eyes on it. In fact, I've never had a need for it before."

"Well, don't worry. You can contact Broward County where you were born. They'll send you a legal copy."

"I'll do it first thing in the morning."

After the supper dishes had been placed in the dishwasher, Kim retired to her bedroom to go through the rest of the letters. There could be a name dropped, or another clue revealed as to the writer of these notes.

This whole day had been more than taxing. Being alone in the house had been traumatic enough by itself. Sorting through her parents personal items added to the difficulty. Now, the letters. The match in the kerosine.

She didn't realize something like this could upset her so. But it had.

As a child, Kim knew her mother always seemed to have her own agenda. She worked when she felt like it. She took time away from the family when she wished. Where Kim's dad exuded warmth and love, cool and dominating described her mother much better.

Now, the thought that her own dear dad might not be her flesh and blood blossomed in her mind like a creeping scourge.

She went through more of the letters, but there was never a hint of who had written them.

In final desperation, Kim closed the box, put it aside and prepared herself for bed. Perhaps a good sleep is what she really needed.

Chapter 12

In the morning, Kim called Broward County and requested a copy of her birth certificate.

Gloria had already left, so Kim decided she would put some of the other things she needed to attend to on hold, bite the bullet and go check out the Boat Tours. This Melvin Thomas person whom Aunt Patricia had commissioned to take over the managing of the business had been Daddy's right hand man. In all respects, her aunt had felt him well qualified to take over. But from things she'd heard in town, had aroused her interest. She needed to see what the business looked like and how Thomas had handled it.

It turned out to be a beautiful, balmy day, sunny and bright, not too hot. Tourists were already filling the parking lot when she arrived. A line snaked up to the building where they waited to purchase their tickets to glide the saw grass wonderland.

Kim chose a spot near the back of the main building, away from the patrons' vehicles. She parked beneath a large cluster palm where the area had been cordoned off and marked "Staff only". Nine vehicles were already parked inside the allotted section. A side entrance allowed her the privilege of bypassing the gathering crowd.

Swinging her purse over her shoulder, Kim headed toward the door marked "Employees' Entrance". A long hallway led past a number of what appeared to be office doors. Closer to the front where patrons waited for their tickets, a large office, bright with sunshine filtering through half-tilted Bermuda shades, a middle-aged man sat at an oversized metal desk. He was smoking a large cigar and looked up as Kim passed.

"Beg yer pardon, ma'am. Jes' where do y'all think yer goin'? This here area's off limits to the public." He rose and started in her direction.

"I ... I'm here to see Mr. Melvin Thomas."

"Yer lookin' at him, missy, and you should of come through the front door where one o' ma 'sociates would of notified me proper like."

"I'm Kim Alexander." She stared at the paunchy man with the scraggly mustache and thick dark brows. His deep brown hair was beginning to show signs of gray while his sideburns were almost white. A short-sleeved plaid shirt hung over the top of baggy, wrinkled shorts.

He said nothing at first. His eyes were busy taking her in from top to bottom. Kim's full, ankle-length, multicolored silk skirt swirled above her bare, sandaled feet. The sheer, low-cut turquoise blouse did nothing to hide the embarrassment and intimidation she felt as Melvin's eyes seemed to undress her from head to toe.

"Well, I reckon it's 'bout time y'all showed up. I heard ya was in town." He expressed no apologies. "Come in, and we kin talk." He removed the cigar from his mouth and used it to direct her into his office.

"I didn't realize I had a deadline," she said following him into the cluttered office. "I've been quite busy getting settled." She wished she'd had Gloria with her to put him in his place.

"Don't matter." He stubbed out the cigar, but the foul smell of cheap tobacco still lingered as small puffs of smoke drifted toward the ceiling. "There's a lot to talk 'bout here, and we all need to get a few things straight." He picked up a glass filled with brown liquid. "Wanna drink?"

"I'm good, thank you." She pushed aside a pile of newspapers and magazines that had found their home on a small couch opposite Thomas' desk and sat down.

"Yer aunt informed me y'all was comin'. I'd like ta know how we'll be handlin' thin's now y'all are in the piture." He sat down in his chair, brushed aside some papers on top of his desk and hoisted up his feet. "First off, I'm gonna need a raise. Ain't been nothin' mentioned for a few years now, and the business been doin' very well, thanks to ma good management." He took an immense swig of the brown drink. "I presume yer aunt tol' y'all I've made this place into a viable business. I hire he'p I kin trust or they're outa here. They don' fool 'round 'cause they know the rules; have to be kind to the customers, keep the place lookin' neat an' clean and put in a honest day's work." He tapped the wooden arm of his chair with the top of his pen, clicking it in and out while he spoke.

"Mr. Thomas, if the place is making money, that's certainly to your credit. I don't need to change things. I have plenty to do myself, and taking over your position is not one of my priorities or desires." Kim steadied her eyes on his, pushing aside the intimidation she felt in her gut.

"I hope not, 'cause we got us a airtight contract." He gave her a Cheshire cat grin, exposing a large gold front tooth. The forefinger of his right hand roamed across the unkempt mustache.

"Oh?" Kim replied. "My aunt hadn't mentioned that. Anyway, the fact remains that I have no intention of taking over your job. As for a raise in salary, we can discuss that after I've had time to look over the books."

There was a moment of silence as the two studied one another.

"I'd like to tour the place at your earliest convenience, Melvin. I want to meet the staff and observe the operation of the business. And finally, I'd like to have a look at those records."

Thomas didn't answer for several seconds while he continued to scrutinize Kim.

"Ya know, missy, yer purdy young to be into the operation of a well-established business such as what I have here. I'll be more than happy to take y'all 'round and introduce ya to the staff, but

I've been successfully runnin' this place since y'all were a gangly ten-year-old, and I wouldn't expect ya to know the firs' thin' 'bout how to operate it. Le's jus' say, I don' think y'all need to look at the books since ma bookkeeper handles all that fer me and does a mighty fine job, at that.

" Seein' as how y'all own the Boat Tours, I agree ya should look 'round and meet ever'one. Then, leave the rest ta someone what knows what they're doin'." He swung his legs back to the floor and stood.

"Now we had our little talk, I'll show y'all 'round and introduce ya to Karen." He headed toward the office door, leaving Kim wondering what hit her.

She followed Melvin down the hall and into the main room. A few dozen men, women and children still waited at the cashier's booth to purchase tickets. A clerk at a central cash register rang up sales on articles from tables and shelves loaded with a mixture of souvenirs. Six circular racks held tee shirts and shorts, many with logos depicting the boats in action, or a variety of Everglade wildlife. Stacks of hats topped the center of these racks. Sunglasses occupied a turntable on top of a glass case where rings, necklaces, bracelets, and earrings displayed their brilliance. Several large cases dispensed canned drinks, candy and nuts. It was a going concern and appeared to Kim to have everything an insatiable tourist could desire.

Melvin didn't bother acknowledging any of the employees as he escorted Kim around the room. "Y'all kin see I've improved the whole place; brought the business into the technological age, and made a place what commands attention. Brings in a nice piece o' change, as well."

He steered her past benches and through double glass doors to the pier where air boats waited to take customers on the ride of their lives.

Potted palms lined the boardwalk to the restrooms. The exterior of the structures displayed attractive, colorful artwork. Tables with shade umbrellas were located near a stand that sold hot dogs and sandwiches. When the aroma of barbequing pork made Kim's mouth water, she knew it was an irresistible addition. On one side of the main building, an area had been sectioned off for a small exhibit of alligators and other native creatures. It would seem that Melvin Thomas had pulled out all the stops.

Impressive and well presented, she thought. Though the place didn't belong to him, he had taken care of it as though it were his own. In fact, Kim was beginning to think this man believed he held the governing share of stock. The so-called contract would tell her the real story.

After she inspected the books to find the profit margin, which she had every intention of doing, she would consider a possible raise for Thomas.

Melvin interrupted her thoughts. "If y'all have seen enough, we kin go meet Karen."

"I'd like that."

He led Kim down the hallway past his office to an adjoining one, much smaller than his, but very neat and organized.

A pleasant-looking young woman sat at a white pine desk in front of her computer. She appeared to be in her late thirties with straight brown hair pulled back in a short ponytail. She wore a green, sleeveless cotton shirt and knee-length beige shorts.

She looked up and smiled when they entered the room. "Good Morning."

"I'd like ya to meet Kim Alexander, Karen."

"Ohhh. I heard you were in town. We were expecting you, weren't we Mr. Thomas?"

Kim extended her hand and smiled.

"I give her a quick tour. She kin meet the crew later since they're all busy now. In fact, that kin be your job when they're on break, so as they won't be usin' work time." He started to leave, then turned back without so much as a smile. "Take a early lunch, and let me know when yer done. I have a bunch o' work for y'all. I'll be in my office."

Without another word, he left the room.

Kim looked at Karen and raised her eyebrows. "Karen, I don't want to interrupt anything you're doing. Please. I can come back another day, if it would be more convenient. I just wanted to meet the staff, but strictly at your convenience."

"It's no problem, Ms. Alexander. I have their schedules and know when each one has their break. I'm used to being ready at a moment's notice. It's expected of me."

"Well, I'm not quite that demanding, Karen." Kim smiled as the secretary moved over to one of three file cabinets on a back wall. "He sounds like a tough taskmaster."

"He has his way of doing things around here, and every employee knows it." She looked over at Kim and gave her a warm smile. "Nobody disputes his word or gives him an argument ... if you know what I mean. He's THE boss."

"Well, I'm the owner, Karen, and, by the way, he's already informed me that I didn't need to look at the books ... mainly because he doesn't think I know anything about the business and am too young and inexperienced. He said I need to leave those things to him."

Karen turned around to look at Kim. "Surely, he didn't say that to you, did he?"

"Emphatically, but I suppose he's forgotten who owns the place."

Karen walked to her office door and closed it. "Everyone who works here knows how Mr. Thomas is. They respect the fact that he gives the orders and manages the payroll. They all seem to get their jobs done, but most of the staff have a better sense of how to go about treating the customers than he gives them credit for. They do a lot on their own when they recognize it's the right way ... without the big boss knowing it."

She removed a large book from the file cabinet and placed it on her desk next to a vase of fresh cut lavender gladiolas. "Regardless of what Mr. Thomas says to you, he knows how and where the salaries come from. I'm showing you my records because this is your business, not his." She brought out a folding chair from a closet and put it on the other side of her desk.

Grinning, she patted the chair. "Sit here and you can look these over for a start. If there are any questions, I'll do my best to answer them. There's a copy machine behind you if you need one."

She handed Kim a scratch pad and slid over a white metal, blue heron decorated container filled with pens and pencils.

"Thanks. I appreciate this."

Kim settled into looking through neat computer printouts, while Karen went back to her monitor.

"While you're doing that, I'll just finish my ordering. I don't want to get on the bad side of you-know-who." Her brown eyes sparkled.

"He seems to have a handle on what works and what doesn't." Kim lifted her head slightly to observe Karen's reaction. The secretary turned up the corners of her mouth and continued with what she was doing.

"How did it go with Melvin Thomas?" Gloria asked when she got home from work.

"Okay," Kim replied as she cut up cucumbers and tomatoes for the salad she'd started. "The place is a picture of success and good business practice. I can't complain about that. It's raking in a tidy sum of money. Everything seems to be well organized and clean. Melvin is a strict boss. Seems to control everything right down to how much air the employees breathe. I suppose that's good working policy as long as he doesn't have personal contact with the customers." Kim turned from the sink. "He doesn't exactly have a winning personality."

"I've heard rumors," Gloria grinned. She removed an apron from the pantry and put it on. "You had a chance to look at the books, then?" She opened the refrigerator and grabbed out a bottle of Miller Lite.

"Oh, yes. His secretary is accommodating and exceptionally neat and efficient. I made copies to look over at my leisure. Next time, I'll check out the cash register tapes. It's not that I don't trust Karen. I just think that Melvin needs to know whose business it is. He's had far too much freedom with no one looking over his shoulder. And, I get the feeling he thinks I'm just some punk kid who doesn't know what it's all about."

She put chopped lettuce into a bowl and placed it on the table next to a tray of assorted cut fruits from Winn Dixie.

"Well, WOW." Gloria sat down and kicked off her shoes. "Sounds like you're getting right with it. Not gonna let that bozo off the hook. Make him sweat a little. He probably deserves it. I've heard nasty stuff about him … like some of the employees call him Simon Legree. Don't think the guy endears himself to many folks."

"Well, he doesn't know yet that his secretary made me privy to the books." Kim removed a package of cold cuts from the fridge and arranged them on a small plate. After she put two dressings on the table, she poured herself a glass of iced tea and sat down.

Gloria followed suit. "My idea of the perfect summer supper. Thanks for doing this. It's been such a busy day, it feels good to relax."

After supper and cleanup, Gloria excused herself to finish a report for the next day. She wanted to shower and retire early for a change.

"You're checking out the Johnson residence tomorrow for an Open House on Sunday?" Kim asked. She refilled her glass of tea.

"Yeah. I don't want any surprises. Have to make sure that Johnson guy isn't boozin' again."

"Do your thing, Gloria. I want to get back to some of those boxes of Grandfather's anyway."

Gloria picked up her shoes from the floor where she'd dropped them. "I'm coming home early tomorrow afternoon to get ready for the big dinner with Brad's parents. I'll see you about four."

Chapter 13

Late the following afternoon Brad called to say that his parents had arrived, and he would pick the girls up about seven for reservations at seven-thirty.

After her shower, Kim dressed in an ankle-length chartreuse and yellow chiffon dress, sleeveless with delicate ruffles around the neckline. Flat heeled, jeweled sandals finished her outfit. She piled her hair high on her head, leaving several tendrils of auburn locks caressing her bare back. Gloria had come home early and just finished dressing when the doorbell rang.

Brad stood at the front door at six-fifty. His parents waited in the car.

"Wow. Who have we here?" His eyes locked onto Kim when she opened the door.

She felt the heat of her flush. "Do you think I'm overdressed, Brad? I wanted to look nice when I met your folks after all these years."

"No, no, no. You look … absolutely … well, too good for Glade City, but my parents will be impressed."

When Gloria appeared in a black sheath and braided gold choker, Brad said to Kim, "I see your partner is none too shabby, either."

The evening went well at one of the town's finest restaurants, Glade Gardens. Brad's parents were easy to be around, and Kim felt instantly comfortable with them.

"Are you planning on staying in Glade City?" Brad's mother, Mariah, asked.

"Absolutely. I've always loved it here. Those were the best years of my life ... until ..."

"Say no more, dear. We understand." Mariah said. "Your Aunt Patricia must have been a great blessing. Did she ever marry?"

"No. She always said carving out a career kept her busy enough. Then I came into her life and, well, I guess I must have filled some kind of void. At least, that's what she always told me." Kim giggled. "I think what she really meant was that I was a bundle of unleashed energy that she hadn't been used to dealing with. But we didn't take long to bond. She's a very warm person."

Kim toyed with her salad while the others dug into their meals. "Actually, Aunt Patricia has been more of a mother to me than my own mom who always seemed to have other things to do. Thinking back, I don't believe she had motherhood in mind when she had me. Not that I loved her any less. Children just didn't seem to be her thing. Dad was different. I guess I was his shining star, more like I had been to my grandfather. Dad used to hover over me. He made sure he knew where I was and who I was with when he had to work. That's what he liked about Luz. He knew she was the next best thing to his taking care of me."

Brad's father, Jeffrey, had been quiet up to now, leaving most of the conversation to Mariah while he finished his ribs. He used the finger bowl and napkin, and then turned to Kim. "Have you heard anything from Luz and Felix? You know that they occasionally helped us out when they weren't working for your parents."

The bus boy picked up the empty plates, and the waiter brought the dessert menus.

"Nothing for me, thank you. I'm so full I couldn't eat another bite," Kim said.

"I know, Kim. You have to watch your girlish figure," Mariah smiled.

"That's so the rest of us can enjoy it, too," Jeffrey added.

Mariah nudged him. "Don't embarrass the girl, Jeffrey. As for me, I'm well past worrying about my figure, thanks, so I'll order the Brownie Surprise."

"Why don't we make that four altogether? Okay Dad, Gloria?" Brad said.

Gloria put up her hand and shook her head. "I'm with Kim. I'm stuffed."

The waiter left to get three Brownie Surprises as the conversation continued.

"You were asking me about the Ramons, Mr. Kimbal."

"Just call me Jeffrey, Kim. Mr. Kimbal sounds so ... stuffy."

Kim smiled and nodded. "I heard that they had moved to Ocala years ago to be close to Luz's mother. I'd love to see them again. In fact, since their son, Justin, is getting married soon to a young lady here in Glade City, I might be able to see them sooner than I had expected."

"I sincerely hope you'll be able to." He took a deep breath. "Changing the subject, Kim, Brad tells me you and Gloria have been doing some investigating on your own. The police never did turn up any concrete evidence, did they?"

The waiter brought the three desserts as Kim started to answer. "No. I don't think anyone had the technology at the time, or the manpower, to solve the case. As far as investigating, Gloria and I have started to dig into things back at SandHill. We also found some information from the newspaper archives at the city library.

"The police declared it a cold case since there was almost a total lack of evidence." Kim watched Jeffrey enjoying his Brownie Surprise. He wiped his mouth and pushed away his empty dessert plate.

She looked down at her glass of water and then back to Jeffrey. "I want to know who hated them enough to do such a horrible thing. And what triggered such an act of violence? Who were the people Mother and Daddy were involved with at the time? I've asked myself these questions for years, and I still have no answers. Now that I'm here in Glade City, I'm going to make sure I look into every possible aspect of the case." Kim moved her glass around in little circles on the table.

Brad's father said, "There was an incident back when Leslie had been visiting …"

"Jeffrey," Mariah started, "Please."

"No, go ahead, Jeffrey, if you don't mind." Kim said. "If there's anything at all, I'd like to hear it. Even if it doesn't sound important, it could be a piece of the puzzle."

"Well," he began, glancing at Mariah, "it happened one time when you invited Leslie to stay overnight. Your mother had finished her work at the office for the day."

Kim nodded. "Mother usually did the books in the morning while I was in school. If there was no school, I had to go to the office with her until she finished. Pretty boring, but sometimes Dad let me go with him while he checked the boats and the workers to make sure they were doing what they were paid to do. But please, I didn't mean to interrupt."

"Well, she had you with her when she came to pick up Leslie. I told her I'd get Leslie in the morning. Your dad had to go to Jacksonville on business and would be gone for two days. That Melvin Thomas used to take over on occasions when your father was out of town. A gruff character, that one." Kim nodded as he continued.

"Leslie told us that you and she were in your bedroom. You had gone to bed late, talked and laughed until well past midnight. Leslie excused herself to go to the bathroom, the wall of which was right next to the Master bedroom. She could hear your mother talking on the telephone. Bits and pieces of the conversation came through, enough to sense that she wasn't talking to your father. She heard your mother say something about the fact that Charles would be gone for several days. Leslie hurried back to the bedroom where you were waiting, afraid to tell you what she'd heard.

"After you both went to sleep, something woke her. It sounded like car tires crunching on the gravel and moving slowly. She got up and peeked out of the bedroom window. She saw taillights disappear around the rear of the house. She described it as being like whoever it was, they were trying not to wake anyone. After that she refused to go back to your place again. She said she knew something was going on and it frightened her. We let it go. She said she was okay with you coming to our house because she really liked you. Why that person was coming in the middle of the night had nothing to do with you. It wasn't long after that when your parents were … both … found dead."

No one said a word.

Finally, Kim broke the silence. "I've found some … things … that ring of … " She looked at her napkin, folding and twisting it. Moments passed before Brad spoke.

"Don't let it eat on you, Kim. You had no control over what had been going on in your parents' lives."

"I know that. I'm just feeling a bit ashamed of what must have been happening behind my father's back … my totally sweet, loving dad."

Brad reached over and put his arm around Kim's shoulders. "Let's talk about something else so we don't spoil the pleasantness of the evening."

"It hasn't spoiled it for me, Brad. I'm just so grateful that Jeffrey had the foresight to tell me. It confirms things I've thought about a lot over the years. My mother never seemed overly loving towards my father. If there *was* another man in her life, there's a distinct possibility that it might have had something to do with the murders. At this point, I just don't know"

"Let's get out of here," Brad offered. "We can go to my place and finish talking there."

Chapter 14

The next day Kim visited Thompson's drug store to inquire about the two prescriptions she'd found. Mr. Thompson looked much the same as Kim remembered him except that now his hair was pure white.

"So you're little Kim Alexander? I'd say you're a few inches taller than the last time I saw you, and now you're all grown up. Look something like your dad used to. A lot prettier, though." His eyes crinkled at the corners. "And, you've got that Sanderson red hair, same as your grandfather and your pretty Aunt Patricia." He placed his elbows on the counter in front of Kim, not taking his eyes from her. "So, now what can I do for you, young lady?"

"If you don't mind, Mr. Thompson." She removed the two bottles from her purse. "I've been at the old homestead cleaning and came across these in the medicine cabinet. Can you tell me anything about them?"

"Well, I'm not so sure how ethical it would be for me to discuss a customer's medication, but, in your case, since it *was* your mother's and she's no longer with us …"

"Don't worry, Mr. Thompson, whatever you can tell me will stay with me. I just need to put some questions I have to rest."

"Only thing I can really tell you, Miss Kim, is that Dr. Evans prescribed both of them. She had been on these two drugs for years, as far as I know." He stopped to wipe a drop of perspiration from his forehead. "As a friend, I mentioned it to her several times that she was playing with dynamite. You can easily become addicted to Valium, which I could see had already happened from the amount she had to purchase. As for the codeine, well, same thing basically. Might kill the pain, but has a lot of nasty side effects. Personally, I can't understand that old quack writing her prescription after prescription for that stuff."

Kim shook her head from side to side, eyes fixed on the druggist.

"Don't know the real reason behind it, but your mother had been a pretty persuasive person when she put her mind to it. Must have gotten hooked on the stuff and just couldn't get off. With Valium, once you become addicted, it's hell to get out from under." He removed a handkerchief from his pocket and wiped the back of his neck.

"Well, Mr. Thompson, I appreciate your time and helpfulness. I just thought you might have known some little thing that could enlighten me as to why? And, now that I find out they weren't just an odd prescription or two but something she had been on for years, it makes me wonder even more."

"You're most welcome, Miss Kim. Glad to be of service. Too bad Dr. Evans is no longer with us. He might have been able to answer some of your questions."

"Possibly, but I wouldn't want anything to do with him. He only aided my mother in her habit." She handed him a slip of paper with her cell number on it. "Thank you, Mr. Thompson. If you should think of anything else, please give me a call."

"Don't be a stranger now, you hear, young lady?"

Chapter 15

The weekend arrived before Kim felt mentally prepared for her meeting with Dr. Wagner. She'd gathered as much information as she anticipated needing, organizing it all neatly into a small briefcase.

The rest of the time seemed to have lined up nicely, though. A friend of Brad's in Miami owned a car dealership and had offered to pick them up after Kim turned in her rental vehicle. He agreed to take them back to his place of business where he had several new PT Cruisers at excellent prices and in different colors.

Kim walked into the kitchen where Gloria sat with a cup of coffee, a bowl of Frosted Flakes, and the morning paper. "There's hot water in the tea kettle, if you'd like. I have to open this morning with Brad being off."

"You don't mind him driving me to Miami?" Kim took out a mug from the cupboard and a tea bag from a canister.

"No way, honey. Brad's my friend and my boss. No more. No less. I just haven't found Mr. Right yet, and Brad has a few dates here and there, but no one special. The way I see it, he's already got you in his sights, the way he fumbles all over the place when you're around." She took a big bite of cereal. "You go, get the info you wanted, and enjoy the day. Brad is an easy guy to be around."

"You think I look appropriate enough to meet with this doctor whom I've never met before?"

"You look very nice and very tropical this morning," Gloria replied. She checked out Kim's short-skirted dress with spaghetti straps. "That lime green color is like a breath of fresh air on this hot, sultry morning. You also look confident and comfortable with who you are, and, I might add, very attractive."

Kim smiled and leaned down to hug Gloria. "You're a great friend, you know. I'm not sure when we'll be home, but I could give you a call if you'd like."

"Don't worry about me. I've got plenty of work to keep me occupied. Just go. Have some fun while you're in the big city."

"I'll do just that." She sat down to have her tea when the doorbell rang. "I think Brad's a bit early," she said and hurried down the hall to the front door.

Chase stood at the door dressed in light blue shorts and a tan muscle shirt. "I hope I'm not interrupting anything at this early hour, but I thought I'd see if you'd like to go to Naples with me this morning."

"Oh, Chase. I'm sorry, but I'm just getting ready to leave for Miami on business." A nerve in her cheek started to twitch. This young police officer seems more than accommodating, she thought, in fact, maybe even a bit too accommodating. Or was it her imagination that he always seemed to turn up when she least expected him? "But, thank you for the invitation." Her voice caught in her throat.

"It's my day off, and I thought it would be nice to have some company. I guess I should have asked sooner." He hesitated and then quickly continued. "Actually, I don't have to go to Naples. I could drive you to Miami if you'd like. That is, if you're going alone. Or is Gloria going with you?"

"No, she has to work today."

Brad's dark blue Lexus pulled into the driveway. Chase turned and looked first at Brad and then Kim.

"You're going with … ?"

"Yes. Brad offered to drive me since I'm not familiar with the city."

He flushed, turned sharply to Brad and said, "I stopped to see if Kim wanted to go to Naples with me, but I see she has other plans." He looked back at Kim. "I'll be on my way, then. I'm sure you'll have a good day together." He turned abruptly and left.

"Brad, I had no idea Chase was going to show up on my doorstep."

"Not your fault, so don't apologize. I think I detect a little green-eyed monster."

"I … don't know what to say. He *has* been very kind to me, and helpful in getting some information I needed." She shrugged her shoulders.

"I wouldn't worry about it, Kim. He's always been a loner. Probably is beginning to crave companionship."

Kim held the front door open for Brad. "Let me finish my tea first. I'll get my purse and the rental car keys, and we can be off."

"As a matter of fact, I haven't eaten anyway. Why don't we stop on our way for a bite?"

Brad pulled up to Glade City Family Restaurant and parked. As they got out of the vehicle, Kim grabbed Brad's arm.

"That's Chase's red Mercedes just going around the block. Do you think he's spying on us, Brad?"

"Who knows, Kim. He won't be able to follow us out of town. He'd stick out like a sore thumb, and there's not enough traffic around here to hide behind someone else. I think he's just trying to see what's going on. Just shows you, he is interested in you." Brad smiled and steered Kim toward the restaurant. "Let's eat and forget him for now. We've got other things to accomplish today, right?"

Chapter 16

Brad's friend, Michael Fenton, turned out to be a gem. He met them at the Econo Car Rental and waited for Kim to take care of the paper work. He drove them back to his place of business and had one of the brand new PT Cruisers ready and waiting for them. It was a metallic candy apple red, and Kim immediately fell in love with it.

After the business for the car purchase finished and Michael went over some of the important details with them, Brad and Kim thanked him and asked about directions to Dr. Wagner's office. Her address was one in an affluent area of Coral Gables. Michael got them started in the right direction.

As they neared the location, the foliage became lush with mature overhanging Jacarandas, Royal Poinciana's and a variety of palms. Waterways teemed with privately owned boats and water toys. The address for Dr. Wagner's office fell just beyond a golf course alive with weekend golfers.

"Here it is." Kim pointed to a two-story pink stucco building that sat two hundred feet back from the street. Two vehicles were parked in front.

Brad pulled in and parked close to the entrance. "I'll see you to the door, and then I'll leave for my client's place. Don Jefferson. You have my cell number, so when you're close to being finished, just give me a call."

Kim nodded.

"Will you be okay?"

"I'm sure. The doctor sounded like a nice person."

She picked up her briefcase and purse and walked to the entryway. She had her hand on the handle when the door opened and a pleasant-looking, petite woman in her early forties appeared.

"You must be Kim Alexander." With a warm smile, she extended her hand. "Jillian Wagner. Please come in and bring your friend, too." She stood aside to allow them entry.

"Thanks, but he has some business to attend to, but I'd like you to meet Brad Kimbal, Dr. Wagner."

Brad reached out to shake her hand. Her small frame barely came up to his chest. "I'd love to join you both, but business always seems to come first. I'll be back later for Kim, though. So, take your time. I'm in no hurry."

After Brad left, Jillian led Kim past the secretary and through to a bright solarium at the back of the building. It faced a garden of flowers, shrubs, figurines and a small pond. Mature Poincianas canopied the back garden invitingly.

Jillian had a tray with a pitcher of lemonade and glasses on a small round coffee table. She motioned to Kim to sit on a love seat next to the refreshments.

"Now, what can I do for you?" She brushed the feathered bangs of her short brown hair away from her forehead, poured two glasses of the beverage, handing one to Kim. "You really have my curiosity working overtime."

"Thank you, Dr. Wagner," Kim said accepting the cool drink.

"This isn't a medical visit, so why don't you just call me Jillian?"

"Thank you. Your father apparently was the doctor to some of my family when they were living in Miami in the late seventies and early eighties. I'm sure you're wondering what that has to do with me now." Jillian nodded when Kim hesitated. "Well, I've been delving into every aspect of my parents lives because they were both murdered in their bed as they slept when I was ten-years-old. Whoever did it has never been apprehended."

Jillian gasped. "I'm so sorry. I'll do whatever I can to help."

"It was a devastating period in my life. Fortunately, I have a wonderful aunt who has since devoted her life to raising me and seeing to my education."

Kim hesitated long enough to sip some lemonade. She picked up her briefcase and opened it on her lap.

"My grandfather willed me his business and the home he had built for my grandmother when they were first married. After he passed away my parents moved from Miami to take charge of both places, each of which were to be turned over to me when I came of age. In the meantime, my parents were designated caretakers."

"I don't quite understand what my father's practice had to do with all this."

"I see your point, but, please allow me to finish. The whole thing is pretty complicated, and I'm probably confusing you. Let me just add that the local Glade City police had been in charge of the investigation without State assistance. No one really seems to know what happened, but if there had been any evidence, it was destroyed or lost. We may never know.

"I've obsessed for many years over *why* someone would commit such a crime and who. I have always held the thought in my heart that somewhere buried in the thread of their lives there has to be an answer, some sort of clue. Was it a hate crime or one of passion or jealousy? I know it couldn't have been a random killing."

"How can you be so positive?" Jillian was sitting forward in her seat, elbows on her knees, studying Kim.

"I was in the house that night, and whoever it was would have killed me if they could have found where I was hiding. Without a doubt, they knew the family well enough to know there was a child, and that this child needed to be disposed of, as well.

"The rage and anger were quite evident as I was the silent witness to it. Right now, I'm looking into everything I can; everyone they knew and associated with. Someday, something will turn up, some piece of the puzzle that's been missing all these years. This is where I believe your father comes into the picture."

"But Kim, you said my father was the family doctor when they were living in Miami. The crime was committed in Glade City. Is that correct?"

"That's true. However, I believe there were ties to Miami; ties we didn't even realize existed.

"You see, since my parents were hard up when they lived in Miami, my grandfather paid them to board my aunt while she attended college. It gave them extra money every month and allowed Aunt Patricia to be with family."

From the briefcase, she pulled out some of the canceled checks she'd found and paper clipped together. She handed them to Jillian.

"When I was going through my grandfather's papers, I found these. My parents never bothered with the library of the estate where my grandfather stored files and most every piece of paper he felt should be saved. So, everything had been left exactly as Grandfather had intended."

Jillian studied the checks. Her eyes opened wider. "These are very large sums of money, Kim, but why was your grandfather paying the doctor bills?"

"That's the part I don't quite understand. The deal was to put Aunt Patricia through college and help my parents through some of the tough times. My father worked for an outfit that didn't pay much, so my mother got a job to help out. Grandfather probably agreed to pay doctor bills, which normally should have been pretty routine. But this … ." She motioned toward the canceled checks Jillian held. "Someone must have either had a bad accident or one of them had been very sick. And then there is the huge check to the Palm Medical Clinic and Private Hospital. I can't find any reason for those payments … unless Grandfather had to pay my mother's doctor bills and hospitalization when she was pregnant with me. I have no way of knowing, since nothing had been notated about what the checks covered."

Jillian looked at Kim. "I have no clue personally, because I didn't know my father's patients that long ago. I would have been attending the university myself at the time. The dollar amount certainly could relate to your mother's pregnancy.

"This building was my father's place of practice. More than anything, he wanted the two of us to work here together.

Unfortunately, he passed away not long after I finished my residency and began to establish my own clientele, but I still have all his records and books stored upstairs."

She rose from her seat and motioned to Kim. "Let's go up and have a look. Since you're directly related to those patients, I know my father would be in agreement, God rest his soul."

She led the way to an elevator in the hallway. The second floor opened into a large room similar to a living quarters. Two doors branched off that room, and Kim could see one held another bathroom.

The open room housed a maze of file cabinets and a desk that looked as though it must have belonged to the good doctor. One wall was completely filled with bookshelves.

"My father's medical library," Jillian said, as she noticed Kim studying the books. "Let's see what year those checks were written." She looked at the earliest check. "This one was written August 31, 1979. The Palm Clinic check was made out on February 26, 1980. The large one to my father was made out on March 25, 1980. Let me pull those files and you can have a look."

Jillian moved over to the cabinet that was marked with an A and slid it open. She began looking through the crammed drawer. After what seemed to be endless minutes, she pulled out a manila file.

"This could be one that you want." She handed the thick file to Kim. "I'll check the Sanderson file now." There was a pause and then a sigh. "You know, Kim, these files only go through the P s. I'm afraid the other files may have been left in our old office storage area by accident. I'm so sorry I won't be able to provide you with the information you wanted today. That room has been locked for years and the keys are in a vault on a timer. It can't be accessed until Monday morning. I'll try to get to it as soon as possible, though. Mondays are busy, but I promise you I won't forget. "

Kim looked up from the Alexander file that she had begun to scan. Jillian's words gripped her skull like a vise. *So close, and yet so far*, she thought. *I have to be patient.*

"Since I seldom get up here, I didn't realize all my father's files weren't stored here."

"Not your fault, Jillian. You've been kind enough to help me. Perhaps this file will be all I'll need."

"Right now, I'll get out and give you a chance to sort through the records on your own. I'll check back shortly to see if you need any help. Take the file over to the desk and be comfortable while you're looking."

Jillian left, and Kim settled down at the desk.

The file disclosed nothing out of the ordinary: normal visits for check ups, blood pressure, prescribing some medications, mostly for Kim's mother. "She must have felt she was under a lot of pressure with working and being pregnant," she mused.

Nothing else presented itself that might answer any of her many questions. She put the file back in the order she found it just as Jillian returned with a tray of fresh cut papaya, strawberries, and a pitcher of ice water with two glasses.

"A little something from my office kitchen. I thought you might like a pick-me-up."

"It looks very refreshing."

Jillian pulled up a folding chair along side of Kim. "Can I help you with anything?"

"I think I've seen it all. There's not as much here as I had hoped for. I guess I'll have to be patient until I get information from the Sanderson files." She hesitated, and looked at the doctor. "I truly expected to find something in the Alexander file, but I'm so grateful for your kindness, Jillian. I'll give Brad a call, and we can be on our way and out of yours."

"It's no problem. I'd certainly like to see you able to resolve some of your issues."

When Brad came to pick up Kim, he showed Jillian the address of Max's old residence at The Breezes and asked if she might know the best way to get there.

"I'm not familiar with that place, but I know the district. It's an older area of Miami, but well kept and clean. I'll show you which main street to take, and you can probably get the exact location from any service station."

"Sorry, you didn't find what you were looking for, Kim," Brad said as he threaded his way through the Miami traffic. "Chances are something will turn up in a place you least expect."

"You could be right. If I can locate Max, that would mean a lot to me. He might be able to shed some light. And, this trip has been fruitful so far; Jillian turned out to be a very nice person, as well as your friend at the dealership, and I have the new car I've been wanting for a while now." She gave Brad a bright smile.

Jillian's directions proved to be right on target. It didn't take Brad long to find The Breezes, even without stopping for additional inquiries.

The apartments were close to the Inland Waterway, built on a piece of property now probably worth millions, but more affordable at the time of construction. The grounds surrounding it were well established with towering palms, Bird-of-Paradise, Pigmy Dates, and Geiger Trees with their brilliant clusters of orange flowers. Red Bougainvillea clung to some of the fencing.

Brad drove into the parking area of the complex where a large portico covered with lavender trumpet vines sheltered the main entrance. A series of sliding glass doors led the way to a lobby outfitted with easy chairs and end tables. It was a pleasant-looking room, dated, but well kept and clean. A small desk in the far corner supported a telephone and a backdrop for keys. On the counter a sign read, "Please ring for Manager."

Kim touched the buzzer adjacent to the sign. It rang from behind a door near the desk. A middle-aged man dressed casually in a Navy blue golf shirt, light blue jeans shorts, and white deck shoes emerged from the door.

"Can I help you folks?"

"I hope so," Kim answered as she withdrew the piece of paper with Max's address and phone number on it. "I was given this address by a friend in Glade City. I've tried calling the phone number, but it apparently is no longer a working line. Mr. Young was a friend of my deceased parents, and it would mean a lot to me if I could make contact with him." She handed the paper to the manager.

"Ah, yes," he said, checking out the name and phone number. "He moved about a year after I came here to work. I'm just not sure if anyone around here might remember him or know his whereabouts. I do recall him living alone. Said his wife had died some years before he came to live at the Breezes."

"I didn't know he had been married," Kim said.

"I'm sorry, Miss. I really don't know much about him. He kept to himself for the most part. Let me check with Al, our maintenance man. He's been here forever."

He picked up the phone and dialed a number. "Al, do you happen to remember Max Young?" He paused, listening. "Good. I have a party in the lobby inquiring after him. Can you spare a few minutes?" He listened a moment and then hung up. "He's on his way. He was just getting ready to check the pool anyway."

In less than five minutes, a tall, gray-haired man in jeans-shorts and a bright orange tee shirt strolled through the front door and greeted the manager.

"These the folks wanting information on Max Young?" He looked at Brad and Kim. "What did y'all need to know, not that I'm privy to much info on him myself?" He pulled a package of cigarettes from his shirt pocket and proceeded to light one while he studied the two visitors.

"I would like to contact Mr. Young because he was an old friend of my parents who are gone now."

"Don't know if I can help you folks or not." He took a long drag on his cigarette and blew out a ring of smoke. "Max didn't hang around Miami after he moved out of the apartments here. Said he had an old friend, a lady, who lived in Ft. Myers and was going to look her up. He called me once after his move and said that he found his friend. Gave me an address and phone number in case I wanted to get out of Miami and visit him for a few days. That was about four or five years ago."

"That would be a great start, if you wouldn't mind sharing that with me," Kim smiled.

"I'll see if I can locate that number. I probably have it in an old telephone book in my quarters." He turned to the manager. "Maybe Dick here, could get you folks a cool drink while you're waiting."

"No problem," the manager replied. "I have iced tea or lemonade."

"How about lemonade?" Brad said.

Kim nodded. "I'd like that."

As soon as Al made his exit, the manager said, "Make yourselves comfortable while I get the lemonade."

Brad nudged Kim and whispered, "Maybe we'll get lucky."

In a few minutes Dick returned with two glasses of beverage. "I have some business to attend to, so I'll leave you two. Al should be back shortly."

Brad nodded. "It's nice and cool in here, so please don't let us hold you up."

"And thanks again for your help," Kim said.

Twenty minutes later, Al returned with a piece of paper in his hand. "This is it, a copy of what Max left me. I certainly hope you can find him. If you do, say 'Hi' for me. I might still get there one of these days. I'd like to see the Gulf coast for a change."

Kim thanked him, and she and Brad left. It was almost five o'clock and had been a long, busy day, although she felt they had accomplished a lot.

"You look tired, young lady. I think I need to get a good meal in you, lift your spirits and get you refreshed." Brad said. "How about we look for a nice restaurant and relax a bit before we start home?" He gave her a bright smile as the Miami sun set off sparks of fire in his brown eyes.

"It sounds just like what the doctor ordered." Kim returned the smile.

On the trip home, Brad did most of the talking; about the business and what he hoped to achieve, about Gloria and what a great gal he thought she was. He often wondered why the men weren't all flocking around her, since she was pretty, intelligent, and fun to be around. "She's a great person to work with. I never see her moody or withdrawn. She always seems to be upbeat, energetic, and willing to go the whole distance for her clients."

"What about you and Gloria, Brad?"

"We're simply very good friends, have been for years, and as far as work goes, I never want her to leave. She's a real asset to the company and my right hand. It wouldn't be the same without her."

"She's most special to me, too, Brad."

He nodded and pulled into Gloria's driveway. "Please don't say anything to her yet, but I'm planning on offering her a full partnership ... if she'll accept." He hit the garage remote, which Kim had transferred from her rental car.

"Mum's the word." Kim's smile said it all. "I can see that she would be the perfect partner; dedicated and accomplished." She picked up her purse and started to open the Cruiser door when Brad beat her to it. "I can't thank you enough, Brad. I certainly enjoyed the trip much more than if I'd had to fight traffic and follow directions by myself. It's been a rewarding day in many ways."

She stepped out, and Brad handed her the keys to her shiny, new car. "The feeling is mutual. I've been putting off this trip for a few weeks now simply because when you go as often as I have to, it gets pretty boring. It was a great excuse for me and made my day. I've enjoyed our time together." He started to his parked car, stopped, and turned back. "Maybe we could do this again someday?"

"I'd like that, Brad." She watched his tail lights disappear before she hit the switch to lower the door, but not before her eyes picked up a small red vehicle parked across the street several houses away. Her mind playing tricks on her again, she reasoned.

Chapter 17

Sunday morning, Gloria walked into the kitchen. Her dark blonde hair had not been combed. She was barefoot and still had on her short cotton pajamas. Kim was already up and dressed. She sat at the kitchen table with a bowl of corn flakes, a cup of tea, a pad and pencil.

"Well, aren't you the early bird?" Gloria said, pushing hair back from her face. She took a can of coffee from the cupboard, a filter and proceeded to fill the glass pot with water. Sitting opposite Kim, she said, "I need a good strong cup of coffee to rev up my jets. None of that wimpy tea stuff you indulge in." She chuckled and looked at Kim.

"Tea's much better for you, my dear. You'll see, one of these days."

"Can't wait."

While the coffee brewed, Gloria got out butter and strawberry jam from the refrigerator and made herself two pieces of toast.

Kim smiled and said, "Cereal would be better for your arteries."

"I'll take your word for it," Gloria said, slathering butter on her toast. "Tell me, what's on our agenda today?"

With an already brilliant sun in the sky, birds chirped, oblivious to warmth and humidity. Wispy breezes moved the sheer curtains at the window by the table.

"I'm waiting for a decent hour to try this number for Max. If I can make contact with him, do you want to go to Fort Myers with me?"

"I wouldn't miss the opportunity," Gloria answered as she poured a cup of her fresh brew. "I've been waiting for a reason to get out of town and see new horizons. Yesterday was so hectic. I need a change of pace."

At that moment, the front doorbell rang.

"Would you be a sweetheart and get that, Kim?"

"No problem," she replied. She got up and walked down the hall to the front door.

Chase stood at the door in his uniform. "I just wanted to know if you had any success reaching Max. I came around last evening but no one answered the bell."

"Gloria was still working, and I didn't get home until nine. I'd invite you in, Chase, but Gloria isn't dressed yet."

"That's okay. I'm on duty anyway. So, did you find him at the address I gave you in Miami?"

"No, but we discovered he moved to Fort Myers. I have a phone number, if it's still a working one."

"Do you have a new address as well?"

"Yes, but who knows? That lead may be as cold as the one you so kindly got for me. I'll see what happens when I try the phone number."

"Will you let me know what you find out?"

"Of course. I appreciate your getting us the original number. Without it, we would still be in the dark."

"My pleasure," he answered and turned to go. "I'll be in touch," he called over his shoulder and stepped into the idling squad car at the curb.

At nine, Kim dialed the number she'd received from Al at The Breezes.

A woman's voice answered sleepily. "Yeah?"

"I'm looking for a Max Young. Do I have the right number?"

"Who wants to know?" was the curt reply.

"My name is Kim Alexander, but I'm not sure Mr. Young would remember me. He was acquainted with my parents years ago. I would be much obliged if I could speak with him … if he's around."

"Well, he ain't here right now, sister, but I'll give him the message when he gets back."

Kim's heart skipped a beat as she realized she had struck pay dirt.

"I would appreciate that. I'll leave you my cell number in case I'm not home when he returns."

"Wow, that's a piece of good news." Gloria said after Kim hung up. "Are we still going to drive to Fort Myers, or do we have to wait for Max to return your call?"

"As long as you've already taken the day off, let's be on our way. If he calls my cell, we'll just be that much closer."

Gloria was gone in seconds, heading for a quick shower. In twenty minutes she returned fully dressed in shorts and a sleeveless top.

"Didn't have time to blow dry, but in this weather, my hair will dry in a heart beat."

"Actually, I like it that way," Kim said as she touched her friend's damp curls. "It reminds me of when you were a little girl."

"Thanks." Gloria's blue eyes flashed the mischief that was part of her ongoing charm. "We're off then."

The day, still strong with sunshine in a crisp blue sky, created a picturesque contrast to the typical billowy clouds of south Florida as the girls headed out on the Tamiami Trail. Past Naples and Bonita Springs, they continued to Fort Myers, both girls chattering endlessly about the days after they met at school in Glade City and the close relationship they'd had before Kim had been taken to Seattle.

"I sure suffered a loss after you left with your aunt," Gloria said. "I don't know what I would have done if it hadn't been for Leslie. Have to admit, I was always a little jealous of her 'cause I wanted your attention all to myself." Gloria sighed as they drove up Cleveland Avenue looking for a good spot to stop for lunch. "She was always a nice young lady, more sophisticated than the rest of us, but a good and loyal friend. Pretty, too. She helped me over my depression after you left. When you're a kid, you just naturally expect things to remain status quo."

"I know," Kim said as she slowed to pull into the Edison Shopping Mall parking lot. "My existence changed so dramatically from a happy and satisfying life with my school chums, Mother and Daddy, and a place I really loved, but Aunt Patricia couldn't have been better to me. She bent over backwards to make me as comfortable as possible. She took me to all kinds of places to keep me amused, my mind off my loss and missing friends and places back home."

Gloria watched Kim pull into a spot near Ruby Tuesday's restaurant. "I remember seeing your aunt that one time when she came to take you back with her. I could definitely see the family resemblance; exceptionally good-looking lady with beautiful strawberry blonde hair."

"She still has it, too, as well as her good looks."

The girls got out and entered the mall near the food court. Looking over the variety of fast foods offered, they settled on Chinese and found an open table in the center of the dining area.

Before Kim had a chance to take her first bite, her cell phone rang.

She looked at Gloria, her hand shaking as she answered.

"Kim Alexander? This is Max Young."

"Mr. Young, I'm so glad you called back. I've really been anxious to meet you and talk to you about my parents since you all had been friends back in Glade City."

"Doris told me you wanted to talk. I don't get down to the Glades anymore, so maybe we could just do this thing on the phone."

"To tell you the truth, Mr. Young … "

"Max, please."

"Well, Max, my friend and I are actually here in Fort Myers. Perhaps we could meet or you could direct me to your place and … "

"Where are you now?"

"We're at the Edison Mall Food Court having lunch."

"Stay there, and I'll meet you. What are you wearing?"

"Look for a red-head and a blonde in the middle of the seating area."

He hung up and Kim gave Gloria a big smile. "We've actually made contact. I can't believe it. I'm so nervous, I don't think I can eat a bite."

"Nonsense. You should be relieved enough now to eat every bit and want some of mine. Put your fork in that chow mein and raise it to your mouth. Now, I say." Sunlight streamed through the skylights of the food court creating streaks of gold in Gloria's hair.

"Yes, *Mother*," Kim answered. She popped a forkful of the Chinese noodle dish into her mouth.

They were finishing when a tall, deeply suntanned man with graying sideburns and rugged good looks approached their table. Bulging muscles showed below the straps of his sleeveless tank top. "Ms. Alexander?" he said in a strictly business-tone.

"Max? I'm Kim and this is my friend, Gloria Latham. Won't you sit down?"

"Pleased to meet you both," he said, his eyes moving from one woman to the other with meticulous concentration. He removed his baseball cap and pulled out a chair. "You have some of your father's features, but with the Sanderson red hair."

"I'll accept that as a compliment." Kim lowered her eyes slightly.

He folded his cap and placed it in a back pocket. "I'll tell you right out I didn't want you to come to the house with Doris there. She's … well, she's a very jealous person, and a bit on the gruff side. Never know what's coming out of her mouth." He sat down next to Gloria.

"I don't mean to be too hard on her, though. She helped me out when my life seemed to be crumbling around me."

"I understand, Mr. ... Max. Could we get you something to eat or drink?"

"Thanks, but I just had lunch before I called you. How did you find me, anyway?"

"Your ex-partner got us your old number in Miami, and those people had your information here in Fort Myers."

"Ah, yes, Chase. I haven't seen him since I left Glade City. I assume he's doing well."

Kim nodded. "Seems to be. I met him when I first came back to Glade City several weeks ago, and he's been very helpful." She paused, taking a deep breath. "I plan to take over the old Sanderson home, SandHill. You may remember that name. The place has a very special meaning to me because my grandfather built it for my grandmother."

"I believe most folks in Glade City knew the story of your grandparents, and how SandHill got its name. I was told your grandmother's maiden name was Hill."

Kim laughed. "People used to call it the Sanderson-Hill House 'til it finally became shortened to SandHill. Grandfather liked it, so it stuck. Until I'm able to have it cleaned up, I'm staying with Gloria."

Max flashed Gloria a quick look. "I think I remember seeing you once when you were staying overnight with Kim." He looked down at his hands momentarily. When he raised his eyes again, he directed his conversation to Kim. "Mrs. Alexander had called the station on several occasions thinking she'd heard a prowler when Mr. Alexander was out of town. The chief sent me to investigate since the Alexander's were special people in his book, and the home was situated out of city limits."

The memory was as clear to Kim as if it had happened yesterday.

Mother opened Kim's bedroom door and looked in. "Kim, Gloria," she said, eyes serious and unblinking, "Lock this door and stay in here until I let you know everything is okay."

"What's the matter, Mother?" Kim asked, sucking in her breath.

"Someone's been trying to break in. I heard them rattling the back door, and then a beam of light passed by the kitchen window going toward the front of the house. I've called the police. They're sending someone out." With that, she closed the door and left.

Kim and Gloria looked at each other. Gloria went to the door and locked it behind Kim's mother. Then she snapped off the lamp next to the bed and moved over to the window that overlooked the front lawn.

"Come here, Kim. You can see as clear as anything with the light off." She pulled the ruffled curtain aside as Kim crept closer to be next to her friend. "Maybe we'll be able to see who it is."

"I don't want to look," Kim said. "Whoever it is might see us."

"No way. It's all dark up here."

"But the moon's bright and shining right in the window."

"Don't be a sissy, Kim. No one will think of looking up here."

Kim edged closer and onto the yellow chintz-covered cushion of the window box. She peeked around the curtain Gloria held open. Not a wisp of air stirred. Shadows from the large Australian pine covered a portion of the lawn, and there was no person in sight.

Gloria had her face pressed against the screen when lights loomed onto the gravel driveway. A police car slowed, pulled through the open gate, and parked in front of the porch.

"I can feel my heart pounding in my throat," Kim whispered, reaching for Gloria's hand.

"Everything will be okay, now," Gloria said.

Twenty minutes later there was a knock on the door. Gloria called out, "Who's there?"

"Police Officer Young. Can you open, please?"

Gloria ran to the door and unlocked it.

The tall uniformed officer took a step forward as the door opened. "Just checking to see if you girls were okay. I've taken a look around the premises and there's nothing. No one to be found." He scanned the bedroom, eyes stopping on Kim by the window. "Everything will be fine, now," he assured. "I'm going to stay for awhile to make certain the prowler doesn't come back."

He left, and a few minutes later Mrs. Alexander popped her head in the door. "I want you girls to go to bed and get some sleep. Your father will be home early in the morning, Kim." With that, she closed the door, and Kim heard her footsteps going down the hall to her bedroom.

❦

"I often wondered if there really was a prowler or if the whole incident was a figment of my mother's imagination." Kim mused.

"Not to change the subject, girls, but I don't have a whole lot of time to spend, otherwise Doris is going to be ringing my cell phone." He touched the instrument in his shirt pocket. "Sometimes I really don't care if she rants or not, but it just makes life easier to go along with her. So, what was it you wanted to talk to me about?"

"I'm sorry, Max," Kim apologized. "Since you were the chief investigating officer in my parents' case, I'd appreciate hearing anything you might remember. There was very little in the newspapers to go on."

"I can't tell you much more than what you've probably heard or read. Chase and I searched the place over for any clues or fingerprints and were never able to find anything substantial. Whoever it was had to be mighty knowledgeable about not leaving any clues behind that could identify or incriminate him ... or her. No other blood except that of your parents turned up. There were no fingerprints found, no piece of clothing, cigarette stubs, nothing at all. We went over the place like pigs digging for truffles; used all the tools available to us at the time. Technology back then wasn't what it is today. I'm sorry I can't enlighten you any more than this, Kim."

"When the station got the call from me that next morning, they sent the coroner and you and Chase out to check the crime scene?"

"That's right. A small town doesn't have the resources a big city has. We did the best we could with the limited help we got from the county sheriff's department. After the coroner left with the ... bodies ... " Max looked at his hands again and didn't look up for a long moment. Reaching into his shirt pocket, he pulled out a package of cigarettes, fumbled with the wrapping, then replaced it without opening it. "I forgot, no smoking here." He concentrated on the surface of the table, avoiding eye contact with either of the women. "Sorry, but that was a pretty rough time for me. You understand ... two good people I'd known for quite awhile."

Kim nodded as the hideous scenes flooded back to mind, scenes she had never been able to erase, pictures that flared up at any given time reminding her she could have been murdered, as well.

"I understand," Kim murmured. "You started to say," she prompted.

"That's when Chase and I went to work. We took pictures, a pillowcase with blood, a piece of Mr. Alexander's torn pajamas ... also bloody. We picked up anything and everything we thought might be used as evidence. It was all taken to the county crime lab. We don't know what happened with the investigation after that. I inquired several times, but the chief told me it was out of our hands once they took over."

Gloria changed the subject. "What about the prowler who had been reported on several occasions? Were there ever any clues as to whom that person may have been? Or were there ever any more incidences along that line?"

"There was one time that something odd happened." Max stroked his chin with a thumb and index finger. "You remember Luz and Felix Ramon, of course?"

"I could never forget those two. Luz was like a second mother to me," Kim said.

"Well, according to what I was told, Luz was downstairs in the kitchen when Mrs. Alexander came racing into the driveway from town one day. Felix had been in the tool shed behind the home when your mother jumped from the car, screaming. Even left the motor running. Something had frightened her, badly. She said someone had followed her and tried to run her off the road and into the swamp. She wasn't able to identify the vehicle when the police came to take a statement. No one ever found out who the culprit was."

"Do you think this person could be the murderer?" Kim asked softly. Gloria reached across the table and put her hand on top of her friend's.

"I honestly don't know. It just seemed that there were a number of strange happenings, things that didn't add up. Your father reported once that they had been getting late night phone calls with nobody on the other end. He finally had the number changed to an unlisted one."

"I wonder if the Ramons might remember anything more? I'd certainly like to talk to them," Kim said.

"I don't think they stayed around Glade City very long after your parents' deaths. As a matter of fact, I believe they went to work for the Kimbals for a short time. I don't know what happened to them after that."

"You mean Brad's folks?" Gloria piped up.

"Yes."

At that moment, Max's cell phone rang. He pulled it out and looked at the screen. "I figured it had to be her. She's getting pretty possessive lately. Pardon me, ladies, if I don't bother to answer this." He put the instrument back into his shirt pocket.

Kim smiled. "I understand. We shouldn't have kept you so long."

"I'm afraid you probably don't understand. I've known Doris for years ... since I returned to Miami to live. She was a private nurse to a very close friend of mine who died of cancer. She moved to Fort Myers after that to get out of the big city, but we always kept in touch. When hard times hit me, she offered me a roof over my head and some personalized therapy. No strings attached. At that time, I felt I had really hit bottom. I welcomed the opportunity, and it was good for me, then." He pulled out a water bottle from his hip pocket and took a long drink while Gloria and Kim quietly observed him.

"She's been a great help over the years, and I am grateful for what she's done for me; giving me a roof over my head, feeding me until I managed to find a job and pay my own way. Since she never married, there's never been a man in her life until she invited me to come and stay with her. Doing chores around the house gave me the feeling of repaying some of the kindness she'd extended to me." He paused, looking at the girls.

"I suppose you both think I'm an ingrate. I hope I'm not, but lately, she's been changing, acting more like a jealous wife, and that doesn't fly with me."

Gloria glanced at Kim. "Maybe, change of life, Max," she said. "She probably can't help it."

"It could be, but it's making my life miserable. We've always been good friends. Our arrangement has been based totally on that and not on sex. I'm afraid I just don't understand her anymore."

"I'm sorry, Max." Kim said. She reached into her purse and pulled out a small pad of paper and wrote a number on it. "This is Gloria's home phone number where I'm staying.

You have my cell phone number. If you think of anything else, I would really appreciate your call."

"I only wish I'd have had something more substantial to tell you." He got up and put out his hand. "I'm glad I got to see you again after all these years, Kim, and to have met you again, Gloria."

He started to leave, hesitated, and then turned back, looking directly at Kim. "Does Melvin Thomas still work for the boat tours?"

"Oh, yes. He's still there, as acting manager. Why do you ask?"

"I remember when your father hired him as his assistant to free up some of his time. Somewhere, I heard something about bad blood developing between the two. I don't know if it was over more pay, position or what. You might want to check that out." He studied Kim's face. "Just a thought," he added, then turned and disappeared into the crowd.

The two women stared at each other for a moment before Kim broke the silence. "The thought never occurred to me. Melvin seems so uneducated, and yet, he's very egotistical. I have to give him credit though. He's kept the business looking good and attracting customers." Kim picked up her purse and stood. "If you're ready, Gloria, I suppose my business here is finished."

She retrieved the car keys from her purse as she and Gloria headed for the mall exit. "Max seems nice enough, but we don't really know much about him. Did you notice how he reacted when he was telling about the murder scene? Unusual for a hardened police officer from Miami, don't you think?"

"Yes," Gloria agreed, "but he did give us a good reason. He'd known your parents for many years."

"Right, but it happened over fifteen years ago. It can even affect me after all these years, but they were *my* flesh and blood. They were only acquaintances of *his*."

Gloria opened the glass exit door, and they moved outside. "I see what you're getting at."

As they headed for the PT Cruiser in the parking lot, Gloria said, "Wow. The heat today is unbelievable." She wiped her brow with the back of her hand. "The car will be like a flaming oven after sitting in the sun for so long."

"I'll get the air on right away," Kim said. She unlocked the car door.

Chapter 18

Monday morning after Gloria left, Kim decided to face the inevitable; she needed to go back to the Boat Tours and find out exactly how Melvin has been handling the money. Not only did her last visit make her anxious, but also Max's mentioning bad blood between her father and Melvin raised many questions.

What, exactly, had caused this "bad blood" between them? As far as she knew, her father had always been fair in his dealings with others, so what could have occurred to cause bitterness between them? Who else could possibly know about this, and how would she be able to find out more?

Questions continued to hammer away in her head while she fixed a cup of tea. She needed to get some fresh air in her lungs and prepare herself for a new meeting with Melvin. Merely thinking about him stirred up strong emotions and frustrations. A brisk jog in Gloria's Spanish Lace complex might be just what she needed, she decided.

She put on shorts, a tank top and jogging shoes, put the house key in her pocket, and strapped a small water bottle around her waist.

As she locked the front door behind her, morning calm filled the streets, still early enough for limited neighborhood activity. The road to her left lead out of Spanish Lace and into town. If she turned right it began a gradual curve left for four blocks and then dead ended into the main highway to town. She could jog that far and then turn back in time for a shower and light breakfast before going to see Melvin.

The piece of highway that bypassed Spanish Lace had been built like a floating bridge over the swamp, running close to the SandHill property on the west to a mile from Glade City's outskirts on the east. On one side, a ten foot high cement block wall separated the road from the housing development. The opposite side paralleled the murky waters of the swamp where a low fence of steel warned motorists of the potential danger.

Several cars passed by as she jogged the blocks in the lane facing traffic. From behind, she heard another vehicle approaching. Slowly. Too slowly. A chill ran up her spine, and she stepped off the street onto the grassy parkway. Keeping up her pace but not wanting to look behind her, she sensed its close proximity. Why hadn't it already passed her? Perspiration beaded on her forehead.

A police cruiser pulled along side her, and Chase rolled down his window.

In a flash of anger, she wanted to protest, but relief in itself quickly cooled her thoughts.

"I could arrest you for public endangerment," he said without a smile.

"Just wh ... "

Quickly interrupting her, he said, "You'll have all the young guys running off the road trying to get a better look." The curve of his mouth exposed white teeth.

She walked over to the vehicle and to his open window. Suppressing a grin of abatement she answered back. "If you're not careful, I'll call the police and report you for molesting the innocent. In fact, I know a police officer who'd handle this for me."

"And that would be ... ?"

"I don't think I should tell you."

"Well, what does this officer look like?"

"He's rather tall, blue eyes, reasonably good looking."

"I think we should discuss this situation over, say, a meal or a drink when that officer isn't working."

"I'll have to take that into consideration."

"All kidding aside, I have something rather interesting to tell you."

"Well, let's have it." She leaned her arms on the edge of the window and looked directly into clear blue eyes.

"I got a call early this morning, at the station. Max. He found out I was still here in Glade City and asked me to do him a favor." He hesitated.

"Go on. Don't let me hang here."

"He wanted to know if I knew of any jobs around. Says he needs a change of scenery and wants to get out of Fort Myers."

"Wow. That *is* interesting. Did you have any ideas?"

"There's a new senior housing development opening soon on the east side of town called Pelican Landing. They're looking for a security guard. I told Max I'd run over there today and put in a good word for him. With his background I doubt anyone else will stand a chance of getting that job." Self-satisfaction seemed to flow through his words.

"So, he's ready to leave Fort Myers?"

"He's more than ready. I invited him to stay with me until he gets situated, and he grabbed the opportunity. Said he'd be here tomorrow."

"So, it's a deal, then?"

"I'll have him a new job by this afternoon."

"You're sure of yourself, aren't you?" Kim shook her head, smiling. A bit conceited, she thought.

"I'll let you know," he told her as he put the cruiser in gear and moved off down the street.

While she showered, Kim assessed the day's development. It was looking more and more like the stage was being set, but for what? Would this be a good thing or would it change the plans she'd already had in mind?

She put on a plain, straight cotton skirt, flat shoes, pulled her hair back into a neat little bun, and then checked her image in the mirrored closet door. Maybe this would give Melvin no cause to make crude remarks or make her feel uneasy with his intense stare.

When she reached the parking lot at the boat tours, it was already full of cars and two tour buses. She realized more than ever that this place was indeed a profitable enterprise, more than Aunt Patricia seemed aware of. She threw her purse strap over her shoulder, locked the car and marched toward the back entrance.

Making her way directly to Karen's office, Kim found the young woman sitting at her desk with a pile of papers in front of her.

"Oh, come in, Ms. Alexander. It's good to see you again."

"Likewise, Karen. Please, just call me Kim. Am I interrupting anything important?"

"No, no. Mr. Thomas just dropped these off to me. But, there's no hurry. He doesn't need them 'til closing."

"I wonder if I could check cash register tapes against the books. Nothing against your bookkeeping, Karen. Just good business practice for me. My aunt never seemed to get much of a monetary report from Mr. Thomas."

"I don't mind at all. He always takes care of the cash drawers and gives me the closing totals every night." She got up and went into the closet to a vault. "Please sit down, and I'll be right back with the records."

In a moment she returned with a container the size of two large shoe boxes. "These are the totals for this past year to date. From these I get my figures for the computer printouts. I pay most of the bills and work up the balance sheets."

"Thanks, Karen. Do you mind if I sit here like I did before? If I have any questions, I'll have you here to help me." Kim looked up and smiled. "Go ahead with what you were doing. And, please, relax. I'm not here to make you uncomfortable."

"I know, ma'am. I don't worry when you're here." She hesitated. "Mr. Thomas, he's another matter. He does make me nervous sometimes. He's such a task master." She set the box on the other side of the desk in front of Kim.

"I didn't realize he had that affect on you. You seemed so … cool with him last time I was here."

"I try not to let it show. I'm okay with him as long as he's not breathing down my neck. He has this way about him, so I try not to let him see that he upsets me."

Kim put her hand on Karen's. "I think I understand what you mean. And, what you say to me, stays with me." She gave Karen a quick grin and then started on the box.

Several minutes later she looked up at Karen. "These are only the daily <u>totals</u> from each cash register. What I'd really like to see are the actual cash register tapes. I can tell what items have been selling, what, if any, need to be dropped from inventory, and figure the profits on each category."

"Oh, Mr. Thomas keeps those in his safe. He says he has to protect them because of income tax."

"So, he gives you only the totals from the end of the day, and you do your books accordingly?"

"Yes, Ms. Alexander, I mean, Kim. He jots down the totals of each cash register for me, and then puts the original tapes in his office safe."

Kim resumed looking at the papers Karen gave her. Melvin could put anything down, and no one would be the wiser, she thought.

A whiff of cigar smoke attacked her nostrils. She looked up to see Melvin walking into the room.

"Ms. Alexander. Y'all gettin' settled in?" The gold tooth grin again.

"I am, thank you." Kim looked up, smiled and resumed going over the items in the box.

"There somethin' I kin hep ya with … or is Karen doin' the job fer ya?"

"Well, there is one thing. I've asked Karen to show me the actual cash register tapes so I can see the progression of business, … important to me. It seems that Aunt Patricia never did receive much information in this respect. Karen has only daily totals that you have written out for her."

Melvin's attitude changed abruptly. "Yup. Thas right. I keep them records in the bank vault for tax purposes. Them're the 'xact figures from the tapes, so ya won't need ta look no further. No need to waste yer time on the humdrum stuff 'cause I already sorted through it fer ya."

"I don't mind pouring over the humdrum stuff, Mr. Thomas. I believe that's part of my job, keeping abreast of how my business is run." Kim held his gaze.

Melvin stared back. "Sorry, missy. Y'all'll have to take ma word fer it. Them's the figers you need, and them's all yer gonna git fer now."

"How soon can I expect you'll be able to produce the cash register tapes for me, Mr. Thomas?"

"They're not 'vailable right now, missy." He walked over to Karen's wastebasket, stubbed out his cigar on her glass-covered desktop and dropped the dead butt into the container.

Karen blinked. She looked down at the ashy mess on her writing space, pulled out a wet wipe, and cleaned it up without saying a word.

"Why aren't they available right now?" Kim persisted in a soft, even voice.

"Them's in ma bank in California for safekeepin'."

"Would it be too presumptuous of me to ask why you don't use a bank in Glade City? Wouldn't that be more convenient for you?"

"Thas the bank I allus had fer years. Why should I change?"

Kim never took her eyes off Melvin. "My father used the local Bank of the Everglades, and my grandfather before him. I'd assume when you took over the management you'd do the same. Especially since the business is still in the Alexander name."

Melvin didn't flinch. "Since I'm legally in charge o' managin' this here place, I got the right to use any bank I wants."

"That means you've transferred all the business funds from Glade City to somewhere in California? Under your name?"

"Not quite." His eyes flashed fire as he continued. "The funds're under SawGrass Boat Tours with me as actin' manager of the account."

"I hardly think that's legal, Mr. Thomas, nor ethical. My aunt would never have agreed to that, I'm sure. How do you manage daily funds ... cash and deposits?"

"Got it set up at Bank of the Everglades for change and daily deposits. Funds git transferred once a week ta California. I FedEx the cash register tapes maself." He spoke through clenched teeth. "Legal? I'm afraid it's very legal, missy. I got a ironclad contract what says I manage the business AND the bank account anyways I sees fit. Now, if y'all'll excuse me, I have more 'portant thin's ta 'tend to." He turned to go, slamming the door behind him, and leaving Kim and Karen with their mouths agape.

Kim closed her mouth, got up, went to the door, opened it, and called out, "Mr. Thomas. A moment, please."

Melvin stopped and turned. "What, now?" he growled.

"Perhaps a better way would be for you to save me the daily tapes, and I'll pick them up each Friday morning. Then you won't have to bother sending for the ones in California."

Melvin scowled. "I wasn't plannin' on sendin' for them tapes." He glared briefly at Kim before continuing. "I thought y'all wasn't goin' to change nothin'. Mebbe I should jus' let ya do the registers yerself. Would thet suit ya?"

"I'm not trying to take your job, Mr. Thomas. I want to see how the business is going from day to day, what the best selling merchandise is, what's profitable, what isn't, and so forth. I'm sure you're doing your best, but since it's my family business, I feel this would put me in touch with the overall running of the place. I have to learn it someday."

"Thet ya should, missy. Y'all don't know nothin' 'bout this place. I'm twenty years ahead o' ya in runnin' Saw Grass, five o' those as yer father's right-hand man. I know this business inside out and run it the way it should be run. Shoulda been run this way when yer father was handlin' it." He spoke without taking his eyes from Kim's.

"I don't think it's necessary to disparage the dead, Mr. Thomas. My father did the best he could, considering he'd had no previous experience in this type of business."

Melvin moved his index finger across his untidy mustache, glaring at Kim for several unspoken moments. When he finally broke the silence, he snarled, "Pick up the tapes Friday, then." With that, he stalked off down the hall without another word.

Karen's face had turned pale. "I don't know what to say, Kim. I'm sorry. That's just the way he is sometimes."

"You're not responsible for his actions, Karen. Don't let it bother you. He's only trying to intimidate both of us, especially me, because I'm his biggest threat. Well, I'm not going to let him get away with it. And, if I were you, Karen, I wouldn't let him pull another trick like he did a few moments ago." She pointed to the spot on Karen's desk where Melvin had stubbed out his cigar. "He can't do anything to you as long as this place belongs to me."

Kim shook her head and looked down at the box of daily totals she'd been working on.

"You know, Karen, I think I'll just wait until after I've picked up those tapes and have a chance to look them over. These don't tell me what I really need to know."

She got up to leave. "I'll see you later then, and don't forget what I told you. That man is going to have to learn the hard way."

Karen smiled. "I can't wait to see that."

Chapter 19

After Kim left SawGrass Boat Tours, she still had several hours of afternoon left. She had the address and phone number of the law firm where Tricia Carson, Jason Ramon's fiancée, worked. In her car, she dialed the number and asked to speak to Tricia.

"May I say who's calling, please?"

"My name is Kim Alexander. Could you tell her that Jason's parents worked for mine over fifteen years ago, and I'd really like to speak to her for a few minutes if she's not too busy?"

Moments later another voice came on. "This is Tricia, Ms. Alexander. I have some spare time. Why don't you come over, if it's convenient?"

"Thanks. I'm just a few blocks away."

She had no trouble finding the cement block building that housed the law firm of Hayden and Michels, and parking was readily available. She found Tricia at the door waiting for her.

"This is a pleasant surprise," Tricia said as she put out her hand in greeting. "Come on back to my office. It's too bad Jason isn't here. I know he would love to see you again."

The petite five-foot-two blonde led Kim to her office and motioned to a cushioned chair. She took a seat behind her desk facing Kim. A framed picture sat on one side of the desk.

"You might enjoy seeing this since you haven't seen Jason for many years." She handed the picture to Kim.

"What a handsome young man he's grown into," Kim said as she viewed the picture of Trish and Jason together.

"Our wedding is this weekend. I know Jason would love to have you attend and so would I, if you're free."

"I'd like that, but I'm staying with my friend, Gloria, so let me see if she minds … "

"By all means, please invite her, too. I'm so happy you called when you did. I'm only here today to finish things up before I leave permanently. After our honeymoon, we'll be living in Ocala where Jason's job is."

"Thank you so much for the wedding invitations. I'm sure Gloria would love to attend. She hasn't seen the Ramon family since I left Glade City. When are Luz and Felix getting here? I'd like to talk to them if they have some time to spare before the wedding."

"They'll arrive Wednesday afternoon, so why don't you come to my house in the evening? It'll be a nice reunion."

"That's perfect," Kim said. "I appreciate your taking time to see me. We can talk more Wednesday."

Tricia jotted down directions to her home and handed the paper to Kim.

When Kim got home, there was a blinker on the phone. She pressed the button to hear the message. "Kim, this is Jillian Wagner. I wanted you to know I've found the files you asked to see. I FedExed them this afternoon, so you can expect them tomorrow. Just return them when you're finished. No hurry."

A shiver of excitement traveled through Kim's torso. It would be hard to control her feelings this week with so much happening; seeing the files she's been waiting for, visiting with the Ramons, the wedding coming up, Max's arrival tomorrow. A full week. Slow down, mind, she told herself. All in good time.

Gloria wasn't home yet, so she decided to have another look at the box of letters while she waited. She went to her bedroom and sat down on her bed with the letters and began to open them. They seemed to be much the same as the first two she'd opened, just a mention of where to meet, when, etc. along with bits of personal information. Nothing that gave her any clues as to a name. These were all dated before the two she had read earlier with Gloria.

She was almost finished with the box when she noticed something that had either slid or been placed alongside of the others, between their edges and the side of the box. She pulled it out and opened it. Since this letter had no date, it could be out of sequence. Or was it? She read:

> *My darling Mag,*
> *It's been too long since we've seen each other. I'm going out of my mind. I'm begging you to face Charles and tell him the truth about us. We'll start over, just the three of us. I make more than enough to support us comfortably. You won't have to worry about getting a job again.*
> *I know you were afraid of what Charles might do if he found out about us. We should have told him together.*
> *Now we're all suffering from this unholy mess. I know your time is limited now, but please don't put us aside. Write me. Surely you have time for some sort of note. I've kept the Post Office box, and I'll be waiting.*
> *Let's make our plans. Please, darling. Don't say no.*
> *Love always,*
> *Me*

Kim was breathing hard, now. Emotions displaced oxygen, and she felt stifled. She had to know who "Me" is or was. Is he still around? What happened to him? Could he be responsible for the murders? Yes, if he had followed them from Miami to Glade City. What had been happening between the time in Miami and when her parents had moved to The Everglades? And the biggest question on her mind: When he mentioned the "three of us," it was obviously after her birth … , wasn't it?

Chapter 20

Tuesday noon Kim headed to the real estate office to meet Gloria for lunch. A note taped to Gloria's office greeted her. "Sorry, got sidetracked with one of my slightly weird clients. Back as soon as I can. Make yourself comfy. Gloria"

She started to open the office door when a hand reached from behind her and pushed it shut. "Nobody home, but I am ... with time on my hands. Join me."

She turned to see a smiling Brad. "I shouldn't be taking up your time, Brad. Who knows how long she'll be?"

"I do." He took her hand and pulled her toward his office. "She called me a few minutes ago and asked me to entertain you for a while 'til she got through with her clients. She said, if she isn't back by twelve-thirty, I'm to take you to the restaurant across the street."

"You're sure?" she said, allowing Brad to lead her into his office and sit her down in a chair next to his desk.

"It's my best opportunity to get more acquainted with you, Kim. Can I get you anything to drink while we wait?"

"I'm good, Brad. So, who are these quirky clients of Gloria's?"

"I'll let her tell you. I'm glad she's the one stuck with them." He laughed heartily. "She can handle them. Don't think I could."

"Now, you're making me curious."

"Forget them. I want to know how you're doing with your sleuthing."

"I'm uncarthing some things ... slowly. They're beginning to line up, you might say."

"Well, if you need any help, I'm at your disposal."

"My biggest problem at the moment is Melvin Thomas. I'm not quite sure how to handle him, but I'm determined to put him in his place, even if he quits. I'll do what it takes."

"Atta girl. I've heard you aren't the only one he gives a hard time. There have also been rumors about ... " He stopped in mid-sentence.

"Don't stop there Brad. What rumors?"

"I probably shouldn't be telling you things that might only be hearsay. You know how folks in a small town are. They pick up on the least thing and soon, it's blown way out of proportion."

"That's okay. Let me be the judge of that. It might be helpful, no matter how insignificant it seems."

Brad took a deep breath and continued. "I've heard it from more than one source, so I take it there's something to it. Melvin had a crush on your mother from the time your dad hired him. He'd been seen following her at times when she left the boat tours to go home. I'm not sure whether or not she ever told your father, but she must have known what he was doing because one of the girls who worked there overheard a conversation between your mother and Melvin. This person was on her way to the office when she overheard your mother reading Melvin the riot act about following her."

Kim didn't say anything for a few moments, just kept her eyes on Brad. "I never knew ... never suspected. My mother didn't like him, either, then. I'm sure my aunt may not have heard anything since she wasn't living here at the time."

Brad said, "Let's forget about it for now. My stomach has been telling me it's almost twelve-thirty. Time to go to the restaurant." He didn't wait for her reply, but went around the desk, pulled her up from the chair and waltzed her out the door.

"This is the first place I stopped when I arrived here from Miami," Kim said after they were seated at the Glade City Family Restaurant. "I needed directions to the police station, so I stopped here for a cup of coffee and some info. I had a brief conversation with a nice waitress named Marsha."

"Oh, yes, Marsha. She's the mainstay at this place. Been here since the place was built. She's a great old gal. Hardly ever seems to take a day off … except today," he said, scanning the room.

They had just ordered when Gloria walked in.

"Whew, what an ordeal," Gloria said, breezing over to their booth. "Those two were not the easiest people to deal with. I'm just happy to be away from them for a while; especially the Mrs. They about wore me to a frazzle. But I've got them thinking."

She giggled, set her purse on the end of Brad's seat, and then plunked herself down next to Kim. "I'm dying of thirst. I need a tall lemonade, and then I'll tell you something funny."

When the waitress came back with the drink orders, Kim watched as Gloria drank half of hers in one long swallow.

"You *must* have been thirsty," Kim said. "Now, let's have the story. I'm ready for a good laugh."

"That was the Robinsons, right?" Brad interjected. "I thought she was ready to make an appearance before the Queen. She must have had diamonds on every finger, as well as on her ears, wrists and around her neck."

"Right. She plays that part to the hilt. After the third place I showed them, she said that her real interest was the big house on the southwest side of town. She called it the 'Sander's mansion.'" Gloria made a face. "Yes, I corrected her and said it was 'Sanderson.' She immediately told me she didn't care what the name was, she just wanted to have a good look at it, because it might very well be just what they had in mind. I told her it wasn't for sale, but she insisted. Said everybody has their price, and they had the cash to negotiate."

"How'd she know about it?" Kim asked. "It's not exactly on the main route."

"Evidently, they'd been snooping around. They saw it when they were surveying the area. She said they'd gotten out of the car to take a closer look, but the high fence kept them from seeing much." Gloria chuckled. "It did my heart good."

The waitress brought their order, and Gloria continued while they ate. "I told her that was why it was fenced, to keep inquisitive folks from getting in. When she gave me a dirty look, I said 'Of course, I didn't mean you people.' I tried to explain that owners must protect their property from would-be vandals or thieves." She took a breath and a bite of her sandwich.

"She still wasn't going to drop the subject. She insisted that I contact the owners to ask what they would take for it, to which I replied, 'I will do my best.'"

The rest of the meal continued as the three laughed, chatted and enjoyed their food.

Gloria looked at her watch. "Guess I'd better get back and do some work for the Robinson's. I need to come up with some excuse and maybe another place for them to view."

"I have to get back home, as well, guys," Kim said. "I'm expecting a package from Jillian Wagner."

Brad grabbed the check. "This one's on me, ladies."

As they got up to leave, Chase and Max walked through the door.

Chase was not in uniform, but in shorts and a tee shirt. "I'm glad we bumped in to you folks. I was going to call you, Kim, and let you know that Max arrived this morning about eleven-thirty."

Max smiled and said, "Kind of feels like old home week. Happy to see you two ladies again."

Chase introduced Max to Brad and then turned back to the girls. "Pelican Landing is definitely interested in Max. They said if he's all I said he is, he's got the job. We're going there right after we eat. We've just been to the station where I introduced and showed him around. I think he's impressed." Chase looked over at Max, who smiled and nodded his head.

"Who wouldn't be impressed with that building? It certainly is a far cry from the one I worked out of."

"I'll let you know what happens when we get to Pelican Landing, Kim," Chase added.

As Kim neared Gloria's place, she saw a FedEx truck parked on the street and a uniformed man standing at the front door. She pulled into the garage and hurried back to the porch.

"Good timing," the fellow said as he handed her a package.

Circling back to the open garage, she pushed the button to close the door and entered the house with her special parcel. Could it contain answers to some of the mysteries plaguing her?

As soon as she got inside, she went to the dinette table and sat down to view what she'd just received. It contained a good-size file and would take time to check each paper. She went to the fridge, got out a pitcher of lemonade, poured herself a tall glassful and settled down to begin her search.

There were records from the time Patricia first came to Miami to begin college and stay with Margaret and Charles. The first item in the file was a letter from her grandfather asking Doctor Warren Wagner to please handle any medical needs of his daughters, Margaret Alexander and her husband, Charles, and Patricia Sanderson, who would be attending Miami University and living with her sister and brother-in-law. He would pay by return mail upon receipt of the doctor's billing. If there was anything unusual, he asked the doctor to let him know so that he could approve service and payment.

She flipped through a number of items such as annual physical check-ups, immunization shots, ones for pneumonia, all the normal things one would expect of normally healthy subjects. Then at the beginning of Patricia's fourth year at the University, the doctor began giving her monthly examinations. Kim tried to read and understand the notes, but there was too much medical gibberish impossible for her to interpret. She tagged these with Post-it notes to check out later.

As she attached one of the notes, her eyes jumped ahead to words she could understand. The paper stated: Full term pregnancy. Mother will give up child for adoption.

Kim gasped, rubbed her eyes and reread the lines. No way, she thought. There had never been a hint of this before … that Aunt Patricia had ever been pregnant. So, were these files correct? Or had they been mixed with the Sanderson medical files by accident?

She knew a child of the Sanderson family would never be given up for adoption. This had to be some gigantic screw up.

She put the papers down, put her hands to her forehead, took deep breaths and tried to clear her mind, to think rationally. If what she read were true, then Kim would have a cousin somewhere out there, a real flesh and blood relative she needed to find. All these years she had believed that she was the end of the Sanderson line. Only she and her aunt were left. She felt Patricia would probably never marry, and if she did, she would not have a child at this time of her life, even if she were physically capable. Kim didn't see it as part of her aunt's nature.

She heard the garage door open and moments later, Gloria walked in.

"Sorry, I'm late. Got involved in a … My God, Kim, you look like you've seen a ghost." Gloria dropped her purse on the kitchen counter and came over to Kim's side.

"I think I have," she said. "I think I need one of your strong cups of coffee. No! Maybe something like wine or … "

In bed that evening, Kim tossed and turned trying to catch an elusive night's sleep. The revelation of Aunt Patricia's pregnancy refused to be put to rest, yet … She rolled it over and over in her head trying to conjure up any and every possible answer to the questions jabbing at her mind: Who was the father? Someone Patricia met in college? Someone who wouldn't or couldn't marry her? Perhaps <u>she</u> wasn't ready for marriage yet, or could it have been rape? What had Margaret and Charles thought when Patricia turned up pregnant, living under their roof and in their care? What about Grandfather? How had he and Grandmother felt about this … embarrassing situation? How had they dealt and coped with it? Who had made the decision to put the child up for adoption? Patricia, herself, or Kim's grandparents? In her wildest imagination, Kim couldn't picture her aunt in this position. Simply put, Patricia had never exhibited this side of herself.

Exhaustion finally claimed its victory, and in the morning, Kim was more tired than she had been when she'd gone to bed.

Chapter 21

She didn't wake up for hours after Gloria left for work. A cool and refreshing shower helped her shake off the fog that occupied her brain. She wanted to have a pleasant visit with the Ramons this evening. Seeing old friends again, she hoped would help to push those haunting questions off stage.

After supper, Gloria set up her home computer with some work she'd brought from the office. As Kim got ready to leave for Tricia Carson's home to see the Ramons, Gloria came over and gave her a big hug. "Don't go worrying about that long lost cousin of yours. If he or she is still around, you'll find out. It'll happen, my friend. You've uncovered quite a bit of puzzling information so far. More will come."

"I hope so, Gloria. I promise I won't be thinking about that this evening. I'm going to try and enjoy seeing Luz and Felix again."

When she pulled up to the curb, Luz came rushing out before Kim could lock the car. "My little Kim Alexander." She wrapped her arms around the young woman still standing in the street. "You're all grown up now, and prettier than ever."

Luz's face had matured, and her short dark hair showed streaks of silver, but the petite frame, sweet face and sparkling brown eyes were still the same.

"It's been such a long time," Kim said, returning the hug. "And where's Felix?"

"He's inside waiting for you."

They went in and joined Justin, Tricia and Felix.

"This is a great treat, Kim," Felix said, jumping up to greet her.

Tricia came over. "I'm so glad you could make it, Kim. Justin and I were just leaving for a very short while to make some last minute wedding arrangements. This'll give you all some time to get reacquainted."

After seeing that Kim and the Ramons were comfortable, Justin and Tricia left. Kim sat in an easy chair across from Felix and Luz where they talked and laughed for about an hour, catching up on what had been going on in each of their lives.

"I still have fond memories of the great tamales you used to make, Luz. I've never tasted anything close to them since."

"It's an old family recipe handed down from my grandmother and her mother, and so on. It's work, but I haven't found an easier way to get the same results."

"Gloria remembers them, too."

"How is she and what is she doing with herself ... married or engaged?" Felix asked.

"She's been in real estate, doing okay, but I guess Mr. Right hasn't shown up yet. She's coming to the wedding, so you'll see her there. Right now, she's been helping me with a project I've had in mind for years. We've been looking over SandHill and going through things in storage. I've always felt there must be some overlooked clues in my parents' deaths." Luz was nodding her head. Kim went on giving them a brief rundown on the state of the home and what she'd been doing.

"That's one thing I've been wanting to talk to you two about. You both knew the family well; their routines, their daily work, and most of the folks who came to visit. Was there ever anything you remember out of the ordinary that might have sent signals to make you suspicious?"

Luz raised her eyebrows. "I don't know what you mean, sweetheart. Felix and I don't have any more information than you."

"What I mean is this: Maybe there's something you've forgotten, something that might not have struck you at the time, but thinking back, it could have meant more than met the eye."

Luz started to shake her head when Felix interrupted. "Luz, do you remember the time when Mrs. Alexander came home from work one evening, slid the car into the driveway like a crazy woman, slammed on her brakes and jumped out. Even left the engine running. She tore up the porch steps screaming for Luz or me. I'll never forget what she told us."

Margaret left SawGrass late that afternoon. In fact, early evening dusk had already set in as she climbed into her car to head for home. Fortunately, traffic was nil. She moved right along the highway without interference. The floating bridge over the swamp loomed close when she detected headlights behind her. The vehicle had moved up quickly and stayed directly behind her. Why didn't it pass? she reasoned, assuming the driver had been in such a rush.

It came closer to the rear of her car. Then she felt the thud as it made contact with her rear bumper. Her vehicle lurched slightly to one side as she held the steering wheel so tightly her knuckles turned white. What was this insane driver trying to do? Did he want her to plunge into the swamp?

Panic swept over her like an icy blast. More than anything, she'd always feared the swamp and the hungry alligators that lurked in its murky depths.

Then another thud, this time harder, with a twist to her left toward the swamp. Her vehicle began to sway. With all her strength she pulled the steering wheel back to her right, simultaneously jamming down on the accelerator. Her car pulled away, obviously surprising the other driver. Her foot hit the floorboard, carrying her car careening down the highway and away from her would-be assailant.

In her rear view mirror she saw the lights of the other car straighten out and head in a direct path toward her. She held the pressure on the gas pedal. Straight along the swamp bridge road, past it and around several curves she flew until SandHill materialized ahead of her. Down the welcoming gravel path, she passed through the open gate and up to the front porch, slammed on the brakes, spraying gravel everywhere. Leaping from the car, she screamed for Luz and Felix, not bothering to switch off the ignition.

Porch lights flooded into the dusk as Luz threw open the front door. No vehicle could be seen behind Margaret.

"Max Young told us about that," Kim said. "Whoever it was tried to push her into the swamp. I remember how she feared that portion of the highway."

"She shook for hours after that. It took all I had to calm her down," Luz added. "Felix and I didn't dare leave her until Mr. Alexander got home."

"Did anyone ever find out who it was?" Kim asked.

"Not to our knowledge. Because no other vehicle had been seen. I think Mr. Alexander may have wanted it forgotten thinking it might have been Mrs. Alexander's imagination, again. Luz and I never brought it up after that."

They were all quiet while the impact of what could have happened sunk in. Then Kim spoke, "Do you know if my parents ever had any company over for meals, drinks, cards or just old-fashioned conversation?"

Luz answered first this time. "I don't think they socialized much at all. They seemed to be tied up with the business most of the time."

"There is something else comes to mind," Felix said, and looked at his wife. "Remember that Melvin Thomas, Luz?" She nodded. "He came over one evening after Mr. Alexander got home from work. I was just putting some things away in the tool shed on the north side of the house. I heard someone drive up so I popped my head around the corner in time to see Melvin getting out of his pickup. He looked like he'd had one too many. Your dad didn't ask him in. They just stood outside on the porch … arguing."

"Do you have any idea what it was about?" Kim's eyes sparked at the mention of Melvin's name.

"No. Mr. Alexander, he never discussed any of his business with me," Felix said. "Before Melvin's arrival, I had been getting ready to get Luz and go home. When I realized the disagreement was getting pretty heated, I thought I'd better stick around until I knew Mr. Alexander would be okay."

"I was upstairs," Luz added. "I had seen you to bed and was folding some clothes in the spare bedroom next to yours, Kim, while I was waiting for Felix. I heard the commotion outside. It frightened me. I went back to check on you. You were sleeping like a baby."

Kim looked at Luz with questioning eyes. "Where was my mother all this time?"

"Where she often went after supper … in her room, with the door closed. I have no idea if she was listening or saw them from her bedroom window. She could have been taking a shower, for all I know. But she never came out of her room."

"Sounds like my mother," Kim spoke up. "If that had been the other way around, my father would have been the first one to see if I was okay or asleep. So, you never found out what the argument was about?"

Luz started to say something and then stopped.

"Please, Luz, if you heard anything."

"It's just that, you know how the spare bedroom is directly above the porch? Well, when I heard all the loud voices and I was in that room with the window open, I could hear enough of the words that I knew it was about money and position. Melvin wanted a jump in salary and the title of manager. Your father told him he couldn't afford to pay him any more right then, and that Melvin was already functioning as his assistant."

"And, <u>that</u> happened <u>when</u>?"

"Only a couple of weeks before your parents were … killed."

Kim was quiet for several moments. She looked at Luz and said, "These are things I've needed to know. I'm hoping someday it will start to come together for me." She brightened then and smiled. "Enough about that. I want to hear the more positive stuff. Tell me how plans are progressing for the wedding." She settled back in her chair to hear the details.

Chapter 22

When Kim got home that night, she found Gloria sitting at the dinette table with a newspaper unfolded in front of her. She sat down next to her friend. "I had a nice visit with the Ramons, and learned something new, as well."

Gloria folded her paper and pushed it out of the way. "I'm all ears, honey. It sounds like it must have been important."

Kim related the two incidences told her by the Ramons. "I knew Mother didn't have much use for Melvin, but the part about Melvin and my dad is all new to me. That must have been the bad blood between them that Max mentioned. And who was trying to push my mother's car into the swamp? Or was that person only trying to scare her to death? And who? Could it have been Melvin?"

Gloria got up, reached in the cupboard and brought out a bottle of Merlot. "I think you could use a shot of this stuff to ease some of that tension."

Kim put up her hand. "A good cup of tea would do much better for me. Wine gives me a headache."

"Tea it is, then. I'll have a latte."

With cups in hand, the two girls made themselves comfortable at the dinette table.

"This evening proved I have to consider things outside of the conventional." Kim sipped her drink. "What the Ramons told me about Melvin changed my way of thinking."

"I don't believe there was ever any love lost between your parents and Melvin to begin with," Gloria said. "I think he was only a means for your father to get some work relief, and at the time, Melvin filled the bill."

"According to Aunt Patricia, my father relied heavily on him. He was, no doubt a royal pain, but capable and reliable, they thought. Good help in a small town can be hard to find. He might sound uneducated, but he's clever. He knows how to get a job done and how to get work out of his employees. Yes, he did do the job. But, at what cost? Melvin evidently realized how my father counted on him. So, in his convoluted mind, he decided to get more money out of Dad. Maybe he wanted to set himself up for a more desirable sounding position than as an assistant." She wrapped her hands around the tea cup, staring down into the steaming liquid. "Long ago, Aunt Patricia told me something else about Melvin that made me wonder."

"What was that?" Gloria leaned over her latte, attention fixed on Kim.

"She told me the reason she'd put Melvin in charge of the boat tour operations. My dad called her less than a week before he was killed and said he wanted my aunt to know he planned on making Melvin a full partner and share profits accordingly. If anything should happen to prevent him from running the place himself, it would be adequately handled, and the family would still have income. Dad felt Melvin knew the business almost better than he."

"But did your aunt mention any legal papers being signed?"

"She said Dad had papers drawn up by his lawyer. He had Melvin sign them, but he hadn't returned them to the law firm to make them official. She says I'm the legal owner, have always been, but when I wanted to check on the business, Melvin treated me like I didn't have any say in its operation."

"Maybe after your dad and Melvin had their talk and he signed the papers, he figured on making the business come his way a little sooner," Gloria said.

"Now, that's a scary thought."

Chapter 23

After Gloria went to work on Thursday, time seemed to drag. Kim knew she was putting off what really needed to be done: taking charge of having the estate cleaned and renovated. The cash register tapes at SawGrass would have to wait until Friday evening when she could collect them for the whole week. She decided to ask Brad for suggestions on whom she might hire for the cleanup job. In the meantime, she could go through more of Grandfather's papers.

Sitting cross-legged on the floor in Gloria's den, she placed one of the big boxes in front of her, checking one piece of paper at a time and placing ones with no special meaning in a wastebasket at her side. She did the same with two more full boxes. No startling revelations turned up until she came to the last container. An old cigar box in the bottom had been taped shut. She removed it. The dried, curled tape offered no resistance.

Inside was a small notebook. When she opened it, she recognized her grandfather's handwriting. It seemed to be some kind of journal, almost as a young girl might keep a diary.

The first page started with an accounting of moneys paid to someone called James Parker in 1979 and 1980. The figures totaled $9,000. Who on earth could this James Parker be? she thought. What possible service could he have rendered her grandfather for this kind of funds? Or, had it been for a purchase? A stretch of the imagination … Could it be blackmail? Was there another explanation? The sheet had nothing else on it. Perhaps a deep, dark secret that nobody else in the family knew anything about? But, there she was, letting her imagination run away with itself. Or maybe it could be something entirely innocent, such as someone working for him on the estate, maybe a carpenter or a painter. That had to be it, she told herself. SandHill would have required too much upkeep for Grandfather by himself since he worked daily at the boat tours.

She went on to the pages following, hoping they would reveal the answer. There were three canceled checks tucked between page one and two. They were dated the same years, 1979, and 1980, all made out to James Parker. Kim turned them over to look at the signatures on the reverse side. They had been cashed at the Bank of Miami, not in Glade City. What was this James Parker doing for Grandfather in Miami? The mystery was gaining intrigue. The only connection that her grandfather had in Miami that Kim knew of was her parents and Aunt Patricia.

She started to turn to the next page when the phone rang. She'd been so engrossed she hadn't noticed the time, past noon.

"Kim, there's a big Chamber of Commerce affair this Saturday," Gloria's voice rang through. "Brad and I are obligated to go, but we can bring guests, if we wish. Would you … "

Brad swept onto the line taking over Gloria's conversation. "I'd be very honored, Ms. Alexander, if I could be your escort for the evening."

A moment of silence and then, Kim giggled. "This is rather sudden, isn't it? Give me a second., please. I'll check my busy schedule." Two second pause. "I think I might be able to squeeze you in," she said, "providing you help me out on two other counts. I need to find a cleaning crew for the estate and a person by the name of James Parker in Miami."

"You drive a hard bargain, girl, but I'm your man."

"Give me that phone, Brad Kimbal." Gloria's voice took over on the other end of the connection. "Boy, some people just can't let a girl have her own conversation. You butt right in on my quarter," she scolded. "As I was saying, KIM, it should be a nice affair. We might have to put up with a boring speech or two, but the food is always good. It's in the Glade City Hotel Ballroom. They're having live music for dancing and listening."

"It sounds like fun, Gloria. I'd love to attend."

After she hung up, Kim picked up the notebook she'd left on the floor. Was there anything further concerning this James Parker? The pages following contained many other notations on billings from companies or individuals Grandfather must have hired for various jobs. One company repainted the estate in 1978. Other payments were listed monthly, such as the garden service for SandHill, Jackie and Company Home Cleaning, South Florida Commercial Cleaning Company for SawGrass, and Glade Maintenance for upkeep on business equipment. He had several pages of men's names listed for "possible consideration as business assistants". Further along, a small section had been designated as "Jobs Completed and Paid". Her grandfather had a knack for being thorough in his detail, so much so he'd almost completely filled the notebook.

Her eyes were growing tired. She felt like finishing another day, but she was too close to the end to set it aside. The folded papers in the bottom of the cigar box would have to wait for another day, but she could finish the last pages of the notebook. One page had been titled "Reports Received from James Parker."

Finally, she'd found more on Parker. The page notated: Services provided from September through November 1979, $3,000. paid by check #4092. Services from December 1979 through February 1980, $3,000 paid by check #4135. The final entry: Services from March through May 1980, $3,000 paid by check #4176. A notation on the bottom of the page stated "Reports filed in safe". The rest of the pages were blank.

So, what safe, and where is it?

Chapter 24

Early Friday morning Kim heard Gloria stirring around in the kitchen and went to see what was up.

"Fresh brew," Gloria said when Kim came through the door.

"You're all bright and cheery so early." Kim smiled.

"Have some printing jobs I have to get done ASAP. The doves woke me up early having a gabfest outside my bedroom window. I closed it and put on the air. It's going to be stinking hot today anyway."

"Thanks for the coffee offer, but I'm going to have OJ and a banana. I want to get down to SawGrass as early as I can. I'm anxious to go through those cash register tapes."

"Well, good luck. I'll see you later." Gloria threw her purse over her shoulder and left.

Kim sailed into Karen's office at ten minutes past nine.

"Boss in yet?"

Karen had a stack of papers on her desk and looked a bit harried. "Are you kidding? He's always here. I swear he sleeps in his office, ... and his clothes. He must want to dream up as much work as he can so no one gets a break."

"He sounds like a pretty dedicated person, but a tough taskmaster."

"Yeah, but I'm sure he has his reasons, more than we know."

"How so?" Kim pulled up a chair and sat opposite Karen.

"Well, I know this business is very profitable ... and busy, but you couldn't tell it from the way Melvin dresses or from the vehicle he drives. I'm sure your aunt has always paid him well. So, what's he do with the money? He's not married, has no family to support."

"Aunt Patricia told me she pays him a percentage of the profits. He couldn't be that bad off."

"In that case, sales last week broke a record, so he should be dragging in a bundle."

Karen fiddled around in her desk drawer and came up with a new pencil. "Hasn't been this good as long as I've been here."

Kim studied Karen. "Was it unusually busy last week or were there some large sales in souvenirs and clothing?"

"Well, I don't go out on the floor often during open hours, but it didn't seem like it was any busier than usual. It's just that the sales receipts were over the top. As I see it."

"That's okay, Karen. I'll just have a look over the cash register tapes. I should be able to see how the business is faring."

Kim stayed at the desk next to Karen, as each of the two handled her own business. Just before lunchtime, the door to Karen's office opened, and Melvin stepped in. His shirt looked like he'd worn it too many times. Karen and Kim glanced at each other, Karen mouthing the word, "See?"

Kim winked at the secretary and turned a smile at Melvin.

"Well, y'all findin' what ya needed?" he said, his face showing no emotion.

"The tapes are very enlightening, Melvin. It seems that this is a very lucrative business. More so than it ever used to be. Aunt Patricia claimed it to be a money-maker, but neither of us realized how much."

"Seems ta have picked up of late, prob'ly the way what I've took care o' thin's. Mah hard work's payin' off."

"Yes, I think you've done nicely. Aunt Patricia will be happy with my report." She turned back to the tapes and her tally sheet.

Melvin yanked down on his shirt and brushed his hand across the front of his hair, flattening some of the stubborn wisps. "Kim, what 'bout I take ya out ta lunch … kinda so's we can get more acquainted? Mebbe we got off on the wrong foot. I think we all need ta pull tagether." His mouth turned up slightly at the corners, like friendly wasn't a familiar habit.

"I … don't know, Melvin?" Kim suppressed the smile that played behind her lips. "I wouldn't want to put you out or … anything."

"Ain't puttin' me out none. I jus' feel it's 'bout time we git tagether an' iron thin's out a bit. Thet way, y'all be able ta see I operate a clean ship, what makes 'nough money fer us both. I'll see ya get the tapes ever' week on Friday. Y'all won't have ta bother yer pretty head 'bout comin' in alla time. Y'all got plenty 'nough ta do without spendin' time on a place what's run proper-like."

Karen got up and excused herself.

"Maybe just a quick lunch, if we don't go far."

"Lemme go check on the rest o' the staff, an' I'll be back in a half hour."

Melvin left and Karen returned.

"Well, that's a first," Karen said. "He must figure he'd better be nice since you're the one holding the real purse strings."

Kim sat back in her chair. Her smile said it all. "I just wondered how long it would take before he started to treat me with some respect. Could it have anything to do with the fact that he feels I'm checking up on him, and maybe I'll find out something he doesn't want me to?"

Karen looked at Kim with resignation. "He's been known to have his moments, but if I were you, I'd keep a close eye on him. He can be a real bugger, so watch your back."

"Thanks for your input, Karen, but it's broad daylight, so I don't think I have anything to fear that way. Besides, if he acts up, he's out of here, 'cause I won't be putting up with any of his nonsense."

Karen grinned. "I'd like to be a little mouse in your pocket."

When Melvin put in his appearance at twelve-thirty, he had changed to a Hawaiian shirt printed with red and yellow hibiscus. His usual tousled hair, no longer uncombed, lay in a perfect gelled coif, his unruly mustache neatly trimmed.

"Thought I'd take ya ta Eldora's on the east side o' town. She's a nice woman. Ain't been open too long, but serves up a mighty fine meal."

"Wherever you choose, Melvin. You know Glade City much better than I."

He nodded, and led her out to where his older model Chevy pickup was parked. He walked to the passenger side, opened the door and helped her in.

When they reached Eldora's, it looked akin to something out of old world Germany; like a Hansel and Gretel house. She greeted them warmly at the door in a peasant-looking dress, complete with a bib-top, and embroidered white apron. She lead them to a quiet corner by a window.

After they ordered, Melvin said, "I know I didn't make no good impression on ya, Kim, but I had the feelin' mebbe ya wuz goin' ta take mah place, an' I'd be outa work."

"Why on earth would I do that, Melvin? You've done a good job handling the place. It's made money, and it looks good. Everything seems to be in workable shape. You couldn't have done a better job if you'd owned it yourself all these years."

"Yeah, I been here fer 'bout seventeen years now, fifteen runnin' the place on mah own. I jus' felt … kinda like it wuz mine." He ran his right index finger over his mustache. "Mind y'all, thet don't mean what it sounds like. Lemme 'xplain. When I first come here, yer daddy an' mama wuz runnin' the place, an' yer gran'daddy before them musta done a right good job to start with. I know he had that big ole house o' his built fer yer gran'mama, and he had good ideas an' all. Same with the business here. I wuz tol' he wuz the genius what built the business from scratch. Anyways, back ta when I wuz hired by yer daddy. He wuz al'ays good ta me, and I 'preciated thet." He took a huge drink of water and continued. "Yer mama … well, she wuz different. A beautiful woman, but cold. Very cold like. I don't mean ta hurt yer feelin's, Kim, but thet's the way I seen her."

"It's okay, Melvin. I remember her. I loved her, but I understand what you mean. My father was warm and loving, demonstrative. I miss him, still. Miss them both, even now."

"Ms. Alexander, she used ta come ta the office an' work on the books. She'd come in after ya went ta school, an' leave in time ta get home afore the bus dropped ya off. She hepped yer daddy a lot. When he hired me, I wuz kind o' like a jack-o-all-trades. He had me to do a bit o' ever' thin'."

Eldora brought the lunches on a large round tray. To Kim she handed a picture-perfect garden salad and an iced tea. Melvin had a barbeque pork sandwich and a glass of tonic water with ice.

"I'd have me one o' them good German beers, but I still got work 'head o' me, yet."

Melvin dug into his sandwich and continued where he'd left off. "I enjoyed doin' all them different jobs fer yer daddy. My time wuz never borin' an' I learned a lot. Hepped me when I wuz on ma own after they wuz ... gone.

"When yer aunt come ta take ya back with her ta Seattle, she made a special stop ta see me an' ask how I wuz doin', if I wuz handlin' the business okay. She seemed satisfied 'nough I could manage it an' offered me a percentage o' the profits if I'd stay an' be the manager. I liked the idea. An', pardon me, Kim, but I'm mighty proud I wuz able to keep up the place, make money for the family, and still have it look great."

"I agree with you on that, Melvin, and I don't want you to think I'm trying to take your job from you. I have an agenda of my own, and right now, it doesn't include me managing the air boat business. You'll be making money for both of us, anyway." Kim worked on her salad while Melvin polished off his sandwich with gusto.

"Thanks. 'Preciate thet. I come here with nothin' an' I worked hard ta do thin's right." He wiped his mouth and beckoned to Eldora. "Cup o' coffee, ma'am. Now, don't go rushin' on my account, Kim. I al'ays been a fast eater, an' I need to relax a might anyways."

He was quiet for a long moment, looking hard at Kim until she felt like squirming. "I hope ya don't mind ma saying this ta ya, but beauty must run in yer family. I thought yer mama wuz the most beautiful woman I ever seen 'til I met yer Aunt Patricia. You look a lot like her."

"My mother, you mean?"

"No. More like yer aunt."

"Well, people in Seattle who didn't know Patricia before I came to live with her, never questioned the fact I wasn't her flesh and blood daughter. That's fine with me. After all, she's been a mother to me for longer now than my own mother. In all those years we never had an argument. She's a warm and extremely fair-minded person. My mother always seemed too preoccupied with her own schedule."

She finished the last bite of salad. Melvin pushed himself back against the corner of the booth and put his legs across the seat.

"I'd light up a cigar, but Eldora don't 'llow no smokin' in here. Tha's okay, though. I'll jus' have one when I get back ta the office. Now, you wuz tellin' me 'bout Patricia."

"That's about all except I still love my mother very much and would like to see justice served. As for Aunt Patricia, I've always felt responsible for her never getting married. Between her position at work and taking care of me, she didn't seem to have time for men." Kim's eyes swept the interior of the German-style restaurant to avoid Melvin's penetrating gaze.

"I used to kid her about going out with her big boss, but she'd only roll her eyes and say she had enough of him at work." Kim picked up the almost empty glass of tea, swirling it gently.

"Wish I coulda got ta know yer aunt better, but her meetin' with me wuz pretty short. She sure had a different personality than yer mama. She treated me with respect, an' was fair 'bout running the business." Melvin glanced at his watch.

"Well, guess I need ta git back ta the flock. So if yer done, we can go."

"I think we understand each other a little more now, Melvin. I'll just finish my work in Karen's office and then be off. There are lots of other things I need to be doing."

"So, don' ferget, Kim, ya don't need ta be awastin' yer time at SawGrass seein' as how I'm runnin' it right professional-like. You can still pick up them tapes on Fridays, if ya want."

Melvin paid the tab, and they thanked Eldora as they left. The place had filled up while they'd been eating, and Kim thought it looked as though it would become a nice addition to Glade City.

Chapter 25

K im spent the balance of the afternoon checking out the cash register tapes, comparing them with the books, and conversing with Karen, whom she felt more comfortable with every time they were together. In fact, the more she had to do with Karen, the more Kim realized how much she knew about the business and what an asset she was.

"By the way, Kim," Karen said looking up from her paperwork, "I hope Melvin was a gentleman when he took you out for lunch." She picked up the ledgers Kim had finished examining and replaced them in the closet safe. "He's not known for his winning ways, you know."

"He took me to Eldora's and happened to be on his best behavior. I believe he finally realizes that he works for me and not the other way around. Of course, he's had fifteen years of handling this place with no one looking over his shoulder, and maybe it was some sort of shock that suddenly he has someone checking out his business ethics." She placed the cash register totals in a small brown envelope and handed them to Karen. "Here, Karen. I don't want anything to happen to these. I'll come back another day and do some more."

When Kim finished at SawGrass, she headed for the real estate office to see Gloria. She couldn't wait to tell her about her lunch with Melvin.

Gloria was putting things away in her file cabinet. "Just getting ready to hit the bricks."

She glanced over her shoulder at Kim. "Let's get out of here. We can throw something together for supper, and you can tell me how your day went at the boat tours while we're eating."

Kim giggled. "Guess who I had lunch with today."

Gloria stopped dead. "No!" She glared at Kim. "You didn't."

"Yes, I did. Go on. I'll follow you home and tell you while we're fixing supper."

Supper and the evening rolled by quickly while the two girls discussed the events of their days with an emphasis on Melvin. "That old coot," Gloria chuckled. "He's never had much of a winning reputation around these parts, but I think he's beginning to get the big picture. Just don't let your guard down, but keep him reminded about who owns the joint."

At ten Kim said to Gloria, "You look tired. I think you've been working too hard."

Gloria opened her mouth wide and yawned. "Tomorrow's going to be a busy day, again. I think I need a few extra winks so I'll be ready for our big night at the real estate banquet."

"I'm for that," Kim added. "I've had too much on my mind lately, too. I need to put it to rest for a bit. So, are you working Sunday, Gloria?"

"No way. I made other arrangements 'cause I figured Saturday night would be a late one. Why?"

"I need to make a trip to SandHill. According to what I found in some of Grandfather's papers, he had some special reports from that James Parker I mentioned yesterday. He made a notation that they were in the safe, and I have no idea where that safe might be."

All Gloria could say was, "Wow."

Chapter 26

When she first got to Gloria's house from Seattle, Kim had called her Aunt Patricia to let her know she'd arrived safely. She'd also promised to call her again in a few weeks after she'd visited the estate, the boat tours, and made a few plans. Saturday morning seemed a good time to catch her aunt at home since she worked weekdays. Kim let the phone ring four times before the answering machine kicked in.

"This is Kim. I'll be busy most of today, so I'll try you tomorrow. Love and miss you."

She'd hardly put the phone down when it rang.

"Glad I caught you home, Kim," Chase said. "Thought I'd let you know that we're getting Max settled in. He starts his new job next week."

"Well, that's super, Chase. Does he think he'll like it?"

"I'm sure he will. The company built a great little house for a hired security person to live in on the property. Perfect size for a bachelor, *and* everything is new. It's fully furnished, including pots, pans and linens, and it's all included in his monthly salary. I think he's got a good deal."

"Well, I'm very happy for him, and you, too. You'll have an old friend living close."

"How about if Max and I pick you up this afternoon? We can show you the grounds of Pelican Landing and Max's new home. You're going to be impressed with the whole place. It's outstanding."

"I'd love to see it, Chase, but maybe we could make it another time. I have plans for the day, and I need to relax for a while first. I've had a lot on my mind these past few weeks. I'm afraid it's catching up to me."

There was a noticeable pause on the other end of the line. When he finally spoke, his words were laced with disappointment. "Sorry you can't make it today, Kim. I'll have to check with Max. It seemed like a perfect day to go there before he starts work." Another moment of silence followed. "What about tomorrow? Max is still free. In fact, we were going to move in some of his personal belongings, but that won't take long."

"Oh, Chase, I *am* sorry. Gloria is helping me at SandHill tomorrow. She has the day off."

"Guess my idea will have to wait then. Since I have the whole weekend free, I thought it would be a great opportunity to show you around." He hesitated, then said "Why don't I call you when I have my next day off?"

"That would be nice, Chase. Thank you for thinking of me, though. And I'm very happy for Max."

After they hung up, Kim made herself a sandwich. Breakfast had been a light one. Now she needed some brain food, time to organize her thoughts for tomorrow, and to rest up for tonight.

Brad arrived just as Kim was adding her perfume. She grabbed her evening purse and hurried to the door to open it. She had to stifle a gasp when she saw him. He looked more handsome in his casual clothes than he did when he was working. At the office he was always the picture of professionalism; neat, light-colored suits, shirts to match and ties perfectly knotted. Tonight he wore light blue gabardine slacks and a short-sleeved, silk shirt with his initials embroidered on the pocket.

Gloria came down the hall, shoes still in hand. She stopped, leaned against the wall and put one on, then the other.

"Well, if you two aren't the picture in my dreams." Brown eyes weren't missing a thing. He let out a big sigh, shook his head and said, "Okay, girls. Let's make haste. Time's a'wastin'." He took each one by the arm and escorted them to his Lexus.

They headed to town, and Brad pulled into the parking garage of the Glade City Hotel.

After he'd found a spot and turned off the engine, he got out and went around to help the girls. .

With one on each arm he marched to the elevators on the main floor. "Man! Am I ever going to make an impression … the two best looking women in Glade City with me."

"Get off it, Brad." Gloria popped him a gentle slug on the shoulder. "We know you love us both and have eyes for no one else."

Brad grinned and gave both girls a gentle squeeze as he pushed them into the elevator. "There's no possible way I could, Ms. Gloria."

The banquet room took up the whole back end of the restaurant and had been artfully decorated for the occasion in a 1940's style theme. A podium stood up front for the guest speakers, and instruments for the five-piece band were arranged on the small stage to the rear.

The two guest speakers were both humorous, the meal a culinary delight and the band a huge success. Kim hadn't had this much fun in years. She wished the time wouldn't fly so quickly.

Brad took turns dancing with both girls until one of the guest speakers came over and cut in on his dance with Gloria.

When Brad got back to their table, Kim asked, "Do you know him?"

"Know of him more than know him. He's new to these parts. Hails from Miami, I hear. They hired him as the new sales manager at Drake Realty, on the other side of town from us. They say he's extremely knowledgeable. Knows real estate inside out, and that's just the tip of the iceberg. That's how he came to be one of our guest speakers."

"He looks like a heart-breaker," Kim smiled. "But then, looks can be deceiving, you know. I'll have to keep an eye on my friend."

The band ended one set and started up with a lively rendition of "New York, New York".

Brad and Kim sat at their table watching Gloria and her partner swinging around the dance floor. When a medley of Latin music began with "Green Eyes", Brad stood and held out his hand to Kim. "In your honor, my pretty one, we must have this dance."

Despite Kim's five-foot-six frame and her high heels, she still had to reach up to Brad's shoulders. "I meant to ask you before, how tall are you anyway?" she asked.

"I believe I was six four last time I measured. At least, that's what my driver's license says."

Dancing around the floor the two seemed to meld in perfect unison. When the set ended, Brad led Kim back to their table. "I haven't danced for so long, I almost thought I had forgotten how," he said as he pulled back her chair for her. "But with you, Kim, it seemed pretty easy."

"Thank you. This whole evening has been such a welcome break for me. I'm so glad Gloria invited me."

Gloria's place remained vacant. Kim scanned the ballroom and the now all but empty floor for her friend. She was nowhere in sight. "Where was that guy's table? I don't see Gloria anywhere."

"You mean Andy Wikstrom? He was sitting at the head table, but I don't see him now."

"Excuse me, Brad. I'm going to the ladies room to see if Gloria may be there."

She moved quickly across the floor and to the hall where the bathrooms were located. There was no sign of Gloria. She went into the private cocktail lounge next to the banquet hall. Several couples and three single men stood at the bar laughing and telling jokes. Still, no Gloria.

She went back to the table where Brad waited. "Now I'm getting worried," she said, falling into the chair beside him.

"She's probably out back in the parking lot necking with Andy."

"Oh, Brad. Don't be funny. I'm concerned. Nobody knows this Andy that well."

She picked up her cocktail glass and drained the last drop. "He could be a serial rapist for all we know."

"Honey, I'll go outside and have a look around. I'm sure I'll find her."

He started to get up when Kim grabbed his arm. "There they are now, coming this way, laughing and talking as if no one is worried at all about them," she said flatly.

"So, you two finally decided to show up," Brad chuckled as the two walked up to the table. He put his arm around Kim's shoulders. "This one has been wanting to call out the militia, I believe."

Gloria looped her arm in her escort's and said, "Kim and Brad, I'd like to introduce you to Andy Wikstrom."

Andy put out his hand to Brad who took it and gave him a hearty shake. "I've heard about you through the grapevine, so it's a real pleasure to meet you Brad. And you, too, Kim."

"Likewise, Andy," Brad said.

"Andy was showing me his new Porsche. What a piece of machinery."

"I wanted to take her for a spin, but she put me off. Another time, I guess."

"Sit down and take the load off," Brad said, patting the chair next to him.

"Don't mind if I do." Andy looked at his partner. "Okay, Gloria?"

"By all means, be my guest."

Before they knew it, the band was playing "Goodnight, Sweetheart", and then began to take down their equipment.

"Well, it's been a super evening," Andy said. "Can I drive you home, Gloria? I don't really want the evening to end just yet. I feel like I'm just beginning to appreciate Glade City."

"Thanks anyway, Andy. I came with Kim and Brad, and I'll go home with them."

"Then, how about if I call you soon?"

"I'd like that," Gloria replied.

When Brad stood up to shake Andy's hand as they were all saying their goodbyes, his six-foot four frame seemed to diminish Andy's thin, six-foot structure making him seem almost small by comparison.

Brad laughed as the three of them walked out to his car together. "I'd say tonight was a huge success."

"Best time I've had in years." Gloria added.

Kim was quiet for a moment and then said, "It was for me, also, until I thought Andy might be a serial rapist." With a serious face, Kim stared at Gloria and Brad, then burst out in a grin. Brad and Gloria laughed until they reached the Lexus.

Chapter 27

Sunday morning sun slithered through Kim's bedroom shades. It's late, she thought, opening one droopy eye. Too much sun to be early.

A knock came on her bedroom door. "Hey, wake up sleepy head. Rise and shine. Shake it up, or whatever it takes to get you going. It's ten thirty and you wanted to get to SandHill sometime today."

"Come in, Gloria," Kim said jumping up and throwing on her shorts and a tank top. "I guess I had too much night last evening, but I don't regret a moment of it."

"Don't worry. I'm in no big hurry if you aren't. I had a great night, too."

Gloria had an extra cup of coffee while Kim took tea and a bowl of shredded wheat. They talked about last evening.

"Brad certainly is a good dancer," Kim giggled. "He didn't step on my toes once the whole evening." She paused to look at Gloria just sitting like Miss Relaxation herself. "So, you liked Andy?"

Gloria eyed Kim. "What do you think, my friend? What's not to like? He's knockout gorgeous, has money, a good position, a super personality, and he's not married or in a relationship. Feels like a winner to me?" She got up, put her cup in the dishwasher and started straightening things. "There haven't been too many eligible bachelors around these parts, especially anyone who would interest me."

"Well, I wouldn't know. I haven't been here long enough. Would you go out with him again?"

"You don't think I've lost my mind completely, do you? The answer … in a heart beat." Gloria's eyes flashed with sparks of pleasure. "If you promise not to tell anyone, I think I'm infatuated."

Shortly before twelve, Kim went to Gloria's den to retrieve the cigar box she'd found on Thursday. Beneath the notebook had been some papers she'd been too tired to finish. The thought had occurred to her that the papers could hold the answer to the whereabouts of the safe.

She lifted the notebook and pulled out the papers. Disappointment stifled her hopes when all four pages turned out to be blank. As she was about to replace them, something shiny caught her eye. It was wedged in one corner of the box and appeared to be a key of sorts. Turning it over and over in her hand, she noticed the black plastic cap was imprinted with letters "Secure Sentry." Could this be for the safe? She put it in her pocket and replaced the notebook and blank pages in the cigar box.

She went back to the living room where Gloria waited. "I'll be ready to go as soon as I give Aunt Patricia a quick call."

When Patricia answered, she sounded excited. "I could hardly wait 'til I spoke to you, sweetheart. I've been almost too exhilarated to relax. My boss gave me three weeks off, and I'm hoping you won't mind if I come to visit you."

"Aunt Patricia, you know very well before I left, I begged you to come down as soon as possible. Don't worry about a place to stay. Gloria has assured me that she'd like you to bunk up in her third bedroom. She uses it as a computer room, but not all that often.

That is, if you don't mind sharing with a desk and some office equipment."

"That would be just perfect, honey. I'll make reservations after we hang up. We can catch up on what's been going on when I get there. I've missed you so."

"Not anymore than I've missed you. If you can arrange to fly into Ft. Myers, I'll pick you up there. It's an easier airport for me to get to."

"I'll call as soon as I've made arrangements."

"Great news, Gloria," Kim said after she hung up.

"I think I know. Patricia's coming down."

"I want her to quit that job in Seattle, and come down here to live. Once I have the estate cleaned up, we'll have oodles of space. We might even turn it into a Bed and Breakfast."

"Now that's a great thought."

The girls laughed and talked as they made their way to SandHill. Exciting things seemed to be looming on the horizon.

When they reached the estate, Gloria unlocked the iron gate for Kim, re-locking it after she drove through. "You want to look in the library first, don't you?" she asked.

"That would be logical, I believe, although sometimes things in this case haven't turned out to be as justifiable as I would like."

They made their way to the library, slid open drapes to let in more light, and started searching the room and closet. "I don't remember seeing anything in here that looked like it could have been a safe," Gloria said.

"Neither do I, unless it was hidden behind a picture or a false wall"

An hour passed as the two girls, tapped all the walls in the storage closet and in the library, pulled out furniture, looked in the cupboards and moved throw rugs from the floor. There was nothing.

Gloria dropped into one of the easy chairs next to the desk. "How about upstairs?" she suggested. "Is there somewhere your grandfather could have stashed it on that huge third floor?"

"Well," Kim mused, "I don't know why he would do that. It wouldn't be convenient at all." She pulled out the desk chair near where Gloria sat.

They rested, thinking and scanning the room as if a safe might mysteriously materialize by osmosis. "What about that key you found, Kim? It must fit something in the estate."

"Since it was hidden away in the cigar box, I would think it would be for something Grandfather didn't want prying eyes to see." She leaned forward, elbows on the desktop. "So, there has to be a safe box someplace. Or a piece of office equipment? Or a metal container to keep sacred things, or ... " Kim's voice trailed off as she became lost in thought.

Gloria watched as Kim moved her arms over the top of the desk.

"What about that?" Gloria said.

"About what?"

"The desk. We haven't pulled it out yet. I know it's as heavy as cement sacks, but together we could do it, I'm sure."

Kim looked down at the desk. "I know we cleaned it out when we were here before, but we didn't think about looking behind it."

"We didn't have reason before," Gloria said. She stood. "Come on. Let's give it a try."

Kim got up and went around to the opposite side from where Gloria stood. "Anything's worth a try."

Together they pushed and pulled until they had moved the desk far enough to be able to look at the wall behind it.

"Oh, curses," Gloria exclaimed, squinting behind it. "The wall is as clean as a ... Now what?" She sank back in her chair.

"Gloria," Kim started slowly, "you know, all the drawers didn't seem to be as deep as the desk. I never gave it a thought before. I wonder ... " She went back, sat down and pulled open the top drawer. She looked and then felt inside. Nothing. Then the second drawer. Again, nothing. The bottom drawer didn't feel as deep as the others. She put her hand inside. The back felt closer than the rest.

Gloria came around to her side. "Let's take it out," she said.

The two pulled and lifted the drawer onto the floor. The back third of the drawer had been skillfully sectioned off and enclosed. A wooden panel mimicked the true back. Gloria put her hand on the panel, tapping around the perimeter until it loosened and dropped, revealing a small lock box with a key slot.

"Pay dirt!" she cried out.

Kim grabbed the key from her pocket and fit it in the slot. "Voila!"

She lifted the small lock box onto the desktop and removed the contents. The first part that came out was the James Parker Report. Kim sat back in her chair and placed the papers in front of her. She handed half to Gloria. "Just scan them if you want, Gloria. I'm interested in what his basic job was for my grandfather."

Silence reigned for several minutes as the two studied the pages. "It appears that Mr. James Parker was a private detective. His job was to follow this particular party, check on 'her' movements and where she went." Gloria thumbed through more papers.

Kim picked up from there. "He says here that, quote, 'your daughter seems to be meeting someone on a regular basis' unquote. Oh, God, it has to be my mother. The letters, Gloria. The letters."

Gloria was reading now. "She left the library at 12:30 P.M. and walked to the coffee shop two blocks away. I waited until 1:10, at which time a uniformed young man came in and sat next to her. They seemed to be having an intimate conversation. I was unable to sit close enough to overhear. They left together at 1:20. She went back to the library, and he disappeared into the police precinct around the corner." Gloria looked up at Kim. "Holy cow," she said.

"I haven't seen a name mentioned, yet," Kim said, "but the report seems to be filled with her meeting him at that coffee shop. Oh, here's one where he goes into the library. 'I followed him in and pretended to study the magazine section. He asked her something, and she led him to a section that was marked Science Fiction. They stayed in that aisle for a while until the head librarian must have gotten wise. She found them, and the young man left immediately. I believe your daughter must have made up excuses since she went back to her job sorting through the book files.'"

The girls kept reading, each report shedding more light on the activities. One notated that Parker followed them to an apartment building where they disappeared for a little over an hour. He remained outside until they emerged.

"I feel terrible, Gloria. It's like I'm peeking into their private lives, but I feel compelled to go on. I need to find the name of the young man."

"Well, look no further, honey. This report mentions Margaret's name, which you've already figured out. And we know that the guy is a policeman, but who? I'm almost to the end of this report. There should be some solution soon. Parker worked off and on over a nine month period, not every day, but an average of one or two days a week. This one is dated May 1980." Gloria took a deep breath and continued to read silently. Suddenly, she sucked in her breath, paused and stared intently at Kim. "You won't believe this, Kim. Parker finally entered the name of the young policeman."

Kim dropped her paper and jumped up to read the report in Gloria's hand. "Max Young," she uttered, and then collapsed back into her chair at the desk.

"Are you alright, Kim?" Gloria moved to her side. "Let me get you a cold drink."

"I'm okay, Gloria. I just need a minute or two to get my bearings. I have too many wild thoughts running through my mind. The most incredible one is that Max could be my father!"

"I know. It's a shock after all these years, but when we read those love letters we found in your mother's closet, we both had the thought that this letter writer could be your father."

"You're right, but I assumed it would be someone I didn't know, someone I would never meet, a total stranger. This is different. I feel so bewildered." When Gloria put her arm around Kim, she said, "I'll be fine. I just need time to adjust to the idea."

"Well, let's get these papers back in the lock box, gather our stuff and get back home. I think you could use a little break time. Get away from all this for a while. Clear your head."

"I think I need that. In fact, I probably need one of your lattes, or something stronger."

Gloria started to put the reports back in the box when she stopped. "There's something else in here, Kim. It looks like a birth certificate."

A few moments of silence followed while Gloria unfolded and looked over the document.

"Patricia's child?" she whispered. Kim sprang up to see what Gloria had found.

"My cousin. I've been wondering how I could track him or her down. Wow! This day is turning into one startling discovery after another."

Gloria pulled the certificate from the box and placed it in Kim's hands. "Perhaps you'd better sit down again, Kim. New information seems to be moving more rapidly than your heartbeat."

Kim took the paper from Gloria and sat down. She read aloud, "Place of Birth: Dade County, Florida; City of Miami at Palm Medical Clinic and Private Hospital; Full name of child: Kimberly Lynn Alexander, Female. Date of Birth: May 20, 1980." Kim looked back at Gloria. "*My* Birth Certificate! Hidden away all these years. And for what reason?" She read on. "Father: Charles Paul Alexander. Mother: Patricia Lynn Sanderson." Kim dropped the document on the desk, staring at it and the line she'd just read. "No, Gloria. No. This can't be. There has to be some mistake."

Gloria stood up and put her arm around Kim's shoulder. "You know, if you think about it, Kim, it makes sense. This Parker guy, he never mentioned Margaret being pregnant while carrying on an affair with Max Young. And, why on earth would Max be interested in a woman pregnant enough to be giving birth in May of 1980? Unless … *he* figured he was the father."

"Oh, my God," Kim said putting one hand to her forehead and massaging it. "This whole situation is going beyond my wildest imagination. But why, Gloria, why? My mother, or, I mean, Margaret committing adultery with Max. My father and my aunt? Was everyone going insane? I don't know what to believe anymore." She wiped a tear that clung to her chin. "Patricia's the only one alive, outside of Max, who knows what was going on then. Do I ask her about this, let her know I've discovered their secrets? Or do I just pretend nothing's happened?"

Gloria massaged Kim's shoulders. "Honey, if I were you, I'd let nature take its course, and do nothing for the time being. If Patricia wants you to know the truth, she'll broach the subject. If not, then it might be best left unsaid." She leaned over and gave Kim a big squeeze. "The last thing you want is to damage the great relationship between you and Patricia. At least, you do have one parent alive and loving you. That's worth more than anyone can put a price tag on. Right?"

"That's true, Gloria. Knowing my aunt, I mean Patricia … Boy, this is going to be hard trying to switch from calling her Aunt to Mother."

"Just don't change anything yet, okay? At least until things come out in the open. But, you started to say, knowing your aunt ... "

"Yes. Understanding her, there's probably a logical and decent explanation. At least, I'm trying to convince myself of this. She certainly doesn't fit the picture this paints."

Sleep did not come easily when Kim finally got to bed. Dreams dominated her subconscious, a jumble of scattered thoughts, none of which made any sense. After waking and getting up several times in the night, she decided to take a mild sedative to relax. She got up and went to her medicine cabinet where she had a bottle of herbal capsules that help to relieve anxiety. Within half an hour, she fell into a deep sleep, but not without an accompanying nightmare.

She was a young girl again, living at SandHill with her parents. Her surroundings were vivid, which included her entire bedroom, canopied bed and all. Again she heard those unfamiliar sounds that had awakened her once before. She opened her eyes to the moonlight-filled bedroom, afraid to move as the sound of footsteps coming down the hallway froze her with fear. She pulled the covers close to her neck as she lay beneath the veil-covered four-poster. Terror choked off some of her breath when she looked toward the bedroom door where the hall nightlight seeped beneath it. There was that shadow again. As before, it passed, returned and hesitated just outside the entrance to the room. Perspiration covered her face and neck. She ducked her head beneath the sheet, praying this intruder would not find her. She tried to stifle the cry in her throat as she realized that the door would burst open any moment like it had years ago and reveal the person who had butchered her parents.

She felt herself hit the floor in her attempt to hide from the fiend she knew it to be. When the door exploded inward she saw the face in the moonlight and understood something more chilling than anything she could have imagined as recognition washed over her. She knew this person, knew that he was still in her life, still a threat and would remain so, unless ...

Gloria rushed into Kim's bedroom.

"Honey, I heard the thud. It frightened me. What happened?" She reached down to help Kim up from where she lay crumpled on the floor.

"Just a nightmare, Gloria" Kim gasped.

"You okay? You didn't break anything, did you?" She brushed off Kim's pajamas, checking her arms and legs.

"I think I'm still in one piece, Gloria. I'm sorry I awakened you. I didn't mean to startle you like this."

"Don't worry about me, honey. I'm concerned with you."

Kim started to laugh, a relief to the ordeal she had been through. Then Gloria joined in. They both sat on the edge of the bed, unable to stop giggling for minutes.

In the morning, when Kim awoke from a fitful but dreamless sleep, the first thought that came to her mind was the nightmare. It's over now, but not forgotten, she determined. During the dream, she had seen the madman's face, and strongly sensed she knew him. He was a part of Glade City, part of her current existence, a fiend masquerading as a normal person, but who? What were his intentions? Is she to fear for her life as long as she remains here, or could he believe she is no longer a threat to him? No. She couldn't possibly think that her life wasn't in danger. Her subconscious knew this person, knew him to be a ruthless killer, but her cognizant self wouldn't bring forth his image or his name.

Chapter 28

"Why don't you come into the office with me this morning?" Gloria put her breakfast dishes into the dishwasher. "I don't have any clients I need to meet or take out today, only a little paper work to catch up on."

"You know, that sounds pretty good to me. It would give me the change of pace I need. Maybe you or Brad can help me find a company to clean up the estate."

"Brad knows a lot more about stuff like that than I do, honey. He'd probably be tickled to help you out." Gloria grinned as she peeked at Kim out of the corner of one eye.

When they reached Gloria's office, there was a flasher on her answering machine. She sat down, grabbed a pen and hit the play button.

"This is Potter Denks speaking. You don't know me, but I've been referred to you by an old friend who trusts your integrity." Gloria looked at Kim and winked. "I need to find a large house, an estate, if you will, preferably not directly in town, one with possibly six to eight bedrooms … if at all possible. I would appreciate any help you can give me. Please let me know what's available and call me at 305-555-2468. I'll be awaiting your call. Thank you."

"Well, maybe I could find him a Taj Mahal out here in the Everglades. I'll go over my large estate book to see what's currently listed." Gloria snickered as she reached over to turn on her computer. "That's a Miami area code. I suppose he thinks we're running the big city a close race for oversized homes. Guess I'll have to call him back and tell him there's no such kind of place around here, unless you want to sell him SandHill."

"Not on your life, pal. My grandfather had that built just for my grandmother, and he did a lot of the work himself."

"Just kidding. I know the place holds a special meaning for you." Gloria picked up her phone dialed the number left by Potter Denks and put on the speakerphone.

A woman's voice answered, "Denks and Associates. How may I help you?"

"This is Gloria Latham returning Mr. Denk's call."

"Oh, yes, Miss Latham. Mr. Denks had to go out on a business call. I'll give him the message as soon as he returns. He's very anxious to speak to you."

"Do you have any idea when he'll be back?"

"Sorry, I don't." She lowered her voice to almost a whisper and said, "He's escorting one of his very wealthy clients around, so it could be rather late. Will that be a problem?"

"Actually, I should be in the office most of the day … except for lunch. Just have him call when he gets back."

She hung up and moved to face her computer. "Let me get some of this stuff out of the way. Go see if Brad's in his office. He can help you find a cleaning crew."

"I'll do that. If he isn't there, I'll just mosey around outside for a while, maybe walk in the garden behind the building. It's really lovely out there." She left her purse on a chair in Gloria's office and went next door to find Brad. He wasn't in, so she headed for the rear exit.

Brad was just coming in from the parking area. "Hey, this is a pleasant surprise," he said, grabbing Kim's arm and whirling her around to the direction of his chambers before she had time to say a word. "As long as you're not busy, come on back with me and have a cup of something."

A little shiver tingled her spine at Brad's touch. His eyes were warm and friendly, not like Chase's sometimes-icy scrutiny. In fact, Brad was Mr. Easy to be around with his casual, unpretentious manner.

"Actually, I was looking for you to get some help finding a cleaning crew for SandHill."

"Leave it to me, sweetheart. I'll find you the best that Glade City has to offer." He opened the door and ushered her into his office. "I'll get that drink and then call the Bestway Commercial Cleaning Company. What'll you have? Coffee, tea or Sprite?"

"Tea would be fine."

Brad heated a mug of water in his in-office microwave oven, took a tea bag from a cupboard and set them in front of Kim. While she fixed her drink, he dialed a number and spoke to someone at Bestway. "They have a cancellation Wednesday at three for an estimate. How's that sound?"

"Great. The sooner, the better."

"They'll meet you at SandHill at three, then," Brad said after he hung up.

"Thanks, Brad. I'm indebted to you."

"Enough to have dinner with me one evening?"

"I … uh, that sounds nice, Brad, but I'm not sure when my aunt will be flying in to Fort Myers. If we can figure out a right time, yes. "

When Kim returned to Gloria's office she heard the phone ringing.

"Gloria Latham here. Oh, yes, Mr. Denks. You're back sooner than I expected." As Kim entered the office, Gloria winked at her and reached over to engage the speaker.

"Yes, as a matter of fact, Ms. Latham," Denks said, "my business meeting was with an important client, the one who wishes to buy the large piece of property I spoke of in my message. He's been interested in Glade City for some time now and has enough funds to offer a substantial down payment and a complete remodel, if necessary." He took a deep breath before continuing.

"As a matter of fact he's sitting here in my office as we speak."

"Well, Mr. Denks, I'm afraid there's no such place around here that would come close to what your client has in mind. The only alternative would be to find some appropriate land and build to his satisfaction."

Ignoring what Gloria said, he continued as though she hadn't uttered a word. "I'll call my client, Mr. Smith, who wishes to remain anonymous. He's familiar with some of the area around Glade City and knows of one place in particular that he would like to acquire. It's a three-story home, probably fifty years old or more, has a large piece of property with it on the outskirts of town, a perfect setting for his needs."

"As you probably know, Mr. Denks, I've been in real estate for long enough that I know there's nothing around here for sale as large as Mr. Smith has in mind." Gloria looked at Kim, smiled, and rolled her eyes. "In fact, the Glade City area has only one three-storied home, and I know for a fact that it's not for sale."

"Well, ha, ha, everyone has his price, Ms. Latham. What, in your estimation, would it take to get the owner or owners to change their minds? What could we offer to nudge them into selling?"

"At this time, Mr. Denks, I honestly couldn't tell you. I will, however, try to get you more information and also see if I can locate some suitable property to build on."

"I appreciate your help, Ms. Latham. We're most anxious, so please call me at your earliest convenience. Thanks again." He hung up.

Gloria pushed her chair back from the desk and looked at Kim. "Some people just don't know when to take 'no' for an answer. I'll let him stew for a few days, and maybe I can find him some available land."

Kim placed her cupped hand beneath her chin and mused aloud. "I wonder who this 'client' is and why the secrecy. I'd certainly like to know what they have in mind." She glanced over at her friend who had picked up a pen and was doodling on a piece of paper.

"You know, ... I was thinking," Gloria said, "there might be a way we could find out."

On the way home that afternoon, Kim's cell phone rang. It was Aunt Patricia.

"If it's not pushing you too quickly, sweetheart, I found a flight I can take into Fort Myers tomorrow with an arrival time of 8:05 P.M." Kim heard the excitement in her aunt's voice.

"Aunt Patricia, I'll be there waiting for you. The timing is good for me, too; nothing pressing until Wednesday afternoon."

Patricia gave Kim the Flight Number and itinerary from Seattle to Dallas/Ft. Worth and to Fort Myers. "I'm packed, anxious, and ready to see you tomorrow evening. Love you, baby."

As she disconnected, Gloria turned into the driveway and hit the remote to open the garage door.

Kim sat in silence until they pulled into the garage. "Guess this is it. I'm nervous about seeing her after finding out she's my birth mother. Do you think I'll give everything away, Gloria? Will she suspect I've found out, or read something in my eyes?"

Gloria switched the ignition off and turned toward Kim. "Face reality, honey. You both love each other. That much is undeniable. She can't blame you for discovering the truth. And none of this is your fault."

"I know, Gloria, but ... "

"No buts, Kim. Be yourself. Don't act any differently. Things will work out in the right way, I know."

"You're always so positive, Gloria. I hope some of your attitude rubs off on me."

After supper, the two went into Gloria's guest bed/computer room to make sure everything was ready for Patricia's visit. They pulled open the hide-a-bed, made it up with sheets, a light blanket, two pillows and a lacy lavender spread that matched the curtains.

The closet had ample room for whatever Patricia would bring with her. A three-foot high bookcase adjacent to the bed served as a nightstand and lamp table. Gloria put fresh towels in the bathroom across the hall from the bedroom and opened the windows in both rooms to freshen the air. Everything seemed to be in order for Patricia's arrival.

Chapter 29

After breakfast Tuesday morning, Kim showered and laid out the clothes she would wear when she and Gloria drove to the airport. The rest of the morning she could use to look over notes she had made to prepare for the Best Way Cleaning Company estimate tomorrow.

The morning sunshine had all but vanished, turning the sapphire sky to a marbled gray by the time Kim was ready to organize what she needed for Best Way. Rain clouds had blotted out much of the daylight. Pulling one of the curtains aside from a kitchen window, she peeked out at the threatening thunderheads building to the east. She switched on the tiny chandelier over the dinette table, and laid out a pad of paper, a pen and notes she'd previously taken at the estate. By 12:30, she had an easy to follow list of what needed to be done and what should be left untouched.

Yawning, she stood up and stretched. When she looked at the clock, she realized fixing a bite to eat might calm her rebellious stomach.

Leaving her notes and list on the table, she went to the fridge and got out a loaf of sandwich bread, a jar of mayonnaise, a package of shaved ham, and some lettuce. The front bell rang. When she opened the door, Chase stood there in slacks and a sleeveless tee shirt.

"Hope I'm not interrupting anything, Kim. I started working the graveyard shift, so I haven't had a chance to call."

"I was getting ready to make a sandwich, Chase, but come on in. Have you eaten yet?"

"Actually, I haven't, but I'd love to take you out for lunch, if you can spare the time."

Kim glanced at her watch. It was close to two. "Why don't I make you a sandwich here? It's a little late and Gloria and I are driving to Fort Myers around 5:00 to pick up my aunt at the airport."

"Aunt Patricia's on her way, then? I'm sure that makes you happy." He gave Kim one of his disarming smiles, adding, "The sandwich sounds fine, Kim, if you'll promise to let me buy you dinner soon."

"Oh, come on in, Chase. And yes, you may buy me dinner one of these days." She put out her hand and pulled his arm.

He followed her down the hall to the kitchen and sat at the dinette table watching her make the sandwiches.

"So, when did you find out your aunt was coming?"

"This weekend. She told me her boss has given her three weeks off, and she called me yesterday with her airline information."

"That's great. Maybe we can show her around, reacquaint her with Glade City, and take her over to Max's place. He might be able to join us when he has some free time."

"Let's wait 'til she gets here before making any plans." Kim put a deli-style ham sandwich on a plate for Chase and went to the fridge. "Beer, wine, milk, or pop?" she asked, getting out a can of root beer for herself.

"What you're having, Kim. You know, I would have offered to drive you to Fort Myers myself, if I'd known. I could have arranged my hours."

"No problem. Gloria wanted to go, anyway." She scooted in on the side of the table opposite Chase and took a sip of her root beer. "So, how does Max like his new job?"

"I think he'll be happy there. He says the work, to him, is a piece of cake. And, best of all, he's out from under Doris's scrutiny." As he spoke, his eyes were drawn to the notes Kim had jotted for the clean up crew. "You found a company for working on SandHill, then?"

Kim reached over and pulled the pad of papers toward her. "Yes. Brad knew a firm that could handle it," she said. "He arranged it for me." She looked up at Chase who showed little emotion at all. His eyebrows knit, then straightened.

"I see, " he replied. "I could have done that for you Kim, if you'd have asked."

"No worry. It's all taken care of now. and it's been arranged for a time tomorrow afternoon for an estimate. Much quicker than I'd anticipated. I'll be so happy to see the place getting a good cleanup. Aunt Patricia can see the before and after."

A flash of light followed by a huge crack of thunder made Kim jump. "Boy, I'm not used to this anymore. None of this stuff in Seattle. When it rains there it might drizzle or mist all day."

"You know, Kim. Maybe I should drive you this evening. I'm used to this weather, and I can be back before my shift starts. What do you say?"

"We should be okay. Gloria's used to the weather, too, and she's taking the Caddy."

He looked at her for a moment. "I want to make sure you're safe. I don't mind, really. "It would be my pleasure. I can borrow Max's rig. There's plenty of room with the crew cab. He has a four-wheel drive, as well. Good for this slick weather."

A double flash of lightning hit this time, followed by an ominous rumble of thunder.

Kim stared out the window as the rain started falling in gigantic drops at first, then changed into a heavy, steady downpour. "This is pretty frightening. Do you think this might delay the flight or force a cancellation?"

"It could," Chase said.

"I'll call Gloria and see what she says."

"I hate to say this," Gloria said after she listened to Kim, "but it might be the best plan. A pickup with four-wheel drive is probably a lot safer way to go. I would certainly call the airport first to be sure the flight's on time." Gloria sighed. "I wish I had something more positive to tell you. Unfortunately, these storms can materialize quickly and disappear just as fast. Let me know what happens, or if you want me to ride along."

"I will, Gloria."

Chase made arrangements with Max to trade vehicles, and then let the station know his plans in case something should arise to delay their return. "Call the airport and check on the ETA while I switch rigs with Max. We can get an early start and take our time." He got up, took Kim's hand and said, "Don't worry, Kim. We'll bring your aunt home in good condition." When he smiled his blue eyes danced.

When Chase returned with Max's pickup, Kim was ready to go. She threw a raincoat over her shoulders while Chase stood at the front door with an open umbrella.

"I called the airport," she said. "There's been no delay, as yet. But, they said it was possible the flight could be late if the pilot had to reroute because of the thunderheads."

After they climbed into the truck, Chase put the umbrella in the back seat along with Kim's raincoat. She buckled her seat belt and settled back. "Max didn't mind you borrowing his pickup?"

"He said he was happy to do you the favor. He wasn't going anyplace anyway, and he uses the company vehicle to police the area."

"Thank you, Chase. I realize now how much the weather could affect us in a car. A person can see so much more from up here in the cab. Did you hear a weather report at all?"

"They're predicting it should be over by mid-evening," he replied.

"I hope they're right. We could do with a little less of this." She looked out her side window. It felt like peering through a wall of water, but Chase was taking his time; carefully staying toward the middle of the road.

They drove along in silence for a few minutes while Chase adjusted himself to the rigors of the road. Kim saw the intensity with which he gripped the wheel, and realized he was well aware of the pitfalls and dangers of customary Florida downpours. She began to relax, feeling safe in his hands.

After they reached Highway 41, Chase glanced at Kim. "Do you mind if I ask you a question about your family?"

Kim turned toward him. "Depends on what you're going to ask."

"What's Max got to do with your family, other than he knew them in Miami, before they all ended up in Glade City? It's just a matter of curiosity and the fact that … I've been thinking a lot about your situation, your trying to find answers, and I'd like to help you in whatever way I can. A little assistance from my trained point of view could turn you in the right direction. I've always been good with investigations." He hesitated for a few moments and then continued. "Why don't you let me help you, Kim? Because we're friends." He took a quick glance in her direction. "We *are* friends, aren't we?"

"Of course we're friends." She hesitated, looked out the window as she considered her reply. He did seem sincere, but … She turned back to observe him concentrating on the road ahead. "The thing is, Chase, both you and Max had been the original investigating officers. Why would I think you would possibly have any more evidence or answers for me than you turned up at that time?"

A noticeable moment of silence followed the question. She concentrated on his face which showed no emotion. He had a talent for being able to mask his feelings, she thought, at least, *some* of his feelings. As she watched, a slow smile crept across his mouth.

"You're right on that score, Kim. I guess I can understand you're thinking I couldn't have any substantial answers, that is, as far as evidence found at the time. But, as I see it, two things come to mind. That happened years ago when my youthfulness made a big difference. Neither Max nor I had been trained for that kind of police work, as no one else at the station had been either. Max had his issues over your parents being friends of his. My dedication to thoroughness and Max's many more years of experience than mine, or almost any of the other officers in the squad, made us as good a team as the chief had at his disposal." He took a deep breath without taking his eyes off the road or his grip off the steering wheel.

"The second thing I see is this: Physical evidence is one thing, but the fact remains that someone really had to have had a vendetta against the family to have done what they did." Silence claimed a few moments while only the windshield wipers broke the lull inside the cab of the truck. "Perhaps by checking the people your parents associated with at the time might reveal … "

Lightening flashed just ahead of them, followed by a loud crack of thunder. Chase tightened his grip on the wheel without continuing his sentence.

"The truth is, Chase, I've had that fact at the back of my mind for years. I'm working on that angle as I go through the papers left at SandHill by my grandfather. It's a complicated mass of information, but I'm determined to wade through it all.

"I appreciate your offer, but, truthfully, I believe that this is something that only I can make head or tail out of.

"However, I do feel Max knows a lot more than he told me when Gloria and I met him in Fort Myers. I think my parents and Max were more than casual friends. It went deeper than that. I feel it in my bones. Getting more information along that line from him might be impossible, because he's not likely to take me into his confidence." She shifted in her seat, eyes back on the road.

"At the time Gloria and I spoke with him, he seemed quite shaken when we quizzed him about the police investigations after the murders. He said he was sorry, but it had been very hard on him, because of their friendship."

Chase interrupted her, adding, "I remember when the chief assigned us to the case. Max became unglued. He tried to talk the chief into getting someone else to do it, but the chief was firm, since we'd been the officers who answered the 911 call. I had to wait until he composed himself before we could take off. It was even worse when we found your parents. I hope I never have to go through anything like that again." Chase reached over and put his hand on Kim's shoulder. "Sorry, Kim."

She drew in a deep breath and acknowledged Chase's sympathetic touch with a sideways glance.

"It must have been hard on both of you, Chase," she said, knowing what she had witnessed back then would never disappear from her memory, although she'd managed to keep it below the surface of everyday life.

"Grandfather told me that Max knew my parents in Miami. Mother and Dad had struggled for years to get ahead, but it'd been tough on one salary. That's when my mother decided to get a job. She started working for the local library. She and Dad used to meet for lunch, when they could, at a little café about a block from her work. It happened to be across the street from a local precinct. A lot of the police used the place as their coffee house, and that's how they met Max."

Chase never took his eyes off the road as she spoke. "Go ahead."

"Later, when Grandfather died and left the business and home to our family, Mother and Dad moved to Glade City. I was just about five, so I remember those times. It wasn't long after our move that Max was transferred here from the Miami force."

"I recall Max saying that he knew the Alexanders from Miami," Chase said. "But how did you know about Max's transfer to Glade City? You would have been too young to realize things like that."

"It's strange the way I found out. An old friend of Brad's had been visiting him from out of town. Brad mentioned that I was back living in Glade City, and he'd met me through Gloria. This friend told Brad he remembered the murders because it had been the talk of the area. He knew about my aunt leaving Glade City following high school graduation to attend Miami University, and later about Officer Max Young's transfer from Miami to Glade City. It all seemed an odd coincidence this friend knew … "

A sudden flash and the horizon filled with a jagged streak of lightening followed by a roar of thunder seconds later. Kim stopped in mid-sentence, her throat constricting. She glanced at Chase who kept his cool concentration on the road through wipers slapping back and forth full speed.

"Don't worry, Kim. I've got the pickup under control. We'll be okay. If I have to, I'll pull over, maybe to a restaurant along the way." His voice never wavered.

"It's … it's so frightening when it comes that fast, … and loud." Glancing from side to side, her eyes concentrated on the downpour around them.

"Go on, Kim. Let me worry about this." He motioned with his right arm, indicating the surrounding sky. "You mentioned that your aunt left Glade City following high school graduation to go to Miami U."

"Yes. That's what Grandfather wanted. He made arrangements for her to board with my mother and father."

"So, what happened after she finished University?"

"When I was old enough to wonder and ask questions, I was living with her in Seattle. She mentioned that by her sophomore year in college she began yearning to get out of Miami and seek a position in the Northwest after graduation. She felt there was greater opportunity there. She began putting out feelers and inquiries, and received some good responses." Kim hesitated for a moment to catch her breath. "My grandfather did *not* like the idea of her moving so far away, and gave her a difficult time. In the long run, she finally convinced him it was in her best interest."

"Did Patricia ever talk about her life in Miami … when she was living with your parents and going to college?"

"The subject came up occasionally. She gave me bits of information over the years. That's when I learned that Grandfather had asked my parents to put her up while she attended college. It satisfied him to know she was with family. He paid them for Patricia's room and board." Kim stared out her rain-soaked side window.

"Wow," was all Chase could say.

At 6:30 Chase pulled off Highway 41 to a small restaurant a ways south of Fort Myers. Only two other couples had been brave enough to venture out in the inclement weather to eat. They could have been traveling, as well, Kim thought. The storm had let up from a downpour to a steady rain. They'd have some time to unwind from the strain of driving and enjoy a leisurely meal.

"How far are we from the airport?" Kim asked.

"Fifteen minutes, tops."

She took out her cell phone. "I'll give the airport a call and find out about the arrival of that flight." When she closed the phone, she said, "The flight is only twenty minutes late."

"Time enough to take off your shoes," Chase said, cracking one of his smashing smiles.

He certainly is a different person when he's not so serious, Kim thought.

At the airport, Chase parked in one of the short-term lots and reached into the backseat for Kim's raincoat and the umbrella. He went around to her side of the pickup and helped her out. "It's actually not too bad at the moment," he said. "Maybe we'll be lucky on the way home."

They sat down on seats near "Baggage Return" to watch for Patricia. There was still time before the plane's delayed arrival.

"So, are you finding clues you were hoping to uncover, Kim?" He turned slightly in his seat so he could look directly at her.

"I can't say I've unearthed anything I could classify as a clue, Chase. Gloria and I have poured through a lot of personal things: recipes, receipts, bills, old papers my grandfather had saved, for what purpose, I don't know. I'm hoping something will eventually turn up or make sense, information the casual looker, or investigator wouldn't deem important. Know what I mean?"

"I think I do. You haven't found any of your mother or father's letters or notes that would give anything away then? Things that could lead to a whole new discovery?"

Kim hesitated. "Nothing I could say struck me as being important." Then she added, "Only some very personal things that I'm not at liberty to share."

"Sorry, Kim. I didn't mean to pry. I thought if there was something we could get our teeth into, I could help you. I'm just as interested in you discovering who committed this crime. For closure," he added.

"I would like that. Right now, I can't say anything else."

Suitcases began to rotate on the conveyor belt as they spoke. Chase tapped Kim's arm. "Check out the guy in the gray suit next to the good-looking woman with hair the color of yours."

Kim punched Chase lightly on the arm and jumped from her seat. "That's my Aunt Patricia."

Chapter 30

After hugs and kisses with introductions, the two women settled down to wait for Patricia's luggage. When they appeared on the conveyor belt, Chase grabbed the cases, and the three of them were off. Outside, rain fell quietly, having spent itself to a drizzle.

"Who was that good-looking gentleman next to you at 'Baggage Return'?" Kim asked as they made their way to the pickup.

"He was nice company. Got on at Dallas and had the seat next to mine. He's heading for Naples as soon as he picks up his rental car."

"Hmm," Kim said, smiling mischievously at Patricia. "Just wondered. Would you like Chase to stop someplace for supper or a snack? Or did they feed you on the plane?"

"I bought something in the airport at Dallas, sweetheart. Besides, I'm too excited to be hungry. I could hardly wait to see you."

The women talked nonstop on the way home while Chase took charge of driving.

By the time they reached Gloria's, everyone was tired. Chase parked in the driveway, helped the two women out as the garage door rolled up, and Gloria rushed out to greet them.

"Boy, I thought you guys would never get here. Come on in," she said, putting her arms around Patricia and hugging her. When she released her, Gloria took a hard look at the older woman. "I must say, you and Kim's mother have similar features except for the hair color. I remember Margaret well, since I frequently stayed over with Kim."

She led the way to the bedroom they'd set up for Patricia. Chase followed, hauling two of the suitcases. He put them next to the closet door and went back for the third.

After he brought in the last suitcase, he said, "I'd better be going, ladies. I still have a shift to pull." Turning to Kim, he said, "I'll talk to you later."

She followed him down the hall to the garage exit. "I can't thank you enough, Chase. You've been so helpful."

He turned as he reached the door. "It was my pleasure, and I must say, your aunt is as pretty as your mother was, a difficult feat to accomplish."

"She's a lovely person with a great personality." Kim walked as far as the edge of the garage with Chase. "I'm indebted to Max for the use of his pickup. I'll thank him later."

Chase hesitated before leaving the garage. "I'm glad everything worked out so well, Kim. Let's get together soon, maybe with Max. Okay?" Looking into her eyes, he suddenly wrapped his arms around her and quickly kissed her on the lips. She objected with a push of her hands, but he sprinted off to the pickup before she could catch her breath.

A flush of bewilderment swept over her. She brushed her lips with the back of her hand, wondering if the others would notice her lost composure.

Chapter 31

The next morning Kim got up when she heard Gloria leaving for work. She knew it was later than her normal time to rise, but yesterday had been a strenuous day. Patricia was still sleeping, and Kim imagined she'd be in bed for a while. Seattle time was only 6 A.M.

She dressed and went into the kitchen to put the kettle on for tea. She sat down with a bowl of fresh mixed fruit Gloria had prepared yesterday. Her raisin toast popped out of the toaster as Patricia entered the kitchen.

"You *are* an early bird today. I expected you to sleep at least until noon."

"I'm too excited, I guess. Can't seem to settle down or unwind, or what-have-you."

Kim studied Patricia, observing her in a new light. Though she already knew they looked related, the similarity in their looks was still amazing; the soft natural curl to the auburn hair, inherited from Grandfather, the green eyes, fair skin, slim nose and oval face. Margaret, on the other hand, had been a brunette with deep blue-gray eyes taking after Grandmother Sofia. She had been smaller than Patricia, but a Norwegian beauty none-the-less, a woman who attracted attention wherever she went.

"Would you care for a cup of tea and cereal, toast or something else?" Kim asked.

"Just tea for now, thanks, sweetheart. Tell me more of what you've been doing at the estate. I've wished so many times, I could have taken a long sabbatical to help you organize the house renovation, go through some of the things that were left after we went to Seattle." She stopped talking, taking a long, hard look at Kim. "I've missed you so much that I considered quitting my job and moving down here."

Kim studied Patricia's glowing face. "You don't know how I've prayed for something like that to happen. I want you here more than you know."

"I've been in Seattle so long that I've made many friends. Unfortunately, most of them work a full schedule, so we don't have that much time to spend together. Besides, there's nothing like family." Patricia sat down in front of the cup of tea.

"I felt the same. Before I got to Gloria's, I worried about whether being so far away from you and what I've known as home for the last fifteen years was going to work. Thank goodness for my good friend here. She and Brad, and Chase, too, have been so supportive. I also think keeping my mind and body busy by going through Grandfather's things and planning for renovations has helped me to stay on track."

"Who is Brad? I don't know him at all."

"Brad is Gloria's boss as well as a good friend. I actually had a crush on him when he was in high school and his sister, Leslie, was in my fourth grade class. We used to have sleepovers occasionally. That's when I first met him."

"Ooohhh," Patricia said sucking in the word. "Do I detect something besides just friendship?"

"You never know." It was hard to hide the smile when Kim thought about him.

"And Chase?" Patricia asked. "He's certainly a handsome one."

Kim hesitated, still feeling the confusion of last night's kiss. "Chase is a nice guy. He's helped me discover things I couldn't have found out without him. I think his biggest problem is being too good looking for his own best interests."

"I understand. Now I remember how I recognized that name. He was one of the young investigating officers for the murders, wasn't he?" Patricia paused, stared out the window at the landscaping in Gloria's back yard; a split-leaf philodendron clung to a corner of the screened lanai while colorful bromeliads adopted support from a traveler palm on the opposite corner. When she turned back, she said, "I believe his partner was Max Somebody. He'd been with the police force in Miami when Margaret and Charles were living there."

"Max Young," Kim added.

"Yes. I met him once when he came to our apartment in Miami. He seemed very nice."

"Yes, he is," Kim said.

There was a lull in the conversation and then Kim decided to risk letting Patricia in on some of the things she'd discovered. "You wanted to know what I've been doing at the estate."

Patricia nodded.

"Well, I started out by cleaning out the closets, the medicine chest in the master bathroom, books and recipes downstairs in the kitchen desk. I've been going through everything of Grandfather's. You couldn't begin to guess how many boxes of papers, notes, paid bills, canceled checks, old Income Tax Returns I've been sifting through. But, of course, everything was neatly filed. It all had a place with Grandfather, though I have my doubts he ever threw any of it away."

"That was my father. He was always Mr. Persnickety. So, Father had that much for you to go through?" Patricia watched Kim as she finished her toast and placed the plate in the dishwasher. "I thought most of that stuff would have been destroyed or thrown out by your parents after they moved into the house because Father seemed to keep every little paper no matter how inconsequential it seemed.

"Since Margaret hated clutter, I would assume she'd have thrown out even some of the important things along with the garbage. So many things went into the trash bin with her. I know Father had that room off the library where he stored his files. I wouldn't doubt that he even had papers in there from when he and Mother were first married."

Kim finished at the sink and sat back down at the table opposite Patricia. "I don't remember my mother ever sorting through any of Grandfather's boxes and files. Knowing her, she wouldn't have been bothered with that stuff. And, you know … out of sight, out of mind. It was a place that she could shut off from the rest of the house; one room she could ignore because she didn't believe it held any relevance for them.

"Some canceled checks led me to a Dr. Warren Wagner in Miami." In her peripheral vision, Kim noticed Patricia flinch. "I discovered that he was deceased, but a Doctor Jillian Wagner was listed in the Miami phone book. When I called the number, I found she was his daughter and had taken over his practice. She was so kind. She invited me to meet her on her time off and allowed me to check out some of her father's records."

Patricia interrupted. "Why would she do that? Isn't that … unethical?"

"I told her how I've been searching for reasons why my parents were murdered. Since nobody in the whole state of Florida seemed to care that the authorities never came up with a suspect, I explained I've been researching on my own. The first thing I felt I needed to do was to check out their lifestyles. Somewhere there could be clues as to who hated them enough to do the unthinkable. I think the good doctor felt sorry for me and thought if it helped me, it could be a way to right a terrible wrong."

Patricia sat quietly, looking out the window, concentrating on the sky and drifting clouds this time. She said nothing for long minutes while Kim waited for some sort of response. Finally Kim put her hand on Patricia's arm and said, "Are you all right, Aunt Patricia?"

She cleared her throat, turned, and focused on Kim. "You've discovered the … the ugly truth, haven't you?" She had paled, her eyes moist with emotion as she searched Kim's face.

Kim leaned over and put her arms around Patricia, hugging her tightly. "I wouldn't call it the ugly truth," she whispered. "I'd say it was a happy truth, for me. I haven't lost my mother, after all."

Kim paused for a few long moments, finally taking up the conversation from where they had left off. "I have to say this, though,

I've had a difficult time dealing with the whole situation. I loved you so much as an aunt and, to tell the truth, I often wondered why my mother had been the difficult person I knew and not at all like you. I loved her, never-the-less, but she lacked the warmth I craved. I've been trying hard to push away the resentment I built up since I uncovered the truth. I mean, why did you have to give me up? Especially, knowing how your sister, Margaret, could be, selfish and unemotional … Did you really think she could be a good mother?"

"Circumstances were different then, sweetheart." Patricia dabbed her eyes with a tissue. "I would have brought shame to the family. Your grandmother, Sofia, was not a well woman. My father was afraid knowing all this would shorten what life she had left. And he was the strong one. He decided that having me disappear while pregnant and then having Margaret and Charles adopt a child would be the perfect solution. It would allow me to finish my schooling and get a position in Seattle, the city of my choice, give Margaret the responsibility of a family, possibly creating a stronger marriage for his oldest daughter. He knew she was unfaithful to Charles, and this had a very negative affect on him."

Kim interrupted. "What about Charles, my dad? What did he know about all of this?" Her voice had lost its softness. "And, biggest question of all, how … did you two get together? Wasn't it bad enough that Margaret had been carrying on an affair, and now, you and Charles? I'm sorry, but nothing wants to add up."

"I know, sweetheart. Please, let me ex …"

"When I found out the truth about my birth parents, I had some very negative thoughts about … you, and why you would give me up to Margaret, knowing her personality."

"You'll never know how hard it's been for me not to tell you, sweetheart. I didn't want you to think less of me, but the longer I kept that secret, the easier it was to let myself believe the story we'd all agreed on."

"And, what do you mean by the 'story you'd all agreed on'?"

"A *long* story, sweetheart. It was your grandfather's idea. Since he was paying all the expenses, I believed he had the right to say what he thought would be in the best interest of all concerned." She stopped speaking, looked down at her hands for a moment before she continued. "But, tell me, how did you come to find the truth?"

"The doctor's records," Kim said. "They stated that you were pregnant, under his care, and he delivered the child, a girl. It also revealed the child was to be given up for adoption. When I found my birth certificate in one of Grandfather's secret hiding places, we knew who my birth mother and father were."

Patricia flushed. "Another story I need to tell you. The only positive in the whole messy affair was the fact that by giving you up for adoption to my own sister and brother-in-law, you would remain part of my family. You'd have your own biological father and a grandfather who adored you from the first day he set eyes on you. And what better arrangement than with another blood relative? Margaret." She took a deep breath before going on.

"Charles had always longed for children, but Margaret wanted none of it. Personally, I think she didn't want to lose her figure, but your grandfather was very persuasive. He had been keeping the wolf from their door for years. Charles's job wasn't that lucrative, and it was expensive to live in Miami."

"So my grandfather put the pressure on Margaret to convince her adoption was the right and only choice?"

Patricia nodded, shifting in her chair, she continued. "Charles and Margaret could raise you as their own. After your birth I would leave Miami and take a job in Seattle. Father made arrangements so that people acquainted with the family would think you were really Margaret's child."

"But … but what did Margaret think about your pregnancy, since you lived right there?"

"Before I even showed, I decided to tell my father the truth about Charles and me. There was no sense trying to avoid it. He would find out sooner or later. He made immediate arrangements for me to take up residency at the private hospital in Miami where you were born, in their wing for unwed mothers. I told Margaret that I had been accepted at the University of Seattle and would be moving there within a few weeks. Not the whole truth and not that she seemed to care. I'm sure she enjoyed the thought of having me out of the way.

"I completed my college courses the last six months by mail, because I was 'ill' and couldn't attend. Father arranged that, too. It was all a cover up, but it was the way he wanted it. I didn't feel I had other options. He paid for everything. He called all the shots. We could hold our heads up without shame … he thought. My shame would live with me a long time. This was partly done so that my mother, your Grandmother Sofia, wouldn't know. Father always protected her from anything unpleasant or negative."

Kim dished up a bowl of fruit, pushed it towards Patricia and filled her cup with hot tea.

"I want you to eat something … for your own good."

Patricia nodded her head and took a spoonful of the mixed fruit. "This *is* refreshing. I guess I need this, after all."

"Go on, please," Kim said, taking her seat again next to Patricia.

"Before I showed," Patricia continued, "Father said I should go to Glade City and visit my mother. He suggested I tell her about the job offer I received from a Seattle department store in the executive offices. He asked me to assure her once I had settled and had a couple of weeks vacation time coming that I would fly back to see her. I never got to see her. She died before your first birthday. I went back for the funeral, and that was the last time I saw my father alive." A tear rolled down Patricia's cheek. She pushed it aside with a finger. "He passed away when you were five. I flew back for the services and saw what a beautiful little girl you were. I cried all the way home on the plane … for missing out on you, for not seeing my father before he passed away, and for knowing I would probably never return to Florida. Margaret and I had lost any sisterly love we'd ever had for each other.

"One memory that continued to haunt me was the knowledge that Margaret had been unfaithful to Charles."

Kim put her hand on Patricia's. "I discovered that through letters Margaret must have buried behind the towels in their bathroom linen closet. We also found reports from a detective Grandfather hired. He revealed who her lover had been."

Patricia nodded. "I knew. There were signs. This all happened several years before you were born. She'd found a job at a library while Charles was working for Miami Caribbean Cruises. If he had to work late or stay over night aboard ship, she often wouldn't come home. She never offered me an excuse, but I knew by the way she acted I'd better stay out of it. Sometimes she'd show up minutes before Charles was due home. She'd barely acknowledge my presence, would walk back to their bedroom and get into her pajamas. I'm sure she probably pretended to Charles that she'd been home all evening. I have no idea what she told him."

"All this time, my dad never suspected anything? There must have been indications somewhere along the way. Was Margaret a smooth liar, or was Dad just plain blind?" Kim studied Patricia's face for an explanation.

"Not blind. Blinded by his love for her. Margaret never let on anything to me about what was going on. Never asked me to keep what I saw to myself, just went on as if I didn't matter. I was only a boarder who helped with their rent and wouldn't have any influence on Charles."

"So, Dad was so in love with her that he chose to ignore any signs of infidelity? And, if he was so in love with Margaret, how did ... " Kim's voice trailed off as she stumbled for words.

"How did he and I get together?" Patricia finished the question for her.

"Yes." Kim flushed. "I'm trying to understand it all. I know this has to be difficult for you, too."

"One day Charles got off early and came home to surprise us. It was one of those days when he expected to be overnight on the cruise ship." Patricia stopped speaking, took a deep breath, and looked at Kim. "You need to understand that Charles and I were *not* having an on-going affair." She wiped her eyes again.

"That night Margaret was gone, doing her 'thing', and I was at the kitchen table studying. When Charles came in, he asked me where she was. I told him I didn't know, which I didn't. He sat down opposite me and laid his head in his arms on the table, face down. I could see he was shaken. I assumed he suspected what was going on. When he finally looked up, his eyes were red and swollen. He said, 'I've lost her, Patricia! I've lost my love.'

"He was so pathetic. I didn't know what to say or do. I tried to decide whether I should tell him what I knew or keep it to myself. Actually, I decided it was none of my business. We both sat in silence until I couldn't stand seeing him in such a state. I got up from my books and and moved around to comfort him."

Patricia turned away from Kim, her body quietly shaking.

"He'd always been the greatest brother-in-law a girl could ever want. He worked long, hard hours. I never heard him complain. He treated Margaret like a queen, yet, she was totally unfeeling toward him. She had her own way of being. When we were growing up, she'd always been that way, cold and calculating.

"It wasn't easy for me living under those circumstances, but I knew one day I'd finish school and be out of there and on my own."

Patricia picked up a strawberry from the bowl. She toyed with it for several seconds before putting it in her mouth. After she ate it, she said, "When I put my arms around Charles' shoulders, he turned toward me, shaking, almost uncontrollably, and hugged me back. After a while, he seemed to calm down and regain some composure.

"We sat there for the longest time talking, with our arms wrapped around each other. I truly don't know what happened or why, but Charles leaned over and kissed me, not like a brother, but like a lover. He said, 'Patricia, you're what I had expected to find in Margaret and never have.' He was gentle and sweet, and somewhere in the back of my mind I knew I'd always hoped I could find a man like Charles. He'd been my idol for years; I had feelings I was ashamed to admit, but careful to hide. After all, he was married to my sister."

She continued sipping her tea, but left the fruit. "Something happened when he kissed me. Neither of us tried hard enough to stop what came next."

Patricia looked up at the ceiling. "I never wanted you to find out, Kim. At least, not like this. It only happened that once, but that's all it took for you to be conceived." Again, she sniffed and wiped the moisture that had accumulated beneath her eyes.

"Giving you up was the most difficult thing I've ever had to do."

"Please don't torture yourself over the past." Kim rubbed her fingers gently over Patricia's hand. "What happened, *happened*. It can't be changed. We're both here today, and that's the only thing I'm concerned with. I've always loved you, and that will never change."

"I know, sweetheart. I feel the same. They say confession is good for the soul, so my soul should soon be feeling much better."

"What about Grandfather? How did he take this?"

Patricia studied her cup before continuing. "He had always loved Charles, like a son rather than an in-law. He had been crushed when he found out about Margaret's affair. So, before you were born, your grandfather and I discussed what needed to be done. We both decided the best thing was to give you up for adoption to my sister and brother-in-law. Charles would have the child he'd always wanted and Margaret wouldn't have to go through a nine-month pregnancy and spoil her beautiful figure."

"And my mother, I mean Margaret, never suspected the child they were adopting was yours?"

"She knew nothing about my pregnancy, thought I'd left town to finish college in Seattle. Father came to Miami to check out the adoption arrangements and then drove me back to see my mother. When we returned to Miami, he and Charles accompanied me to the airport."

Patricia returned her attention to the garden outside the window.

"Was there any communication at all between you, Grandfather and my dad while you were in Seattle?"

Patricia returned her gaze to Kim. "Before your grandfather died, he called regularly to see how things were going. He told me how he lived for your visits with him in the Everglades. He was a lonely man after your grandmother passed away.

"After your grandfather died, Charles brought the family to Glade City to manage the business and care for the estate, as Father had previously discussed with the family and set up in his will. Charles called me several times a year to keep me up to date on your development. One time, he sent me your school picture. Of course, Margaret knew nothing about this. He also mentioned that the assistant my father had hired, Melvin Thomas, knew his stuff and was a great deal of help to him, but he suspected Melvin had a crush on Margaret. He hung around her office far more than necessary when she was in. It didn't seem to bother Charles, though, because he knew Melvin wasn't Margaret's type. She wouldn't have given him the time of day if he'd gotten on his knees and begged. In fact, she was downright nasty to him most of the time."

"Other than that, my dad didn't have any problems with Melvin?"

"Not to my knowledge," Patricia answered. "Personally, I wouldn't have known what to do without Melvin there to carry on after they were ... gone. He was a blessing in disguise for me."

Kim reached over and rubbed Patricia's shoulders. She said, "I'm sure all this has been very exhausting for you. I have to meet a cleaning company rep this afternoon at the estate. I want you to rest up, and then tomorrow, I'm going to take you to town to meet up with Melvin again. He's quite an enigma."

Chapter 32

After lunch, Kim showed Patricia around the house and garden to familiarize her with her new surroundings. She made certain Patricia was comfortable before she left for SandHill to meet with the manager of the Bestway Cleaning Company.

"I won't be long, Aunt Patricia. I'm anxious to get this job started."

"Don't worry, sweetheart. I have clothes to hang up, and after that, I think I may stretch out on the bed and read my book."

"Good girl," Kim said, leaning down to give Patricia a peck on the cheek.

On the way out, she picked up her purse and the tablet with notes for the cleaning company. It was a little early, but she didn't want to keep Mr. Simms waiting.

Allowing herself enough time to open up before Simms' arrival, she pulled into SandHill's driveway at quarter to three and parked inside the iron gate and left it open for the manager.

She entered the house leaving the front door ajar for fresh air and for Simms. Ten minutes still gave her time to go upstairs to her old bedroom and decide whether or not she wanted to have the broken furniture restored after the cleaning crew finished.

As always, mounting the stairs brought back haunting memories, no matter how hard she squeezed her mind against them. Pausing at the bottom, she willed herself strength to overcome those persistent demons. This would have been so much easier had Gloria been here to accompany her, but right now, knowing it was part of the therapy she needed, she placed one foot on the bottom stair and urged herself upward. It was time to depend upon herself.

Sun from the skylight and the open front door built her confidence as she mounted the stairway. When she reached the top, she silently congratulated herself. She was one step closer to conquering her fears.

As she started down the hallway toward her bedroom, through the open front door she heard the crunch of gravel grinding beneath shoes. A bit early for Mr. Simms, she thought, but she could put off the decision on her bedroom furniture until another time. Retracing her steps to the staircase to meet him, it occurred to her she hadn't heard a vehicle at all. So, where had he parked?

She looked over the banister. A man's shadow, not moving, reflected on the open front door. No one else had any business being here except Simms. So who was this? She watched in silence, trying to make sense of it. Of course, it couldn't be Simms.

Moments passed. The shadow didn't move. No one attempted to enter the house. She wanted to call out and ask who was there, but panic gripped her. Her heart started to pound. Common sense cautioned her to heed her gut feelings. She turned and hurried toward her bedroom. Closing the door quietly behind her, she locked it, and tiptoed to the window overlooking the front of the house. Her car stood where she had parked it. There was no other vehicle in sight.

As she pulled her cell phone from her purse to call for help, a pickup turned off the highway, came down the driveway, through the gate and parked. A sign on the side of the vehicle read, "Best Way

Cleaning Company." She threw open the window and called to the man getting out, "I'm upstairs. Please come in, and I'll be right down."

"Yes, ma'am. I'm on my way."

Tiptoeing back to the door, she listened with caution. Nothing but silence. Reminding herself that help was only stairs away, she turned the lock and twisted the knob. The door slid away. She eased into the hall, looking in both directions. The passage was clear, but he could be hiding in one of the rooms along the corridor. She rushed toward the staircase, never feeling her feet touch the floor. The man from the pickup was coming through the open front entrance as Kim reached the head of the stairs.

At the bottom, breathless and heart pumping double-time, Kim managed to smile and extend her hand. "I'm Kim Alexander. I'm so glad to see you."

"Larry Simms," he said, taking her hand. "Is everything all right, ma'am? You look a little … pale."

"Did you see anyone outside when you drove in?"

"Yes, ma'am. A man was going around the side of the house when I pulled off the highway. I didn't get much of a look. Seemed to be in a … hurry. Was that your husband, ma'am?"

"I'm not married, and I don't know who it could have been. A prowler, I suppose. He frightened me half to death because he was standing near the doorway shortly before you arrived." Kim wiped perspiration from her brow. "I was upstairs and saw his shadow on the open front door. Thank goodness you arrived when you did. I think you saved my day."

"Do you want me to have a look around? Or call the police?"

"That sounds like a sensible idea. I should report this."

She took out her mobile phone and rang Chase's cell number. After four rings she disconnected and rang the police station to report the incident. "Is Officer Grey there?"

"Sorry, ma'am. Officer Grey is off duty. Could I help you?"

Kim reported what had happened.

"I'll have one of the other officers come right out. Best we check these things out while they're still fresh."

"Thank you, sir." Kim hung up and turned to Larry Simms. "I don't want to keep you, so we might as well get started. The desk officer is sending a patrolman right now." She put her phone back in her purse and retrieved the tablet with notations.

The two finished going over the living room, library and kitchen when, through the window above the sink, Kim saw a squad car pull up and park. A tall, dark-skinned officer stepped out, gun in hand and ready for action. By the time Kim reached the front door, he was disappearing around the side of the house.

"Guess I'll let him do his job. I feel better knowing he's checking the place," she said to Simms.

"You're right."

Before they went upstairs to finish, the police officer stopped in to tell Kim he'd found no evidence of a prowler.

"I'll report this to the chief when I get back," he said. "I imagine he'll order extra surveillance for the time being."

When Kim finished with Larry Simms, she asked if he would mind following her into town.

"No problem, ma'am. I have to go that way anyway. I could follow you right to your home if you'd like. It might be safer."

"I'd appreciate that very much."

The two walked out together. Kim secured the house, backed out after Simms moved his pickup beyond the fenced area, then locked the gate and got back into her car. She moved ahead of Simms, and he followed her back to Gloria's.

Simms stopped behind Kim when she pulled into Gloria's driveway. Leaning out the window, he said, "You okay now, ma'am?"

"I am, and I'm grateful."

"You're more than welcome, ma'am. I'll get my crew together as soon as possible and give you a ring next week sometime to set up a starting date."

"Great." She pulled into the garage next to Gloria's Caddy.

Gloria sat at the dinette table sipping from a Starbuck's cup. "I just got home a few minutes ago. My client, the gentleman, and I use that term loosely, was determined to ask me every question in the book. I don't think he had any intention of buying from me. He just seemed to be … nosy." She offered the paper cup to Kim. "Yeah, I know. Don't say it, friend." She grinned at Kim. "I know I can't expect to sell everyone."

Kim turned down the offered cup and went to the wine cupboard. "I need something stronger than that." She rummaged around until she came up with a small wine cooler. She filled a tumbler with ice cubes and emptied the bottle in to it.

"Well, that's a first." Gloria watched Kim take a swallow. "Did something happen?"

"Have you seen Patricia?" Kim turned to look at Gloria.

"It's been quiet as death since I got home. Her bedroom door was open, so I peeked in. She was sound asleep with a book clasped in her hand on her chest. I didn't wake her. No doubt she needs the rest."

"Good. I don't want her to hear this." She sat down next to Gloria and took another sip of the sweet drink. "I had quite a scare this afternoon," she said.

Gloria put her cup down on the table and stared. "For God's sakes, Kim, now what?"

Kim related to Gloria what had happened, adding, "I don't think this was just a random incident. What if someone knows what I'm doing, when and where I am at all times?"

"Well, you're not going there anymore by yourself. If I can't be with you, I'll get Brad to accompany you."

Kim took a larger swallow of her cooler. "I'm not going to take him away from his business. I thought about this on the way home, and I know I need a plan if I have to go back to the estate. I'll figure out something. The officer on duty at the station said the chief might post extra surveillance, if necessary. Above all, I don't want to frighten Patricia. She doesn't need that right now."

The two sat in silence, each cloaked in her own thoughts.

Gloria was the first to break the lull. "Thing is, most everyone in town knows you're here and that you've been going through the house. People still talk about the murders as though they happened months instead of years ago, and no one can understand why the person or persons responsible have never been caught. He or she could easily still be living in Glade City, waiting to see what you're going to do next. If you get too close to the truth, your life could be in grave danger."

"I've considered that."

Chapter 33

When Kim awoke the following morning, the sun had not yet made its appearance. A dull overcast sky greeted her. It might not be so melting hot and humid today, she thought.

She took a quick shower, dressed and went into the kitchen. Gloria and Patricia were already sitting at the table enjoying coffee and conversation.

"Too bad some people sleep so late they miss out on all the good stuff," Gloria giggled.

Kim took a mug and tea bag from a cupboard. "I don't know what happened to me. I guess my brain didn't know it was time to get up."

"The water in the kettle just boiled," Gloria said.

Patricia got up and poured herself another cup of coffee. "I'm still a bit tired myself. Change of time and weather probably working on me. Now that I'm here, I can't seem to control my excitement. I want to see everything." She spread strawberry jam on a piece of toast. "Everything tastes so much better here in Florida than it did in Washington. I love being back."

"It's the newness. It'll probably wear off by noon," Gloria said. "I have to get to the office by Eleven. Brad has to be in Naples by noon on business and may have to stay over. He'll call me later. Didn't want to disturb you two yet, but he's anxious to meet Patricia."

She got up, grabbed her purse and keys from the counter. "If you run out of things to do, stop in at the office. I'll be stuck there for the day, unless Brad gets back."

"Thanks. We'll see how it goes."

When Gloria left, Kim turned to Patricia. "Would you like to go to the Boat Tours first?"

"I'm ready when you are."

When they pulled into the parking lot at SawGrass, it had just begun to sprinkle. Customers were scarce, chased off by the weather. Kim led Patricia to the employees' entrance and down the hall toward the main room. As they passed Karen's office, Kim tapped lightly on her door.

"Please come in."

"I want you to meet my aunt, Karen."

"So happy to finally meet you. Please sit down, and let me get you some tea or coffee."

"Not right now, thanks, Karen. I want my aunt to meet Melvin first."

"Sorry, Kim, but I haven't seen him since yesterday morning, early. He's almost always here before I arrive. So, I really don't know what's going on. He hasn't called. I tried his cell phone a little while ago and didn't get an answer." She picked up her phone. "I'll try him again. He might have forgotten to turn it on."

"Fine. In the meantime, I'll take Aunt Patricia around the premises. We'll check back when we're finished."

Kim escorted Patricia around the gift section of the business and introduced her to the staff. Outside rain continued to spit, building puddles on the docks.

"Let's just pop around town for a while until the weather makes up its mind. It's too early for lunch but we could drive out past the estate, if you'd like. We don't have time to go in today, but I can give you a good look at the property."

"I'd like that, sweetheart. I'm ready for whatever you decide. It's all new and exciting to me."

The two walked back toward the parking lot exit. As they passed Karen's office, she beckoned them back in. "I just got hold of Melvin. He apologized and is on his way. He's asked me to have you wait." She went into her closet and pulled out a folding chair, placing it alongside the upholstered one in front of her desk. "Sit down, please. I know Melvin won't be long."

"Could I trouble you for some water, Karen, please," Patricia said.

"Nothing for me, thank you," Kim said patting the comfortable chair for Patricia.

As Karen walked out the door, Melvin came in. "Hello, ladies. Sorry, I had some urgent business ta 'tend ta, but I'm sure I told Karen 'bout it the other day. She jes' fergot." He turned to Patricia. "Though our meetin' was brief an' a few years have passed, Ms. Sanderson, I still think I'd know y'all anywheres."

"Thank you, Mr. Thomas. It's nice to see you again … and under more pleasant circumstances. I think you've done a nice job keeping the place profitable and looking good."

"I try. It's a mighty big 'sponsibility, but after all, when customers come in, what they see reflects on me. I say, if yer in the business, ya'd best take care of it, and I reckon I'm in it to stay."

Karen walked through the door with a bottle of cold water and handed it to Patricia while Kim's mind registered Melvin's appearance; he wore a thin, short-sleeved cotton shirt, no tie, jean shorts, sandals, and a light lime fragrance; his neatly combed hair, parted on one side, and freshly shaved face seemed a bit out of character, but he did know of Patricia's arrival in town. Probably a show for her.

"Karen tells me y'all took yer aunt 'round before I got here." He directed his gaze at Kim. "Anythin' else I could show ya or do fer y'all?" He switched focus to Patricia.

"I think Aunt Patricia has seen enough for now, until the weather shapes up. I planned on taking her around town this morning before lunch. Is that still okay with you?" She turned to Patricia.

Patricia started to answer when Melvin interrupted. "I'd like ta treat ya both ta thet meal, if I could. Mebbe Ms. Sanderson might have some business thin's to discuss with me."

"That's very kind of you, Mr. Thomas. It's entirely up to Kim."

"It's jes' I'm mighty proud o' my business here, and it'd be nice if we could have a good sit down and discuss it over a meal."

Patricia looked at Kim who shrugged her shoulders. "Whatever my aunt wants, Melvin."

"It's a date then," Melvin added quickly before anyone had a chance to say anything different. "Meet me back here at one, an' I'll take y'all ta a nice place."

"I guess it *is* a date then," Kim added, stifling a sigh.

The two women left, heading for the parking lot and Cruiser. Pools of water sparkled in the sunlight. The wet ground and sun had created a greenhouse effect.

Kim unlocked the car. "Let's get in quickly, or we'll be the ones dripping soon."

They jumped in, Kim put the key into the ignition, and started the engine. In moments cool air blasted from the vents, and she took off to give Patricia a tour of the town.

After an hour of driving the streets of the city, Patricia turned to Kim and said, "I'd say that Glade City has grown quite a bit since Margaret and I were kids. Not too many landmarks left, or they've been swallowed by time and progress. Still, the memories march on," Patricia sighed, "most of them pleasant, but others, not so much."

"Such as?" Kim prodded.

"Well, Mother and Father were great parents in every way, but they did have strict morals and rules. There was never a problem as long as we met their conduct code. I was the shy one and worried about doing exactly as Mother and Father expected of us. Margaret was not of that mind, and that always bothered me. She'd do things she wasn't supposed to, and then make me promise I wouldn't tell. It made me crazy. I didn't want to tattle on her, but I also didn't want to get blamed for her indiscretions."

"What 'things' would she do?" Kim pulled into a parking space in the town mall and turned off the engine.

"It mostly involved boys. The five year's difference between us made me vulnerable to her whims. Because of the house size, we each had our own wings on the third floor. A huge space spread between our bedrooms. Father allowed her a telephone in her quarters when she turned sixteen. A big mistake. She did some devious things, then let our parents think it was me. I didn't even realize what was happening until Father would begin to question me.

"One time when she was thirteen and I was eight, she took money my mother had set out on the kitchen desk to pay the gardener. When Mother discovered the money missing, of course she questioned both of us. We were the only other ones around that day. Margaret feigned complete innocence. Mother and Father both thought it was me, even though I cried and said I hadn't taken it. Father never touched me, but I had to stay in my room every day after school, and over the next weekend. I was devastated because, at the time, I didn't know anything about Margaret taking the money."

"How did you find out the truth?" Kim prodded. "Did Margaret confess?"

"Not Margaret. Not likely. She had one of her girl friends over for the evening, and I wanted to join them. But, as I neared her bedroom I overheard them talking and laughing about how Margaret had taken the money, and I'd gotten blamed for it. I was crushed. After that, I never trusted her again."

"Mother, I mean Margaret," Kim started, "was never the most demonstrative parent. I loved her, of course, but when I was a bit older, I wondered why she was often too busy to pick me up at school when she only worked a half day. Luz picked me up most of the time."

Patricia locked eyes with her daughter. "Did you ever find out why?"

"No. I never questioned her activities. Under the age of ten I don't think most children would suspect their parents of wrongdoing. At least, I didn't."

Patricia nodded. "As an adult living with Margaret and your father in Miami, I found many things to be suspicious about, but

I never had any proof. Only the things Charles told me that night confirmed to me the fact that Margaret had someone else."

"What kind of things did my dad tell you?" Kim studied Patricia's face. "You know I found letters Margaret must have hidden where she thought Dad would never find them. They weren't in his handwriting, and they weren't signed. Who knows how many men she had on the side, both in Miami and Glade City? Some one of them could have become angry if he thought Margaret was giving him the run around. Or, maybe she decided to call off their little affair, and he became infuriated, unreasonable, lost his temper. They could have had a big blow up. Maybe he came back to see her that night … to make up, or take care of her one way or the other. Didn't know my father was already home, walked into the bedroom where they were both sleeping, and did …" Kim took a deep breath.

"Wait, wait, sweetheart." Patricia put her hands on Kim's. "Please don't jump to conclusions because of what I've told you. I only know how things were in Miami. I had no idea what went on in their lives here in Glade City."

"I'm sorry, Aunt … Mom. I have so many unanswered questions on my mind, I sometimes tend to push too hard." She started the car and backed out of the space. "Remind me, and I'll show you the letters when we get back to Gloria's. In the meantime I think we'd better get back to the Boat Tours. It's getting close to one o'clock."

When they pulled into the SawGrass parking lot, Melvin was standing next to his Ford Ranger, an arm stretched out on the hood, fingers drumming the metal. Kim parked, and Melvin walked around to Patricia's side and opened the door.

"Kin I hep y'all, ma'am?"

"Thank you, Mr. Thomas. That's kind of you."

He took her arm and led her to the open door on the passenger side of his pick-up, directing her to the middle of the front seat. He then helped Kim to the seat next to the door.

Kim suppressed a smile, as she watched Melvin maneuver Patricia next to himself.

"Well, ladies, 'less y'all had a special place ya'd' like ta eat, I'm gonna take ya ta ma favorite place, Eldora's. Y'all've been there with me afore, Kim." He smiled as he pulled his door closed and turned the key in the ignition.

"It's fine with me, Mr. Thomas. Everything around Glade City is new to me anyway." Patricia fastened her seat belt.

"Jes' call me Melvin, ma'am."

"Done," she replied, "if you'll call me Patricia."

"Eldora's 'tis then." He put the Ranger in gear and headed east to the outskirts of town.

"I'd have y'all over ta ma place, but it ain't too special. Like ta change thet someday. Have ma eye on a spot, but I'm still 'gotiatin'." As he drove, he put his right arm on the back of the seat behind Patricia.

Patricia moved a little closer to Kim. "Are you sure we're not crowding you too much, Melvin?"

"Hey, sweetheart, not 'tall. I'm honored ta be able ta escort two such beautiful ladies at the same time."

"Where's the place you're hoping to get?" Kim asked as they started down the highway.

"I'm not at liberty ta say, jes' yet. But, I figger once they hear ma offer, it'll be a done deal." He looked over at the two women.

The cat has swallowed the canary, Kim thought, observing the light in Melvin's eyes.

"What've you ladies been doin' with yerselves?" He glanced at Patricia. "Been out ta SandHill yet?"

"No, but soon, I hope. I'm anxious to see it again after all these years."

Melvin pulled into the restaurant parking lot. "I'd be happy ta run y'all out there after we eat."

"I'm planning on doing that myself, later, Melvin. No sense in you taking more time away from the business." Kim opened her door and stepped out.

"Ain't no problem. I got Karen trained good. She knows what ta do when I'm not there, an' she best do it right." He got out and went around to help Patricia.

Kim started to object, but Patricia said, "It's generous of you to offer, Melvin, but that's up to my niece."

"It's settled then." Melvin took Patricia's arm and led her toward the restaurant. "When we finish here, I'll run y'all out there."

"It needs a lot of cleaning and fixing before it's ready for anyone to see or live in it," Kim said.

"Not ta worry, missy. I have a good eye when it comes ta pitchurin' thin's."

The restaurant was almost full, but Eldora, in her unique little Swiss costume, found them a quiet corner booth.

After they ordered, Melvin brought up the estate again. "I won't git in yer way, ladies. I'll jus' mind ma own business, let y'all have a good look 'round."

When Melvin pulled into the circular driveway of SandHill with the two women, afternoon still lingered on their side. Kim got out of the pick-up, unlocked and opened the gate, allowing Melvin to drive through.

"Come on, ladies, we're 'bout ta take the plunge." He opened the passenger door, and offered Patricia a hand while Kim opened the old teak front door.

"I take it the inside isn't in as bad a shape as the exterior," Patricia said, crossing the threshold with Melvin close behind.

"Outside of a layer of mold and mildew," Kim said, "it doesn't look too bad. Gloria feels sure there won't be a problem in bringing it back to its old glory. As for the outside, that'll require a lot of work. Next week, a crew will be coming in to clean and get rid of the mold. Then I'll have air conditioning installed to make sure the mildew won't return. I can't wait to see it restored."

Patricia gasped. "What a job this is going to be." She turned slowly taking in the complete once-grand entryway.

Kim took Patricia's arm. "I wanted you to see the 'before' picture. In a few weeks we should be able to see a great change." She looked back at Melvin who seemed to be transfixed with the size of the hall.

"I never reckoned this here place bein' so grand." Melvin followed the two women into the open area. "If y'all take ma advice, missy, I think it's goin' ta be too much fer a young lady such as yerself ta take on fixin' a place o' this size. Seems ta me, it'd be much easier ta sell it an' let somebody else worry 'bout it. Even like 'tis now, y'all could turn over a healthy bundle o' cash. Probably 'nuff ta keep y'all comfy fer the rest o' yer life." Melvin turned his gaze back to Kim. "Sellin'd let y'all keep the money an' not have ta shell out fer all these 'spensive fixin's."

Kim crossed her arms over her chest. "Melvin, I don't think you understand. My grandfather built SandHill for my grandmother. It has a special meaning for me because he was an extraordinary part of my life."

Patricia grabbed Kim and squeezed her tightly. "Look, sweetheart, I'm sure Melvin sees his suggestion as being in your best interests."

"Tha's right, li'l lady. I jes' thought it looked like more than … Well, more than y'all should have ta worry 'bout, 'long with ever'thin' else." He reached over and patted her back, adding, "Why don't y'all do yer thin', an' I'll have a look 'round fer maself."

"I'm sorry, Melvin. I'm probably being overly sensitive, but I've dreamed so many years about this place, about my parents and grandparents. I feel it's only right for me to restore it."

"I understand." Melvin nodded and cracked a half smile. "Now, y'all go, an' I'll jus' be hangin' 'round, takin' it all in."

"Help yourself, Melvin." She turned to Patricia and said, "Come on. Let's go into the library."

Kim took Patricia's arm and moved her in that direction. "I want to show you Grandfather's special storage room," she said when Melvin was out of earshot on his way up the winding staircase.

"I can imagine what it might look like. Father never threw out much of anything. It was a place that was off limits to us girls, and Mother never bothered his 'little' room. She'd say it was his idiosyncrasy, and he could do what he wished with that room because he never bothered or cluttered her space."

Kim headed directly to Grandfather's storage place while Patricia continued. "He even kept boxes of his canceled checks."

"I know that, for sure," Kim added.

"Mother had a lot of photo albums she kept up, but after she died, I think Father just stored the rest of the family pictures in a big cardboard box. It wasn't his style to organize anyone else's collections."

Kim opened two folding chairs that were standing against the wall. "I've spent a lot of time going through the boxes here, but I haven't come across any loose pictures yet." She motioned for Patricia to sit. "Grandmother's photo albums are arranged chronologically on one shelf in the library, but I've been so busy with other matters I haven't looked those over yet."

"I'd like to look at them sometime before I leave."

"Please don't say that word 'leave'. You just got here, and I don't want you to ever go." Kim looked over at Patricia who seemed in awe of the mass of stored items.

"I am very tempted, sweetheart, but I did leave the company with the promise I'd return in a few weeks."

"I'll convince you yet, Mom. You need to be here. This place is part of your life, as well as mine. I think Grandfather would have agreed."

Patricia peeked out into the library. "Remember, call me Patricia for now," she whispered. "We've got extra ears around."

"You're right." Kim clasped her hand over her mouth and giggled. "I need to be more careful. Let's go ahead and look over the rest of the house. When we leave we'll take some of those albums home."

"Good."

The two women began to check out each room on the main floor and then started up the stairs, deciding to take in the third floor first. Melvin was just coming down.

"I'll meet y'all downstairs, ladies. Ain't no hurry. Take yer time."

Kim nodded. "We won't be long, Melvin."

As they ascended, Patricia reminisced. "Margaret and I had the third floor, her bedroom on one end and mine on the other."

"How about my room on the second? What was that used for?"

"Strictly a company bedroom with its own bathroom. Mother wanted to keep that for special guests. Margaret and I could do what we wanted upstairs without bothering anyone."

Kim escorted Patricia around the two floors while Patricia reminisced aloud about her childhood days in the Everglades.

They were finished and descending from the second floor when the front door burst open with a deafening crack. Patricia grabbed the banister, and Kim put her arm out to support her. They both stood paralyzed as a hand with a gun moved into the opening from one side of the door.

"Hold it right there," Melvin shouted from the living room. "I have a gun, too, an' it's pointed right at the door."

The gun edged around the corner of the door revealing an arm followed by a uniformed policeman. Chase entered the home and lowered his weapon. Glowering at Melvin, he said, "Put that damned thing down, Melvin. I trust you have a permit for that weapon, or I'll have you at the station before you can count to ten."

"I sure 'nuff do, officer." Melvin stood his ground. "An' what're y'all doing here, anyways?"

Kim got her breath back and started down the stairs again.

Chase continued to glare at Melvin who showed no signs of intimidation. "The station still has orders to keep an eye on this place, and I'm carrying out my duty. When I passed the property I could see a pickup parked in front, not one I believed I recognized. The precinct hadn't been notified of a change in arrangements."

"That's my fault, Chase," Kim said. "I'm sorry, I should have called. With Aunt Patricia being here we were busy doing other things, and I didn't think. I'll call the station later with my apologies." She looked over at Melvin who was scowling at Chase. "Actually, the pickup is Melvin's, and he was kind enough to escort us here so we wouldn't be alone."

Chase looked from Kim to Melvin and back. "In that case, Kim, I'll apologize, even though I'm only carrying out orders. I understand getting busy and forgetting." His eyes softened as he spoke to her. Then he turned to Melvin. "I realize now you were trying to protect the women. However, you'd better be a damned site more careful with that gun in the future, or this could have resulted in a tragedy."

He turned to Patricia and said, "Nice to see you again, Miss Sanderson. I only hope I didn't frighten you ladies too much."

Patricia nodded, smiling warmly as she and Kim reached the bottom of the stairway. "It gave us quite a turn for a few moments, but you had your reasons," she said.

"Yes, ma'am. I'm sorry about that. Can I do anything at all for you folks?" Chase kept his eyes on Kim and Patricia while he spoke.

"I think I kin handle thin's here maself, Officer, if ya don't mind. I'm the one what brung these ladies here, an' I'll see ta their safety." Melvin moved toward Patricia and took hold of her arm.

"I'll be on my way then." Chase started to leave.

"Chase," Kim said, "thanks for your concern. I'll make sure to let the station know the next time we're planning on being here."

Chase tipped his hat, smiled at Kim and left.

"He certainly does seem taken with you, Kim," Patricia whispered after he'd gone.

"I must confess, Aunt Patricia, Chase has been very considerate, and I like him." To Melvin, she said, "I think perhaps we'd better get back. I appreciate your taking time to escort us."

Chapter 34

The following morning Kim had an early breakfast before Gloria came out dressed for work.

"What are you up to today, honey? You look like you're ready to conquer the world." Gloria grabbed a bowl from the cupboard, filled it with raisin bran, a dash of milk, and sat down.

"What, no coffee this morning?" Kim said.

"In a hurry today. What about you?"

"I'm going to pop in to see Karen at SawGrass, maybe catch her before Melvin knows I'm around. I told Patricia to get some rest today because I have business at the Boat Tours."

"Right. If you have time, stop by the office when you're finished."

Kim walked into the side entrance of SawGrass Boat Tours and made her way to Karen's office. She found her sitting at her desk looking through a ledger. She looked up as Kim stopped in the open doorway.

"I'm glad you came by," Karen said, getting up to close the door behind Kim. "I've been going through some of the records, the daily totals that Melvin gives me and adding them up. I'd never noticed anything wrong before, but something kept piquing my interest, something that never seemed quite right. He always gives me the day's totals and handles the ordering of supplies himself; repair parts, gift store items, and new equipment. He takes care of returns. I handle most of the rest; payroll, taxes, bills, etc."

She pulled out a chair for Kim. "If he should come in, please pretend you just stopped in to chat, okay?" Kim nodded. "I don't know why I thought about this. It never occurred to me until you were checking the cash records. Then I began to realize that his returns never show up anywhere, as … credits." She looked at Kim. "I can show you, if you'd like. I need another opinion."

Just then, the door opened and Melvin stuck his head in. "This here a private meetin'," he said, "or is anyone invited?"

"Come in, Melvin," Karen said. "Kim just dropped by to say 'hello'."

"Join us," Kim added. "I'm still fantasizing over that delicious salad at Eldora's yesterday. She should build up a great clientele with food like that."

"I liked ma lunch, as well. 'Course, it coulda been the company what he'ped." The corners of his mouth curved up slightly.

Kim's mental note told her his clothing looked a bit neater than it had when she first met him although he had fixed himself up for his luncheon dates.

He didn't offer to come into the room. "I was jus' on ma way to see what ma boat mechanic found out 'bout a bit of a problem he had, but thanks fer the invite anyways. I'll see y'all later, Kim." He was off and Karen fanned her face with a sheet of paper.

Kim turned back to Karen and said, "Before Melvin came in, you were saying when he returns things, they don't show up in the records."

"Exactly." She pulled out some papers from a bottom drawer. "I can balance everything, and that's no problem, but there should be evidence of any returned items, shouldn't there? We should show credits to our accounts."

Kim stroked her cheek with an index finger. "That's wrong. Not the way legitimate business is conducted. You were right to bring it to my attention. Melvin seemed so sincere when we talked at the restaurant. I was actually beginning to feel like he wasn't nearly as bad as I'd imagined."

"He has his moments. I truly think he feels in his heart that this business should belong to him because he's put so much of himself into it. He once told me that he thought the old estate should have gone with the business. He said it was a crying shame the place was left out in the boonies to wither away when someone like himself could care for it and keep it up.'"

"Really?" Kim said. "Interesting quirk of his personality. Well, don't say anything. Just keep your eyes open, and let me know if you find any returns starting to show up. One way or another I'll get to the bottom of this."

She said good-bye to Karen and headed for Gloria's office.

Kim took a seat in front of Gloria's desk. "You mentioned you thought you might have a way to find out who was after the estate. What was your idea?"

"I've thought about it, but then I decided you might not go for it."

"Let me decide that."

Gloria studied her friend's face. "What if I told Denks you might be interested in selling after all, but only if his client would meet with you in person?"

Kim stroked her chin and was quietly pensive for a few moments. "It might work," she said. Then, "Let's go for it. It certainly can't hurt to let him think I might be willing to part with the property." She smiled, and Gloria reached for her notes and the phone.

Gloria dialed and waited several moments. "This is Gloria Latham calling you back concerning the property you were interested in. Please give me a call at your convenience."

After she'd hung up, she said, "He's out of the office, but he'll be calling back. He's hot for that property. I can smell it."

Before the two women had a chance to say two more words, the phone rang, and Gloria picked it up. "Oh yes, Mr. Denks. I do have some new information for you." Gloria grinned at Kim and put the phone on speaker.

"I've been waiting patiently for you to call, Ms. Latham, because my client is very anxious." The hearty voice of Potter Denks filled the office air space.

"The large three-story home you referred to just outside of town, well the owner will consider a sale."

"That's wonderful news, Ms. Latham." His words were woven with excitement. "Have they mentioned a price? When can we see it?"

"Just a moment, Mr. Denks. I said the owner would *consider* selling. I didn't say it was a positive. No price has been discussed. The owner will entertain the idea only if a meeting can be arranged with your client in person."

"Oh, no, no, no. He wants to remain anonymous. He probably could be persuaded to negotiate via telephone, though."

"No deal, Mr. Denks. I said only consider a sale and only in person." Her words reflected her resolution.

"Well, I don't … I'm not at all sure he'll agree to that. I'll have to inquire. Please ask the seller not to make a deal with anyone else until I can get back to you, okay?"

"I'll arrange it, Mr. Denks. Let me know as soon as possible." She barely had time to hang up before she burst into laughter.

"He sounds like such a fuddy-duddy," Kim said as she wiped tears from her eyes. "I must say, at least he lightened up the day."

"From his voice, I can just picture him," Gloria said. "He's about fifty, short with a bulging gut, balding, small, round, thick glasses, and a nervous twitch around his mouth."

"I think you're very good, Gloria. Fits my impression. Guess we'll just have to see if Denks can convince his client to meet with us."

The office door opened and Brad stuck his head in. "Lunch, ladies?"

"Actually, I need to get back to Gloria's place. I left my aunt alone, but perhaps another time, Brad."

Brad walked into the room and stood next to Kim. "I have some free time, and after my last two days in Naples on business, I'm in need of some feminine intervention, preferably, the Kim Alexander type." Brad reached down and took hold of her hand.

"Sorry, Brad. It sounds good, but I hope you understand."

"In that case, why don't you call your aunt and tell her we'll pick up something at Hattie's Pork Barrel and bring it to the house? After all I've heard about her, I'd like to meet this pretty lady."

"She'd probably enjoy that," Kim said, liking the idea herself. "I'm sure she'll be happy to meet you, too." She took out her cell phone and called Patricia while Brad led her out to the parking lot.

When Kim hung up from speaking to Patricia, Brad said, "Leave the Cruiser." He steered her toward his car. " When we're finished, I'll bring you back here to pick it up, and maybe Patricia would join us."

Kim nodded. "A nice thought, Brad."

After their purchase at Hattie's Pork Barrel, Brad headed to Gloria's place. "How are you doing on your sleuthing?" He glanced at Kim as he drove west to the Spanish Lace area.

"The whole thing is getting more involved all the time. I can't help thinking there's much more to this than meets the eye. Too much doesn't add up, at least, in my mind." Kim sighed and went on. "For instance, the Ramons mentioned that Melvin Thomas came to the house one evening to speak to my dad. They stayed out on the front porch where a lot of shouting went on. Felix Ramon said they didn't know what it was about because he couldn't hear the conversation. But, it definitely was an argument. This happened only days before … my parents were murdered."

"Do you know if the police checked out Thomas at all?" Brad kept his eyes on the road ahead as he spoke.

"No, but I doubt it. I don't think the police were equipped for an investigation of this caliber. Blood samples were taken at the crime scene, but all they discovered was they belonged to my mother and father.

"I also wonder about Max. He comes off as a nice person, but he could know things he's not letting us in on. He avoids discussing his past. He closes up or changes the conversation as he did when Gloria and I met him in Fort Myers."

"What about Chase?" Brad said. "He was Max's partner when they handled the investigation. I've heard he has a hair-trigger temper."

"Gloria and I have never seen that side of him, Brad. Besides, he never knew my parents in Miami." Kim's eyes were fixed on a place beyond the road as she considered the facts. "He wouldn't have known Patricia at all. He was only a rookie fresh out of police academy when he and Max were partnered here in Glade City."

"How about that prowler you said the Ramons mentioned one time?"

"Another dead-end, " she added. "A report had been filed, but there was no information regarding the culprit; whether it was a male or female."

"This Felix Ramon, you think he's perfectly guilt free?"

"I don't think anyone in the world could accuse Felix of doing something not above board."

Brad sucked in his breath and drummed his fingers on the steering wheel as he drove into the Spanish Lace complex. "Kim, let me do some scouting around. I know a few people in Miami and I know a lot of folks here in Glade City. Maybe we can turn up information no one thought relevant."

Kim sighed. "I've begun to feel so lost with information that doesn't make sense. When you talk like that, it's just like ... I can't quite explain it, but like a little of my burden has been lifted, ... or shared."

Brad reached over and put his hand on Kim's. "If there is anything in the world I could help you with, I'd do it." His brown eyes lit up when he looked at her. "Let's pool all our resources and go after some answers."

"Thanks, Brad."

As they pulled up to Gloria's, Patricia came to the front door and held it open. "I'm so glad to meet you, Brad," she smiled. "I've heard a lot about you."

"All good, I hope," He placed his hand on the door for Patricia to go back inside.

"Of course. Now, come in. I've made some lemonade to go with the sandwiches."

"Sounds like what the doctor ordered." Brad smiled and gave Patricia a big hug.

After lunch was over and the three had had a lively conversation, Brad asked Patricia to join them when he drove Kim back to pick up her PT Cruiser.

"The change of scenery will be nice," Patricia said.

Brad pulled alongside the pygmy date palm where Kim had left her car. "Let's get together for dinner one evening, Kim. I'd like to take you both out for a nice meal and get better acquainted with you, Patricia." He jumped out, went around and opened the passenger door to help the two women out. "I'll ask Gloria, too."

"Give us a call when you're ready, Brad. It should be fun." She unlocked the Cruiser for Patricia.

"Just promise me one thing, Kim. Please don't go back to the estate without someone, preferably me, to accompany you. I don't think it's safe. Things seem to happen that shouldn't."

"I'm not planning on it, but if I need to, I'll call on you, Brad. Thanks." She smiled, kissed his cheek and slipped behind the wheel.

"Where to now, sweetheart?" Patricia settled herself next to Kim and fastened her seat belt.

"I thought we could run over to the construction company to schedule a time to begin work when the cleaning crew is finished."

Chapter 35

Kim awoke before anyone else was stirring. Sleep hadn't been easy. She kept thinking about Brad, and what an easy person he was to be around. She tried to keep her mind on the things at hand, but somehow Brad's face kept interrupting her other concerns. She hadn't planned on anything like this happening, but here it was; feelings getting stronger every time she saw him. She'd never had a steady in college because it hadn't been a part of her planned agenda, and falling in love was not what she had considered something she needed at the moment.

Yet, here he was: Mr. Brad Kimbal, tall, handsome, great manners, trustworthy, *and* a very good friend to her best friend. Had she been holding him at arm's length? And where was all that hidden resolve of hers, anyway?

She rubbed her eyes, got up quietly and dressed. She needed to get outside, exercise, see blue sky, drink in fresh air, and try to get her head on straight.

She dressed in her jogging gear and went into the kitchen to get a bottle of cold water. With sunglasses and her house key, she took off on the four blocks toward the back end of the Spanish Lace complex.

The area past the homes gave way to stands of Australian pines and melaleucas, dead-ending onto the highway that bordered the swamp. She could jog a short distance here before having to turn back, which gave her a chance to clear those cobwebs from her head and to think over all the unanswered questions of this uncompromising mystery.

New information has since entered the mix, most of which concerns Melvin. What is his role in all this crazy intrigue? Why has he suddenly turned from a rude, inconsiderate person to someone kinder and more courteous? What is his motive? Maybe he thinks he can get further with honey than vinegar. Why doesn't he want her to check out the cash register tapes? Has he been siphoning off some of the profits? When he spoke about Margaret and Patricia, there seemed to be something odd she couldn't quite put a handle on. She felt he had also been making a play for Patricia. Last, but not least, what about the argument between her father and Melvin? And only days before the murders? Could that have precipitated a reason to kill?

Could this so-called transient who tried to break into the estate and frighten the residents or rob the place have anything to do with the murders? The occurrence made enough of an impression on the Ramons to never forget it. Could it have been a complete stranger or perhaps someone known to Mother and Daddy? Certainly not the fiend who destroyed her bedroom, or the one she sees in her recurring nightmare, the one she believes responsible for it all, and the one her subconscious knows.

Max comes across as a nice person, but she feels he also has issues to hide. Why would a person like that carry on an affair for years with another man's wife? Then there's Chase. He is showing more than just a passing interest in her, and he isn't exactly hamburger, either. Despite his good looks, Chase lacks the warmth that Brad exudes. And, he had been in Glade City when her parents were still living.

A flock of snowy egrets landed in one of the cypress trees on the swampy side of the highway as Kim reached the junction. They set up quite a clatter, breaking her train of thought. Their white feathers gleamed as they caught rays of sunshine that filtered through the foliage of the marshlands.

She jogged on, not wanting to break her pace until a movement in the water alongside the railing attracted her attention. A large gator glided silently through the murky depths, only the tip of its nose and eyes showed above the water until it disappeared into a thick shelter of mangroves. Her first sighting of one of the swamps most fearsome creatures was quite a thrill, but she was grateful to be safe on the bridged portion of the route.

When she got back home, Patricia and Gloria were both having coffee. Gloria put her cup down and dabbed a napkin on her lips. "Whatever you two are up to today," Gloria said, getting up and putting her empty cup in the dishwasher, "stop in the office around noon, and we can go to lunch together. I need some diversion from that place."

"Nothing special on our agenda today," Kim said. "We'll see you at 12:00."

"I think I have a surprise for you both," Gloria said as Kim and Patricia walked through her office door at a quarter of twelve. "Someone you haven't seen in years, Patricia, just dropped by to say hello and is in Brad's office at this moment."

Kim raised her brows as she looked at Gloria. "Well, don't keep us in suspense."

"Someone I haven't seen for years? Hmmm," Patricia mused. "It must have been someone I knew in Miami because when I came back here to pick up Kim, I didn't stay long enough to get acquainted with anyone. I made arrangements with Melvin Thomas to manage the boat tours. After I spoke to the authorities and dealt with the funeral director about my sister and brother-in-law, I set up a patrol schedule for SandHill." She paused again. "From then on, it amounted to getting Kim and her belongings together in order to get back to Seattle. I just can't imagine … "

When there was a light rap on Gloria's door, she called out, "Come in, please."

The door opened, and Max Young walked in.

"Patricia?" he asked, extending his hand while not taking his eyes off her. "It's been a long time, but, I think I'd have recognized you anywhere."

Kim cast a quick side-glance in Patricia's direction. Her face was pale as she opened her mouth to answer. "Max, I am ... Yes, it's been a very long time. I would say, perhaps twenty-five or six years. I must say, you look in good health."

"I'm doing okay and feeling pretty good, as well, and I'm very happy to be back in Glade City." He took her hand and squeezed it. "I hope you're going to be a permanent resident here, as well."

"That remains to be seen," Patricia added with a smile.

Max turned to Kim and said, "Good to see you again, young lady. I hope I'm not intruding on anything important. I had time off and thought I'd stop and say 'hello'. Gloria's been kind enough to invite me to lunch with you ladies, if it's okay with you?"

"I think it sounds like a nice idea," Patricia said. "What do you think, Kim?"

"Definitely. I'm glad you had the time off from your new position."

"Sit down for a few minutes, before we go to lunch," Gloria said. "I just have a letter to address and get off in the mail today." She pointed to an extra chair for Max to pull over. He positioned it next to Patricia.

"I believe we only met on that one occasion in Miami," Patricia started, "when you came to the apartment to see my sister and brother-in-law."

"That's pretty much what I remember." A handsome face surrounded the broad smile.

"It was thoughtful of you to stop by, Max," Kim said. "By the way, how is your new job coming along?"

"I like it. It keeps me busy, puts money in my pocket, and the perks are good. If you ladies have some time, I could show you around the complex. It's brand new, just opened to the public, and it's very good looking."

Gloria grabbed her purse. "Let's go, people. I'm finished and famished, and we can get to the restaurant before it gets too busy. You all can ride with me."

As they pulled out of the parking lot, Gloria said, "I figured the Glade City Family Restaurant might be a good spot to have lunch. They're fast, and the food's good."

Minutes later they were parked and heading for the entrance.

"There's Marsha," Kim said as she spotted the waitress scurrying about serving customers. "I met her the first day I pulled into Glade City. She seems a likeable person."

"I see her almost every time I come here," said Gloria as another young lady seated the group at a round corner booth. "I wonder if she ever takes time off."

After they made their choices, Marsha came over to take their orders. "Afternoon, Ladies, and Gentleman. What can I get you all today?" Looking over the group, she poised a pen above her order pad and focused on Kim. "I remember you, young lady. Did you have any trouble finding the new police station?"

"None whatsoever, thanks to your directions."

"I like to be helpful when I can." She looked at Patricia and then at Max. "You two new in Glade City?"

Kim answered. "This is my aunt, Marsha. She's visiting, and Mr. Young has a new job in town, so he'll be around."

Max put down his menu and nodded to Marsha.

"Say, don't I know you from someplace?" The waitress studied him intently. "You look pretty familiar."

"I … don't think so. I haven't been around much since I arrived here."

"I don't mean recently. This is from way, way back. I'm thinking it might have been when I worked at the Gator Reserve Club. I was there 'bout twenty or twenty five years ago. My first waitress job." She gave a broad grin. "Real special place, out of town, and out of the way of most Glade City folk." She chuckled. "Probably some wouldn't admit to knowin' the place, with its little private rooms and all."

"I … I'm sure I don't remember it. I was a policeman here about that time. Maybe you just remember me from around town." He grinned, adding, "Maybe I gave you a ticket."

"Never got one of them things in my life. All's I can say is I never forget a face, even if it's been years. Well, folks, sorry about this. Just don't pay me no mind."

She took the orders and returned quickly with their drinks, continuing to study Max. Finally, she said, "I just gotta say one more thing, Mr. Young. I think I might remember you when you used to come out to the club once in a while with that beautiful, brunette lady." She placed a glass in front of each person. "A real knockout, she was. Used to think to myself, those two were meant for each other."

"I think you must be mistaken, Marsha." Max didn't look up at her. Instead, he busied himself with squeezing lemon into his ice tea and stirring in a cube of sugar. "I'm not familiar with the club at all."

"Not to worry. It really don't matter none to me. Just so sure I seen you before. Sorry to bother you."

When Marsha returned with the orders everyone settled into eating their lunches, chatting non-stop, with Gloria being the one who always seemed to have the most to say. She looked over at Max. "You have to forgive Marsha, Max. She's as down home as she can be and likes to carry on conversations with all her customers."

He wiped moisture from his upper lip with his napkin. "It's okay, Gloria. I hardly think I would have forgotten her if I'd seen her before."

"Well, maybe you don't remember because she's so plump now. When I was a kid, she used to work at a lot of different places, but she was very slim. Rather pretty, too, with a nice figure. I think that's why she worked at the Gator Reserve Club." Gloria kept her eyes on Max. "I remember Dad talking about the women who worked there. Said they probably were making money on the side. I didn't know what he meant at the time. Since then, I figured it out."

Lunch hour breezed by, everyone seeming to enjoy the camaraderie. Nothing more was mentioned about the Gator Reserve Club or what went on there.

Gloria pulled into the parking lot next to Kim's red Cruiser. "Don't worry about time, ladies. I have stuff in the freezer to feed us tonight, so do whatever."

They all got out to go their separate ways. Max thanked them for inviting him to lunch.

"Keep in touch, Max. You know where to find us," Gloria said as she walked toward the office building.

"Thanks. I'd like that."

After he left, Patricia turned to Kim. "Max seemed a bit upset when Marsha thought she recognized him, don't you think?"

"I had the same feeling. I could almost see perspiration on his forehead, but maybe my imagination was running away with itself." She unlocked her car and the two women slid in. "No matter what I found out about him and my moth … Margaret, he still exudes that nice guy personality. But you know what they say about still waters?" She turned the key in the ignition to start the air conditioner.

"He's a very good looking man, Kim. In a way, I can understand why Margaret's eyes wandered, even though I don't condone her actions, especially when she was already married to a great guy." She paused and looked at Kim. "You said Max never married?"

"I guess not. Remember, I told you he said he'd lost the love of his life?" Kim backed out of her parking spot and headed to the street. "He did live with some woman for a while after he left Miami, but I'm sure it was not a love situation. He was rather down and out, and this Doris person took him in as an old friend."

When they were on the avenue, Kim turned to Patricia. "I'd like to go to SawGrass while we still have some afternoon left. I want to get the cash register tapes from Melvin. Would you mind?"

"You do what you have to, sweetheart. I can browse around the souvenir stands and maybe watch the boats take off. It'll keep me busy."

"Thanks, Mom. I need to check up on Melvin."

She headed for the Boat Tours.

When they arrived, Patricia headed toward the boat launch, and Kim went to Karen's office. When the secretary saw Kim in the doorway she put one finger to her lips. "He's next door in his office," she whispered. "Sit down, and I'll get you some ledgers." She went into the closet where she kept the files, brought out several books and placed them on the opposite side of her desk in front of Kim, and then closed her office door.

"If you look these over from the last several years only, you can see there are no entries for returns; no credits."

"You said Melvin handles all the returns himself?" Kim thumbed through the books.

"Yes. He said he'd take that off my hands. One less thing for me to worry about, he told me. I never questioned him, because it's none of my business or my job description." She sat down opposite Kim. "Employees have been instructed to put all their returns into a certain storeroom, and Melvin would handle them. I pay most of the bills, balance the ledgers, and make out payroll."

She handed Kim an envelope. "Melvin gave me these cash register tapes to give to you. The totals are the same as those he's given me."

Kim took the envelope and went through the tapes comparing them with those Karen had posted. "I see the totals are the same, but what about the tapes before I arrived? Who's to say if they match the figures he gave you?"

Karen shrugged her shoulders. "I can only tell you the business has picked up since your arrival, Kim. It's been a remarkable few weeks."

Just then the door opened and Melvin walked in. "Didn't know ya was here, missy. Karen give ya them tapes okay?"

"Yes, thanks, Melvin. By the looks of it, business has increased quite a bit. Is this a seasonal thing?"

"Not to worry 'bout thet, ma'am. Happens alla time. Folks vacationin' an' all. Never know what makes 'em spend more money one time or 'nother. Jes' the way business runs sometimes." He grinned at Kim, and said, "Where's yer Aunt Patricia today?"

"She's here, Melvin, out looking around while I'm with Karen."

"Well, I cain't have a pretty lady like thet with nothin' ta do. I'll go find her. Mebbe she'd like a air-boat ride while yer workin'."

"Great idea, Melvin. She might enjoy that." Kim winked at Karen as he turned and made a hasty exit.

"You're a trusting soul with your aunt." Karen grinned at Kim, then looked back down at her work.

"Aunt Patricia can take care of herself quite well, thanks. Besides, this will give me an opportunity to check out Melvin's office." Kim smiled this time and hurried out.

230

She walked down the hall to the main room, peeked to see if Patricia was anywhere in sight. Melvin had her by the arm and was steering her through the doors that led to the boat launches. Kim smiled again. This may work out well, she thought.

Melvin's office wasn't any tidier than his clothes had been when she'd first met him. Stacks of magazines cluttered the two available guest chairs, as well as one corner of his desk. Several stale cigar butts filled an ashtray on the other corner, one still smoldering and leaching a vile odor into the room. Kim wrinkled her nose, but sat down in his desk chair anyway. She wouldn't move anything that might cause Melvin to become suspicious. And her opportunity had a limited time frame.

Several empty cans of root beer, a half-cup of coffee, and a paper plate with remnants of some kind of sandwich added to the clutter on Melvin's desk. The wastebasket brimmed with wadded sheets of paper and discarded mail.

A local map, yellowed with constant subjection to tobacco smoke, covered a small space on the wall opposite Melvin's desk. A picture of the downtown area had been thumb tacked to the wall next to the map. Upon close examination, Kim realized it was not an updated picture since the old police station still stood on the main street in town. The wall behind Melvin's desk served as a bulletin board with numerous reminders and cutouts from the local paper push-pinned directly to the painted surface. It was hard to believe that someone demanding fastidiousness from his employees would be such a slob in his own office.

She slid open the large drawer in the middle of the desk. A jumble of pens, pencils, rulers, and push-pins filled the interior. One by one, she opened the drawers on the right side of the desk. Nothing of any consequence: size 10 envelopes, a few blank note pads, a box of paper clips, staples and a registry book with blank checks. Could his checkbook records be tucked away in the safe? That would be where someone like Melvin would hide information he wanted to keep secret, especially if it didn't correspond with Karen's records.

The top two drawers on the left side of the desk opened easily. The first held a box of cigars and a container of wooden matches. In the second, she found a Handbook for Loan Payments and Amortizations, and a pad of scratch paper, the top few pages of which contained a jumble of numeric figures, crossed out and rewritten many times.

She reached down to pull open the bottom drawer. It stuck. Pushing it back in, she pulled again, this time trying to make sure it lined up straight. It still resisted, but she repeated the procedure. It finally gave in to her persistence. Filled to the top with old letters and pictures, the drawer seemed to overflow with things Melvin did not want to part with or maybe didn't care to deal with for the present. Some of these had jammed together and caused the sticking problem. She started to close it again, afraid to change anything lest Melvin suspect someone had been rifling through his personal belongings. As she attempted to shut it, something jammed again, preventing closure.

A bead of perspiration rolled down her nose and dripped onto the calendar/date cover on the desk. Nerves tingled as she reminded herself she wasn't doing the right thing by nosing into Melvin's personal belongings.

Gently, she straightened the top papers so the drawer would close. She moved one hand down the side of the items, trying not to disturb or rearrange them. Something had become stuck along the side and seemed to be the problem. She tried to release it without tearing whatever it was. It remained stubborn, probably because of the thickness. After several minutes of attempting to change its position, she finally succeeded in loosening it. Carefully she extracted it from the drawer. Once free, she could then slide it between the other items and Melvin would never be the wiser.

As she withdrew it, she could make out snapshots bound together with a large rubber band. Shock smacked her between the eyes as she observed the top picture being one of her mother, Margaret, close to the time the family first moved to Glade City. Her mother sat at her desk in the office that now was Karen's. She bent over papers in front of her, seeming to be unaware of being photographed. In the next picture, she stood on the docks where the tour boats took off. The picture framed her perfect profile. There were others taken randomly around the business. Then, out of sync, the last one appeared to have been taken through the chain link fence in the back garden of SandHill. She lay on a blanket on her stomach, head to one side, in broad sunlight, obviously sunbathing and nude.

What was Melvin doing with pictures of her mother? Perhaps they were old pictures that had been left when her folks were still running the business. But the one of her sunbathing on her back lawn nude? No way would that have been allowed to be taken, if her mother had known.

Picture after picture in many settings turned up, mostly around the business area. In none did she appear to be aware of the photographer.

Another bizarre twist. What could it mean? From everything Kim had ever heard or seen, Margaret would never have encouraged any of this. If Melvin had been the photographer, Margaret did not seem conscious of it. Was he stalking her? Have a fixation on her? How far had he carried these feelings? Had she rejected him causing him to lose his cool and commit murder? A double murder?

A wave of fear swept over her. How safe were she and Patricia since Melvin was showing definite signs of interest in Kim's birth mother? So lost in thought, she hadn't noticed Melvin's and Patricia's voices coming down the hall. She was trapped.

With one swift move she swept the batch of photos back into the envelope, replaced it where she'd found it, and closed the drawer. Now, the only thing she could do would be to find a reasonable excuse to be in his office.

The cigar smoke. Of course. She had smelled it and thought something was smoldering in his office. She pulled the ashtray close to her and stood in front of it, preparing to be caught in the act.

The voices continued on down the hall to Karen's office. A cold sweat ran down her neck and throat. She scurried to the open door, and the few steps to Karen's office.

As she neared the open door, she heard Karen telling Melvin and Patricia that Kim had stepped out to go to the Ladies Room.

Kim walked through the doorway. "I'm back now. Thanks." She pushed the hair back from her forehead, wiping the beads of perspiration away with the action. Trying to sound as casual as possible, she said, "Hope I didn't keep you waiting."

"We jes' got back, anyways, missy. I think yer aunt enjoyed the ride." He put his arm across Patricia's back. "Tomorra I wanna take her out ta see where the 'coons and gators play. Them all like hidin' in the mangrove roots."

Kim felt the blood drain from her head. "Patricia and I have an appointment tomorrow, Melvin. Perhaps another time."

"That's right." Patricia nodded at Kim. "I did enjoy the ride, Melvin, and I thank you for your time spent but, after all, I'm here to be with my niece."

"Don' y'all worry, ladies. I kin git her after yer appointment. Mebbe take her out fer a bite ta eat. Now, you'd like thet, wouldn't ya ma'am?" He focused on Patricia.

"I'm sorry, Melvin, but Kim and I have some other matters to attend to after that." Patricia took a step away from Melvin. "Isn't that right, sweetheart?"

"Well, don' worry yer pretty li'll heads over it. I kin git Patricia day after tomorra. Gimme a extra day ta git ever'thin' planned out perfect-like, so's she'll be havin' a right great time." He turned to go. "Got me some special business ta 'tend ta anyways. I'll call an' let y'all know what time I'll be pickin' ya up, darlin'." He smiled, turned and disappeared out the door.

The three women stared at one another. "Is he always so persistent?" Kim said.

"Once he sets his mind to something," Karen said, settling back to her bookwork, "that's the way he is."

As soon as they left Karen's office, Kim turned to Patricia and said, "When you get in the car, Mom, make yourself comfortable. I have something to tell you that you may find bizarre and hard to believe."

Chapter 36

"Melvin never ceases to amaze me," Patricia said as they pulled into Gloria's garage. "He's rather a slick kind of person, don't you think, taking all those pictures of my sister on the QT? And I, for one, don't always know how to handle him." She looked at Kim before she stepped out of the Cruiser. "I wonder how Margaret coped with him, having to work around him every day ... or at least, part of most days."

"For one thing, Mom, don't forget that Margaret had a very different personality than yours. She probably wasn't about to put up with any of Melvin's guff, or whatever. I'm sure she didn't know anything about those pictures. Melvin was only fantasizing. He wouldn't have dared let Dad know what he was up to, or he would have been out of there in a heartbeat."

"Well, sweetheart, it isn't as if he did or said anything out of the way to me, but he just seems to make me uncomfortable with his over attentiveness."

"I know, Mom. He makes my skin crawl at times. But, he did handle the business for us when we needed him. I'm not sure how well, but that remains to be seen. We'll try to keep you out of his clutches, if possible." Kim broke into a broad grin. "I never thought I would have to safeguard my own mother from the likes of big, bad Melvin."

After dinner and after Kim related to Gloria the findings of the snap shots of Margaret in Melvin's office drawer, the three settled down to a relaxing evening of watching a movie on one of the premium television channels.

When Patricia started to yawn, Kim got up, turned to her and said, "I say we would be smart if we all got a little extra rest tonight by getting to bed at a decent hour. I, for one, have some odds and ends to take care of tomorrow and feel it best if I start out early. Mom, would you like to hang out with me while I do my errands, or would you prefer to stay home to do whatever you feel like doing?"

"I'll be fine here, sweetheart. Just do what you have to," Patricia said. "I can go with you another time. I still have my book to finish and some undies to hand wash."

"Right. If you need me, call my cell phone or Gloria's office. I probably won't be back 'til afternoon. Lounge around and don't worry about a thing. I'll fix supper when I get home."

Chapter 37

When Patricia got up in the morning, both girls were already gone. She made a fresh cup of coffee and took a doughnut from the fridge, sat down and read several articles in the local newspaper before taking her shower. Dressing in a short skirt and sleeveless top, she felt she could beat some of the heat without having the air on all day. She went to the living room, sat in a bright orange chintz covered recliner and picked up the book she'd brought with her on the plane.

She hadn't read more than two pages when the door bell rang. Putting down the book, she went to the front door. Max stood there casually dressed in teal green twill shorts and a sleeveless beige tee.

"Hope I'm not interrupting anything." He grinned broadly and removed a neat cotton baseball cap with the Pelican Bay Condo's logo embroidered across the front. The fragrance of a leather cologne drifted through the open door.

"You're only disturbing my doing nothing." Patricia moved back from the door. "Come in. The girls aren't here right now, but I could call Kim's cell phone if you need something."

Max stepped through the door. "I have the day off, and it was actually you I was hoping to see. Could I take you out for a little drive? Maybe we could both get reacquainted with Glade City and later stop for a latte or something? I've been feeling a bit lonely since I moved from Fort Myers. Kind of left most of my friends behind, but guess that's life when it calls for a change of scenery."

"That's a very thoughtful idea, Max, but I'd better call Kim to see if that fits with her plans. Come sit down while I try to reach her."

When Kim answered, Patricia told her about Max's offer.

"By all means, Mom. Go out and have a bit of fun. I'm sure Max will treat you well. So, please don't worry about me. Enjoy yourself 'cause I love you."

"Thanks, honey. Love you, too."

After she hung up, Patricia turned to Max. "Let me get my purse and sunglasses, and I'll be right back. Is there anything I can get you before we leave?"

"Just the pleasure of your company. Got any place in mind you'd like to see or revisit?"

"I haven't lived here since I graduated from high school, Max. Why don't you make the call? Your history is more recent than mine."

Max held the screen door open while Patricia locked up and then escorted her to his dark blue Ford pickup.

"It's not fancy, Patricia, but you've ridden in it before, so I know you're familiar with it."

"I'm just happy to be invited."

He helped her into the passenger seat. When he'd settled himself, he said, "How about if we take a tour of the place where I'm working, first?" He pointed to his cap.

"Sounds like a very good choice. But, that might be like a bus man's holiday for you," Patricia said.

"Not what you'd think. I enjoy the job and surroundings. They've given me a small, one- bedroom, furnished cottage as part of my salary. It's comfortable, and the whole complex is well done. I think you might enjoy it."

"Let's do it then." Nodding, she smiled.

Max headed toward the east end of Glade City.

Patricia watched the scenery unfold for several minutes, and then said, "Did you like Fort Myers, Max?"

"I did. I lived near the Caloosahatchee River. It's convenient to Fort Myers' Beach, the Gulf, Sanabel Island, good shopping. The airport is close to town, as you may remember. There are boats for hire that take you out on the Gulf for fishing or sunset/dinner excursions. No, I didn't have any problems with the area at all. Did you ever get out that way when you were growing up?"

"No. My father was very dedicated to making the business grow and prosper. My mother was a stay-at-home mom, the way Father wanted her to be. Margaret and I went to school here in town. We could attend functions, maybe have a friend over on occasion. Nothing too exciting. Since Mother didn't drive, it was up to the servants to take us places that required traveling farther than we could walk."

"I knew your father through his business, because I transferred to the Glade City police from Miami before he died." Max stopped at the gates of Pelican Bay Condos. "I saw him often on my beat. He was a good person."

A uniformed man at the Guard House waved them through. The condos were enveloped in a mass of greenery and color: assorted palms, bright red and purple Bougainvilleas, and other tropical plants. The buildings, a variety of pastel colored stuccoes with wrought iron steps and balconies, were draped in wisteria vines. A swimming pool, tennis and shuffleboard courts were part of the clubhouse area. Sidewalks wound around the buildings, adding to the charm.

"It must be quite a chore to work in a place like this," Patricia grinned, catching a sideways glimpse of Max.

"Yeah," he chuckled. "And real tough living in the old dump they provided for me." He pulled up in front of a small cottage and parked.

"It's compact, efficient, and affordable. Just what an old bachelor like me needs." He climbed out and went around to help Patricia. "Come on in, and I'll show you around the place. Takes almost a whole minute. And I have some lemonade I just made this morning."

He led her through the front door into a sunny living room where windows and skylights added hominess to the small interior.

"Everything is so bright and cheerful. I think you've done very well for yourself," Patricia said as she looked around the neatly furnished room.

"Have a look behind you. It's the Master, the one and only, bedroom. The bathroom with shower is the door to the left, and ahead of me is the large," he chuckled, "kitchenette where I can be chief chef and bottle washer."

"I like it very much, Max. I'm happy for you."

"Sit down, and I'll get you a drink."

"Anything I can do?" She stood by one end of the couch.

"No, just sit."

He moved to the kitchenette and reached into a cupboard to pull out two glasses, which he filled from a pitcher out of the fridge. Sitting down in a chair opposite Patricia, he said, "So, tell me, do you think you'll stay here in Glade City?"

Patricia sipped her drink and looked at Max. "I have an obligation to my bosses in Seattle, but it certainly is tempting to want to be with my only family. I'd have to relearn survival in the heat and humidity of the Everglades after Seattle's moderate climate, but anything is possible if one wants it badly enough. How about you, Max? Will you settle here, or is this only temporary?"

"I'm still thinking about that. This town's tiny by comparison to Fort Myers or Miami." He took a large swallow of lemonade. "I'm beginning to adjust, though. After all, I did live here some years ago after my transfer from Miami. And, I'm under much less pressure here. Easier traffic, and I'm enjoying my quarters, as well as my job."

"I feel that way, too. Traffic is getting bad in Seattle, and I still have to commute." She looked around the cheery room. "I truly love being with Kim. She's been a part of my life for a long time, and I know there's no way I'll ever get her back to Washington, not with her inheritance and her heart here in the Everglades." She finished her lemonade as Max tipped his glass for a last swallow.

"Shall we go? I'll show you where they're starting to build a new water park." He stood up and took the glass Patricia handed him.

"Sounds interesting," she said.

The rest of the morning slipped by quickly as Max escorted Patricia from place to place.

"How about some lunch? Are you getting hungry?" Max said, as they drove back through town.

"I don't want to keep you, Max. You've been very kind."

"You're not keeping me from anything. It's not often, I'm privileged to have such nice company."

"Thank you," Patricia smiled.

"Breakfast seems a long time ago," he said pulling up in front of the Flamingo Restaurant.

He got out and went around to Patricia's side. "I think you'll like this place."

"I'm thinking so already. Something smells awfully good."

As the two entered the restaurant, Chase in uniform beckoned them from a nearby booth. Max looked at Patricia. "It's up to you, Max. After all, you two are old friends."

"Of sorts," Max replied. "We worked together for a few years, and he *did* influence me to come back to Glade City, for which I'm very grateful." He put up his hand to acknowledge Chase, and led Patricia toward the booth.

"Nice to see you two out enjoying yourselves," Chase said, pushing away his empty plate. He picked up the ticket the waitress had left him and scooted out of the booth, beckoning for the two to sit down. "I wish I could stay and chat, but duty calls." He stepped aside for Patricia and Max to sit down. "Are you getting settled in okay, Max, or might you need some extra help?"

"I'm doing fine, thanks. Didn't have that much to do. Come on over some night this week when you have time off." They shook hands, and Chase left.

After Patricia and Max finished their lunches, Max asked if he could order Patricia a piece of Key Lime pie. "It just so happens, I hear it is the house specialty here. I'm anxious to try it."

"How could I resist? One of my favorites since my childhood days in South Florida."

After they finished their pie, Max pushed his empty plate to one side and concentrated on his guest. "Do you remember much about Glade City, Patricia?"

"Of course. I was born and raised here until I moved to Miami to go to college."

"That's when you lived with Margaret and Charles, right?"

"Yes. Not the best of times, though. I missed Mother and Father, and Miami's bustle was totally foreign to me after this little town." She hesitated before going on. "Living with Margaret had its drawbacks, but Charles was always congenial, hard working, and very much in love with my sister, in spite of how she … " She stopped abruptly and looked away, focusing on the luncheon crowd as people chatted and laughed, and waitresses scurried about the room carrying full trays. At last she turned her eyes back. "I'm sorry, Max. I shouldn't be discussing my family, my sister."

"I didn't mean to pry. I knew them both, remember? And whatever you say stays with me." Max leaned back against the support of the booth's corner, not appearing to Patricia to be in any hurry to leave.

His easy demeanor disconcerted her, but she managed to pull herself together. "I started to say, in spite of the way she treated Charles. He was always so good to her."

"They seemed like a well-matched couple," Max said. "When they lived in Miami, she had a job, so she must have been trying to help out. When I met up with them in Glade City some years later, she was working at the Boat Tours during the hours Kim was in school."

"I knew she worked with Charles after they moved to Glade City." Patricia played with her glass of iced tea. "I had no idea how she treated him then, since I was already living in Seattle. My only contact was an occasional phone call I would make to see if they were doing okay." Patricia swallowed the last of her drink and pushed the glass aside. "Margaret never bothered to call, but Charles phoned occasionally, when he had the time to report how the family was faring. He also sent pictures of Kim so I could keep up with my niece's growth. He was very proud of her."

"So Margaret never discussed her life in Glade City with you?"

"No. Like I said, Margaret never called to say anything. She basically ignored me like I didn't exist anymore, and I only knew whatever Charles was willing to share."

"I guess Kim is still bent on trying to find out who murdered her parents. She seems to be a very determined young lady. That whole thing was a terrible shock to the community. Rumors surfaced for years before and after I left Glade City, according to my old friends at the station. Do you know how she's doing on that score? Is she making any progress? Any clues she's been able to uncover?"

Patricia was silent for a moment before focusing directly into Max's eyes. "I don't pry into Kim's business, Max. If she feels like telling me something, I listen. Otherwise, I don't ask questions."

"Sorry, I didn't mean to sound nosy." He looked away momentarily, flushing slightly.

"Kim is a very nice young woman, and I'd like to see her fulfill her goal and settle that part of her life. I know how she feels about accomplishing that, because she and Gloria came to see me when I was still living in Ft. Myers. She was seeking any information I might have remembered. Anything at all concerning the investigations Chase and I handled that might give her extra insight into … Well, you probably know what I mean."

"I'm sorry, Max. I didn't know that. And yes, she is a very determined young lady. I just don't want to see her get into trouble over this, and I especially worry about her putting herself in any kind of danger."

Patricia picked up her purse from the seat next to her and looked at her watch. "I've had a very lovely time, Max, and I want to thank you for taking your day off to escort me around the area. But, I think I should be getting back."

"Please, Patricia. The pleasure is all mine … Really." He hesitated, eyes steady on the woman sitting across from him. "Actually, I have a confession to make. I wanted to become more acquainted with you. After all, I'm sure you'll probably be coming down here to live one of these days."

"I have no idea what the future holds for me, Max. I'm just taking it one day at a time."

Max rose to help her from the booth. "I hope we can do this again someday, soon."

"You home, Mom?" Kim called out as she brought in a bag of groceries and set it on the kitchen counter.

"I'm here, sweetheart." Patricia walked in from the living room and began to help Kim put things away.

"So, how was your date?"

"I wouldn't call it a date, honey, but it was pleasant." She paused. "Up until the last."

Kim folded the empty grocery bag and looked at her mother. "What do you mean by 'up until the last'? Did something happen?"

"Not really," Patricia put the frozen vegetables in the freezer and sat down at the dinette table. "Max is a very nice person, accommodating and easy to be around. He seems to be good company, but … "

"But what?" Kim took out two bottles of chilled water, set them down on the table, and took a seat next to Patricia.

"Nothing specific. I just had the feeling Max was trying to pry information out of me, concerning you."

"How so? What did he say?"

"He asked me how you were doing in finding clues on the murder of your parents. It gave me an awfully strange feeling inside, like he might have an ulterior motive."

"Oh, Mom. I wouldn't worry about Max. Since he and Chase were the two officers at the scene, it'd be natural for him to wonder if I had turned up anything they had overlooked. Right?" Kim reached over and patted the back of Patricia's hand. "Gloria and I spoke to Max in Fort Myers, and when we questioned him about the murder investigation he lost his composure. He said he was sorry his emotions slipped out, but the Alexanders had been friends of his. Later when we asked him if he'd ever married, he told us no, because he'd lost the love of his life. And we both know who that was, don't we? The thing is, Max doesn't know we know."

Patricia watched her bottle of water as she pushed it around in little circles on the table. Finally she raised her eyes to Kim's. "I guess you're probably right, sweetheart. I shouldn't be so suspicious. He *is* a gentleman and tries to make one feel comfortable."

Kim got up from the table and went to the fridge. "Gloria will be home shortly, Mom, so I'm going to start supper now. When we're finished eating, I'm going to run down to SawGrass for awhile. Karen's leaving some things out on her desk for me because Melvin's gone 'til tomorrow afternoon."

"Do you want me to go with you, honey?"

"No. Stay home, rest, and keep Gloria company. I won't be that long."

Chapter 38

Total quiet prevailed when Kim pulled into the SawGrass parking lot, her first time there after hours. Lights flooded the parking area and exterior of the building. She stepped out of the Cruiser, hit the lock button, and took out her key for the back door of the business. It felt strange being here with no one else around, but it afforded her the best opportunity to get things accomplished without interruptions and fear of alerting Melvin.

She entered the building, locking it behind her, and headed for Karen's office. True to her word, the secretary had left a pile of files and papers on one side of her desk. There were boxes on the floor marked by each year, plenty to keep her busy far longer than she had time for tonight. She put down her purse and keys and made herself comfortable in Karen's chair.

Sorting through all the files, she put the older ones on top to look at first. Karen had brought out everything from the time she had started working for Melvin, including Income Tax Returns.

She began with the first return after Melvin had taken over, and brought out the last one made by her father. The profits had dropped off considerably, but taking into account that the murders had had an adverse impact on the business, it didn't seem too far fetched. Perhaps the following year would show an improvement. It did, but only slightly and not what she had anticipated.

She continued her search, making detailed notes in her journal. Minutes turned into hours. She looked at her watch. Quarter past eleven. Her mother and Gloria would be wondering what happened to her. Time to close up shop. She would call Karen in the morning so she could put the files out of Melvin's sight in case he came in early.

As she picked up her purse and keys, she heard something in the hall. She froze, holding her breath, hoping what she thought she'd heard to have a simple explanation; perhaps a small animal, or better still, her imagination. She groped in her purse for her cell phone while she kept her eye on the opening to the hall. As her fingers came in contact with her phone, a shadow moved across the open door.

Chase walked through in uniform.

"My God, Chase. You frightened the living daylights out of me."

"I *am* sorry, Kim. I didn't mean to scare you. I'm on my beat and noticed your car in the parking lot. I wanted to make sure you were okay. You know, this time of night it just isn't safe for a young woman to be out alone."

"Well, I'm safe, as you can see." She stopped, turning questioning eyes on the young officer. "But, I locked the door behind me, so how did you get in?"

"Locked doors have never stopped me." He grinned.

She sank back into the chair where her purse had been. "I'm sure I must have sprouted my first gray hair, Chase. It's spooky enough being in this big, old building alone without a sudden fright like this."

"Again, I'm sorry, Kim. What can I do to make it up to you?"

Kim closed her eyes and shook her head. "Give me a few moments to catch my breath."

"What's going on, anyway?" He moved closer and sat down on the chair next to her.

"Just checking up on my esteemed employee, Melvin. I think he's been ... adjusting the books."

"I wouldn't trust that old SOB for any reason. You know, Kim, he's never had a particularly good reputation in town. If it weren't for the employees handling the shop and boat tours, he wouldn't have any business at all. He keeps out of the way while they take care of the the customers." He scooted his chair closer to Kim's. "Most folks never come into contact with that old weasel anyway. Word of mouth is that the business people in town hate his guts."

Kim stared at Chase. "I can believe that by the way he treated me when I first arrived. But how come I've never heard the rest?"

"Guess nobody thought it was their business to inform you."

"I know Karen just puts up with him to keep her job, although I've assured her she doesn't have to worry as long as I own the place." Kim began to relax, feeling safe with Chase's presence. "She's a good employee. I'd trust her with anything. In fact, she's capable of running the business on her own."

Chase reached over and put his arm across the back of Kim's chair. "Who knows? She may have to if you get fed up with him and find out he's been embezzling. Whatever happens Kim, know I'm in your corner. I'll do what it takes to protect you and the business."

"Thank you, Chase."

She stood, picked up her purse and journal, and turned off the overhead lights.

"Let's make sure you get off okay," he said, taking her arm as he escorted her to the rear entrance.

She locked up while Chase stood guard next to her. When she got out her car keys, he took them from her, walked her to the Cruiser, unlocked the driver's door, and held it open. "I'm going to follow you home, just to make certain you get there okay." He swung the keys back and forth before relinquishing them. "At this hour, the streets aren't safe for anyone alone."

"Thanks, Chase." She put one arm around him and patted him on the back. "I appreciate your concern. You *are* a good friend."

Patricia and Gloria were in the living room in their pajamas when Kim reached the house and hit the remote to open the garage door. Gloria jumped up from her recliner, skipping quickly down the hall just in time to see the police car pull away from the curb. "I was just about to call your cell phone, honey. You had us both worried sick, Kim." Her eyes shifted to the disappearing police vehicle. "Did you get stopped by the police? Is that why you're so late?"

"Sorry, Gloria, but I got so involved in discovering what Melvin's been up to, I couldn't quit. I think I have a good enough case against him to put him away for a long time."

"But, what about the police. What happened?" Gloria insisted.

"Let's go sit in the living room, and I'll tell you all about it." She hit the button to close the garage, and took Gloria's arm to lead her back to the living room.

Kim sat next to Patricia on the couch. "Forgive me, please, both of you, but I became so engrossed in what I was uncovering that I almost forgot about time. I'm sorry I had you both worried, but I'm convinced Melvin has been embezzling. And for a long time. Probably ever since he's been in charge.

"And, no, Gloria. I didn't get picked up by the police. That was Chase you saw leaving. He's on duty tonight and spotted my car in the parking lot at the Boat Tours. He came in to make sure nothing was wrong, and then, escorted me home."

Patricia put her arms around Kim. "Promise me you won't go back there anymore at night, Kim. It makes me nervous. Thank goodness Chase was looking out for you."

"Especially since you're evidently not doing it yourself," Gloria said with a hint of a smile.

"I needed to look over the books Karen left for me without Melvin knowing what I'm doing. I think I have most of the evidence I need now."

"I feel badly about this, sweetheart," Patricia started. "To think that I hired him to do the job, and he's been stealing from you all these years."

"Not your fault, Mom. Who would have guessed? Besides, what other choices did you have at the time? He was the most logical. And he knew the business." Kim yawned, got up and stretched. "As long as I'm forgiven, can we all get to bed? I'm feeling exhausted right now. It's been a long day."

"As long as you don't pull that trick again, honey." Gloria got up and went to Kim's side. "After all, I can't let anything happen to you now. Especially, after I just managed to get you back in my life again."

"I promise, Gloria."

Chapter 39

S tress had taken its toll. Kim felt drained and too keyed up to close her eyes and claim the much needed sleep. Her mind whirled in rhythm with her heartbeat as everything melded together out of focus. The past became the present while the present seemed a threat to her future. She tried to will herself to sleep, but it wasn't happening. Too much information fluttered about wanting to organize itself into neat little answers.

Foremost was Melvin with his game of milking the business for his own greed. What were his plans for the money he must have accumulated? How could he think he could get away with actual theft? Just because he'd stopped embezzling for the time being, did he think he could cover up what he'd already stolen? And just what is he trying to pull with Patricia? Even though her mother treated everyone fairly, Kim knew she would never consider Melvin as anymore than just hired personnel.

Then, there was Chase who had turned into a real friend; considerate, well mannered, uncommonly handsome, he continually displayed that he had her best interests at heart. She knew she could count on him if Melvin so much as showed an ounce of disrespect or hostility toward her. He knew the townspeople had it in for Melvin, and, knowing Chase, he would give her plenty of back up.

And, Brad. A friend plus much more. She had begun to realize what a blessing he is, and how she has grown to appreciate his quiet integrity and gentle nature. How lucky could she be to have Gloria, Brad, Chase, and now Patricia, her birth mother, in her corner of the world?

So many things to think about. Exciting things. Soon, the estate would begin to have a new look, a dream coming true for her. If the mystery of the murders would unravel, it would complete what she had set out to do.

Outside her bedroom window, the moon presented itself as a symbol of the night; a torch to guide the weary on a gentle path to slumber. It seemed so peaceful as moonbeams danced through her filmy curtains. Why then couldn't she find the sleep she needed so desperately?

Sliding on her slippers, she crept through the house to the back door and stepped into the night. A bit of a breeze lifted her bangs, moving them out of her eyes. Night whispers reminded her of when she was a girl staying with Grandfather on the estate before she started school; just the two of them sitting on the front porch on a summer evening, listening to the geckos chirp, the night birds talk, drinking in the beauty of the moment with its dancing stars and moon hanging low over the cypress and mangroves. Those were such wonderful days, she thought as she moved through the garden toward the back of Gloria's property. Grandfather had always taken time off from his business to spend with Kim when she was allowed to visit him. He seemed to have as much fun as his granddaughter.

With that thought in mind, she turned back to the house feeling as though sleep would not be far off. Moonlight and shadows played tricks with her mind, and the night whispers grew louder as unseen breezes rattled the palm fronds. For whatever reason, the garden no longer seemed as friendly as it had when she first came out. She had foolishly tossed caution to the wind and left the safety of the house. It was a stupid move, but sleeplessness had blocked natural respect for the unsecured area.

The house stood in darkness as it had when she left the doorstep a short while ago. Stars pierced the black sky giving the moon a respite from being the only light in the night. It all helped but she felt the space from her position in the garden to the back door to be three times the distance it had been when she left her safety zone.

A car creeping by on the street out front appeared to loiter. Her heart raced again when the engine cut. Realizing what a senseless thing she'd done, she hurried back, forcing herself not to break into a run. She entered the house and locked the door behind her as her foolishness surged through her body like stinging nettles.

Back in her bedroom, she slipped between the sheets again, thinking she had absolutely no reason to act like she had. She'd had one scare tonight. She didn't need anymore. On the other hand, there had never been any threat to her life at Gloria's. So why the worry now?

Her eyes drifted to the window where starlight kept the room from sliding into darkness. She watched the shadows making patterns through the curtains as gentle breezes moved the outside foliage back and forth. But one shadow remained stationary, not affected by air movement. It seemed to look like the figure of a man. But, she had to be mistaken, hadn't she, her imagination playing mind games with her again?

Chapter 40

Kim's cell phone rang at eight A.M. The cleaning company had a cancellation and could start this morning.

"I'm beginning to get so excited," she said to Gloria when she walked into the kitchen.

"I guess you well deserve to be, honey. It's been a long time coming." Gloria reached into the fridge and brought out a small coffee cake. "So, what happens now?"

"I'll meet them at the estate and leave the manager my extra key. They can open and close at their convenience, and I won't have to run back and forth to do it for them."

"Great idea." Gloria cut a piece of the cake for herself and pushed the rest toward Kim. "So, what do you think you might do about Melvin, the old poop?"

"First of all, I have to organize all my information and hire a lawyer. The thing is, I want to know where that money is before he's on to me."

"Well, that makes sense. The way his mind works, he could do a lot of things if he got suspicious of you. He could just plain disappear with the money, or even more scary, he might end up doing you bodily harm before you could present your case to the authorities."

"That's true, Gloria. I've considered that more than once. When I think about him having free reign over the whole business, I realize how naïve we were, and he knew it. Mom had no way of knowing. She'd never had anything to do with the boat tours when she lived here, and she trusted Melvin to take care of things." Kim cut a slice of the coffee cake and placed it on a plate Gloria had put out for her. "I don't think he's embezzling now. He probably realizes it's too risky. And that's probably why the profits seem to be much higher than they have been for years."

"Well, I just hope you can put that slime ball where he deserves to be ... in the big house."

"I'll get him, one way or another." Kim sucked in her breath.

"Why don't you ask Brad to help? I know he wouldn't put up with Melvin's bull for a minute."

"Not a word yet, please, Gloria. If Melvin suspects anything, I don't know what he might do. As you mentioned, he could be dangerous. Remember the argument he had with my dad just days before the murders?"

"You're probably right, Kim. We'll keep a lid on it for now." She finished the last bite of her slice of coffee cake, put her dishes in the sink, and grabbed her purse. "Bring Patricia in later and we'll have lunch. Gotta run. I'm expecting a client, and two important phone calls."

When Kim returned from meeting the cleaning company at the estate, she found Patricia at the dinette table, sipping a cup of coffee and reading the Sunday Seattle Post Intelligencer, which she had forwarded to her once a week.

"Any good news, or is it all the same old thing?" Kim laughed and slid onto the bench opposite Patricia.

"I thought it a good idea to keep abreast of the Seattle news for when I have to go back."

"Pleeeese don't mention leaving again, Mom. I need you to stay here."

"Don't worry, sweetheart. I have to go back one of these days to turn in my resignation and give the company time to replace me. Then there are my things I have to pack and ship, but I'll wait 'til the estate is ready for us. I can't put Gloria out. And storing them would be double handling." She beamed. "Anyway, things are starting to happen, right?"

"Knowing that, Mom, makes me feel a whole lot better. Now, get your purse. Gloria wants us to meet her for lunch. She and I need to discuss a real estate deal we've been working on. I'll tell you about it on the way downtown."

As she drove toward town, Kim told Patricia about Potter Denks and the mystery person interested in buying the estate.

"You're considering selling, Kim?"

"No way. I didn't say that. This Denks guy is a real estate agent in Miami who has a client interested in buying the estate at any cost without disclosing his identity. Denks is very persistent, no doubt because of the commission involved. Gloria and I decided to try and flush out that person by telling Denks that I would *consider* selling if I could meet with his client in person."

Patricia watched Kim as she threaded her way through the downtown noon traffic.

"And they fell for it?"

"No, but Denks asked us not to sell to anyone until he conferred with his client to see if he'd be willing to reveal his identity. We haven't heard back yet. But I've decided to ask half of the price in cash for a down payment in lieu of revealing his identity. I doubt if whoever it is can produce that much, in which case, he might be willing to come forward rather than lose his chance of acquiring the property. If he *is* able to produce the cash, I simply won't sign a contract. I want to find out who this interested party is and why the secrecy."

Kim pulled into the real estate office parking lot as Patricia was shaking her head. "It all seems so strange," she said. "What difference could it possibly make to allow you to meet with him in person, unless he has something illegal in mind?"

"Well, either the whole thing will blow over, or I'll find out who this anonymous buyer is."

Brad sat in Gloria's office when Kim and Patricia arrived.

Gloria looked up and beckoned them in. "More news, Kim. Do you remember Andy Wikstrom?"

Brad rose and offered Patricia his chair.

"Do I remember him? How could I forget? You were all over him at the Chamber dinner dance." Kim suppressed the smile that lurked behind her lips.

"Guess I was at that." Gloria giggled and went on. "He called a little while ago. The agency he works for is sponsoring a concert at The Blue Heron auditorium this Friday. He has tickets and has invited all of us, including Patricia, to go with him. He says he can use the company van, so he'll have plenty of room for everyone."

"I think I'd like that, Gloria." Kim turned to Patricia. "Wouldn't you?"

"It certainly would be refreshing."

"Then, I can call him back and tell him we've accepted his invitation." Gloria started to pick up her phone. "He wanted to know if we would mind meeting him here in the parking lot to save time."

"I don't think that's a problem," Kim answered.

The phone rang in Gloria's hand.

"Ms. Latham, this is Potter Denks regarding the three-story home."

"Yes, Mr. Denks."

"I'm very sorry, but my client still does not wish to reveal his identity at this time."

Gloria looked at Kim and mouthed the words, "Plan two?" to which Kim nodded.

"I'm sorry about that, Mr. Denks. Fortunately for your client, my seller has an alternate plan. She will accept half the money up front in lieu of a meeting in person, which is very generous on her part, I must say."

"And that would be … "

"One million, seven hundred and fifty thousand, Mr. Denks … cash."

A long pause followed Gloria's response.

Denks finally answered. "I'll have to get back to you, Ms. Latham. That's a mighty large sum to come up with in cash."

"It's a take-it-or-leave-it offer, Mr. Denks."

"I understand, Ms. Latham. I'll let you know as soon as I can." He hung up.

"As we were saying before our interruption," Gloria said, "Friday evening it is, then."

Friday couldn't come soon enough for Gloria and Kim. Excitement stirred the air all day; Gloria anxiously awaited seeing Andy again, and Kim looked forward to the diversion.

Gloria came home early to shower and change. Patricia and Kim had put together a vegetable salad with sliced ham on the side and were ready and waiting when Gloria walked in.

"I think I might be too excited to eat," she said as she tossed her purse on a chair in the living room where Kim and Patricia sat.

"Nonsense, Gloria. You are going to eat *something*. We haven't been slaving so you could skip taking care of your stomach. One would think this Andy Wikstrom was somebody special." Kim winked at Patricia.

"Yeah, right," Gloria commented. "It's not often a guy like Andy falls out of the sky and lands in your lap. You two go ahead and eat, and I'll shower. If you insist, I'll force myself to have a little salad when I'm finished."

When they were ready to go, Kim looked at Gloria and said, "I'm driving. I don't trust your judgment tonight considering the state *you're* in."

"Okay, okay. Enough said. I'll leave the driving to you."

The three women piled into Kim's car and were off to the real estate office. When they pulled into the parking area, Brad stood next to his car, dressed in beige summer slacks and a dark green silk shirt. Kim felt her heart skip a beat as a warm glow flowed up from her neck to her hairline.

Gloria hadn't missed a thing. "Talk about me, Miss Kim, you can't hide *that* look from your old buddy."

"Hush, Gloria. He'll hear you."

Both girls giggled while Patricia looked on. Moments later Andy pulled up in the company van, and it was Gloria's turn to blush.

After an enjoyable concert, Andy invited them to the Glade City Hotel for dessert and coffee. "A fitting climax for an unforgettable evening," he said as he took Gloria's arm and led the group to a round, damask-covered table near the center of the room. Soft light and a pianist playing romantic hits added to the mood.

As they sat, Andy leaned over and whispered something in Gloria's ear. She smiled and nodded. Andy said, "Okay, guys. Don't look at me that way. I just asked if she would go on a fishing cruise with me out of Naples on Sunday morning."

Kim smiled to herself, enjoying seeing her best friend so happy.

Everything had worked out perfectly, a lovely evening no one would forget. Andy pulled into the parking lot next to Brad's car. "I'll pick you up at 5 A.M. Sunday morning," he said, leaning over to kiss Gloria's cheek.

Brad leaped from the van and cried out, "What happened to my car?"

All four of his tires sat flat against the rims.

Kim, Patricia, Brad, and Andy all trouped out of the van, gathering around Brad's car to survey the damage. Even in the limited light of the parking lot, the extent of damage was more than obvious. Each tire had foot-long slashes.

Kim pulled out her cell phone. "I'm calling the police. They need to see this."

Ten minutes later a squad car pulled into the parking lot and headed toward the group. Chase got out and walked over to have a look. "Son of a bitch!" He knelt beside one of the rear tires, using his flashlight to get a better look. "What kind of an asshole would do a thing like this?" He stood up, dusted off the knees of his uniform and walked around the vehicle, carefully checking out each of the four tires. When he finished, he turned to Brad. "This is a first for this kind of crime in Glade City. I don't see it being a random act, either. I'd say somebody has it in for you, my friend, big time. Do you have any idea who might have done this? Who you might have made an enemy of?"

"I have no frigging idea." Brad ran his fingers through his hair, looking again at the destroyed tires. "Right now, I'm so pissed I can't even think straight. They could have targeted Kim's car, too, but didn't touch it, thank God."

Chase went to the squad car. He took out a notebook and started to write. "I'll get a report out and notify the Chief. I can arrange to have your car picked up in the morning, unless you want to pay premium to have it done tonight."

"I doubt if the lunatic who did this will be coming back this way again. If he wanted to do more damage, he would have done it when he slashed my tires." He put his hands on his hips, shaking his head back and forth. "Why? I can't think of anyone, anywhere who would benefit from doing this to me. And if it weren't a personal thing, what purpose could it accomplish?"

Chase nodded, put the notebook back in his squad, and turned to face Brad. "Have you had anyone work on your car lately?" Brad shook his head. "I'll have the station send out someone to check for finger prints. There could be some other than yours, depending on how careful or knowledgeable the perp is and if he has a record. Let's not overlook any possibilities."

Brad shook his head. "I still can't believe this. To my knowledge, we've never had trouble like this before."

Chase looked around at the group. "There's always a first time."

After Chase left, Gloria grabbed Brad's arm. "No sense in crying over spilled milk. It's a crappy shame such a great evening had to end like this, but we all have to shake our butts back to reality. Standing around like this isn't going to solve a thing. We'll get you home tonight, Brad, and I'll pick you up in the morning for work. You can make arrangements for a rental car from there." She turned back to Andy. "Everything turned out so perfect 'till this." Her eyes took in the mutilated tires. "But, I'll see you bright and early Sunday morning, Andy." As she reached over to give him a big squeeze, he pulled her in close to him, wrapping her in the safety of his embrace.

"Don't worry about all this, darlin'. We did have a perfect evening, and I'm sure the police will get on it. As long as there's been no bodily injury. That's the most important thing, right?" He leaned over and kissed her on the lips.

Chapter 41

Saturday morning, after Gloria had left to pick up Brad, Kim dialed Karen's private number at SawGrass. "Has Melvin gotten back yet?"

"Yes, he got back yesterday. Said he planned to stay here 'til late last evening 'cause he had some catching up to do."

"Oh." Kim didn't say anything for a moment. "Then, he was in town last night?"

"Right," Karen answered. "Any problem?"

"No, no. You have any idea what he was up to?"

"Not a clue, Kim. I was home enjoying my time away from Simon Legree." Karen was silent for a moment and then added, "He was acting a bit strange yesterday afternoon."

"How so?" Kim asked.

"I had to go out on the floor to straighten out some hours for one of the girls. When I passed Melvin's door, he must have just gotten a phone call, and you know how loud he talks." She gave a little chuckle and lowered her voice. "Well, all I heard was, 'Ah sho wish y'all could make yerself more forceful once in a while.'" She imitated Melvin's speech. "When I returned to my office, he was in his safe box in the closet. I couldn't see what he was doing, but it was obvious something had him excited."

"He hasn't been in yet this morning?"

"Haven't seen him, but that doesn't mean he's not around. He can be very sneaky, and I don't always trust him."

"That's all I wanted to know, Karen. Just checking, thanks." She hung up as Patricia walked into the kitchen.

"Did Gloria pick up Brad?" Patricia opened a cupboard and got out two cups. "I sure hope they find the person who slashed his tires."

"Gloria left about a half hour ago. Brad wanted her to take him directly to the car rental place, rather than calling them from the real estate office. He said his insurance should pay for most of the bill."

The tea kettle whistled and Kim got out two tea bags. "It's so nice out, Mom. Let's take our tea to the garden and catch some fresh air before it gets too humid."

"Let's." Patricia got out a small tray and placed the cups of tea and two blueberry scones on it. Kim got some napkins and held the door for her. "I enjoy listening to the mockingbirds and watching their antics. And sometimes it's just relaxing to sit and think."

"There is something mesmerizing about that," Kim said as she pulled two deck chairs close to a small table. "Mind if I ask what you think about?"

"The other day when you and Gloria were both gone, I started thinking about Max."

"Oh, oh. Sounds serious." Kim's eyes crinkled as she smiled and gave her mother a knowing look. "His good looks got to you, eh?"

"Not what you think, sweetheart." She sipped her tea and picked up one of the scones. "I must agree with you, though. He's very easy on the eyes, and I had a pleasant time with him, but … "

"But what?" Kim prompted.

"We talked a lot, nothing special at all, just pleasant, idle conversation. He seems too good to be true, if you know what I mean. I think about the fact that my sister and he were … "

"Mom, that was a long time ago. Margaret's gone. The affair is over. And he's probably a lonely person. You have to give him a break."

Patricia nodded. "You're right, Kim. What have you been thinking about?"

"Not anything so pleasant. I found out from Karen this morning that Melvin got back yesterday afternoon, and he stayed at SawGrass last evening, to catch up, he claimed."

Patricia studied her daughter. "And so?"

"You don't see the significance?"

"I'm not following you, sweetheart. He had some things to get done."

"And what *were* those things? It meant that he was in town last night, easy access to the real estate parking lot. And there's no love lost between Melvin and Brad."

As Patricia stared at Kim, her mouth turned into a little circle, and she whispered the word, "Oh."

The door bell rang and Kim ran inside to answer it.

Chase and Max stood at the front door. "I'm off duty 'til Tuesday, and Max has the weekend free. We thought we'd stop by to see if we could take you young ladies for a bit of a drive and then to lunch."

"Well, I … " Kim started and then hesitated. "... oh, come on in. We were just sitting out on the patio having tea and a scone, kind of resting after last night's … adventure."

The two men followed Kim through the kitchen and out back. "I made arrangements for Brad's car to be transported to Curly's Repair Shop," Chase said.

"I'm sure Brad will appreciate that," Kim said. "Company, Aunt Patricia," she said as she ushered the two to where Patricia sat. "Maybe you men could grab a couple chairs from the corner and bring them over. Could I offer you a cup of coffee and a blueberry scone?"

Max smiled. "I'd like that. Thanks, Kim. Good to see you again, Patricia."

"I'll start the coffee and get some scones while you two tell Patricia what you have in mind."

"Can I help?" Chase started to follow her back into the house.

"No, stay. I won't be long."

When she came back, Chase took the tray from her and set it on the table. "The Chief sent over one of our men to dust for fingerprints before Brad's car got picked up."

"Would that really do any good?" Kim questioned.

"Maybe. Maybe not. Just in case there are any foreign prints. They just have to test out around the wheel wells." Chase stirred some sugar in his coffee. "Enough about Brad's problems. What about you two coming along to brighten our day?"

"I planned on going to the estate today to see how the crew's getting along with the cleanup."

"Couldn't you do that later? Patricia was agreeable when we mentioned taking the two of you out."

"It's okay, Chase," Patricia said. "I'll go along with whatever Kim needs to do."

Max spoke up. "Why can't we take you both to the estate and then to lunch afterward? I wouldn't mind seeing what they're doing with the place."

Kim looked at Patricia. "Would that be all right with you, Aunt Patricia?"

"I don't see why not."

After they finished their pastries, and coffee and tea, the four set off in Max's pickup, with Kim and Chase taking the back seat of the cab.

When they pulled into the driveway of the estate, there were three pickups and a van parked inside the gate. "It looks like this company is pretty serious, Kim," Chase said.

"Three floors of mildew will take a gang to get that under control," she replied.

Max parked and they all stepped out.

"You've never been in the estate before, Max?" Kim led the way through the open front door.

"Ah … no. There was never a reason for me to be here." He fell in behind Patricia as they passed through the entryway and to the winding staircase where they heard the workmen above them. He remained quiet as Kim made her way toward the voices and obvious activity.

They found the whole crew on the third floor. "Slow going men?" Kim said as she came across the foreman and some of his workers back in one of the large rooms.

"Somewhat," he answered, "but once this gang adjusts, they move pretty fast. I think you'll be pleased with the results when it's completed."

"I'm sure I will be. Looks good, so far. I'll check in early next week, and please call if you need me for any reason."

When Kim seemed satisfied that the company's work would fulfill her requirements, she suggested that the four of them could leave.

"How about The Krab Shack?" Max said. "I haven't been there, but I've heard they have super sandwiches and salads."

"A good choice," Chase agreed. "So, let's go."

When they dropped the women back at Gloria's, Chase took Kim aside while Max walked Patricia to the door. "There's something I've been meaning to talk to you about, Kim, but it's not for everybody's ears."

She turned to face him. "You sound serious all of a sudden."

"It's a serious matter," he said.

"About what?"

"It concerns Melvin. Something you need to be aware of. Something the two of us can handle, together.

"Since I have the rest of the weekend off, would you have dinner with me tomorrow, and I can tell you about it then?" Chase's blue eyes embraced Kim's with their usual intensity.

She hesitated for a few moments. "Tomorrow Aunt Patricia, Brad and I are going to Big Cypress Swamp Preserve." Kim glanced up at the front porch where Max and Patricia seemed to be deep in conversation. "My aunt has been dying to spot some of the wild orchids they claim to have."

When Chase's eyes darkened, Kim felt the disappointment they registered. "I'm sorry, Chase. We could make it another day … soon."

He turned dead quiet, and she sensed his answer still in thought.

"This is critical, Kim. I don't know what could happen if the problem isn't solved without delay."

"I've already accepted Brad's invitation, Chase, and he doesn't get too many Sundays off. Could we make it Monday? Gloria will be home in the evening to keep my aunt company."

With an almost inaudible sigh, Chase said, "We'll make it Monday then. I'll pick you up at five."

Chapter 42

Sunday dawned clear and cooler than the past few weeks, a perfect day for the trip to Big Cypress. Brad arrived in his new rental vehicle to pick up the women. They were ready and looking forward to the outing, armed with sunscreen, bottled water, and wearing comfortable walking shoes.

"I've had my nose to the grindstone far too long," Brad said as he headed toward Tamiami Trail and the Preserve. "The dance a few weeks ago and the concert were enough to make me realize what I've been missing." Brown eyes twinkled when he glanced at Kim seated next to him.

He spoke over his shoulder to Patricia. "Did you ever visit the Preserve when you lived here?"

"No, my father wasn't too much on short trips like that, although I remember twice he took the family to Miami for a boat ride to the Bahamas and once to the Virgin Islands. Otherwise, he was always building the business." She giggled when she related how frightened her mother became when she and Margaret got too close to the railing of the excursion boat.

The day turned out to be just what Kim needed; time to forget all the pressures and worries. Brad, the perfect gentleman and tour guide, gave them a running account of what he'd learned about Big Cypress. As they moved along the elevated boardwalk, the Preserve provided an orchestrated background of the wildlife, each species carrying its own melody. One sound resonated above the rest, seemingly akin to a gigantic bullfrog.

Kim and Patricia both stopped, leaned against the railing, and listened intently in the direction of what they had heard.

"Know what that is, Ladies?" Brad came up behind Kim and put his arms around her.

"It sounds familiar, as though I should know, but it simply eludes me. However," she turned back to look Brad square in the eyes, "I have a distinct feeling you're going to tell me."

Brad chuckled and picked up Kim's arm, pointing it in a direction straight ahead of the area where they stood. "It's a big old bull Alligator grumbling at his mate. You won't see him, but you can bet your last dollar that he's back there behind all the brush and overgrowth waiting for his love life."

Kim giggled. "Just like some men. Never satisfied with all the good stuff the ladies do for them." She looked back in the direction Brad had pointed out. "I remember now. Grandfather and I hadn't had the occasion to actually experience it, but he described it quite well, now that I come to think about it. The Alligator grumble, he told me. That's exactly how he explained it. I guess I hadn't thought about it for a long time."

The experience of that day would not soon leave Kim's thoughts. Everything had been exhilarating and relaxing, a total turn around from what she'd been experiencing since she had gotten back to the Everglades, something of which she was sure she could handle a lot more.

Three tired but happy sightseers returned to Gloria's in the early hours of evening. Gloria had not yet returned.

"She should be one tired gal. She got up at the crack of dawn." Patricia fell into one of the easy chairs in the living room.

"But happy," Kim said. "Very happy." She took Brad's hand in hers and led him to the couch. "Come, relax. I'll fix us all a drink. Iced tea or something stronger? We have some nice wine in the fridg. And you stay where you are, Patricia. I've got this one covered," she said as her mother started to get up to help.

Brad relaxed into the comfort of the couch. "Surprise me," he said. "After that I'll need to get home. Tomorrow's going to be a busy day at the office, and I *have* to be there early."

"How about our cavorting little blonde?" Kim called back as she headed down the hall to the kitchen.

"I'm afraid I have to be the early bird tomorrow. She comes in at nine."

When Kim came back, she carried a tray with three glasses of a beautiful, sparkling liquid. "Asti Spumonte, for the conclusion to a delightful day."

"I'll drink to that." Brad smiled and took the offered glass.

When they finished their drinks, Kim walked Brad out to his car. "I had a marvelous day, Brad."

"Ditto for me. I look forward to a lot more of these days." He unlocked the car and turned to Kim. "Life feels awfully good right about now." He reached out, took her arm and pulled her close to him. "I want you in it more than you know." Wrapping his arms tightly about her, he bent and pressed his lips to hers, lingering there while Kim's body tingled with emotion.

And then he was gone, the taste of his mouth still clinging to hers.

When Gloria came home, she looked like she'd been in a windstorm. Her hair was tousled, her face flushed, and she had two white circles around her eyes where her sun glasses had been. "I know. I know. Don't say a word. I had a fantastic day, and I think I'm in love. No. I *know* I'm in love." She straightened her blouse and patted her hair down. "And it's not what it looks like. Andy is a perfect gentleman."

Kim struggled to restrain a grin that lay masked beneath a straight face. "I'm sure he is. There's iced tea, if you want it."

Gloria sighed and sank down on the couch next to Kim. "I'm too keyed up to be thirsty, now, thanks. Just thought I'd tell you something Andy dropped today. He said he got a call last week from the strangest guy, a Potter Denks from Miami."

"You're kidding me."

"Not at all," Gloria said.

"What did he want?"

"He wanted to know if Andy had any influence over the other real estate agents in town."

Kim studied her friend. "That's it?"

"Guess so. Said he had a client who wants a piece of property pretty bad, and the other office, us," she giggled, "is giving him a hard time."

"Oh, oh," was all Kim could say.

Kim snuggled beneath her covers but couldn't get her mind off Brad's kiss and what he'd said. Deep inside, she felt the same toward him but strained to keep her emotions in check. Wasn't it too soon to believe Brad had come this far in his feelings for her? Never-the-less, just the thought of it thrilled her to the core.

With this warm glow cuddling her like a blanket, sleep quickly overtook her.

But not for long.

Intruding into her tranquility the nightmare came, the one that periodically invaded her mind and body. The scene always replayed itself from where the intruder lingers outside her bedroom door and then bursts in to destroy things close to her heart. The most disturbing thought is: She knows him. He exists in her present life; she sees him frequently, and there's interaction between them. The vision of his face in the moonlight-filled bedroom of her youth does not unlock, but something in his actions feels familiar. It nudges her subconscious to uncover this mask of anonymity.

What is it she thinks she recognizes about this murderer? She's only seen a shadow person from between the cracks of the storage bay where she'd hidden that horrible night, not enough to identify him. But he has no way of knowing this, or does he? Is he in her life to find out if she *has* unearthed evidence that could incriminate him? And, what will he do to insure his obscurity? Or, quiet her if he feels she could put the finger on him?

In her mind she again considered the men in her life here in Glade City. Melvin was a creep, crafty, pushy, but she thinks too uneducated to have murdered and gotten away with it. He definitely was not neat enough to hide incriminating evidence. On the other hand, Chase was clever, intelligent, and trained law enforcement. He was Mr. Fastidious himself, the opposite of Melvin and more apt to have the know how and means at his disposal to carry off the murders and conceal or dispose of any damning information that could identify him. Max had been around, also a knowledgeable policeman, with more experience behind him than Chase. And now that she knew, in love with Margaret. Could she have rejected him after all their years of … ? Perhaps he couldn't take waiting any longer for her, or not seeing progress in their relationship. This could have sent him over the deep end. And last, but not least, there was Brad. She couldn't even begin to think of him as a suspect. He was too kind, too gentle. And, he had only been only a teenager at the time. No way could he have been involved with her mother and father enough to have killed them, as far as she could fathom.

When Kim walked into the kitchen at nine A.M., Patricia was sitting in the breakfast nook having coffee and a piece of toast.

"Gloria left, Mom?"

"About ten minutes ago, sweetheart. She said Brad should be there already. He had some important things to get done." She bit into a piece of toast and looked up at Kim."What have you on your agenda today? Anything special?"

"Nothing important at the moment. Sorry, I overslept. I had a restless night. I kept dreaming and waking up."

"That's not so good, sweetheart. I'm sure you needed the rest, though. We had a busy day yesterday." Patricia got up to refill her cup with coffee.

"My own fault, Mom." Kim slid into the booth opposite Patricia. "Will you be seeing Max again soon?"

Patricia grinned. "Why the sudden interest in Max and me?"

"Nothing special. I've been thinking about the different people I've met since being back, and how they've been impacting my life. The only other ones I knew before are the Ramon's, and they don't live around here anymore."

Patricia nodded and finished her last bite of toast. "All I can tell you now is that Max said outside of knowing Chase, he hasn't had a chance to meet many people except those who rent the condos for short periods." She paused, looked at Kim for a moment before continuing. "He asked if he could see me again, because he enjoys my company and thinks we have some interests in common."

"I want you to enjoy yourself while you're here, Mom. He might be very good for you. He's always seemed to be the gentleman." Kim hesitated, searching Patricia's face. "But, tread lightly. I'm still keeping my mind open for any unusual signs, thinking about all the people who were a part of Margaret's and my dad's lives."

Patricia stood in front of the dishwasher. She turned to face Kim. "You don't think Max could have had anything to do with ... ?"

"Mom, I don't think anything at the moment. But, as they say, still waters run deep."

The telephone rang and Kim went to pick it up. "Yes, Gloria. Mom and I were just having a bit of breakfast. What's up?"

"Have you heard anything from Brad?"

"Not this morning. It's still early, though. Why?"

"When I got here this morning, I had to unlock the office. He told me he'd be here by seven and it's almost ten." She sounded rattled. "I've been trying both his home phone and his cell phone for about forty-five minutes. There's no answer on either one."

"Maybe he had some kind of an emergency. Hold tight, and I'll drive to his place and see what I can find out."

"Thanks, Kim. I know I shouldn't be such a worry wart, but this is not like Brad at all. If I should hear from him, I'll call you on your cell." She hung up, and Kim hurried to get dressed.

Patricia followed her into the bedroom frowning. "Anything I can do, sweetheart?"

"Would you like to come with me?" Kim pulled off her pajamas and slipped on shorts and a top. "I'm going to see if I can find out where Brad is."

Chapter 43

Patricia and Kim pulled up to the apartment building where Brad lived. A janitor and the manager were talking in the entryway. Kim parked, got out and went up to the manager. "I'm looking for Brad Kimbal, Sir? Would you have any idea where he might be?"

"If he's not in his apartment, I have no idea, Miss. I haven't seen him since yesterday morning when he said he was off to Cyprus Swamp."

Kim studied the manager for a moment. Then she said, "Sir, would you be able to let me into his apartment? He's not answering either his home or cell phone, and I'm worried something might be wrong."

"I can do that, but I'll have to go in with you. For safety reasons."

They rode an elevator to the second floor. As they approached Brad's apartment, the manager took out a ring of keys and pounded first on the door, then, after waiting for several minutes, unlocked it. Pushing gently, he stepped in ahead of Kim and called out, "Mr. Kimbal, are you here? Anybody home?"

Dead silence surrounded them. He beckoned to Kim. "Look around. Try the bedroom first. I'll go through the living room and kitchen."

Minutes later they met back in the living room. "There's no sign of him there," the manager said. "You have any luck?"

"Nothing in the bedroom or the bathroom, but now I'm really worried. His bed hasn't been slept in."

"No place else where he might have bunked up?"

"No, I'm positive of that. This whole thing isn't like Brad at all. He told us last night he had to be in his office early this morning."

"And he didn't sleep there?"

"No. My friend who works with him is there now. She's the one who called me."

"I'd call the police if I were you, Miss."

Kim thanked the manager, and they headed back outside.

When she got back to the Cruiser, Patricia stood by the side of the car. "I'm so concerned, sweetheart. Did you find out anything?"

"Nothing. Let's go to the office with Gloria. We'll call the police from there."

Kim's cell phone rang as they were getting into the car.

"The police station just rang." Gloria's voice quivered. "Some people driving on the highway called to report a car off the road, partially in the swamp. When the police arrived, they found Brad, head slumped over the steering wheel, unconscious." She uttered a little sob. "Kim, they've taken him to the hospital."

"Mom and I are on our way to get you right now. Don't do anything."

Gloria stood outside the office building when Kim and Patricia arrived. She'd placed a sign on the door, "Closed for Emergency." Kim pulled up to her and Gloria got in the back seat. "I figured we would be going directly to the hospital." Her eyes were moist with unshed tears.

"You bet, Gloria." Kim circled and headed for the hospital. " I've been trying to imagine what happened. Was it an accident, or did someone deliberately force him off the road?"

Gloria wiped at her eyes. "The police said the back end of Brad's car had a good-sized dent embedded with bits of dark blue paint. Whoever did that had the right leverage and push to force him over the edge of the retaining wall and partially into the swamp. The airbags had been disabled. What stopped the car from completely going into the water was a large cypress knee. And this happening only two days after Brad's tires were destroyed. Someone has him targeted, and I'm scared."

"No more than I am, Glo. Someone's playing dirty, and I'm afraid of what it could lead to." She pulled into the hospital's emergency parking area. "Who knows what the motive could be or if any of the rest of us are on the menu?"

The three women got out and headed to the door.

"I'm sorry. Mr. Kimbal's in ICU. No visitors, unless you're next of kin." The woman at the desk looked at her papers and then back at the three women.

"Well, I'm Mr. Kimbal's sister," Gloria said, "and I want to see him."

"May I see some ID, please?"

Gloria handed over her driver's license.

"The last name isn't the same." The woman returned the license.

"That's my married name, ma'am. Now, may we please speak to someone with some authority?" Gloria never broke eye contact with the attendant.

The woman glowered at her, not moving.

Just then, Chase walked through the door out of uniform and came up to their sides. "Is there a problem here, ladies? You all look like … something's wrong."

"Try asking the chief here," Gloria spat. "She tells me only next of kin are allowed, and I've informed her that Brad's my brother."

He turned to the desk nurse in charge. "Miss, I'm with the Glade City police." He took out his ID and handed it over. "I wish to speak to the head nurse, Ms. Constantine. NOW. These people are my friends, and I insist on getting answers for them."

"Yes, Officer." The attendant got up, straightened her skirt, and stalked off down the corridor.

The three women turned to look at Chase. "How did you know about Brad?" Kim said.

"One of my friends at the station called to tell me. He was one of the two officers who investigated the accident. He said he couldn't tell me any more than what the police already told Gloria."

A heavyset woman appeared in the hall, heading for the small group. She walked directly toward Chase. "Good Morning, Officer Grey. What can I do for you?"

"We would appreciate information regarding Mr. Brad Kimbal who was brought in by ambulance earlier this morning, Ms. Constantine."

"The staff is working on him right now, Officer. He's been in a coma since they found him. If there should be any change, we'll be happy to report it to his sister if she'll leave us a phone number."

Chase looked over at Gloria. "Could you do that, Ms. Latham?"

Gloria nodded and reached into her purse. "Could we wait here, Miss?" She handed the woman a card containing her phone numbers. "We're all concerned about him."

"Right now, there's nothing you can do for him. It's just a matter of time. Go home, relax, and leave him to our staff." She smiled and reached out to shake Chase's hand. "Nice seeing you again, Officer Grey. Sorry it had to be under these circumstances." She turned and strode back the way she'd come.

"I don't understand it at all." Kim's eyes flooded with tears.

Chase turned to Kim and put his arms around her. "Don't worry, sugar. He'll be okay. I have some pull at the hospital, so I'll check on him myself." He released his grip, keeping one arm around her waist while he steered her toward the exit, adding, "Come on, folks. No sense in hanging around here."

When they were outside, Chase walked them over to Kim's car. "How about if I come back for you about mid-afternoon, Kim, if our dinner date is still on?" When Kim started to object, Chase continued. "I know none of us wants to think about leaving Brad at this point, but here's how I see it. Our being here isn't going to make him any better, and the hospital has promised to call if there's any change. I still have something to discuss with you concerning SawGrass, so if I may pick you up, we can come back here and check on Brad before we go to eat. Perhaps by then, they'll allow you in to see him. If they give us a hard time, I'll apply a little pressure on Ms. Constantine."

The three women stood outside the car, not offering to get in while Chase spoke. Kim looked first at Gloria and then her mother. "What do you think, Gloria? Does that sound reasonable?" Then, turning to Chase, she said, "Thanks for your help, Chase. I understand you two have known each other for a long time. But Brad is very special to all of us."

Patricia took Kim's hand. "Sweetheart, you need to follow your heart. Do what *you* feel is right. Maybe Chase can help. He has so far, but this should be your decision. We all understand what Brad means to you."

"So, I can count on picking you up this afternoon, Kim?" Chase grasped her arm.

Freeing herself gently from his hold, Kim said, "I guess it's okay. I need to find out those things from you, and Brad doesn't need my help at this point. I do want to see him, though."

Chase arrived at Gloria's place at four to pick up Kim. As usual, he was dressed like a fashion model; impeccably attired in an Italian suit and shoes, a silk shirt and gold neck chain. Everything was coordinated. Kim had changed from her morning clothes to a simple skirt and blouse, suitable for a hospital visit, she thought, but somehow she felt unnecessarily outdone.

On the way into town, she turned to Chase. "Something's been bothering me about what you said earlier, Chase."

He smiled. "What's that, sugar?"

"You said you could exert some kind of pressure on Ms. Constantine because of a favor. What kind of pressure, Chase?" She observed his face as he drove.

" Let's just say, she needed back up for something that went on at the hospital, and I supplied that support. She was grateful."

Kim shook her head. "You always seem to have the right answers, Chase. Just as long as that's all there is to it."

"Nothing serious at all." He pulled into the hospital parking lot, found a spot close to the emergency entrance and got out to help Kim.

When they reached the desk, another woman greeted them.

"We'd like some information on Brad Kimbal."

"I'm sorry, but you'll have to speak to the head nurse."

"Then I need to see Ms. Constantine, please."

"Are you Officer Grey?" She looked down at a piece of paper on her desk.

"Yes, ma'am." He nodded.

"She said to tell you that Mr. Kimbal is still unconscious, but you and your party may look through the window for a few moments. The nurse will open the curtain for you."

"Thank you, ma'am."

"He looks so peaceful lying there," Kim said after they left the hospital. "It's just like he's sleeping." She wiped the corners of her eyes as they teared up.

"I'm telling you, sugar, he'll pull out of it. He'll be fine, you'll see."

When they were seated in the restaurant and had ordered, Kim focused on her companion. "Now, tell me, Chase, what is it that's so important?"

"Melvin has embezzled about $200,000 from the business, and I have the proof."

Chapter 44

Kim searched Chase's face. "I know he's been juggling funds, but how did you find out, and most importantly, how did you find out how much?"

"Can't tell you right now, sugar. You'll just have to trust me. What I've told you is fact. I also know where the money is."

"You *know* where it is? Is it safe? Is it possible to get it back? $200,000 is a lot of embezzling."

"For now the money's safe. And there's more to all this than you think. Things you probably won't believe."

"You *are* going to tell me, though, aren't you?"

Chase's eyes glowed. "You'll find out when the time's right."

Kim studied him for several moments. "It seems to me, Chase, you get some sort of excitement from all this. Right?"

"I'm excited because we're on the path to justice. I want to catch that SOB red-handed." He took Kim's hand. "What's that crook been doing with all the cash he's stolen from your business? He doesn't live like a man with money to throw around. Look at his clothes. His pickup is old. He lives in a cheap apartment, doesn't date or spend anything on women. Surprise is no one's figured him out yet. I'm going to nail this guy to the cross, and put the rotten swindler away where he belongs."

"Hold on, Chase. I've gathered enough evidence to do just that myself, and I don't intend to sit back and let him get away with it."

The waiter brought their order, and the two sat in silence, as they ate.

After Chase finished his soup, he concentrated on Kim. "I don't want you to do anything to Melvin on your own, do you understand me, Kim? He's dangerous. Not to be taken lightly."

She swallowed a bite of salad before replying. "The only thing I'm planning is perfectly legal: All my evidence will be placed in the hands of a good lawyer."

"And in the meantime, should he suspect you're on to him, what do you think he'll do? He's not going to wait for you to incriminate him. He'll try to stop you, something I don't even want to think about." He dug into a thick, rare rib eye steak like a man on a mission, while Kim dabbled at her Shrimp Alfredo.

"I've given a lot of thought to this, and it's my belief there's no way for him to find out what I'm doing. How could he? Karen won't say anything. None of the other employees knows what's been going on."

"Don't be so sure."

She looked up, eyes wide. "What else can I do, Chase? He belongs in prison for what he's done. I have to stop him."

"No, you don't." He took a mouthful of baked potato, not looking up.

"But … "

"No buts. I have a plan."

"No, Chase. This is my problem, not yours."

"I'm making it mine, sugar. You're special to me, and I'm not going to let anything happen to you or what is rightfully yours."

She opened her mouth to say something, but the words solidified in her throat. Finally, she picked up her fork and swallowed her unsaid thoughts.

When Chase pulled into the driveway, Gloria came running out of the door. Tears streamed down her cheeks.

"Honey, Brad took a turn for the worse. They have him on life support."

Kim cried out, "Oh, no." Ignoring Chase as he opened the car door for her, Kim shot past him to embrace Gloria. "Let's go to the hospital right now."

"They're not going to allow you in, girls." Chase walked up behind them and placed his hands on their shoulders. "Stay here. Let me see what I can do. I'll call you if I can get you in."

The two young women stood, arms around each other, until Chase shook them.

"Come on, girls, get a hold of yourselves. There's nothing you can do at the moment, so go inside and keep telling yourselves Brad will be okay." After he steered them toward the porch and open front door, he left.

In the house, they found Patricia on the phone. "I'll let them know, Max. Thanks for your concern." She hung up and turned toward Kim and Gloria. "He just found out about Brad and wanted to know if there's anything he can do. I told him to say some extra prayers, and call back later."

Following a restless night, Kim dragged herself into the kitchen after morning light had crept into her bedroom. Patricia stood in front of the range. "I thought you girls could use a break. Would you check on Gloria for me, Kim? Breakfast's just about ready."

Before Kim had a chance to respond, Gloria walked through the door dressed and ready for work. "I decided moping around won't help anyone, least of all Brad. I'm going to open the office this morning and try to get some things done. But before I do that, I'm going to the hospital and find out what's happening and why we haven't heard a word." She took the cup of coffee Patricia offered her and sat down in the breakfast nook. "Someone needs to do a little shaking up at that place. They should understand how worried we are and call us."

"I'll follow you in and we'll do a little shaking up together. If Brad is … If nothing more is wrong, I'll go on to SawGrass." Kim helped Patricia dish up sausage and eggs. "I've been hoping Chase would call with some news." She sat down next to Gloria and took a forkful of scrambled egg.

The phone rang and Gloria jumped to answer it. "We've been on pins and needles, Chase. What's going on?" Gloria looked from Kim to Patricia. "That sounds more positive than last night. Okay, thanks. I'll tell the girls." She hung up. "Chase says that Brad seems to be responding to life support, and the staff is hopeful that it can be removed later today. We can call after three to see if they'll allow us in for a few minutes."

"Thank you, Lord," Kim whispered.

Kim walked into Karen's empty office, turned and went next door to Melvin's. It, too, was vacant. Moving along to the main room, she found Karen helping some of the clerks with an overload of customers.

Karen waved when she saw Kim heading toward her. "With you in a minute," she called out across the room.

When they met, Kim said, "Where's Melvin?"

"I haven't seen him since Friday. It's not unusual for him to take off a day here and there, but … " She rolled her eyes. "He almost always works Sundays, so I can have time at home. He didn't show then, either. One of the girls called me on her cell phone from here. Said the place was still locked up at 8 A.M. when she tried to get in." She led Kim back to her office and offered her a chair.

"He's pretty much a workaholic. I hate to say this, but I *am* a little concerned, especially after I got no response from his phones. I called the police a while ago to see if they had any information. An officer said he'd have someone check out Melvin's apartment and let me know. I planned to call you."

"He didn't even leave you a note?"

"Not a word."

Kim sat down on the offered chair. "That's odd." She rubbed her upper lip with her index finger. "It's like deja vu … with Brad."

She toyed with a pencil on Karen's desk. "My friend, Brad Kimbal, is in the hospital on a ventilator. Monday he didn't show up for work or respond to his cell or home phone. Some motorists discovered his rental car partly in the swamp with Brad unconscious behind the wheel. They notified the police, who had him taken to the hospital."

"I'm so sorry about your friend, Kim. Does anyone know what happened?"

"The police are investigating." She dabbed a tear from the corner of an eye.

"Well, I'm not a Melvin Thomas fan by any means," Karen said, "but I wouldn't want anything to happen to him … " She tried to suppress a smile. "At least, not 'til we find a replacement."

"I wouldn't worry about Melvin, Karen. He's too ornery to have anything bad happen to him. When he does show up, he might just wish he'd stayed missing."

Karen studied Kim. "You've found out more about what he's doing with the business funds?"

"I believe so. I know you won't say a word, so as soon as I have anything concrete, I'll let you know. When the time comes, would you consider a promotion to manager?"

"I don't know what to say, except YES, I'd love to." Karen's eyes seemed to catch a misplaced ray of sunshine. "And without Melvin being around, it would be a real pleasure."

"It's settled then. Now, tell me where you can use my help the most, and I'll dig in."

"How are you doing, honey?" Gloria's voice came through Kim's cell phone when she answered.

"Keeping busy, working at the Boat Tours right now. What about you?"

"Hangin' in there. I'll call the hospital at three, and if they don't give me some answers, I'm going there and shake something out of them. They should at least have the decency to update us."

"Good for you. If you want me to come along, let me know. It's so hard waiting around not knowing."

"You said you were *working* at the Boat Tours. What do you mean?"

"Melvin hasn't shown up in the past few days, leaving Karen in a lurch." Kim sighed audibly. "She's a dedicated employee, but I can't expect her to run the place on her own."

"Where on earth is he? Maybe he's absconded with the stolen loot and doesn't plan to return, period."

"I don't think so, Gloria. Chase tells me he knows where the money is. It's safe for now. Since I've been busy here, my mind's been working overtime. Lots of things to consider. Karen says she called the police earlier. They'll check things out and let her know what they find."

"What about Chase? Since he seems to know so much, why hasn't he offered to help you?"

"He has. He says he has a plan, which sounds to me like he either knows what Melvin's up to or knows more than we do. I told him this is my problem, not his or anyone else's. Besides, as a member of the police force, I think Chase has an obligation to inform his captain of what he knows."

"Evidently, Chase doesn't think that way," Gloria said.

Chapter 45

Before Kim left SawGrass, Gloria called again. "Meet me at the hospital. They're going to let us in to see Brad. The head nurse told me they've been able to take him off life support because he's breathing on his own. Best of all, he's blinked a few times."

"Great news. I'm on my way."

With Max and Patricia by her side, Gloria met Kim at the front entrance of the hospital. "He's still unconscious, but they want us to talk to him to see if he responds to our voices."

"Max wanted to visit him, too, Kim." Patricia's eyes sparkled in the setting sunlight. "He was kind enough to pick me up."

"Let's go, then." Gloria reached for Kim's arm. "See if we can get a response from him."

As they moved down the hall to ICU, Patricia came alongside of Kim and said, "Has anyone heard from Melvin yet?"

"Nothing. Karen received a call from the police station. They told her that no one has seen Melvin at or around his apartment since the weekend. I'm sure he'll show soon, though." She gave a little giggle. "You know they say a bad penny always turns up."

"For me, it's been a relief, not having to worry about hurting Melvin's feelings or avoiding him."

Kim leaned toward Patricia and whispered, "For goodness sake, Mom, don't worry about hurting Melvin's feelings. Not after what he's been doing to us with the business. If I have anything to say about it, he'll be heading to jail." She looked ahead where Max and Gloria were engrossed in conversation.

Gloria stopped, turned around and whispered, "Hurry up, you two. You're holding up the parade. We're almost there."

The nurse in Brad's room came out as the four reached the unit. She put up her hand, palm out. "One at a time, please. We still need to keep him quiet."

Patricia moved in front of the ICU window. "Max and I can see from here. If Brad responds to anything, I think it would be to your voice, Gloria, or Kim's."

Brad's nurse said, "Which one of you is Mr. Kimbal's sister?"

Gloria winked at Kim and stepped forward. "That would be me."

Kim, Patricia and Max watched through the glass partition while the nurse stepped aside and allowed Gloria to enter.

Equipment dominated Brad's immediate space. There were feeding tubes, oxygen tubes, monitoring apparatus, as well as bags hanging over one side of the bed for draining purposes. An overwhelming feeling of apprehension struck Kim as she watched Gloria place her hand on Brad's arm and lean closer to his face. Her lips moved as she spoke to him and gently rubbed his forearm. Despite the five minutes the nurse permitted Gloria in the room, Brad showed no response.

Surely something should be changing for the better, Kim thought. Why can't he blink again? Just give us a sign he understands we've come to support him? It's been over thirty-six hours.

She touched her forehead with the back of her hand where beads of perspiration had accumulated. Whispering a prayer, she said, "Please, dear Lord, help Brad. He's a good person and doesn't deserve this."

"You may go in now, Miss Alexander." The nurse stood at the door as Gloria passed through.

Kim made her way to Brad's side and bent close to his face. "Please, Brad, show us you know we're here for you." She touched his forehead, pushing a wisp of curl back from his lashes.

"Can you open your eyes, blink? Say a word, anything? We're all so worried about you." She felt his face, his lips with her finger tips and put one hand over his. "I won't have anything happen to you now that I've finally found you. I'll do anything it takes to see that you come out of this."

Straightening up, she picked up the hand she had covered with her own, rubbing it gently to stimulate circulation. Twitching slightly, he shuddered and took a deep, audible breath. Kim froze with the unexpected movement, her eyes fixed on his face, awaiting the slightest indication of consciousness. As she watched, his lips parted, seeming to form a word. Excited, she turned toward the glass, smiling for the visitors outside to see.

The nurse entered the room. "You need to leave now, Miss Alexander. If all goes well, you're welcome to come back tomorrow."

"Please, may I stay a few minutes more? I just saw him move."

"Two minutes then, ma'am. I'm very happy there's been some reaction. It's a good sign, but he may not do anything again for hours. For now, he needs rest."

Kim couldn't keep the smile from her lips when she left ICU to be with the others. " I know he was trying to speak to me."

"He's going to come out of it, Kim. I feel it in my bones." Gloria gave her friend a warm hug. "We'll come back tomorrow, for sure."

She let go of Kim and started to lead the others to the hospital exit when her cell phone rang. "Yes. Oh, Andy, how did you find out? The grapevine, eh? We think he just tried to respond to Kim. At least, it's encouraging." She listened quietly for several minutes. "We'll be coming back here tomorrow afternoon. I don't know if they'll let you in his room, but I'd love to have you here … for moral support." She smiled as the four of them walked through the corridor and out to the parking lot. "Meet me at the office after work tomorrow. We'll pop over to the hospital, and then I want you to stay for supper. I'll cook."

The following morning, Kim got ready to help Karen at the Boat Tours. Patricia offered her assistance, as well. "I actually miss working," she said.

"I'm happy to have your company, Mom."

By the time they arrived there were plenty of customers. Melvin still hadn't made an appearance. All three women were kept busy most of the day, until Kim and Patricia felt they could leave for the hospital without abandoning Karen.

Brad appeared to be about the same with the exception he had moved slightly several times. A positive sign, the nurse reassured them.

The interlude with Andy at supper lightened the atmosphere. He seemed to have a way of putting everyone at ease. "From what I could see through the window, I think Brad looked pretty good this afternoon, not at all what I expected. Seemed to me he was about ready to get out of that hospital bed and come back with us for some *good* food." He put his hand over Gloria's as they sat at the dinner table. "I'd be willing to bet he'll be free of all those wires and tubes within a day or two."

"We're planning on it." Gloria got up and went into the kitchen. She came back with four bowls of chocolate mousse on a tray, which she distributed around the table.

Before he left, Andy asked Gloria if she had heard any more from that strange Mr. Potter Denks.

"He did call to make sure I hadn't sold the property. He said his client was to bring him the cash, but he's still waiting. Denks promised to call as soon as this client arrived with the funds in hand. Personally, I feel the so-called mystery guy probably couldn't come up with the bucks."

Gloria walked Andy outside to his car. When she didn't return immediately, Kim looked at her mother who sat on the couch thumbing through a magazine. "I believe love is in the air, Mom. What do you think?"

Patricia looked up from her reading and smiled without saying a word.

Chapter 46

K im and Patricia arrived at the Boat Tours the following morning along with a light rain. "If this continues," Karen told them upon their appearance in her office, "the business will be sparse, probably only people who want to look over the gift shop items and check out the alligator park. No sense in you gals sticking around for nothing. The other women and I can handle this with no problem."

"There are some things I've been wanting to show my aunt in Melvin's office, Karen. I may as well do that before we leave. And don't worry if Melvin should come back. I'll tell him we're trying to do his job since he hasn't even bothered to call." With that announcement, she took Patricia's arm and led her back into Melvin's office.

"Remember the pictures I told you about, Mom? The ones of Margaret that Melvin had hidden away in a bottom drawer of his desk?" Patricia nodded. "Well, now is a good opportunity to show you without Melvin being around."

Kim sat Patricia down at one side of Melvin's desk while she fished for the envelope in the bottom drawer. She found it where she'd left it, pulled it out, and spread the contents on top of the desk for her mother to view.

Patricia examined the pictures one at a time, the expression on her face growing somber. "My sister. By all appearances, she knew nothing about anyone taking these snaps, especially this one." She held up the one of Margaret sunbathing on the back lawn on a blanket. "Is Melvin some kind of pervert?" She shook her head back and forth. "I know Margaret would have never allowed anything like this. She might have done some uncalled-for things in her day, but posing nude … never, never. That was not her way."

The pause that followed told Kim that Patricia was as puzzled as she.

"I don't know what to say, sweetheart. I knew my sister, and she wouldn't have looked twice at Melvin had he not been on their payroll. More than likely she would have been repulsed by him."

Kim sat quietly studying Patricia and then the pictures. "There are so many things about Melvin that seem to be coming to light lately. My opinion is that he was obsessed with Margaret, stalked her, maybe even propositioned her. She would have told him off or threatened to expose him to my father. That could have angered him deeply. The thought of how she treated him could have festered until it drove him to desperation. I'm thinking he might have gone to the house to have it out with her late one evening when my father was to have been out of town overnight. If and when Melvin reached the house, he may have entered with duplicate keys he had made from those that had been left at the business. He more than likely knew some of their routines and a little about the estate from what he overheard at work." Kim fingered the photos, started to put them back in the envelope she'd found them in. "He could have gone upstairs to where he figured the master bedroom was located, thinking he could overcome Margaret, possibly rape her or try to seduce her in some way. In his mind, he probably had no idea that she would have turned him away. Mainly because he just doesn't perceive rejection at all. Unfortunate for him, he finds my father home ahead of schedule, both of them in bed asleep. Too late to try and back out now since he probably awakened them, Melvin still has an advantage over them. They are in bed and probably not fully aware of what's going on. He's afraid of going to jail for trespassing, so it wouldn't be hard to visualize Melvin with his brute strength taking out his knife and … . " Kim looked hard at Patricia. "After all, the authorities will no doubt blame it on the prowler or prowlers who have been reported in the past."

"Oh, my God, Kim. You don't really think we've been living and working around a murderer?"

"That's exactly what I've been thinking. When Melvin escorted us to the estate, he pulled a gun on Chase. And I've seen him with a hunting knife belted around his waist. He thinks nothing of arming himself, and not secretly.

"It hasn't been just that one thing that's made me consider the fact that Melvin could be the one responsible for my parents' murders. Stealing money from the business has raised the biggest red flag. Then Brad had his tires slashed, and we found Melvin had been in town 'working' late at SawGrass. Could those tires have been cut with the same knife used on my parents? Well, *now where* is Melvin *and* the money?"

"So, now what do we do?" Patricia sat back in her chair and studied her daughter.

"That's what I've been trying to decide. I believe Melvin could be very dangerous if pushed into a corner. I don't think it's wise for me to do anything by myself, so I know I'll need help from the authorities." She toyed with the picture envelope. "I'm positive I can get him on embezzlement, but can I prove he's a murderer? I have nothing to go on except suspicion. Is it possible for me to trick him into admitting he had anything to do with the murders? I doubt it. He may be uneducated, but he's crafty. I think that beneath that backwoods exterior of his he's cool and calculating."

"So, if you can put him behind bars for theft, at least he's where he can't do anybody any harm."

"Exactly." Kim put the envelope back in the drawer. "But that could take months with all the legalities involved. In the meantime, if he suspects that we're on to him for murder, he might decide to take one or both of us out thinking he wouldn't have any more to lose."

"I see what you're saying." Patricia said.

"I've also given this some thought. Chase mentioned that he had a plan, and, at the time, I rejected his help. That was before I felt Melvin was obviously the murderer. I could ask Chase about his plan and what it would take to implement it."

"Do you think that's a good idea, Kim?"

"I need some legal help, Mom. Who better than a police officer who knows all the ins and outs of the law? He'd also have more clout than the average person."

"What about Max? Could he help? After all, he knew your parents before Chase did, and he was also in law enforcement."

"It's possible, Mom. But I think I should find out Chase's plan first."

She closed the desk drawer and stood. "Let's consider the possibilities. We have several options. In the meantime, I want to go to the hospital and check on Brad."

Kim and Patricia went to the gift store area of the business where they found Karen with a customer. After telling her they'd check in tomorrow if Melvin still hadn't shown up, they said goodbye and made their way back to the rear exit.

Chapter 47

Rain continued to fall, but was no problem in reaching the car or getting to the hospital.

One of the nurses on duty in Brad's ICU room approached them, put a finger to her lips and led them to his door. Stepping aside, she allowed them to enter. The head of the bed had been slightly elevated, and Brad's head was raised with an extra pillow. His eyes were closed, and his IV had been removed.

Kim turned to the nurse questioningly.

"Just go in and say something to him. I'll wait here," she said.

She allowed Patricia to follow Kim into the room.

"Brad?" As Kim touched his arm, his eyes opened wide and then closed again.

The nurse came in and stood behind the two women. "Mr. Kimbal regained consciousness about an hour ago. When the doctor came in to check him, he said his vitals are stable. He said we can try him on some Jello in a little while."

She started to leave and then turned back. "Don't stay too long, ladies. He still needs his rest."

Patricia stepped nearer to her daughter's side as Kim took a tissue from her pocket. When she reached down to pick up one of Brad's hands, tears filled her lower lids. She dabbed at them, bent over and whispered, "It's so good to have you back."

With his eyes still closed, the corners of his mouth turned up slightly. He spoke in a weak voice. "I didn't know I'd been gone."

Kim smiled broadly and looked over at Patricia. "You don't have to say anything, Brad. Save your strength. We can talk later. We'll have all the time in the world to talk then." His hand squeezed hers.

He opened his eyes again. "I know. I still feel confused." He looked first at Kim and then Patricia, smiled and closed his eyes once more.

"We'll let you sleep for now, but we'll be back later." Kim touched his cheek with her other hand, then leaned forward and kissed him on the cheek..

"Don't go yet. Stay awhile."

"We would if we could, but … "

Kim felt his hand go limp. His head fell to one side as he drifted off again.

Reentering the room behind them, the nurse said, "Don't worry, Miss Alexander. He'll be better once we can get some food into him. Why don't you come back later?"

Patricia nodded her head and touched Kim's arm. "Good idea, sweetheart. He's just come out of it. He needs time."

Kim nodded and laid Brad's hand back at his side. Stroking his forehead gently, she said, "Thank you. We *will* do that."

On the way back to Gloria's, Kim's cell phone rang. "Answer it, Mom, please."

She pushed her purse toward Patricia.

"Yes?" Patricia listened. "It's the cleaning company, Kim." Several moments slid by. "They would like you to take a quick look to see what they've done so far. Also, they've found something they want you to see."

Kim's eyes flashed toward her mother. "Tell them we'll be there in five minutes."

She changed directions, heading out to the highway and toward the estate.

When she pulled in through the iron gate and parked, the manager of the cleaning company, Larry Simms, met her at the door. "It's just that we'd like your approval for some places we've cleaned and plan to work on next. We don't want to overstep our boundaries."

"I'm sorry, Mr. Simms. A close friend of ours is in the hospital. I guess we've been distracted way more than I had planned."

"I'm very sorry about that. I trust your friend will be okay."

"For now, he's holding his own, thanks. I brought my aunt with me, so why don't we get started?" She turned to her mother. "Come on, Aunt Patricia. You should see this, as well."

The two women followed Simms inside.

"What's this thing you've found?" Kim looked around the entry way, taking in the beauty and brightness of the area since it had been cleaned.

"I'm going to show you." He started up the winding staircase, the women following close behind. Turning down the second floor hall, he headed to the Master bedroom. "I know you emptied all the shelves and bins, but it's our job to clean them inside, as well as out. One of my men was working just behind this door." Simms stopped in front of the bedroom's large closet. "Our policy is to take everything out and clean that area before replacing the sanitized drawers. When he did that, he found this in the space beneath the bottom drawer." He held out his opened hand to Kim.

She picked up what appeared to be an embroidered piece of heavy cloth. Her eyes widened. "It's a police uniform patch."

"Yes, ma'am. Its location seemed to indicate someone had purposely hidden it there."

Turning it over, Kim surveyed the colorful patch. "The stitching that attached the patch to the uniform seems loose or broken."

Simms observed the piece. "Perhaps it was removed from an old shirt and saved."

"We'll probably never know," Kim added.

It was made of a heavy beige twill in the shape of a six-pointed star, embroidered with the words "Police" at the top and "Officer" on the bottom in scarlet. Between the two, Glade City, Florida was stitched in a bright green.

Kim placed the piece in her purse. "Thank you for turning this over to me." Focusing again on Simms, she said, "I noticed the entryway when we came in. It's certainly a far cry from the state it had been in when I first arrived. Your crew is doing a great job. Is there anything else you wanted to discuss with me?"

"I want you to look over the third floor before you leave. We're finished there, and I'd like your approval."

When Patricia and Kim were finally on their way back to Gloria's, Kim glanced over at her mother. "What do you think about finding that patch, Mom?"

"My opinion is, this just adds to the mystery of Margaret."

"We know she had been involved with Max in Miami, and could have been here, as well, since he was on the Glade City force at the time. But, why would she have this patch anywhere around where my dad might have found it?"

Patricia shrugged her shoulders. "Kim, didn't Max tell us he hadn't been inside the estate before?"

"Yes. He said he'd had no occasion to be there." Kim was quiet for a moment, staring at the road ahead. "That could be, Mom. He wouldn't have had to be in the house if Margaret had kept the patch and hidden it away herself."

They rode in silence until they reached Gloria's home. Kim pulled into the garage to keep the car cool until they were ready to go back to the hospital. "It's well past lunch time, Mom. Let's go fix a bite to eat, then we can get back to the hospital."

Kim mixed up a fruit salad while Patricia made two small sandwiches of sliced turkey breast. They each fixed themselves a glass of iced tea and sat in the dinette.

"Why do you suppose my sister had that patch tucked away, anyway? She should have known better than to have remnants of her affair around the house." Patricia squeezed a slice of lemon into her tea and stirred.

Kim dished up the salad onto two small plates. "The question is, did he give it to her, lose it, or what? Maybe she wanted to keep it as a souvenir."

"You're probably right, sweetheart. No sense in trying to figure it out. It's water long over the dam."

They finished up without further discussion about the discovery, put away their dishes, and readied themselves to go back to the hospital.

They found Brad sitting up with a small bowl of green Jello in his hand. "I'm not exactly a fan of this stuff, but, for some unexplained reason, it tastes pretty good to me now." He gave them an "old Brad" smile.

Patricia pulled up a chair next to one already there, patting it for Kim to sit. "We're so glad you're able to eat something. That should help you get back on track."

"I'm beginning to feel more normal." He scraped the bowl with relish. "My thinking seems to have cleared some, as well. It felt like looking through a thick fog. Nothing wanted to come into focus."

"Do you remember anything about what happened to you?" Kim took the empty Jello bowl and placed it on the swing out tray.

"Some of it. I remember driving alongside the swamp on my way home from our outing together at Big Cypress when headlights loomed up behind me. I felt the hit. All I remember is seeing what appeared to be an old pickup through my rear view mirror before everything went blank."

Kim sank back in her chair, eyes wide, mouth slightly opened, staring at Brad in disbelief. "You mean to tell me that you actually saw the vehicle that hit you?"

"That's it. All I know, all I saw."

Patricia looked at Kim who had suddenly focused on her. "What?" she said.

"You don't see the importance?"

"No, I don't know what you're referring to," Patricia said.

"I suppose you're going to think I'm silly, but Melvin's pickup is old, and you'll be saying there are plenty of old pickups around. The significance is that we think it highly possible Melvin is the one who slashed Brad's tires. Now, put those facts together and … "

"Whoa." Patricia's mouth dropped open.

"Whoa … what?" a voice from behind startled the two women.

Kim shot a glance behind her, spotting Chase dressed casually in shirt and shorts.

"How'd you get past the watchdogs?"

"I have my ways." He gave a most engaging smile, blue eyes clear and intense.

"What facts are you putting together?" He didn't wait for an answer, but turned instead to acknowledge Brad. "Good to see you sitting up, fella. You gave these ladies one big headache."

"I seemed to have given myself one, as well." Brad gave a weak smile.

"This has to be a big relief to everyone," Chase added.

"We're all thrilled." Kim rested her hand on Brad's arm. "It's turned out to be quite a week for him; first his tires get slashed; then this accident; Melvin on the missing list and looking guilty as sin. I don't know what to expect next. At least we have this guy back with us, and we're all happy about that." She gave his arm a squeeze.

"Yeah. It was touch and go, all right. Just thought I'd better check in and see how the patient is coming along."

Kim took her eyes off of Brad, moving them to Chase. "There *is* something I want to talk to you about later."

"Talk away."

"Not here. Not now. We don't need to take up Brad's time." She looked back at him.

"I'll stop over tonight before I take my shift." With that, he put both hands on Kim's shoulders and squeezed them gently, then disappeared as quietly as he had appeared.

"That was short and sweet," Patricia said.

"That's Chase." Kim turned her attention back to Brad.

Gloria opened the front door to Chase. "Kim's expecting you. Come on in. She's in the living room."

Kim stood to greet him. "How about some iced tea? Come on in the kitchen, and we don't have to disturb anyone."

He followed her through the hallway and into the kitchen, taking a seat at the dinette table. "What's this all about, young lady? You have my curiosity up."

She put out lemon and sugar, poured two glasses of tea and placed them each on a paper napkin. "I know you don't like Melvin anymore than I do, so I'm going to tell you the latest and ask your advice." She sat down opposite Chase and fixed her drink.

"I've been reconsidering everything I know about Melvin. At first I just believed him to be a nasty, uncouth, embezzling crook. But lately other things keep coming to light.

"I remember what I was told about Melvin having a big argument with my dad on the front porch of the estate only days before the murders. No one seems to know what that argument was about. The Ramons seemed to think it was over money.

"On my first visit to SawGrass, Melvin tried his best to intimidate me. When it didn't work, he suddenly became solicitous." She paused to sip her tea. "A bit too solicitous.

"I've felt certain he's the one who slashed Brad's tires. Brad's only memory of the night he was found in the swamp is that it was someone in an old pick-up that pushed him. Chase, we all know Melvin's truck is an old one, and dark blue like the police had noted from the paint in the dent on the trunk of Brad's car. He's clearly out to do Brad bodily harm." She looked directly at Chase, took a deep breath and continued. "I don't know why Melvin's taken such a dislike to him, except he knows that I … Gloria and I are very close to Brad.

"Then there were all the pictures of Margaret that I found in Melvin's desk, especially the one of her nude. These prove to me he must have been stalking her."

"Wait a minute. Back up." Chase put down his glass of tea and leaned forward to grasp Kim's arm. "Pictures? What pictures? He must be more weird than I thought." He shook his head.

"I'm sorry. I hadn't mentioned that before. It's just that it's a little embarrassing, that's all." She hesitated momentarily, cleared her throat, and then continued. "I came across them accidentally when I was checking out Melvin's office. They certainly confirm any negative thoughts you may have had about the man. From his actions since I've been back in Glade City, he thinks, or acts like he owns the Boat Tours, has a right to it and any profits gained. And lately, he's been focusing on my Aunt Patricia. I'm certain he wants her, as well as the business. As you've told me, he's absconded with over $200,000 of SawGrass profits. And where is he now with all this money?"

Chase swirled the ice cubes in his glass and took a huge swallow without taking his eyes off of Kim.

"What's next? Will he be coming after me? Wanting to get rid of me so he can have these things free and clear?" She sighed. "A good reason for murder, I'd say."

She studied Chase's reactions as his eyes grew dark. He seemed to hang on Kim's every word. What she'd been saying had definitely affected him more than she'd anticipated.

"I'll tell you, Chase, this whole thing is spooky. Not knowing where he is or what he's up to … I don't know what to expect next. Is he plotting something devious? He could turn up here in the middle of the night, break in, and do the unthinkable. I'm afraid for all our lives, Gloria's, Aunt Patricia's, mine, even Karen's. I'm almost afraid to go anywhere alone, even in broad daylight. Look what happened to Brad. I don't know whether or not the police would even believe all this. It sounds so … Or if they'd consider some protection for us. They'll probably think I have a screw loose."

Chase reached over and put his hand on Kim's arm. "I believe you, Kim. I'll be here to protect you. Believe me, when I say I always have been."

Kim took several sips of tea. "I didn't intend to lay all this on you, Chase, but I have no one else I can turn to. Max seems interested in my aunt, but we don't know him well enough to ask him for any kind of protection." She hesitated. "And the worst thing is … " She stopped dead in mid-sentence.

"What?" He sat up straight in his chair. "What's the worst thing, Kim? Don't stop there. Whatever it is, I said I'd help. I'll protect you at all costs."

She looked down at her hands on the table, folded and unfolded her paper napkin. "I … don't know if I should tell you this."

"Come on. You know me well enough to confide in me." He grasped Kim's hands in his. "You are one of the most important people in my life. You should know that by now."

Kim moved her hands from beneath Chase's and placed them on her lap. "It's about a nightmare I had recently. I saw the killer's face in that dream."

Chase put his glass down and scrutinized Kim. "You *know* who that person is, and you haven't told anyone yet?"

"Well, he was in my nightmare, the one from my childhood that has repeated itself to me often. I believe he's in my life right now. The problem is, my conception of him is like many dreams we're prone to have: The person is there, interacting in the scene with you. You know who it's supposed to be without actually having a face to identify. Your mind tells you who it is. As much as I've concentrated on that part of the dream, I can't clear up the image enough to identify him."

Chase took out his handkerchief and wiped his forehead. "Why haven't you told me this before?"

"I don't know. I guess I didn't want to lay my problems on you or anyone else, for that matter. Since all this has transpired with Melvin, I'm positive he's the mystery man in my nightmare. He was in our lives back then, and evidently wasn't happy with his pay, position or what-have-you. He had a thing for Margaret, and today, well history is repeating itself with Patricia and the profits from the Boat Tours. And I'm frightened."

Chase stroked his upper lip and then smoothed his hair in silence for moments while he studied Kim with an icy blue stare.

"What are you thinking, Chase? You're beginning to alarm me."

"Please, sugar. I don't mean to worry you at all." His eyes suddenly softened as he continued. "I'm only trying to put this into perspective. We need to come up with a solution that won't put any of us in harm's way. This nightmare thing has thrown a monkey wrench into the equation." He leaned back in his chair and closed his eyes.

"I'm sorry, Chase. I shouldn't have bothered you with this. After all, it is my problem."

He got up suddenly and came around to Kim's side. "No more talk like that. Do you hear me? I'm going to work this out. I won't have you worrying your pretty little head anymore. Please count on me. I'm going to take care of you. Do you understand?" He sat down next to her and put an arm around her. "You'll find out Melvin won't be a problem anymore." He tweaked her nose, kissed her on the cheek and stood to leave. "I'll be in touch."

Chapter 48

Over the next two days Brad's condition improved rapidly. The doctor reported that if his recuperation continued at that rate, they could probably release him the following day.

"Let's have a little get together at the office for Brad next week." Gloria put away clean dishes from the dishwasher, while Kim and Patricia cleared the supper table. "Something to celebrate his recovery. By then he's going to be climbing the walls to see people. It'll be fun. We'll have the staff in. I can invite Andy, and you two can call Max and Chase, if they're not on duty. Brad will love it."

"You don't think it's too soon?" Kim put a clean cloth on the table after it had been wiped.

"No way. Give him a few extra days, and he'll be a step ahead of everyone else. I've known him too long. Besides, we can keep it low key."

"Sounds okay to me, don't you think so, Mom?"

"As long as you both believe it won't do Brad any harm."

Gloria took a pen and note pad from a kitchen drawer and sat down at the table. "I'll get the staff started on it in the morning. Come on, you two. Let's plan a simple menu to serve."

The wheels were set in motion, and the room teemed with excitement as the three took to the idea. Kim wanted to decorate the reception room with balloons and streamers. Patricia offered to shop for food and drinks. Gloria said she would arrange for some of the staff to set up tables and chairs and help with the food.

Patricia called Max who said he'd make sure he'd be free that evening. Andy thought the idea was a great one. Kim left a message at the station for Chase.

Kim and Patricia continued to go to SawGrass each day to help. Karen still hadn't heard from Melvin.

"I don't think he's planning to return at all," Karen told Kim when she poked her head into the secretary's office the following day. "He seems to have disappeared into thin air. And with the money he's stolen, why should he bother? He could live like a king for the rest of his life, without having to lift a finger."

"That is, if the police don't catch up to him first." Kim stepped into the room. "Chase tells me they have an APB out on him. They haven't tracked down either Melvin or his pickup so far, but it's not going to be too long with that old vehicle of his. It's as obvious as snow in July. Unless he's smart enough to dump it and buy something else."

Karen leaned back in her chair. "He's not exactly the brightest guy, but he's wily enough to get away with a lot of stuff."

"For starters," Kim said, "I'm going to clear out his office. It's a mess, and I'm ashamed of it. I'm surprised he's managed the business so well when he never even bothers to organize his own workplace."

"That's because he intimidated the staff into doing much more than he paid them to do."

"I can believe that, Karen." Kim turned to leave and help Patricia when Karen's phone rang.

"Yes sir." Karen held the phone to her ear and listened for a moment. "Haven't seen him for days. Ms. Alexander and I were just discussing it." There was another brief interlude of silence. Kim stood inside the doorway waiting. "You *what?*" She looked over at Kim, her eyes widening. "Thank you, Officer. I'll let Ms. Alexander know right away. That's all? No trace of Melvin or any of his belongings? Well, please call if anything else turns up." She disconnected, sank back in her chair and looked at Kim. "They've found Melvin's pickup, but not a sign of him or any of his things."

Kim stepped closer to Karen's desk. "Where? Where did they find it?"

"The officer who called said it was discovered in the swamp on the east end of town.

It had been either driven or rolled in. Only part of the cab was visible. They had to tow it out before they could identify it."

"I still don't trust that old crook. He probably pushed it into the swamp to throw us off his track. I'll bet he wants us all to think he's dead, so he can be free to go wherever he pleases."

"You've got a point there, Kim. I've always felt he was more devious than anyone realized."

Chase stopped by SawGrass as Kim and Patricia were about to leave the parking lot. He pulled the police cruiser next to Kim's vehicle and jumped out. "Two things," he said, leaning on the open window frame next to Kim. "I'll be there for Brad's party. I had my shift changed. Second, I heard the station called about finding Melvin's pickup."

"Yes, and I'm still afraid. Nobody knows where he is. This could be another of his cunning schemes."

"I understand your fear, but don't worry, baby. We'll get to the bottom of this." He put his hand on Kim's arm as it rested in the window frame. "At least Brad's out of the woods."

"They released him yesterday with his promise to rest at home for the next forty-eight hours. Aunt Patricia and I were about to go check on him, to be sure he's obeying doctor's orders and all." She smiled and withdrew her arm from the window. "We'd better get going, Chase. We'll see you on party night." She turned the ignition and the car rumbled to life.

Chase didn't move from his position, but stared silently as Kim pulled away from him, heading to the real estate office to first pick up Gloria.

When the two women walked into Gloria's office, she was just getting up from her desk.

"I'm ready. Just finished jotting a couple of things for me to take care of first thing in the morning." She picked up her purse and flicked off her desk light. "This has been a day of happenings. One of the secretaries just turned in her resignation. She's getting married next week and going to Paris with her husband. His job sends him to different parts of the world. Nice work, right?"

"Sounds like an exciting life she'll be leading," Kim said as Gloria locked her door behind them, and they all walked out into the reception area.

Gloria called to a lone female at the front desk, "Ruth, close for me, please. I'll see you in the morning."

While the three made their way to the parking area and Kim's car, Gloria made an announcement. "That dink, Potter Denks, rings me earlier. Says his client called him last week to say he had the cash to buy the estate and would meet him at his Miami office to sign the offer this past Monday. Well, that was three days ago, and he still hasn't shown. Denks wanted to know if I'd heard from the guy, by any strange coincidence." Gloria rolled her eyes. "Shoot, we don't even know who this client person is."

Chapter 49

"It's just as well this mystery man didn't show up, since I had no intention of selling the estate, anyway." Kim unlocked the Cruiser, and they all stepped in. "I do feel bad that I let Mr. Denks waste his time, though. I should have been honest with him."

"I wouldn't worry about Denks, honey." Gloria settled herself in the back seat. "He wasn't exactly up front with us, so why even give it a second thought?"

"I know. Still, I shouldn't have carried it this far. The whole deal would have folded and disappeared if the guy couldn't have come up with the cash the way we figured it would happen. Maybe we won't have to worry about him anymore. We've all had way too much on our minds lately, Brad being on the top of *my* list." She inserted the key into the ignition, started the engine, and headed out of the parking lot toward Brad's condo.

On the way, Kim told Gloria about the police finding Melvin's pickup in the swamp, buried up to the cab. Gloria leaned forward from the back seat and put her hand on Kim's shoulder. "Wow. This changes the whole picture. It means that our suspect isn't who we thought it was." She let out a huge sigh. "It's getting more mind boggling all the time."

"Not so fast, Gloria. They haven't found a trace of Melvin yet. This could be part of his insidious plan to trick us into believing *he* is the victim here."

Gloria sat back in her seat, with a puff of disdain. "Darn. I thought it sounded like we were finally getting some sort of closure."

They were all silent for a few moments while Kim drove toward Brad's place. Finally, Gloria spoke up again. "The thing is, without a body, an investigation will go nowhere."

Chapter 50

Brad continued a speedy recovery. His appetite came back. His color improved. He was doing what the doctor had ordered; sitting around quietly, reading, or watching television and looking forward to the evening visits from Kim, Gloria and Patricia.

Three days after Brad's release from the hospital, Kim received a call from the cleaning company. Larry Simms told her that they expected to be finished in about two days. He would call and let her know the exact time.

"Now I *am* getting excited. It shouldn't be long now 'til the estate is ready to move into," Kim said one evening after the three women left Brad's condo. "And Brad is beginning to look like himself, again. Kind of offsets some of the problems we've had lately. I know there's still the concern about Melvin, but knowing the police are looking for him makes me feel a little safer. If he ever surfaces, he'll wind up behind bars before he knows what's happened to him."

"You're not afraid of him anymore?" Gloria said as the three stood outside the building near their cars.

"I didn't say that. So far, there hasn't been any sign of him returning. I've decided that old thief is more afraid to show his face than I am afraid of him harming any of us. He has to know the authorities are searching for him, and his name will be mud if he comes out of hiding."

Patricia studied her daughter. "I understand that. I just don't trust him not to figure out a way to retaliate."

"Rather than retaliating, he's probably hightailing it out of the country. He has the advantage of having all that cash to spend anywhere he chooses."

Chapter 51

The evening of the party finally arrived. The real estate office buzzed with activity. Kim placed balloons and streamers everywhere. On a folding banquet table, the women set out cocktail napkins, clear plastic cups, and an arrangement of gladiolas and white roses. At one end, a crystal punchbowl brimmed with a mixture of ginger ale, frozen lemonade, ice and frothy orange sherbert. For those who wished something stronger, a bar had been set up in one corner of the room where several kinds of beer would be available. Mouthwatering appetizers of every description Patricia had ordered from Everglade Catering sat next to small paper plates. The final touch: soft music played over the intercom.

Max and Andy conversed in one corner of the office while Patricia and Gloria saw to finishing touches. Kim had already left to pick up Brad when Chase arrived. He wore navy shorts and a sleeveless muscle shirt in an electric blue that made his eyes glitter like a blowtorch.

"Where's our lady fair?" he asked Gloria when he spotted her checking on the hors d'oeuvres.

"She won't be long. She went to pick up Brad."

Chase frowned. "I could have done that. I offered to help her." Disappointment laced his words as he glared at Gloria.

She shrugged her shoulders. "It's her business, Chase, not mine."

He abruptly turned his back on Gloria and headed toward Max and Andy.

As Kim and Brad walked through the reception room door, a huge cheer broke out. The office staff and invited friends immediately surrounded him to wish him well. Chase muscled his way through the group to stand next to Kim.

"Looking good, buddy," he said as he reached Brad's side.

"Thanks. I'm beginning to feel like my old self again." He reached over and offered his hand to Chase.

Kim's cell phone rang, and she stepped away from the crowd to hear.

"It's Larry Simms, Miss Alexander. We're almost finished. The guys say we have less than a day to go. I need you to come and make a quick inspection in the kitchen. There are some specific places I have to show you before we can wind it up tomorrow, and since that's Saturday, the men want to finish early."

"I guess I could do that, Mr. Simms. We're just about to launch a party here, but if you don't think it will take too long ... You and your men have been so dedicated that I want you all to know how much I appreciate your hard work."

"I wouldn't ask if it weren't important. I'll take up as little of your time as possible, ma'am. I'll see you shortly." Simms hung up and Kim went back to the group of well-wishers.

Chase moved in close to Kim and whispered in her ear. "What's up, sugar? You look a bit disturbed."

"The cleaning company," she whispered back. "They need me there for an important decision. I hate to leave because this is Brad's big night, but I won't take long. This party is too important to me."

Chase gave her a hard look. "Well, you're not going alone, sugar. I'll take you. Let's make our excuses and a quick exit. They'll all be busy 'til we get back."

"First let me tell Aunt Patricia and Gloria, and I'll get my purse."

"We'll hold the eats 'til you get back." Gloria looped her arm through Andy's. "Make it as quick as you can."

"My word of honor," Kim replied as she and Chase headed out.

Chapter 52

Chase pulled through the open gates of the estate and parked next to Larry Simms' van, the only vehicle around. Simms stood in the doorway waiting for Kim.

"This is a friend of mine, Chase Grey," Kim said. She turned to her escort. "This is Larry Simms, manager of the Bestway Cleaning Company."

"Nice to meet you." Simms nodded and offered a hand. "Follow me, please, and I'll show you the problem." He turned back inside and lead them toward the kitchen.

"The others have left?" Chase asked as he followed Kim and Simms through the entryway.

"They finished for the day when I called Miss Alexander, but they'll be back early tomorrow morning."

Simms entered the kitchen and went to the range in the island area. Above it, a large metal rack hung from the high ceiling. It held various pots and pans hooked individually on chains. "Quite modern for having been built by your grandfather, Miss."

"Actually, my father had some of the kitchen updated after our family moved in." Kim set her purse on one of the counters and looked at the area above them.

"That accounts for it, then." He switched focus from Kim to the ceiling. "This is the problem area. This large room juts away from the rest of the house, almost like an add-on, although we know it to be original." Kim nodded and squinted up at the ceiling where Simms pointed. "At one time, there must have been a pretty fair storm. Water leaked in severely, damaging the eaves, wooden beams in the ceiling, and the surrounding plaster. It was either not noticed, or it could have happened after the place was boarded up."

"I'm sure it must have happened when the house was empty. It does look bad. I thought it was just a huge water mark that could be painted over."

Simms continued to look up. "Would that it were that simple."

Chase stood behind Kim assessing that portion of the ceiling.

"So, what do we do now, Mr. Simms?"

"I had one of my men go into the crawl space to check it out. The entire area needs to be torn out and rebuilt. There is extensive wood rot, and that will need to be replaced before this whole section falls into the kitchen. You'll need to hire some carpenters. I suggest that we leave this part of the kitchen until it's repaired. At that time, we'll come back and finish our job here." Simms looked back at Kim. "Does that sound okay with you, Miss?"

"Yes, yes, of course, Mr. Simms. We don't want anything like that hanging over our heads. It's way too dangerous."

"I agree. So, with your approval, we'll complete everything else by early afternoon tomorrow." He removed the van keys from his pocket and turned to go. "I'm a bit late tonight, so I'd better get rolling. I'll give you a call tomorrow when we're finished." He headed through the kitchen door, stopped one more time, turned and said, "I can recommend a good company for the repairs, if you wish. Just let me know." With that, he was gone.

Kim stood still surveying the damaged area.

Chase came up close behind her. "It doesn't sound good at all," he said.

"Well, I guess there's nothing more we can do for now. I'll call someone in the morning. Let's get back to the party." She picked up her purse and moved toward the door as Chase followed close behind.

When they reached the front door which Simms had left open, Kim stopped suddenly. "I don't know if I have my set of the estate keys with me or not." She set her purse on the small entryway table, and began to fish around in the bottom. "I should have had Simms lock up for me before he left. Darn."

Moving between Kim and the open front door, Chase stared to laugh. "Ladies purses I'll never understand. They never cease to amaze me." He grabbed her bag and dumped it out on the hall table. "There. That ought to help. Now you can see everything at once. Should be a lot easier."

Kim gasped as her cell phone, cosmetic bag, ball point pen, wallet, and the policeman's cloth patch that Simms' men had found, all came tumbling out in a jumble.

"I hardly think that was necessary, Chase. Now, look what you've done to my personal belongings. You don't fool around with a woman's purse."

Again he laughed heartily as he surveyed the contents spread out before him, until his eyes settled on the police patch. "What's this?" he growled, his attitude changing immediately. He picked up the piece of cloth and scrutinized it. "This is off one of my old uniforms. I recognize the ripped colored thread that it was sewn on with. How the hell did you get it?" He stared at Kim with eyes black as thunder clouds.

Chapter 53

The party at the office warmed up as everyone gathered around Brad, chatting and laughing and expressing their pleasure at having him back amongst them. When a recording of Dolly Parton's famous hit, "Nine to Five" started to play, Andy grabbed Gloria and drew her out into an open area. "May I have the pleasure of this dance, Mademoiselle? I can't resist that beat," he said as he twirled her around the makeshift dance floor.

Max picked up on the idea and took Patricia's arm. "How about it? It's been years since I've had the pleasure of a beautiful partner."

"I'm pretty rusty, myself, Max, but it sounds like fun."

Soon a few others followed suit. The rhythmic beat was followed by some slower and more romantic tunes. The rest of the crew were enjoying the moments of magic when the main office phone rang. Gloria broke away from Andy with reluctance. "It's probably Kim," she said, "or I'd let it ring."

"This is Karen from SawGrass. Is Kim there? She told me they were having a get-together for Brad tonight."

"She should be back any minute, Karen. In fact," she looked at the office clock over the door, "she's long overdue. Can I help you?"

"I was just getting ready to close up shop when the police station called. They told me they'd let us know if they had any new information on Melvin."

"Yes?" Gloria's breath came in short spasms. "Tell me, please."

"They found some body parts near the east edge of the swamp. Some youngsters playing nearby discovered them and told their parents, who, in turn, notified the police. The station sent out a small team to investigate. They reported that what they found was badly decomposed, but when the head showed up shortly after that, they were sure it was Melvin's because of the gold tooth in front. They will, of course, check dental records, as well."

"Do they have any idea how long he's been dead? That is, if it is Melvin."

"Maybe a week and a half, more or less. Decomposition in this heat is rapid."

"Thank you, Karen. I'll let Kim know as soon as she gets back." Gloria hung up and held onto Andy who supported her under one arm. He looked at her questioningly.

"From the lack of color in your face, babe, the news must be ... "

"Scary," Gloria filled in.

Max and Patricia moved in from the dance floor. "You look like you've seen a ghost," Max said. "What's up?"

Gloria started to explain in vivid detail, but before she could finish, Max grabbed Andy by the arm. "Let's go, my friend. We need to get Kim. RIGHT NOW."

Chapter 54

"How did you come by this?" Chase snarled, turning the patch over in his hands.

Kim started to explain and stopped herself. "I could tell you, Chase Grey, but that would only … "

"Only what?" He grabbed her arm. "That patch has been missing for years, and I got in trouble for it, as well as for my torn uniform. Now, *tell me* where you got this?"

"First, you tell me why you're taking this out on me?" Facing him, she stared, unblinking into his eyes.

He shook his head, refocusing on her. "I'm sorry. I don't know what came over me." With glazed eyes he continued to hold Kim's arm in a death grip.

"I could show you, if you would please let go of my arm. You're hurting me."

At the moment he started to release her, Kim turned, swiftly lifting her knee to his groin with all the force she could muster. As she connected solidly, he howled in pain and collapsed in the open doorway. Clutching his crotch with one hand, he grabbed for Kim's leg with the other. Muscular fingers wrapped around her calf. She kicked hard, jerking herself free, and started to run back through the hall when she remembered the only rear exit in the house was always dead bolted. Without her keys, there was no escape there. Turning to the stairs, she took them two at a time, breathlessly making it to the second floor while Chase still writhed and moaned in the entryway.

Flying down the hall, she entered her old bedroom where she knew she could hide. Taller now than when she hid from her would-be assailant fifteen years ago, she prayed she would still fit in the secret compartment Grandfather had built for her toys. She threw up the faded chintz cover, and lifted the wooden seat. With toys and games long gone, she slid into its welcome sanctuary.

Positioning herself on her side, she could see through the same crack between the boards where she'd watched the shadow of the fiend years before. Though her breathing was shallow, her mind whirled in overdrive.

Her first thought was the patch. Chase's, caught beneath the closet drawers, not Max's. Had it been Chase, and not Max, who'd been having an affair with Margaret? If so, how long had it been going on? Had he come looking for her that night to have sex with her? When the family moved to Glade City, Chase was only a young rookie. Margaret had to be at least ten to twelve years his senior. Although this may not have mattered to Chase, Kim felt her mother would not have gone for a young upstart like him in the first place.

Max had more class, but how did he fit into this puzzle? Was he aware of things going on between Chase and Margaret? Or were they both having affairs with her at the same time? Tears spilled as she willed herself not to think that way. She couldn't imagine Margaret in that kind of situation.

What about the night of the murders? If Chase was the murderer, what could have caused him to go berserk? Had he come to the estate to find Margaret and discovered Kim's father home unexpectedly? That would have messed up his plans. He also had to know there was a child. If he killed the parents, then he should have realized he'd have to get rid of the child as well. But he couldn't find her. Had that triggered the uncontrollable rage?

Shivers ran down her spine as mental pictures raced through her head. She kept her eyes on the crack, but there was still no sign of Chase.

But all this was supposition. More tears leaked past her clenched eyelids.

Considering things long gone would not save her. She needed to concentrate on how she could help herself now. The past could wait.

She blinked open her eyes and peered through the slats in the box seat. Quiet and subdued light prevailed with no telltale sounds of footsteps slipping through the evening. Nothing. Surely Chase had recovered enough to search for her. Would he find her? If only she hadn't left her purse with her cell phone on the table downstairs.

Since she first arrived in Glade City, she now realized she'd been too naïve to see through Chase. His handsome face and well-muscled body had nullified any warnings that should have alerted her. And the little voice whispering in her subconscious had been too easy to dismiss. Had they been warnings she'd chosen to ignore?

Regrets weren't going to keep her safe now. She needed a plan.

Chapter 55

Gloria reached out for Max. "What's wrong? Why do you have to get Kim right now? If something's the matter, Patricia and I will go with you." Patricia nodded with eyes large and questioning.

"No. Stay. I'll fill you in later." With that, he rushed Andy through the office and outside while Patricia and Gloria could only stand open-mouthed.

Max headed for his pickup with Andy close on his heels. "I don't understand what's going on. Is Kim in danger?" He threw open the door on the passenger side and jumped in as Max switched on the engine. "Clue me in." He snapped on his seat belt, and stared at Max.

"Without Melvin in the picture, there's only one logical suspect, and I worked with him for ten years." Max threw the pick-up in gear and roared out of the parking lot.

"Chase!" Andy exclaimed. "Why? How? What else do you know?"

"Tell you later. Hang on while I get us out of town."

Filled with hammering questions, Andy sucked in his breath as he watched the heart of Glade City flying by his window.

White knuckled, Max gripped the steering wheel and concentrated on the road ahead. He turned off to the shortcut that passed the swamp. The pickup fishtailed onto the open highway.

In silence, with crazy, racing thoughts, Andy hung onto the overhead strap as Max sped full-throttle out of town.

A siren sounded close behind. Red and blue lights flashed their message in the rear view mirror, and Max reluctantly pulled over.

Chapter 56

K im listened. The silence was deafening, and more than frightening.

So where was Chase now? What was he doing? She knew he would never leave without taking care of her. Permanently.

Time ticked on, and Kim became more fearful of what might be going on downstairs. If he *was* downstairs. He could be lurking anywhere, waiting for her to come out of hiding, waiting for the moment he could grab her and ...

She shuddered as she considered the possibilities.

"Kim." A pleading voice sounded from the hall. "Kim? I'm sorry I frightened you. I didn't mean any harm. Please come out. I'll get you back to the party right away. Kim? Everyone will be wondering what happened to us." The voice drew closer, hesitating at the doorway. "They'll be sending out the militia. You wouldn't want that now, would you?"

He sounded so logical, so well-meaning. But she wasn't going to fall for his bull again.

Chase always seemed to be able to weasel or con his way out of things. Well, this time he wasn't going to trick her. She'd finally seen through him. Maybe too late, but the truth had hit her between the eyes, and she had to command herself to hang tight. Just hang tight, girl. He'll never find you.

Footsteps entered the bedroom, and Kim clasped her hand over her mouth. Could he possibly hear her breathing?

The footsteps moved to her bathroom, paused for several seconds, and then came back. Looking through the crack again, Kim could see him standing in the middle of the room. Slowly, he turned full circle, then stopped when he faced the window and the secret box beneath it.

Moments passed while he continued to stare directly at the window seat. Why?

Her breathing almost stopped. Why was he concentrating on the window seat? It was at that moment she felt a part of the ruffled edge of the cover inside with her. It had caught on her clothing when she jumped in.

Chapter 57

Brad and his guests continued to laugh and talk, munch appetizers and drink punch or beer. Music still played softly in the background. Gloria and Patricia had backed away from the rest of the group in hopes of not breaking up the festivities. Brad looked over at them and beckoned for them to join the crowd.

Gloria waved, holding up an index finger to indicate they'd be joining the rest shortly, but the look on her face spoke volumes to Brad. He excused himself and walked over to where Patricia and Gloria stood huddled next to a file cabinet.

"What's going on?" he asked. "You both look like lightning struck you."

"Please stay with our guests, Brad." Gloria took a deep breath. "We were just worried about Kim and Chase being gone so long. Max and Andy have gone to check on them. Andy promised to call us as soon as they got to the estate. It's probably nothing. Some sort of delay. I'm sure everything's okay."

"If that's what you think," Brad said. "Otherwise, I could have gone."

Patricia put her hand on Brad's arm. "Please, let the guys take care of it. I'm sure they'll all be back very soon."

Brad hesitated. "Chase *is* a cop. He can handle anything that might come up, but I still worry. Kim is more than just special to me."

Gloria gave him a little push toward the guests. "Go. You need to enjoy our efforts. Kim will be fine."

Brad turned reluctantly toward the others, stopped and looked back at Patricia and Gloria, who smiled and waved him on.

Chapter 58

Max pulled over to the side of the highway. He opened his door and started to get out.

"Stay in your vehicle, sir," echoed over a speaker as the cop stepped out of his cruiser.

Max backed into the truck cab at the command, and said, "This is an emergency, officer. A young lady may be in a life-threatening situation." He stared out at the approaching policeman.

"Do you know how fast you were going? I clocked you at ninety-five miles per hour." He strolled up to Max's side of the pickup. "You were not only threatening the lives of others, but your own as well. If this young lady is in danger, why didn't *you* call the police?"

"Officer, there was no time to call. Instinct told me to get there before anything happened to Miss Alexander."

"Kim Alexander? One of our men took the evening to attend a party she's putting on." He spoke too casually to suit Max.

"That would be Chase Grey, and he's the cop who worries me. Please, officer please follow us out to the Sanderson estate. We need your help."

The officer looked hard at Max. "You used to be on the Glade City force?"

Max nodded furiously. "Yes, but never mind about me. I believe Kim's life is in grave danger."

"Then, follow me, sir." He turned on his heel and moved quickly back to the squad car. "I'll lead the way."

Chapter 59

Chase moved toward the window box with great deliberation. "Well, well. What have we here? You wouldn't be hiding from your good friend, would you, Kim baby?" He stopped directly in front of the secret toy box. "A friend who always had your welfare at heart, who considered you much more than just a friend, one who discovered that your employee, Melvin Thomas, had been stealing from your business for years." A measured pause followed before he continued. "He planned to use the money to buy the estate from you without you knowing who the purchaser was until it was too late to do anything about it. Well, you needn't worry about Mr. Thomas anymore. I've taken care of him, and only because I cared for you ... very much. Much more than anybody else could possibly understand." He turned around and sat hard on top of the chintz cover.

Kim sucked in her breath. She was trapped.

"There was a time, I would have done almost anything for you, Kim, because I think I've been in love with you from the first day I saw you standing in front of SandHill Estate. I was lucky enough to have met you before anyone else in Glade City." He paused before continuing.

"If only you would have given me a chance.

"When you went to live at Gloria's and she introduced you to Brad, I felt you drifting away from me. Every time I tried to get closer to you, it was Brad, always Brad. I should have gotten rid of him a long time ago. But, accidents happen, and his next one will be his last." He was quiet now while Kim tried to calm herself, to stop the shaking she felt inside her body.

"I could give you one more chance, but I know now I can't trust you. You're like your mother in that respect. I offered her a good life, but she rejected me. Laughed in my face. Preferred other men over someone who would have devoted his life to making her happy."

He tapped his heel against the wooden box.

"For your information, she wasn't in love with your father, either. She simply liked men, lots of men. I finally figured out she was nothing but a whore. She was seeing Max on the side. No, he never said anything to me. I just found out by following him on days when he knew your father had to be out of town. I think Max really loved her, but she couldn't be satisfied with that. She flirted with anything in trousers, even in front of your father." He took a deep, audible breath. "Melvin was another sucker for her, although I doubt she would have ever had much to do with him. He wanted her, though. Followed her around like a sick, love-struck puppy, 'til your father caught on and threatened to fire him."

He pounded his fist on the wooden seat. "Are you listening to me, Kim? Do you hear what I'm saying? Your mother was a whore, trading on her beauty for favors from the men in her life. She was no more than a beautiful, faithless diversion, who teased and deceived, not worthy of any man's love. One time, when I knew she was home alone, I went to SandHill while I was on duty. I thought she'd be glad to see me, but not Margaret. She put on her airs like she was too good for me. Didn't want me to even touch her. I figured she owed me so I tried to take her, but she only laughed at me. Spit in my face. We had our little tussle. She ended up ripping the emblem off my shirt, destroying the sleeve in the process.

"I knew a lot of things that went on at the Boat Tours because it was one of the businesses on my beat. I spent more time there than anywhere, a lot more time than I was required to. I saw things, heard things, watched the little tramp play her sucker list. When the truth finally hit me, I knew I had to even the score. Trouble was, Kim, your father wasn't supposed to be home that night."

He paused again. This time it was bone-chilling. Kim gasped for breath, afraid of what was coming next. She knew he would certainly be planning on getting her out of the way.

"Being a cop, I knew exactly how to cover up the evidence. Even my clothing. The blood on it made for a good gator snack. You see, Kim, no one ever found any thing because I was too smart for them. My brother always said I was the clever one in the family. I just wish he were around to see me now. He told me once that I should have gotten rid of you a long time ago, and if I ever needed any help, he would come here from Detroit, and do the job himself.

"So, let's just say, you meet with an unfortunate accident. I don't even have to make up an excuse for not having you with me when I return to the party. In fact, I don't have to return at all. I simply go missing, and I have all the money Melvin embezzled from the business. I'll be long gone before anyone's ever on to me.

"You and I, Kim, we could have had it all, a sweet life together, more money than we ever needed, if you only could have seen what was best for you … and who was best for you. To hell with the rest of them, Brad, Gloria, and even your Aunt Patricia."

Once again, he was quiet, a thinking kind of quiet. At last, he stood up and turned around, bending slightly to finger the chintz cover. "I need to check out this seat. It seems to have a piece of the ruffle missing. Or is it tucked away inside a hidden compartment?"

Without further warning, he grabbed the ruffle firmly, and jerked it hard, tearing the material into shreds and exposing the seat beneath it. With the other hand he reached for the wooden cover and yanked it open.

As the lid came up, Kim sprang from the interior, catching Chase off guard. She shoved him as hard as she could. Losing his balance, he stumbled backwards, while she rushed past him down the hall to the winding staircase. She almost made it when he caught up with her tackling her and pinning her arms behind her.

Securing her body with his muscular arms, he struggled with her at the top of the stairs when lights flashed through the open doorway. Gravel flew as two vehicles slid to a halt in front of the entry.

Chase's attention rocketed to the interruption. Her upper body restricted, Kim wrapped a leg around Chase's lower limbs and pulled hard and sudden, upsetting his balance. He let go of her arms and grabbed for the banister, but Kim took one foot and raised it to his rear end, shoving with all her might. He tumbled, head over heels, down the long flight, and landed head first on the tile floor below.

A police officer burst through the door, followed by Max and Andy. Max knelt down next to Chase's motionless body. He touched the artery on the side of Chase's neck. "He's still alive." Leaving him, Max jumped up, taking stairs two at a time to where Kim stood, shaking and clinging to the bannister for support. Andy was close behind.

The cop secured Chase's hands with cuffs and turned to his radio. "We need backup and an ambulance at SandHill Estate."

Chapter 60

"Let me have your car keys, Gloria. Something isn't right, and I have to go to Kim right now." Brad put out his hand.

Gloria started to object. "But Andy and Max are ... "

"Keys, *please*," he repeated as he waved his hand in Gloria's face. "You and Patricia see to the guests 'til I return." He grabbed the keys before she could free them from her purse. "Not a word to the others." He put a finger to his lips and hurried to the exit.

On his way out of town, the whine of sirens followed him to SandHill.

He entered the estate driveway just minutes ahead of the ambulance and two squad cars.

Pulling alongside the other police car and Max's pickup, he jumped out without bothering to close the car door.

Through the front door, Brad could see Max and Andy at the top of the stairway with Kim. Chase lay on the floor below where he had fallen. A police officer knelt beside him.

"My God. What's... " Not waiting to finish his question, he took the stairs two at a time to where Max and Andy supported Kim.

He moved between Andy and Max, and threw his arms around Kim. "Are you okay?"

She grabbed Brad around the neck, fiercely clutching him close to her. "I'm all right, now, but I have these guys here to thank for that."

Four more cops and three paramedics walked through the door behind Brad. One bent down to check Chase. "Let's get this guy in the ambulance. His vitals don't look good at all."

Two of the men brought in a stretcher. They placed Chase on it and carried him outside, while the first cop followed.

The four new officers started quizzing Max, Andy, and Kim on what happened when Brad interjected. "Officers, could we please allow this young lady to go down stairs and sit?"

"Of course," said the one wearing sergeant stripes on his sleeve. "We'll question her later. Have the medics check her out before they leave."

Brad brought Kim downstairs, sat her in one of the hall chairs, and went to the kitchen to get her a glass of water. When he returned, he said, "Officers, I believe Ms. Alexander needs to go home and rest." He squatted beside her and, placing one arm around the back of the chair, reached over and kissed her cheek.

"Scariest night of my life, Brad, but I'm a survivor. Right now, the only reason for me to go home is to get the keys for this place so I can lock it up."

"Let's go, then. Call Gloria, and tell her what's going on, and that we'll be back there as soon as we can."

Max and Andy were still talking to the police officers.

Chapter 61

"What a night," Gloria said, after she distributed cups of coffee to everyone who had assembled in her living room. She sank onto the couch and kicked off her shoes.

Andy sat down next to her and put his hand on hers. "I think we'll all agree on that." He placed his other arm over her shoulder and pulled her head to his.

Max and Patricia sat on adjoining easy chairs opposite the couch. Patricia put a dash of cream in her cup, stirred, and turned to Max. "I've been wondering what made you think Kim could have been in danger with Chase since he's always seemed so solicitous."

"It's a long story and a hunch." He raked his fingers through his dark, wavy hair and looked around the room. "You remember Chase and I were partners for ten years. I knew him well; knew his good points, understood his quirks, and discovered he harbored a lot of resentment for his parents. He kept to himself, more than normal."

He took a deep breath. "But that's getting off the subject. When Karen called to say the police told her they'd found some of Melvin's body parts in the swamp, and approximately how long they'd been there, I knew he couldn't have been responsible for committing the crimes we'd credited him with. It had to be someone else. That's when Chase came to mind. Little things started popping back from when we worked together. Alone, they didn't mean much, but when you added them together … they spelled danger for Kim."

Gloria and Andy sat forward paying close attention to Max.

"I should have recognized the signs of a troubled soul," Max added. "Having partnered together for that long, I always had confidence in Chase and respect for his abilities. He backed me up 100 percent, never questioned anything I suggested we do in the line of duty. But the Chief saw him in a different light; he recognized some instabilities. He insisted Chase see a doctor if he wanted to stay on the force. That doctor put him on Thorazine, a medication which seemed to satisfy the Chief as long as Chase stayed on it and continued to have medical checkups."

Patricia leaned closer to Max. "What sort of instabilities?"

Max hesitated, then went on. "The Chief asked me if Chase ever took chances when we were on duty. I recalled him ignoring caution on a number of occasions. Once he pursued a drunken driver who had run a red light and ignored our signals to pull over. With lights flashing and sirens blaring, Chase tried to ram him from the back. I warned him it wasn't protocol and could be dangerous for us, but he said this guy was a threat to our community. That part was true, but rules are made for a reason and for our own safety." Max drained his coffee cup and set it on a table next to him.

"If someone we pulled over gave him any excuses or back talk, I could see his anger flare. There were times I felt he was ready to do something … unethical, but he'd finally get control of himself. He had a short fuse with felons, but was very protective of me."

Andy stood, picked up the coffee pot from a side table and refilled Max's cup.

Max nodded to Andy and took several sips. When he continued, he said, "It was only in the last year, before the murders, that Chase started acting strange with me, possessive, maybe, or jealous … Who knows? I couldn't figure him. If we were apart, he wanted to know where I'd been, and who I'd been with. I never gave him any personal information. Sometimes I'd tell him, 'It's none of your business, Chase, so drop it.' He wouldn't speak to me until he cooled off. Then, he'd fall back into his normal, non-committal mood.

"On several occasions, when I was off duty, I could have sworn someone was following me. One night, I turned off my headlights and pulled into a wooded area. When my follower passed by, I recognized Chase's vehicle. He was checking me out, all right."

Max stared at a spot on the ceiling without speaking for several moments. "That's about the time things started to get weird. He began to miss days at work, leaving me on shift without a partner. After the Alexanders were murdered and Kim placed the 911 call, the Chief assigned us to investigate the crime scene. It was so bad, I almost lost it, but Chase held up like a true veteran. He took over more than his share. And I let him." He paused rubbing index fingers on his eye lids. "In retrospect, he was damned persistent about collecting evidence on his own."

Patricia reached over and put her hand on Max's arm. "Bringing up your past with Chase must be difficult for you, Max, since you'd been friends for so many years."

"It hasn't been easy." He sighed audibly. "Things weren't the same between us after that. Eventually, I decided I couldn't live here anymore and put in for a transfer back to Miami."

A dead hush filled the room when Max stopped speaking. Gloria jumped up and grabbed Andy's hand and the near-empty coffee carafe. "Come on. Let's make another pot. Kim and Brad should be here soon, and I'm sure they can use a fresh brew." Hand in hand they left Patricia and Max and headed for the kitchen.

With the others gone, Max turned to look at Patricia. He reached over to her face and brushed a wisp of auburn hair from her eyes. "It's hard to believe you're Kim's aunt. She looks so much like you."

Patricia flushed, withdrew her hand from Max's arm, and turned away from his intense gaze. "I guess," she paused and then, with deliberation, looked back at him, "I guess I'll have to have Kim tell you a little story."

Max took her hand in his. "I'm ready anytime."

Patricia's hand quivered slightly. "Why don't you finish telling me about Chase?"

"Not much more to say except I should have seen this coming earlier. Trouble is, when you've worked with someone day after day, you tend to overlook things your subconscious is trying to tell you. It took me a while before I realized Chase had Margaret on his mind. He had the classic signs of a person obsessed.

"I believe he has been trying his best to make up for the past. He did help me get this job in Glade City and got me out from under Doris's thumb. His being so helpful almost made me forget how strange he got before the murders."

"So, back then, you were suspicious of Chase?"

"He knew I had known the Alexanders in Miami." He opened his mouth to say more and then stopped. He rubbed his thumb over Patricia's hand.

"Go on, Max. I'm listening."

"I don't exactly know how to say this, Patricia. I don't want to hurt your feelings, because I've grown to truly enjoy our friendship and look forward to being with you a lot more." He stared intently into her eyes. "What I was about to say is that I believe Chase guessed about my relationship with Margaret when I lived in Miami at the same time the Alexanders were there, although I never told him a thing." He looked down at his hand as he held hers. "I loved your sister then, even though I knew in my heart, I was only another fling to her. I see things clearly now. And I only wish ... " He looked through her eyes and into her soul.

"Wish what, Max?"

"I only wish I'd met you first, Patricia. My life might have turned out quite differently."

"We've each had our share of regrets, Max." She squeezed his hand. "Since we can't change the past, do you think we could put it behind us?"

His only response was a smile that seemed to light up the room.

Gloria and Andy came back in and sat down on the couch again. "Coffee's brewing. Should be ready by the time Kim and Brad get here."

The front door opened, and they appeared. "Got her all locked up, folks. Sorry we weren't able to get back to the party before it broke up. End of story for today." Kim pulled Brad over to the other end of the couch.

"A fitting end, at that," Brad said just as the telephone rang.

Gloria reached over and picked up the receiver from the end table next to her.

"He what?" Her eyes grew wide. Moments passed as she listened. "Well, thank you, officer. I'm sure everyone has been waiting to hear."

She replaced the phone and looked at the others who had focused questioningly on her. She sank back again against Andy and said, "Wow."

"Wow what?" Kim sat up straight. "Don't keep us in suspense."

"Chase regained consciousness a while ago. His voice was only a whisper, but he managed to get the nurse and police officer on duty to hear him out before he died."

"Oh, no." Kim leaned forward. "I'm sorry it had to end this way. He could have been so much more. He had some remarkable qualities."

"Never mind that," Andy said. "What did he have to say?"

Gloria looked around the room at the expectant faces. "They recorded it at the hospital. The officer in charge took the tape to the station. We can go there tomorrow."

Kim jumped up. "Forget tomorrow. Let's go right now."

Brad stood and pulled Kim over to him, wrapping his arms tightly around her shoulders. "Pardon me, young lady, but you've had a full day with all the stress to go with it. You're in no shape to go any place tonight." He leaned down and kissed her on the cheek, looked around the room, smiled and tilted her mouth, covering it with his. When he finally released her, he whispered in her ear, "You were my watch dog for a while, now I'm going to be yours."

"I guess tomorrow will have to do, if you insist." Kim smiled up into a pair of soft brown eyes. "But I do have to drive you home first. Remember? I picked you up for the party, so you have no car."

"Never you mind about that, sweetheart. If Gloria doesn't mind, I'll bunk here on the couch for the night. We'll go to the station in the morning."

"I have dibs on the lounger," Andy piped up. "We can *all* go to the station together."

"Mind if I tag along?" Max looked at Kim and Gloria, and then at Patricia. "I can be back here whenever you say."

"Of course," Kim said. "You knew Chase before any of us did."

At nine o'clock in the morning, six people walked into the Glade City police station to hear the tape of Chase Grey's final words.

"This recording is for Miss Kim Alexander," the officer in charge said.

Kim stepped forward. "That would be me, sir. I brought these people with me to hear it."

"If that's your wish, ma'am. I have an empty interrogation room down the hall. Follow me. You'll all be able to have a seat."

He led them to a room with a table in the center surrounded by four chairs. He had another officer bring in two more folding seats.

When they were settled, one of the cops on duty brought in a player which he placed in the center of the table. "Grey's voice is pretty weak so I've put the volume up as high as possible. If you're quiet, I think you'll be able to hear all his words."

The room became deadly silent as the sergeant engaged the player and the tape began.

A male voice said, "Go ahead, Mr. Grey. The recorder is ready for you."

Softly, just above a whisper, Chase began. "This is Chase, Kim. I have … something to tell you. (A pause) When I first … met you, I believed … with all my heart (longer pause) you were the one I'd been waiting for … all my life."

There was another moment or two of quiet. Chase coughed several times, cleared his throat and continued. "I followed you when I know I shouldn't have." (Another long pause.) "It was my way of feeling closer … to you, a part of your life. But, no matter what I did … for you, you never seemed … to notice."

He hesitated long enough that it seemed as though it was the end. Kim glanced around the room. All eyes were on the recorder. The male voice heard in the beginning spoke. "Would you like a drink of water, Mr. Grey?"

Chase didn't respond to the question but started in again, even slower than before. "When you injured me at … the estate, that really hurt my … feelings. (He coughed again, weakly.) But, I was still willing to forgive you. You should have … chosen me, Kim. You should have chosen … " The words trailed off. There were excited voices in the background and then the tape went silent.

Quiet fell over the room. The tape stopped rolling, and the police officer turned off the recorder. "That's all there was before he closed his eyes and … "

Another cop walked through the door. "We've impounded Grey's convertible, so if no relatives claim it, it'll be sold at auction, and the profits will go to the police fund." He looked directly at Kim. "I thought you'd like to know that in the trunk we found a briefcase imprinted with the Glade City Boat Tours logo which contained a large sum of cash."

Epilogue:

Sixteen months later, SandHill had a new/old look. Fresh white paint gleamed in the Florida sun. Wisteria covered the wrap-around porch and west side of the house, glowing in shades of purple and lavender. A dozen tables with their matching chairs sat around the porch beneath outdoor fans. Grandfather's old rocker near the entryway next to one of a small child's, both restored to their original state, moved gently when stray breezes flowed through the Magnolia trees and scores of replanted bougainvilleas in the front garden. The old iron gate and chain-link barrier around the property had been replaced with a four-foot high white faux wooden fence, now covered with moon vines and plumbago and backed with dozens of fire bush plants and coonties for hungry humming birds and butterflies. Behind the fenced area of the estate, Saw Palmettos had taken over the acreage before it gave way to where the tall Cyprus dipped their feet in the waters of the Everglades. A sign stood just off the highway at the entrance of the driveway. It announced the grand opening of SandHill Guest House Bed and Breakfast, proprietors/hostesses, Kim Alexander Kimbal and Patricia Sanderson.

Inside, the original library had been remodeled into one grand bedroom suite, while an additional room had been added on the opposite side of the living room and functioned as a second Master Bedroom.

The grand entryway greeted overnight or weekly guests in royal style below the magnificent crystal chandelier. The second and third floors of the home had been remodeled into large bedrooms, six per floor, each with its own bathroom facilities. All had a commanding view of the beautifully-kept gardens where a walking path of crushed shells meandered over the grounds.

Close to the center of town, a former yard goods store had been remodeled to house the new business of Max Young Security. Pelican Landing had hired a new man from Michigan to fill the vacated position.

On the enlarged Kimbal Real Estate building, a new neon sign proclaimed: Kimbal, Wikstrom and Wikstrom, as THE Real Estate Agency of Glade City. A group picture showed a smiling Brad Kimbal standing behind Gloria and Andy who were seated side-by-side at a desk.

Last, but not least, in town, the SawGrass Boat Tours' new sign at the front entrance informed visitors that the business now operated under the new general managership of Karen Bishop, former business secretary/manager.

Fini

We hope you enjoyed reading Kim's Story: Murder in the Everglades. This is book one in the Everglades series by Loie Lawless. Turn the page to take a peek at the prologue of her new book: Kim's Story: Terror in the Everglades. To be released Summer of 2013

Kim's Story:
Terror in the Everglades
Prologue.

KIM'S STORY
Terror in the Everglades
(Book 2 of
The Everglade Series)

By Loie Lawless

Prologue:

After he captured the Cottonmouth, he placed it in a small glass terrarium in his garage, keeping it alive by feeding it rodents. It would be well worth the trouble it took to maintain the snake, considering the enjoyment he would have when the time came.

The most pleasure he'd had in far too long came before he'd sedated the woman. He'd placed the terrarium close to her face and played with the secured lid. She'd screamed and cringed in fear, perspiration covering her face and neck. She shook uncontrollably when she'd thought he was going to release it while he reveled in the look of horror on her face. The Cottonmouth gave him the gratification he'd needed. Finally, things were beginning to change for him … for the better.

He took the woman's unconscious body and placed it in the back seat of his pickup. So beautiful, he thought, but some things just had to be done. He climbed into the driver's seat, turned the key in the ignition, the lights on, and headed for the abandoned roadhouse he'd found soon after situating himself in Glade City.

A dozen years prior to his arrival in town, the old highway had been rerouted to bypass a developing dangerous swampy area. No longer accessible to the public, the small but once prosperous jazz joint had been deserted and rebuilt on another property adjacent to the new highway, resuming all its once-held popularity.

The old road, blocked off from access due to the hazardous conditions, had not escaped his devious eye. He'd always been on the lookout for places known to be closed to the public. One never knew when one could utilize such a spot, and he'd often had need for such a place.

Midnight light in the sky, almost nil, produced a good cover for covert operations as he parked outside the blockade. He took a large wheelbarrow from the pickup bed, a heavy duty flashlight, gloves, and his kit with syringes. Pulling the woman from the vehicle, he placed her in the wheelbarrow, alongside a two-gallon bottle of fresh water and a small bag of food. Not an easy push through the overgrown, swampy remains of the old road, but his perseverance never failed him.

About five hundred yards past the blockade, the building had continued to rot in the extreme conditions of the swamp, and the road had deteriorated even more since his last visit. All the more secure for him, he thought. No one in his right mind would want to venture into this thicket of evil: vines, palmettos, mangroves, venomous snakes like his captive cottonmouth, and because of its ideal conditions, the possibility of an alligator nest. Inhabited by a number of other unsavory creatures made an almost positive deterrent for anyone seeking to satisfy his curiosity.

The building itself, unstable, but usable enough to hide his prey, he deemed a safe place to use until the time came to dispose of her. Since the windows and doors had been securely boarded up, with the exception of his own secret entryway, no animals could get in, and she couldn't escape, nor would anyone be able to hear her. He smiled at his own cunning.

When it actually came time for her "untimely death", the snake would do a good job without casting guilt on him. No fingerprints to worry about. No weapons to trace. Only a dead body in the swamp.

A perfect plan that would satisfy his need for power, to torture, and without having to commit the act himself. He could simply be the audience. Pretty clever, he chuckled to himself, even without Bo.

Yes, without Bo. This reminded him of when they were kids. With parents like theirs, at times they had been forced to do what was necessary for survival. Never easy, but he and Bo knew what had to done, and they did it without so much as looking back. Never getting caught only encouraged them and added to the sweetness.

After he situated her on an old table, he left a basket of food: some old apples, bread, peanut butter, and a bag of stale potato chips next to her, along with the bottle of water. That would be enough to keep her alive for several days until he could return. One more shot to keep her sedated for a while, and he could be on his way back to Glade City and his new job; a perfect move to a perfect place.

Watch for Kim's Story: Terror in the Everglades
By Loie Lawless
To be released Summer of 2013

Author Biography

Loie Lawless
Kim's Story: Murder in the Everglades

From an early age, Loie Lawless fantasized about becoming an author. As a child, she delighted in telling "scary" stories to her friends. In junior high school a teacher assigned the class a writing project: Write an ending to the popular story, The Lady or The Tiger. She garnered much praise and encouragement with her assignment, realizing that writing was her true calling.

Loie was a young World War II bride, marrying her Marine shortly after high school graduation. Throughout her marriage and the raising of their four children, she did however steal away time to dabble in short stories in many different genres, from romance, romantic humor, children's fiction to several thrillers. In recent years, Loie wrote a non-fiction story about a terrifying experience her husband had as a Marine Corps prop mechanic on Guam during World War II. This piece was quickly picked up and published in World War II Magazine.

Only recently, as retirement settled in, did she find time to write her first full length novel, the plot of which had been playing in her mind for a number of years. Loie's preference leans heavily toward mystery/suspense/thriller fiction in which she intends to continue her writing. She is currently working on her second novel.

Loie lives in Hemet, CA, surrounded by her large and loving family and her two "best friends" "KiKi" and "Lily" the delightful Chihuahuas who have been her muse's and constant companions since the passing of her beloved husband, Don, in 2011.

Watch for a book of Loie's short stories to be published early in 2013.

www.ingramcontent.com/pod-product-compliance
Lightning Source LLC
Chambersburg PA
CBHW070405260626
47161CB00001B/281